HIS WORDS TORE
THROUGH HER HEART

And then Remie bent to brush her lips with his, and a white-hot fire raced through her blood; and when he pulled her into a firm embrace Soleil was helpless to resist. The feathery kiss became an impassioned one, long and deep. She opened her lips beneath his, and for the moment she was able to put aside his stipulations, to ignore what they must surely mean.

"Will you marry me, Soleil?" he murmured at last.

And even as she heard her own breathy "Yes, I will," she felt the beginnings of the pain that she sensed would remain with her for a long, long time.

WILLO DAVIS ROBERTS

MADAWASKA

W🌐RLDWIDE.

TORONTO · NEW YORK · LONDON · PARIS
AMSTERDAM · STOCKHOLM · HAMBURG

MADAWASKA

A Worldwide Library Book/June 1988

ISBN 0-373-97074-9

Prologue

BY THE SUMMER of 1754, the Acadian people had lived under the rule of the British for more than forty tumultuous years. During that time there had been numerous attempts by the French to retake their New World colony of Acadia. While the Acadians would have preferred retaining their ties to the land from which their ancestors and their language had come, they were not fanatically devoted to France. They wanted mostly to be left alone to farm and to fish and to practice their Catholic religion. Few of them could read or write, and they wished also to be allowed to have priests educated in France to lead them and to interpret whatever written matter they had to deal with.

Since the Treaty of Utrecht in 1713, which established British control over most of present-day Nova Scotia—which the inhabitants then called Acadia—the Acadians had remained stubbornly neutral in all matters of conflict, as the treaty demanded. Concerned only with their own local affairs, they refused to assist either European contender for control over their society. They did maintain an excellent relationship with the local Indians, who were extremely hostile toward the British.

In 1726 the English, fearing that their French-speaking subjects would join with the hostile Indians or the French inhabitants of neighboring Canada to fight against them, required that the Acadians sign an oath of unconditional allegiance to King George I. The Acadians refused to do so unless a clause was inserted into the document that would exempt them from taking up arms against either their French neighbors or the Indians who had befriended them. They also asked that they be allowed to continue to practice their religion with their own priests.

The demand that they sign the oath of allegiance was made numerous times over the following years, and always the Acadians resisted the pressures, insisting that the changes they had asked for must be made.

The Acadians neither understood nor respected their English rulers; insofar as was possible, they simply ignored them. One British commander complained bitterly that his authority extended no farther from his fort than the reach of his cannons; when the Acadians did not care to comply with his wishes, they simply moved out of range of the guns and went on doing things the way they always had.

Thus it was that during the last relatively peaceful time most Acadians would ever know, storm clouds were building on the political front that would shatter their lives forever.

1

SUMMER WAS NEARLY OVER. The hay would be completely harvested in another week, and the marsh grasses were turning russet with the promise of autumn. On the edge of the woods, a single maple flared crimson. Soon the frosts would touch everywhere, painting leaves gold and burgundy and scarlet before the snows followed too quickly after.

The warmth of the sun lingered on her skin, however, as Soleil Cyr walked slowly home, swinging the basket in which she had carried the noon meal to her father and brothers.

She ought to have hurried, because there was the evening meal to prepare and her mother would be impatient for her return. Barbe Cyr was often impatient, however, and a walk such as this was the only time Soleil had to herself. Living in a household with so many other people made it difficult to find the privacy to think her own thoughts.

Soleil had many thoughts that demanded solitude to indulge them. She was fifteen and a half, an age when most of her friends, except for Céleste Dubay, who was six months younger, were already married. People were beginning to make sly remarks, to ask what she was waiting for.

Soleil had no ready answer. It was not for lack of suitors; there were at least four young men of Grand-Pré alone who would have been happy to walk to Father Castin any night of the week and ask that the priest say the banns over himself and Soleil Cyr on the following Sunday. And there was that Garneau fellow from Beaubassin who had danced with her nearly all night at Agathe's wedding, and the one whose name she didn't remember from Annapolis Royal, though of course she would never have considered *him*. She was not interested in a man who could not hold his drink any better than that.

As a matter of fact, she was not interested in any of them. She was not especially eager to be married and in charge of her own household at all, being perfectly content where she was, at home.

But that didn't mean she didn't dream of romance, of being swept off her feet by someone so handsome, so strong, so brave that she would not have to think twice, should he ask for her hand.

The trouble was that no such person had appeared in Grand-Pré, and since Soleil was unlikely ever to have the opportunity to travel elsewhere, she was beginning to wonder how this matter would turn out for her.

Sooner or later, if she didn't choose a man to her own liking, her parents would do it for her.

"Soleil! Wait!"

She turned at the familiar voice, pausing until Louis caught up with her. Her oldest brother was perhaps her favorite, and he'd never made any secret that she was his. He had been ten when she was born, the year Mama had been so ill and nearly died, and it was Louis who had taken care of her, fed and changed her, coaxed her into her first toddling steps, protected her from all dangers. It was to Louis that she would confide, should matters reach a stage where advice must be asked.

Louis, like Soleil, was always recognised to be a Cyr by any stranger who had ever met one of the family. The Cyrs all looked as alike as the grains of sand on the red beaches along the Minas Basin. Except, of course, that they were not red like the sands, but dark. They had black hair, the lot of them, and deep brown eyes, and most of them with dimples, as well. Louis was slower to smile than the others, so his dimples did not show as often. It had occurred to his sister that perhaps that was why he remained sober so much of the time; he thought dimples detracted from his masculinity.

They didn't, she thought, smiling a little now as he came abreast of her. His shirt was soaked with sweat, for he had been swinging a scythe since daybreak; the sleeves were rolled up to reveal muscular arms tanned the color of old leather, the same as his face.

He looked even more sober than usual.

"I'm surprised Papa let you go so early," she remarked, swinging the basket.

"He didn't. I just left. I wanted to talk to you, and there's never a chance with Mama and Madeleine and the children around. Walk slowly or we'll be home too soon."

She nodded, waiting.

Louis brushed back a thick lock of black hair, only to have it fall again at once over his high forehead. He stopped abruptly, putting both hands on her shoulders, and she felt a stir of uneasiness.

"I'm leaving as soon as the hay is in," Louis said.

For a moment his meaning escaped her. "Leaving?" she echoed stupidly.

"Leaving Grand-Pré," Louis stated. "If I thought Papa would listen, I'd beg him to come along, to remove the whole family, but we've argued over it enough so I know he wouldn't be swayed. But I'm going."

Soleil moistened her lips. "Where? Where are you going?"

"To Beaubassin, at first. But finally, I think, to Île St. Jean."

Soleil sucked in a breath of dismay. "So far! Louis, no one in the family has ever been so far!"

"The farther the better, away from the damned English!" Louis said, his fingers digging into the soft flesh of her shoulders. "There will be no land for my sons, no freedom for them under British rule. I won't see them driven out. I'll take them out myself and find a better place for them."

"But Île St. Jean! Louis, have you thought—" She stopped. Of course he had thought. Louis always thought things through, far beyond his younger brothers. And the anguish was there in his face, the knowledge that his decision would have far-reaching effects on all the other members of the family.

Pain swept through her, physical pain. "No one has ever been so far," she murmured. "We may never...see you again."

"Come with us, if you like. Papa won't prevent your going, if you want to come."

The pain grew deeper, as if an arrow had been plunged into her breast. She couldn't bear the thought of Louis going away forever; even less could she imagine being able to leave her entire family behind.

Compassion shifted the planes of her brother's face, so like her own. "No. That was wrong of me, wasn't it, to suggest that you come, too. I was being selfish, because I will miss you, little sister, more than all the rest put together. And you are closer to most of them than I, so your suffering would be greater if you were to go. But I must, Soleil. I have struggled over this for months—no, for a year or more. I cannot stay here under the British heel any longer.''

She tried to pull herself together. "Madeleine? How does she feel about it?''

"She doesn't know yet." Louis dropped his hands and turned away, beginning to walk reluctantly along the familiar path. "I'll tell her soon, but not too soon.''

"She won't want to go," Soleil said softly.

"I know. Yet she's my wife, and she'll go where I go. In time she'll understand why it must be this way.''

Would she? Soleil and Madeleine were as different in temperament as they were in appearance—one dark, one fair—and often had opposing viewpoints. But Soleil knew with a bittersweet flash of intuition how her sister-in-law would react to this news—to leave not only the family into which she had married and with whom she had lived for the past four years, but her own beloved family, as well. Madeleine was very close to her parents and siblings. The highlight of every week was the hour or two she spent with them on Sundays.

Soleil looked up at Louis, and their eyes met in perfect understanding. No promises were asked of her, for he knew she would repeat nothing he had said until he had made his own announcement. And no mention was made of the agony of heart that they both knew must inevitably result for all from his decision.

Shoulders touching briefly as they walked, they strode the rest of the way home without speaking. As she thought of her parents and how they would feel, Soleil wondered if it were truly possible to fall sick and die of a broken heart.

IN THE BUSTLE OF PREPARING and serving the evening meal, Soleil's preoccupation passed unnoticed. Barbe Cyr, a comfortably plump woman of forty-one with streaks of gray in her dark hair, presided easily and volubly over the kitchen with a running stream of orders that Soleil scarcely heard. Hearing was not necessary, since she knew each of the orders by heart, and had since childhood.

She moved mechanically, handing down the wooden bowls to her twelve-year-old sister, Danielle, who might have been her own twin except that she was not as tall as Soleil and was nearly flat chested. Danielle was much chagrined about the latter fact; only yesterday Soleil had caught her squeezing her tiny breasts to make them extend as far as possible, and bemoaning their pathetic size.

"What if they never grow?" she had demanded, and Soleil had laughed.

"They'll grow. Stop worrying about it."

"Your bosom attracts all the boys' eyes. *You* don't have to worry."

"Neither do you. Nature will take care of the problem, given another year or so," Soleil had told her.

"I want Basile Lizotte to notice me," Danielle had said, pouting. "And he looks only at girls who have big bosoms."

"Then he's not worth worrying about," Soleil had assured her, and laughed again when her younger sister had given an annoyed snort.

"He *is* worth it. All the boys look at you. You don't know what it's like to be like me." Danielle had sounded sullen.

She was not being sullen today. She was putting the bowls and other utensils on the long oak plank table that would seat the twelve family members who were old enough to sit on the benches around it, plus half a dozen more, should there be need. She adeptly avoided stepping on the toddlers underfoot and herded ten-year-old Jacques away from the bread she had put out to slice.

She gave her older sister a friendly smile, which Soleil did not even notice. Soleil, instead, was observing Louis's wife, Madeleine, who sat spooning something into young Marc's eager mouth. Not even the sight of Louis's son engaged in his favorite pastime brought a smile to Soleil's lips today.

Madeleine stood out sharply among the Cyrs, for the hair peeking out from beneath her white cap was the color of a newly minted gold coin, and though it did not curl like Cyr hair, it was stunningly beautiful, like everything about Madeleine. It was no wonder Louis had fallen in love with her. Her heart-shaped face was exquisite—perhaps too delicate for an Acadian woman whose lot in life must invariably involve hard work and some degree of privation, though within this family she had been somewhat protected so far.

Soleil studied the animated face of her sister-in-law as she fed
the baby, playing with him, enjoying him to the fullest. Two
infants had been stillborn before Marc; no wonder Madeleine
now took such joy in a healthy, handsome boy.

Soleil's heart twisted. Here at home Madeleine always had
help when she needed it. Barbe and Danielle and Soleil had
been at hand when she lost her babies. Madeleine had never had
the full responsibility of her own household, nor sought it.
Willing hands had always been ready to take over when she
grew too tired to care for her own child, when she needed rest.

Until now it had not mattered terribly that Madeleine was
more frail than most. But Louis contemplated taking her and
the baby to Île St. Jean, many miles away across the slate-gray
waters to the north to a place they had only heard about, the
island the Micmacs called Abegweit, or Land of the Red Soil.
They would have to walk all the way to the shores of the Gulf
of St. Lawrence, then paddle a canoe to the island itself, a
crossing that tested the endurance of even the Micmac braves.

Aside from a few of the local Indians and Father Castin,
Soleil did not know anyone who had ever traveled so far. How
would a woman as fragile as Madeleine hold up under such a
journey?

Marc blew a bubble through the last spoonful of pap, sending a spray over his mother to signal that his belly was filled.
Madeleine wiped at the flecks that had spotted her. "You bad
boy," she reproached, but was unable to contain her flicker of
amusement. "See what you've done to your poor mama! Now
I shall have to wash the stains out of my dress before we go to
the dance tonight, and there will be so little time. Here,
Jacques, take this messy child away and keep him from underfoot until we are ready to sit for supper."

She swept up her son and handed him over to the youngest
of Louis's brothers, still wiping at his face with a damp rag.

Jacques accepted the baby with the ease of long practice.
"Come on, my little friend, let us go outside where the women
will not step all over us. Ah! You are getting too heavy! When
are you going to walk on your own two legs?"

"Very soon now," Madeleine promised, swinging toward her
mother-in-law, who was shifting a kettle in the great stone
fireplace. "Do you want some help with that, Mama?"

The dance, Soleil thought. They were all going to the dance tonight. Would this be the last time that Madeleine knew a carefree evening with the entire village present?

Louis would dance and drink and talk, and no one would know what was inside his head. That was the way Louis was. Soleil didn't know how *she* would get through the evening without someone wondering what was the matter with her; her brother's revelation lay heavily upon her, indeed.

"Soleil, stop mooning about and fetch a platter for the fish," Barbe said sharply, colliding with the daughter who stood impeding her way. Then she paused. "Are you daydreaming about some boy?"

The hopeful note in her mother's voice was depressing. "No, Mama, I'm not."

Barbe's scrutiny was made in seconds. That was usually all the time she could find for such things. "You're looking droopy about the mouth. I hope you're not sickening. Marie Trudelle's lying-in will probably take place within a few days, and I've promised to attend. And with Madeleine breeding again, you'll have to take over here, no doubt—"

"Breeding? Madeleine?" Soleil cast an anxious glance at her sister-in-law, who had not heard the exchange. "Nobody told me."

Barbe sniffed. "She's not told anyone, not even Louis, I'd wager. But you've only to look at her to know. That secret little smile, the way she hums and hugs her belly from time to time. Besides which, she's lost her breakfast the past three mornings."

Barbe swept away to rescue the kettle of boiled cabbage Danielle was trying to lift off its iron hook.

Pregnant. Madeleine was pregnant, and surely not even Louis was aware of it yet. Soleil felt a surge of hope—that this would mean he could not take his family away at once, as he planned. He knew how difficult pregnancy was for his wife, and he loved her very much. He would never do anything to endanger her or their child.

Yet she was uneasy, for men were known to do what they felt they had to do, regardless of the consequences to their families. And Louis was related so strongly to Papa: both of them proud, and stubborn.

"Oh, by the way," Barbe said over her shoulder, steam from the cabbage rising around her already pink face, "Guillaume Trudelle stopped by today to give me the message about Marie. He said that he has a visitor who will be at the dance tonight, his nephew who has been at Louisbourg. Twenty, he is, and handsome as a peacock from the royal gardens. A good catch, Guillaume says."

Soleil compressed her lips. She remembered the last of Guillaume's nephews—or was it a cousin? Also a "good catch," but simpleminded and not at all good-looking.

"Who wants to marry a peacock?" she muttered.

Even though she had spoken under her breath and there was conversation all around them, Barbe heard.

"Well, miss, you'd better be considering some man, and soon. I'll not have it thought a daughter of mine is too ugly—or bad tempered or persnickety—to land a husband. So, look this Remie Michaud over before every other unmarried female in Grand-Pré blinds him to whatever virtues you might offer."

Soleil stared at her mother resentfully and scowled at Danielle's anticipatory grin. No doubt her sister believed that once Soleil was wed, she herself could not be far behind.

In spite of herself, Soleil was moderately intrigued by a man who had been at Louisbourg. She wondered if he had seen the governor's house there, which they said had more than fifty rooms.

"Remie Michaud," she murmured his name. "Well, we'll have to see."

For a short time, then, as she joined the others at the supper table and later brushed out her dark hair and put on her best dress and cap for the dance, she forgot what Louis had told her and wondered about the new young man who was visiting. Remie Michaud. She liked the sound of his name, at least.

2

ÉMILE CYR NEVER FAILED to take pleasure in the sight of his home. It sat snugly against the backdrop of the forest, constructed of square-cut spruce logs carefully fitted together so that the wind could not penetrate between them. Both the thatched roof and logs had been weathered after all these years and now blended into the landscape as if the house had grown there.

Extending from the main body of the dwelling was the entryway, or foyer, common among Acadian houses. Even when the outer door was closed, it was never locked; in this country of bitter cold winters, the entryway provided refuge for any unfortunate traveler caught without a roof of his own. The passageway was unheated, but since it shared a wall with the kitchen fireplace, there was always some warmth to be gained from the heated stones.

The Cyr farm was isolated from its neighbors, and there were seldom unexpected visitors, but if one should choose to take shelter for the night, he would of course be invited to join the family for a hearty meal in the morning when his presence was discovered.

The door stood open now, the tunnellike entry empty of anything except hanging coats and a row of wooden clogs. Émile had been born forty-three years earlier in the main part of the house, the large central section built by his paternal grandfather to replace the smaller cabin that had been the original home. A few years after Émile's parents had married, an addition had been made to one side so that they might have some privacy and the space to raise a family that eventually consisted of seven boys and five girls.

Émile was the oldest, and after his sisters had married and his brothers had all taken up land farther on, he had brought Barbe here as a bride. It still made him smile, to remember Barbe as a young girl. Beautiful, she had been, looking much as Soleil looked now, with those black curls tousled by the wind, her lips red as wild raspberries, and a bosom that made a man want to...

Ah, he had always been a man with an eye for a pretty figure, and his Barbe had had the best. Even now she was only comfortably plump, not fat. And as good in bed—or better—than she had been as a girl of fourteen when he married her.

The latest addition to the house had been built when Louis married. Émile liked Madeleine—no man could fail to appreciate her blond beauty and her sweet disposition—yet he wished his son had chosen a sturdier woman. Any female might lose a babe or two—it was God's will, no doubt, for it happened to them all—but she was ailing too often. Barbe and Soleil and Danielle had never complained, at least to him, that Madeleine shirked her duties in the house and garden, but he knew she did far less than the others. And now, if his wife was correct, as she invariably was, the girl was breeding again. Well, she had given him one fine grandson, and if the good God was willing, there would be more.

He approached the house, hearing the sounds of young voices, a baby crying, and Barbe's voice raised in sharp command. Émile smiled. Barbe's household was at all times under her control, which was the way he liked it.

As he approached, the old man seated on a bench beside the door removed the pipe from his mouth and greeted him genially.

"Good evening, Grand-père," Émile said to his father-in-law with a smile, and then stepped sharply aside.

A basin of water flung out the open doorway had narrowly missed him. François's chagrined face appeared a moment later. "I'm sorry, Papa. I didn't see you coming."

"You have created a mud puddle directly in front of the door," Émile pointed out with little rancor. "Your mother will not be happy with the mud Grand-père and I must now track in."

François and his twin, Antoine, were perhaps the most handsome of his sons in a family where exceptional good looks were taken for granted. Émile shouldered François aside to enter the kitchen, assimilating the aromas of boiled cabbage and fresh fish and the heat of the cooking fire. His eyes met his wife's over the heads of assorted children and grandchildren.

"Ah, there you are," Barbe greeted him, that small secret smile that only he ever noticed touching her lips. "We'll be late for the dance if you don't come to the table at once."

He had forgotten the dance. "One advantage of being the fiddler," he told her, "is that it's hard for the dancing to begin without you. Let's eat."

There was a surge of movement toward the big table, followed by scraping sounds as the family scrabbled to their places and jostled the benches into position, Grand-père still with his pipe clenched between what remained of his teeth.

Émile's gaze swept over them all as he waited for the noise to subside so that the blessing might be said. His broad chest swelled with pride, for there was no finer family in all of the Grand-Pré region—no, in all of Acadia. He included himself in this assessment; false modesty was not one of Émile's short-comings. While he took pride in the height and strength of his sons and the beauty of his wife and daughters, he deducted nothing from the score for his own rather squat build. Was he not, after all, strong, healthy, intelligent and devout?

All the faces were watching him expectantly. Émile bowed his head and began to give thanks for the blessings that God had provided. "Amen," he said at last, and reached for the platter of fish.

While he ate, he surveyed his family members in turn. From Louis, his firstborn, to grandson Marc, he loved them and every day thanked God for them.

His gaze rested for a moment longer on Soleil than on the others. She was the first daughter after five sons—a sixth had been stillborn—and he admitted she had won a special place in his heart. One reason he had not given in to Barbe's mild nagging about the girl's future prospects was his own desire to keep her here a little longer. Yet he supposed the time had come to urge the child to think seriously about choosing one of the young men who flocked around her like the bees around the spring apple blossoms. The Salieres lad, perhaps. He was an only son and would come into a nice section of land; the family farmhouse, though less than half the size of Émile's own, would make his daughter a comfortable home.

Émile sighed. Yes, he would have to broach the subject, and soon. He only hoped that Soleil would prove amenable. Docility was not one of her obvious assets, and the last thing he wanted to do was to force an unwelcome choice on her.

His opportunity came as the family straggled along the track toward the village half an hour later. Louis and Madeleine strode ahead of them, young Marc on his father's shoulders, plump fingers digging into Louis's thick, dark hair. The twins were far ahead of everyone else, the others lagged behind. Only Soleil fell into step with Émile.

Incredible, he thought, that his loins should have contributed to the creation of this beautiful young woman. His throat almost closed at the thought of losing her, even if it were sending her only a few miles away to the care of another man. Yet he made good on his promise to Barbe, though awkwardly, almost unwillingly.

"I've been wanting a chance to talk to you in private," he said, earning his daughter's quick, wary glance.

"Mama's been at you," she guessed, "about my choosing a husband."

He was relieved that he didn't have to spell it out from scratch. "Eh, that she has. You know your mama." And then, lest he sound disloyal, he added, "She's right, you know. You'll be sixteen in November."

"Old, old," Soleil said, laughing. "A disgrace to my family, remaining a spinster so long." And then she sobered. "Papa, there is no one who measures up to you, or to Louis or Pierre or—" She had thought to mention François and Antoine but on consideration decided not to. "All my life I have known only intelligent, devout, kindly men. Am I to choose to spend the rest of my years with someone like—like Marcel Salieres?"

Émile's heart sank. "You don't like Marcel?"

"Papa!" Reproach drew her exquisite face into doleful lines. "He is such an . . . an idiot! So silly! And his mama is even worse. Can you imagine, after being schooled by Mama in keeping a household, going into *hers*? No, no, not Marcel!"

Émile moistened his lips and tugged at his beard with the hand that was not carrying his violin. "Who, then?"

Soleil sighed, and he could not doubt the sincerity of her own concern. "Mama said there will be a newcomer at the dance tonight. His name is Remie Michaud. Perhaps it is too much to hope that *he* might prove . . . interesting."

Émile's spirits rose at once. "Ah, yes! Very handsome, I heard! That is one of the things a girl looks for, no?" He gave her a sly grin. "And a handsome man wants a beautiful girl, eh? He has come recently from Louisbourg; a man of the world." And then, struck by a thought too horrible to contemplate, he added hastily, "Of course your mama and I would not want you to form an attachment to a man who did not intend to remain in Grand-Pré! I could not bear the thought of one of my children going so far away that we could not easily visit between our homes.''

Soleil gave a guilty start, glancing ahead at Louis and his little family, but her father didn't notice.

"No, of course not," she said, sounding subdued. "We can only see what this Remie is all about."

Émile nodded, satisfied. He had spoken to her as promised, and he could report to Barbe that she was receptive to their wishes. There were a few other unmarried females who would also be eager to meet this Michaud fellow, but none of them approached Soleil in either beauty or temperament. If Michaud had any sense at all, the choice would be obvious. And at the reported age of twenty, he was surely considering taking a bride.

Content, Émile stepped out more purposefully, smiling.

REMIE MICHAUD WAS, in fact, not considering any such thing.

Unlike most of the young Acadians, he had not spent his life wresting a living from either the soil or the sea. He was more at home in the woods, and he found hunting and trapping for meat and furs far preferable to breaking his back planting or harvesting crops.

Not that he was not superbly equipped to do heavy manual labor. Of above average height, and long accustomed to fending for himself under often adverse circumstances, Remie Michaud was strongly muscled and vigorous. He simply didn't see the point in working at something tedious when there was adventure to be had.

He had no intention of remaining in the village of Grand-Pré for more than a day or two. He was, in fact, en route from the fort at Louisbourg to the distant walled city of Québec, more than three hundred miles to the north and west. By the time he arrived there, he would have collected the cache of furs he had left with friendly Micmacs, which he would sell for a considerable sum. No doubt Monsieur Braque, to whom he would deliver them, would double the returns before he shipped the furs to France, but Remie was not greedy; he could live with a fair profit, particularly if it evolved from doing what he loved to do.

He was used to being alone most of the time—or had been, before his recent sojourn at Louisbourg. This didn't bother him. Something about the forests and the Indians and animals that inhabited them filled a need deep within him. He was at times aware of the distant possibility of someday meeting a female who would attract him strongly. Indeed, there was a Micmac maiden in the tribe that guarded his cache of furs who sent provocative tremors through his limbs, who stirred him in a way that could not be casually assuaged, for Running Fawn was a chaste young woman, converted by the Holy Fathers, and her father was a friend who must not be betrayed. If he decided to take Running Fawn as a wife, it would be before a priest. He was not yet ready for that, however; there were many solitary adventures still to be enjoyed before he was ready for a family.

His Uncle Guillaume had urged him to stay for a few days. "Marie is soon to be brought to bed with another child, so she will not attend the dance tonight," he had said only this morning. "However, it will be a gay time, with music and laughter. And," he added with a sidewise glance, "our prettiest girls. Of course they're all pretty when a man has just spent weeks by himself in the woods."

Remie had grinned. "I'll stay that long, but don't be matchmaking, Uncle. My feet itch to be on the trail again."

Guillaume grinned, too. "It may be that you will see one female who can change your mind," he suggested.

Remie had risen and headed for the door of the snug log house. "Perhaps," he conceded carelessly, "but don't count on it, Uncle."

Guillaume held his peace and had said no more right up to the time the music began.

Remie stood on the edge of the clearing, knowing he was the center of attention—though it was courteous and unobtrusive enough—and rather enjoying it. He had been introduced to most of the older people and many of the younger ones, as well. His dark eyes were polite in return, his smile genuine if rather perfunctory, and he had not ventured into the dancing.

And then he saw the girl.

Slim, with a halo of dark curls not quite concealed by her prim cap, thick lashes over dark brown eyes and a mouth surely meant for kissing... For a moment he stared, forgetting to be blasé, forgetting even to breathe.

By the good God, she was a beauty!

Their eyes met from a distance of some dozen yards; boldly Remie held her gaze, and she did not shrink from his scrutiny. And then, with deliberation, he at last let himself see the rest of her: small, perfect breasts not wholly concealed by the simple gown she wore, a tiny waist, tanned arms bespeaking days spent working in the sun, hands brown but delicate, sensitive.

A prickle started in Remie's groin and grew more intense.

"Ah, Soleil," Uncle Guillaume said, materializing at Remie's side with the girl herself. "I would like you to meet my nephew, Remie Michaud."

For seconds neither of the young people spoke, then Soleil's full lips curled in a faint smile. "Welcome to Grand-Pré," she said. "I understand you are recently come from Louisbourg."

Even her voice was different: husky, tantalizing, more feminine than any voice he had ever heard.

"I spent some months there," Remie conceded. He caught a glimpse of his uncle's face and realized the older man was amused by the reaction Remie thought he had concealed. Why didn't the old fool go about his business now that he had brought them together?

For her part, Soleil, too, struggled not to appear visibly smitten. It did not do to be too eager.

But she had a fleeting thought: even if Remie Michaud did not hold his drink well, or if his mother should prove a formidable adversary, it might prove worth it to seem interested.

Before this evening was over she would know, she thought with an unshakable conviction.

Or perhaps, deep within the shaking jelly that now comprised her insides, she already knew.

3

THE ACADIANS loved to dance. They liked a strong beat that compelled them to stamp their feet and sway and twirl.

Behind Soleil, the fiddlers had struck up another tune, and those who had chosen partners began to shuffle in the dust. She scarcely heard the music, tipping her head to stare up into those lively dark eyes, mesmerized by this man.

"Hey, Soleil, have you see Jacques? Mama wants him." It was Bertin, her seventeen-year-old brother. She scarcely noticed him; she knew Jacques would come to no harm in this gathering. He was probably with the Indians who stood on the fringe of trees, watching the white men dance, for he was everlastingly drawn by their Micmac neighbors.

Bertin belatedly noted that his sister was engrossed in the newcomer; he flushed and muttered an apology, backing away.

"Would you dance with me, *mam'selle*?" Remie Michaud asked, and Soleil lifted her hand to accept his.

It was as if a current flowed between them as he led her to join the swaying couples. Soleil was only dimly aware of François and her best friend, Céleste Dubay—or was the man Antoine? In the fading light, with the pair moving adroitly through the steps, it was hard to say.

She was filled with excitement, as if wine suffused her blood; she was reluctant to swing away from her partner, eager to return to him, to have his strong hands close around hers, to draw breathtakingly near to the most fascinating face she had ever seen.

His hair was thick and as black as her own; his skin deeply tanned; thick brows over eyes blacker than her own dark brown ones. He had a strong nose and high cheekbones, and a wide mouth that held just the suggestion of a smile. His firm, unbearded chin hinted, perhaps, of willfulness and determination.

The music ended too soon. A hand touched her arm, and Soleil looked around to find Marcel Salieres grinning hopefully.

Damnation, she thought, smothering her irritation. She did not want to dance with Marcel, did not even want to acknowledge his existence. He was only a silly boy, while Remie Michaud was the most exciting man she had ever encountered.

Remie was smiling, and she could not tell if he was as reluctant as she was to end the moment of magic. He released her and stepped away, effectively handing her over to Marcel.

Marcel, whose palms were damp, whose smile was insipid and who smelled strongly of the fir beer that was being passed around amongst the men.

The enchantment—so brief!—was gone, though an after-glow lingered, for Remie Michaud was still there. He had not even yet chosen another partner, and something blossomed in her chest, a warmth, a hope. He stood near the bonfire that had been lighted against the encroaching dusk, accepting a drink, watching the dancing.

Don't dance with anyone else, she begged silently, and let Marcel propel her into the steps as soon as the fiddlers struck up the next tune.

Was Remie watching her? It was impossible to keep track when she was being whirled around so rapidly. She registered familiar faces—Antoine, Louis, Pierre, François, all her brothers except young Jacques and Bertin, who was too shy to ask a girl to partner him until he'd imbibed a certain amount of the beer. All the villagers were there, too, and those from the surrounding farms, yet she was only truly conscious of one tall, broad-shouldered figure, silhouetted against the leaping flames.

And then, as she spun, the figure was gone.

Dismayed, Soleil turned her head from her current part-ner—her brother Louis, who for all his air of sobriety was one of the best dancers of the lot—to seek the newcomer. Had Re-mie already left?

Relief flowed through her when she found him again, in the deepening shadows where the Indians stood observing. He was in earnest conversation with Iron Eagle and Two Feathers, she thought thankfully. She could not bear the idea that he might leave without speaking to her, or dancing with her, again.

Once more the music ended, this time for long enough to al-low the trio of fiddlers to refresh themselves from the keg of beer. A string of small children raced by, giggling and shout-ing; Soleil stepped back out of their way to keep from being trampled and let her latest partner go without regret. She be-gan to work her way around the edge of the clearing, avoiding the spot where her mother sat chatting with a neighbor's wife, attempting to be unobtrusive about approaching the visitor and the Micmacs.

Céleste Dubay, her face flushed with exertion, reached out to grab her sleeve.

"Don't you even see old friends tonight?" she teased.

Soleil stopped, although she was unable to keep her gaze from straying toward her goal. "My throat is dry."

Céleste laughed. A pretty brown-haired girl in a blue dress, she was several inches shorter than her friend. "And Remie Michaud is standing within a few feet of the beer barrel."

Soleil felt the warmth in her cheeks. "Am I so obvious?"

"To me, at least. He's incredibly good-looking, isn't he?"

With Céleste there was no need for pretense. "I've never seen anyone like him."

"He's not staying in Grand-Pré."

Soleil's spirits plummeted. "Are you certain?"

Céleste shrugged expressively. "That's what I heard. *He* hasn't talked to me. I did hear him mention you, though."

Soleil stiffened. "To whom? What did he say?"

"He asked Guillaume how old you are, and if you are betrothed."

"He did?" The excitement was back, spreading through her body like liquid fire. "What did Guillaume say?"

"That you have been left on the shelf at the great age of near sixteen, that no banns have been read over you, ever."

The heat expanded, blossoming in her cheeks. "How humiliating."

Céleste laughed. "He didn't seem put off by it. Remie, I mean."

"What did he say after that?"

"Nothing. He simply stared at you for a moment—you were dancing with François—or perhaps it was Antoine—and then he turned away for another dipper of beer. The next thing, he was jabbering away in Micmac."

Soleil didn't know whether to be elated or chagrined. A glance told her that Remie Michaud was still engaged in a conversation with the Indians, facing away from her in three-quarter profile. She decided to change the subject, at least momentarily. "When are you going to learn to tell Antoine from François?"

Céleste sought the twins out across the clearing, no difficult task since they were standing together, sampling the new keg of fir beer. "It's François on the right, isn't it?"

"No. That's Antoine," Soleil said flatly.

The younger girl pursed her lips. "How can you tell?"

"They don't look that much alike," Soleil said. "Not if you see their faces. I'll admit it's more difficult with only a rear view."

"They look as like as any two eels caught in the weir," Céleste stated.

Soleil's reply was a shot in the dark, for her friend had as yet said nothing to indicate an uncommon interest in either of the twins. Céleste had, however, been partnered at dancing by either François or Antoine more often of late than in the past. "Which one of them is it you've set your cap for?"

Now it was Céleste's turn to blush. "How does one choose between a pair of eels?" she asked with a show of careless bravado that was diminished by the color in her face.

Soleil laughed. "I don't know, but there's more to a man than his looks. My brothers are different, you know. Living with François, for instance, would not be at all the same as marrying Antoine. Their attitudes are far from identical, no matter what they look like."

Céleste sighed. "I know. Antoine is the leader, François the follower. Which would I want? Both are quick and energetic and hardworking. They are both funny. And—" she frowned a little, watching the twins, who were now clowning around near the fire "—they both tend to dip into the beer a bit too often."

As if to prove that statement, the shoving match between the twins sent Antoine reeling backward. He stumbled against the newcomer, so that Remie swung sharply around, his beer sloshing over the rim of his mug.

"Pardon, M. Michaud," Antoine apologized at once. "My clumsy oaf of a brother plays the fool at your expense."

François, too, offered his apologies, though he was laughing. "I only meant to cause my brother to fall into the fire," he explained. "Not to insult a visitor."

Remie was a head taller than either of them. He stared for a few seconds as if memorizing their faces. "Cyrs, are you?" he asked.

At that they both laughed, for anyone could have guessed.

"Apologies accepted," Remie decided. "Though I warn you, should it happen again, I may be the one to throw the pair of you into the fire myself." He was grinning, and he looked past the brothers and directly at Soleil.

Again that shock of excitement ran through her. She forgot Céleste, or the twins, or that the entire village was gathered and might be watching. She was totally engrossed in Remie Michaud.

"Perhaps," he said in a voice that carried clearly to her across an expanse of a dozen feet, "you could influence your beautiful sister to dance with me again."

François shook his head. "We've no influence over Soleil. She makes her own decisions. You'll have to ask her and take your chances, I'm afraid."

Remie made no direct response to that. Instead, he drained the mug, put it down for the next thirsty man and strode directly to where the two girls stood facing him.

"Mlle Soleil, the music is about to resume, I think. Would you dance with me?"

Soleil swallowed, her mouth inexplicably dry. She had been dancing since she was a child, and never had an invitation sent such shivers of pleasure through her. "I would be happy to, *monsieur*," she agreed. And then, as Céleste surreptitiously kicked her ankle, she added, "Have you met my friend, Céleste Dubay?"

He acknowledged the other girl, repeating her name in that voice that somehow managed to send vibrations along Soleil's spine. But it was not at Céleste that he looked, except briefly.

Soleil was swung away to join the other dancers. The faces of the onlookers were a blur; there was Barbe, smiling approval, and Émile, intent on his fiddling but aware, as well, that his older daughter was the object of the stranger's attentions.

It had never bothered her before that it was impossible to be alone with a boy—a man, in Remie's case—but Soleil found herself wishing that there were no spectators, that they could be allowed to get acquainted without chaperons.

Being alone with a man, however, was not a thing that would be permitted. Or so she thought.

Had Remie maneuvered the dancing, she wondered, feeling dazed, so that when the music ended, he and Soleil were at the far end of the clearing, away from the fire and the musicians? Several old women sat gossiping there, but Soleil knew they were deaf as stones; even if they ceased their chatter they would not overhear the words spoken a few yards away.

"Your father is one of the fiddlers, is he not?" Remie asked. He spoke softly, for he did not know the old women were deaf. "The one on the right?"

"Yes," Soleil admitted, attributing her breathlessness to the vigor of the dance.

"And your mama, where is she?"

"Across there. The one with the blue kerchief."

Remie followed her gaze, nodding. "The prettiest one there. I might have known."

Was that a compliment? she wondered, confused. To indicate that *she* was pretty, because her mother was?

"And brothers—you have a dozen of them here somewhere?" His black eyes scanned the crowd of people who were already moving into the steps of the next dance.

Her laugh was shaky, though she was not sure why. It was not as if she were a green girl who had never been shown any attention. The boys had been seeking her out since before she was Danielle's age. What was there about this man that made it different?

"Not so many. There is Louis, over there—the one speaking to his wife, Madeleine, with the blond hair. And the twins you've met, and...over there is Pierre, he is widowed, and those are his two little boys with Mama. Jacques is the one poking at the fire with a stick, the youngest, and somewhere there is Bertin. He is next older than I . . ."

"Not a full dozen, then. That's a relief," Remie said. His hand rested upon her arm, drawing her gently but firmly back into the shadows of the trees. It had grown quite dark by this time, and the firelight was far away. "And there is no betrothed? No jealous suitor?"

"There are would-be suitors," she admitted. "No betrothed."

For long seconds she felt paralyzed with some new emotion as he studied her face at close range in the dimness. When he spoke, his voice was even softer than it had been before.

"You are quite extraordinarily beautiful, Mlle Soleil. In all of Louisbourg I saw no one of such loveliness. But no doubt you have been told that many times, so it is unimportant coming from a stranger."

Nothing about this man was unimportant, Soleil thought. His hand still rested on her shoulder, strong and warm through the material of her sleeve. Perhaps her thoughts would not be so chaotic if he were not touching her . . . yet she did not draw away.

"It must have been . . . interesting, to visit the fort. I have never been anywhere like that, with hundreds of people there all at the same time."

"Thousands," Remie corrected gently. "Thirty-five hundred soldiers alone. Plus another two thousand administrators, fishermen and tradesmen."

Please, God, she begged silently, *do not let my mind go blank so that I appear an idiot. Not now!* She groped for an intelligent response. "So many! Louis . . . my brother Louis has been there, but long ago, and only briefly. He said it was very beautiful."

"It is," Remie agreed immediately. "Someday, if you like, I shall tell you all about it."

Her heart lurched. "I . . . I had heard that you would not be among us for long, M. Michaud."

And then she wished her tongue had not said that, for it clearly revealed that she had been discussing him with others. Madeleine said that *she* had won Louis through modesty and coy glances, never allowing him to know how taken she was with him, not until after he had committed himself. Céleste, too, counseled that course. Yet here Soleil was, blurting out whatever came to mind. Not that very much did, she thought in something approaching despair, and never had it mattered more to her to be able to impress a man.

"I had thought to move on in a few days," Remie said. "But that was before I saw you."

There was a burst of raucous hilarity from the group around the beer keg, and a shower of sparks rose into the night sky as an armload of wood was dropped into the flames. If the sparks had fallen directly onto her, Soleil could not have moved away from this man to avoid them.

What did one say to such a statement?

"I . . . would be most pleased to hear more about Louis-bourg," she managed, and was disgusted with the triviality of the remark, for all that it was true.

"I believe that I will have occasion, tomorrow, to discuss business with your father, M. Cyr," Remie said in that soft voice that had the power to send prickles all through her. "May I hope that I will encounter you, as well?"

Again she spoke without considering how she would sound, and then was sorry. She wanted every word to be significant, yet none was. "What business do you have with Papa?"

He laughed, and never had amusement been so delicious. "I don't know yet. I'll think of something."

Suddenly it was clear to her. He liked her. He admired her. He wanted to know her better. And there was no reason to be coy, to play a silly part. If Remie Michaud was the man for her, he must know her as she was.

"Then come slightly before midday," she told him boldly. "I will be walking out to the hay fields with the noontime meal, and the basket is heavy."

He laughed again. "Carrying heavy loads is my speciality, Mlle Soleil. I shall be there. And now, lest we should linger here overlong and invite unwanted comment, perhaps we should dance again."

Soleil moved with him once more into the mass of stomping, swaying figures, and her heart soared.

4

IN THE CURTAINED BED in which they had slept together every night of their marriage, within which existed all the privacy they had ever had, Louis told his wife of his plans.

He had expected her to be dismayed at the idea of leaving her family—and the one she had married into—for a strange and distant place. He had not anticipated the depth of desperation his words evoked, nor the storm of passionate weeping that followed.

Louis held her in his arms, smothering the choking sobs against his bare chest, stroking Madeleine in the way that ordinarily would have led to a session of lovemaking.

This time, wrapped only in her own despair, Madeleine did not respond to his touch in the slightest. "You cannot do this, Louis!" she protested. "You cannot ask this of me!"

"Shh! You'll wake the entire household!" He tried to draw her closer, but Madeleine resisted.

"What does it matter! They'll all know soon enough, won't they, what a foolish idea you've taken into your head! You can't seriously propose to take Marc and me off into the wilderness where we'll never see anyone we know again! You can't deprive Marc of his grandparents and his aunts and uncles, and me of my parents! I cannot believe that your father will not forbid it!"

Louis sighed and retained his hold on her, though it was now tenuous, and he'd given up any idea of arousing her to compliance with his immediate desires. Indeed, they were fading before the raw pain he heard in his wife's voice.

"My father will not approve of what I do any more than will yours," he admitted. "But you and Marc are my responsibility, Madeleine, and I cannot stay here any longer while all hope of the future sifts through my fingers. There *is* no future for us here; not for us, certainly not for our son. The British are determined to break our backs, to beat us into submission. Perhaps if we go, our families will follow."

This last was a feeble hope—her parents as well as his were firmly wedded to their land—and Louis flinched when his wife actually struck his chest with her small protesting hands.

"They will not! Father Émile and my own papa will never give up what they've labored for all their lives! They would die for their lands!"

"Aye," Louis agreed, suddenly grim. "They may have to, and still not retain them. Madeleine, I have no wish to cause you suffering, but staying here and being beaten down and down is no solution to the problem. In time you'll come to see that I'm right, that we *must* go, and it's better to go now, before the British make it impossible!"

"I cannot!" Madeleine's voice rose so that it must surely have carried beyond the wooden-walled bed, through the hangings on the open side of it to others in the house who were not yet asleep. She had planted her fists firmly against him, holding him off, and there was an intensity in her words that frightened him. "I will not go, Louis."

Never in their four years together had she defied him. And much as he loved her, Louis could not allow her to do it now. He touched her lips gently to remind her once more that her voice would travel beyond their bedchamber. "You are my wife," he told her. "You *will* go with me, Madeleine, because I know it is for the best. I will not have my son crushed under the weight of the British yoke."

It was only then that Madeleine, who had also planned something special for this night when they were alone, remembered. She fought down her panic, for she held a winning card, she was sure.

"There will be more than one son," she told him, her happiness now having taken on a bittersweet quality, "for a new babe grows beneath my heart. By spring Marc will have a little brother or sister, and you cannot possibly expect me, in my condition, to walk for miles through the woods in the fall of the year and in the storms that cross the Northumberland Strait to a strange land where there is no one to help us through the winter. We must stay here at least until the child is born, and we are both strong enough to travel." Some of her anguish had subsided, for she was convinced he must see the logic of this, and during the coming months when Louis was confined to the house, she would be able to work her wiles upon him as she had always done.

For an instant Louis's breathing was suspended beneath her hands, and she thought she had won, at least temporarily.

"You are with child? And all is well?"

"So far."

"When is it due?"

"The end of February, I think." The joy in the impending birth seeped back into her.

"February. By then we will be well situated on Île St. Jean," Louis said.

Madeleine's happiness evaporated. "You cannot be serious! Louis, for the love of God, consider! You know that I have already lost two children, and that while I was cosseted and cared for here at home! In the wilderness, unattended by Mama

Barbe or my own mama, this child will perish, too! I will not allow that to happen!''

"If that is God's will, then so be it," Louis said gently, stroking her cheek with a big finger in the way that she had always loved. "Once we have a home of our own, in a safer place, there will be other children, my love. But we must escape from here, and we must do it now, before it is too late."

She was stunned at his cruel words. "You do not care if the child dies?''

"Of course I care, about both the child and you. But it is right for us to go, while there is still time. We must trust in God to see us through whatever ordeals we may have to face."

"Trust in God!'' Madeleine wrenched herself entirely out of his embrace to sit upon the far edge of the bed, pushing aside the hands that sought to hold her. "Why do we not trust in Him to protect us from the British?''

"Because He has not yet seen fit to do so in all these years," Louis replied, "and I can only conclude that this is one of those matters in which He intends me to use my own judgment. We will go as soon as the harvest is completed, Madeleine."

His hand closed around her slim wrist and he drew her back within the curtains to cradle her as her body was torn with the sobs she could not control.

Gracious God, he begged silently, let me be correct in this. Guide me in this, as in all things. His own tears mingled with his wife's as they clung together in the darkness.

IN HER OWN BED, beside Danielle, who slept quietly, Soleil heard the muffled crying.

He's told her, she thought, and felt her sister-in-law's grief as if it were her own. She does not want to go and she will fight him to stay, if she can, for the sake of the baby she carries, if not for herself.

Yet Soleil did not believe that Madeleine would win out over her husband. Soleil had known Louis longer than Madeleine, and in some ways she knew him better. Her brother would not have announced his plan if he had not made up his mind, and once he had done that, there was little that could sway him— not even the wife he loved. In his own mind he was convinced that leaving was best for her as well as for himself.

She lay looking up into the darkness, remembering the time that Pierre had playfully but inaccurately shot an arrow toward a squirrel that might have gone into the stew; the arrow had instead struck Soleil in the arm.

She would never forget the shock and pain of it, nor the way that young Louis had dealt with the situation. "Hold her still," he had ordered the white-faced Pierre, "and I'll cut it out."

"No!" Soleil had cried, but Louis was adamant.

"It must come out at once. Hold her firm, you damned young idiot!"

Pierre had obeyed and Soleil had obeyed as Louis took his knife and removed the barb projecting from her flesh, then pulled the shaft through from the other side. The wound had bled freely, Pierre had vomited into the bushes, and Louis had bound his brother's shirt over the resulting bloody mess so that they could get Soleil home before she fainted from the blood loss.

Louis had known how much she hurt, but he had done what was necessary. No doubt he would do so again, with Madeleine, for her own good.

Only an hour ago Soleil had walked home with the others through the summer darkness, glad that no one could see her face, see the smile that persisted in turning up the corners of her mouth, or the color that surely suffused her face.

It had been the most thrilling evening of her life. Remie Michaud was beyond doubt the most exciting man she had ever met, and tomorrow he would be here to see her. Oh, he would pretend he had some business to attend to with her father, but everyone—including Émile—would know his real purpose: to further his acquaintance with Soleil.

The smile returned to her lips. No doubt Mama would insist that Danielle accompany them to carry lunch to the boys, because Acadian women were always properly chaperoned. The smile deepened as she recalled how frustrated Louis had been when he was courting Madeleine and her mama was always present. But Danielle could be persuaded to walk well ahead of them, and there would be an opportunity to study Remie in the daylight, to see if the magic remained.

She did not seriously believe that it would not. No, Soleil knew that she had found the man of her dreams. All that remained was to convince him to stay on in Grand-Pré, to speak to Father Castin about the banns, and then . . .

Acadian betrothals tended to be brief. There would be a wedding, with dancing and singing and celebration, and then perhaps . . .

The unexpected disloyal thought was sobering. If Louis and Madeleine had left for Île St. Jean, their room would be available. That would mean that Louis would not be present at the wedding, that she would have lost a brother when she gained a husband. Yet what alternative was there for herself and Remie if they married? It wasn't likely Papa would want to build on another addition simply for the two of them, and having no privacy at all—Pierre and his ill-fated bride had slept on a pallet on the floor of the kitchen for the first six months of their marriage—was not to be thought of.

Soleil laughed softly to herself. How confident she was! So sure that she and Remie were meant for each other, that the good Lord had brought him to pass through Grand-Pré strictly for her benefit!

A few more hours and he would be here. Then she would be sure, the moment she saw him in daylight, she thought. Oh, she had no desire to hurry a courtship. That was something a girl only enjoyed once, and she might as well make the most of it— up to a point—and savor every moment, as all the women before her had done.

Soleil snuggled down beside her sister and was glad that she could no longer hear Madeleine crying as she drifted off to sleep.

BARBE TURNED, flushed from the heat of the cooking fire, in time to see her daughter-in-law pass through the room on the way to the privy.

"What's wrong with her? She was fine when we got home last night, but now she looks as if she spent the night weeping."

Danielle craned her head to see Madeleine's averted face. "I didn't hear anything."

Barbe's shrewd gaze rested on Soleil. "You've a look of understanding about *you*."

"Madeleine hasn't said a thing to me," Soleil stated truthfully.

Barbe nodded. "But Louis has, eh? Don't risk eternal wrath by telling lies."

"I speak no lies," Soleil protested mildly. "If Louis and Madeleine have something to tell everyone, they'll do it in their own time."

"Humph. Here, finish cooking this bacon, and, Danielle, call one of the boys to fetch another bucket of water. Henri!" she called to the little boy who was still rubbing the sleep from his eyes. "See to Vincent, help him with his stockings!"

"Yes, Grand-maman," Henri said obediently, and bent down to draw his younger brother toward a corner where they would not be trampled in the early-morning rush. Pierre was not expected to look after such tasks with his motherless children; there were women around to do that. Henri was three, Vincent was not quite two, both recognizable at once from their dark hair and eyes and deep dimples as members of the Cyr family.

Soleil hoped her mother had been momentarily diverted from whatever was amiss with Madeleine. It was, after all, not Soleil's announcement to make, and she would not be pushed into revealing confidences, but Barbe was tenacious when her interest was aroused.

At the moment she was too busy, however, to pursue the matter. She said nothing even when Madeleine returned, her eyelids newly reddened, her pretty mouth set in an unhappy line, to take up her son to feed him.

Unlike suppertime, when talk flowed freely around the big table, breakfast was eaten in comparative silence except for commands to the younger children and Émile's orders for the day's work. Louis appeared not to notice his wife's face; he stretched out a hand to ruffle his son's hair as he left the table without a word to her and went out into the yard after the others.

Émile, the last of the men to leave, glanced at his daughter-in-law, then at his wife, raising his eyebrows. Barbe shrugged her ignorance of the situation, and he sighed and left the house, too. Sooner or later someone would tell him what was going on, he supposed. Probably it was no more than a marital spat; the good God knew he and Barbe had had enough of those, especially early in their marriage.

Only Soleil was aware of the seriousness of the situation, and even she was not inclined to dwell on it. She cared very deeply what happened, but there was nothing she could do to influence Louis, and besides, there was Remie Michaud.

She glanced at the marks that had been cut into the frame of the east-facing window to designate the time. Four hours, at least, before she could expect Remie to arrive.

When he did, she thought, both she and the house would look their best, and there would be the welcoming aroma of cooking food.

She wiped at Vincent's chin, lifted him off the bench and began to clear the table, an anticipatory tattoo beating wildly in her chest.

5

BARBE WAS far more observant than those around her gave her credit for. Something was severely amiss with her oldest son and his wife, and it went beyond a mere disagreement. Madeleine had been so happy the past few weeks, holding to herself the secret of the new life within her. She had been smiling and content at the dance last night; Barbe had experienced similar feelings often enough in her pregnancies and knew she had correctly identified her daughter-in-law's symptoms.

Louis was harder to interpret because he kept his feelings to himself to a greater extent; his face was not the easily read book that Madeleine's was. Nor even as easy to read as his father's. Émile could never fool her, Barbe thought fondly, though he sometimes refused to discuss a matter with her unless she pried it out of him.

The whole family had been in good spirits when they returned from the dance the night before. Louis and Madeleine had walked hand in hand until tiny Marc grew too sleepy to balance on his father's shoulders, and they had laughingly relinquished their own closeness so that Louis could carry him more securely.

So something had happened after they had all retired, something that had left Madeleine weeping for half the night. The privacy provided by the enclosed beds was only an illusion; sounds carried through the wooden walls built on three sides, and the bed curtains were no barrier to sound at all. How many times over the twenty-seven years of their marriage had Barbe lain awake, hearing and evaluating the nighttime movements of her family—the whisperings, the sobs, the muffled laughter? Oh, she was an expert, even without the added evidence of reddened and downcast eyes, the trembling lip, the exchanged glances on the following morning.

Something was wrong, and it caused deep currents of uneasiness in Barbe. She almost feared to know what it was, because instinct told her that it threatened the fabric of her life, the closeness of her family, which meant more to her than life itself.

And there was Soleil. Though she had as yet made no comment, Barbe had not missed the interlude between the girl and that Michaud fellow when they had faded into the shadows beside the clearing. Barbe had seen their faces as they danced past the bonfire, had observed how their glances clung to each other. So, it was happening.

She had mixed feelings about it. It was time the girl chose a husband, and there was no denying that young Michaud was an attractive devil. But she'd always thought that Soleil would marry one of the young men from the village, a boy she had known all her life, and go to live only a few miles away, well within walking distance. When Soleil was brought to bed in childbirth, Barbe expected to be there. When there was illness or grief, they would support each other. And in old age, which seemed rapidly approaching, Barbe could reasonably assume that her daughters, rather than daughters-in-law, would be the ones to see to her comfort.

With Remie Michaud in the picture, those things did not seem quite as certain as they would otherwise have been. He was a stranger, an unknown factor.

Certainly *that* one hadn't cried all night, Barbe thought, watching Soleil across the room as she swept the floor with the broom Barbe herself had made this past summer of the reeds that grew along the dykes. Even as she watched thoughtfully,

Soleil's mouth curved into a gentle smile, and her mother could imagine the thoughts that accompanied it.

Well, whatever the good God had in mind, that was what would be, she decided philosophically. The only trouble was, sometimes it was difficult to know what was God's will and what was the will of man . . . or woman.

Soleil had finished sweeping the dirt out the front door. She now took up a cloth to dust the windowsills and then the mantel on the fireplace where the stew for the noon meal already bubbled gently, sending out a savory aroma. Barbe's eyes narrowed. When she spoke it was with deceptive casualness.

"Expecting company, are we?"

Soleil started and flushed. "What do you mean?"

"You're uncommonly tidy this morning. Did you, by any chance, invite M. Michaud to visit us today?"

The color in Soleil's cheeks grew deeper as she reached up to tuck an errant curl under her cap. "I did not invite him," she disclaimed. "I would not do that without asking you or Papa."

Barbe astutely assessed the reply. "But you would not discourage a man who invited himself, eh?"

For a moment the girl's face was a study in mixed emotions, then she laughed. "No. I would not discourage a man who invited himself. As long as he was not Marcel Salieres."

Barbe laughed with her. Marcel was a nice enough boy, but she thought his mother a tyrant. Not a mother-in-law she would wish on a child of her own. "Perhaps you should bake a cake this morning. Just in case a guest drops in unannounced."

"A guest?" Danielle asked eagerly, emerging from a bedchamber carrying a load of quilts destined for the kettle that was coming to a boil over the fire outdoors. "Are we having company?"

"It's only a possibility," Barbe told her blandly. "Get on with that washing or the day will be over and our sheets will still be wet. Your father has an aversion to wet sheets. They tend to make him quite irritable."

They all giggled, then, only a few steps closer to the doorway, Danielle paused again. "Is it M. Michaud?"

Soleil's face gave away the answer, and they giggled again.

"Ah, he's so good-looking, isn't he? And he dances like a dream. I don't suppose he would pay any attention to a twelve-year-old, would he? Though he *did* dance with me once."

Barbe made shooing motions. "Get about your business! You are much too young to be worrying about a man. Perhaps next year..."

"I certainly hope so," Danielle observed, and went on out to the yard, leaving her mother and sister smiling quietly at each other.

REMIE APPROACHED the Cyr place with mingled uncertainty and expectation.

The sun was warm, the slight haze of autumn shimmered in the air, and a few trees were turning color already, though for the most part the woods were a rich deep green except for the ghostly white trunks of the birches. Overhead a hawk soared soundlessly across the blue, swooping suddenly toward some small unseen creature that would provide a meal.

Had the girl really been as beautiful as he remembered? In the light of day it scarcely seemed possible. In the moonlight or the firelight, or the dark itself, a woman could be mysterious and tantalizing, irresistible. And a generous measure of drink contributed to the illusion.

Mostly, though, it *was* an illusion. Once a man's head had cleared, the ache dissipated and his senses restored to normal, most females were only that: ordinary females.

Yet he had had no great amount of the fir beer last night, and there had been no moon, only the flickering firelight. And he had seen her first in the full light of early evening, when the very sight had taken his breath away.

And there had been those moments in the shadows, when he had felt the flesh of her arm firm yet soft under his hand; when he had looked into thick-lashed brown eyes at close range, felt the breath from that mouth that looked as if she'd just been eating raspberries, and he'd resisted the urge to take her into his arms and kiss her, right there in front of the whole village.

Insanity. It would have been insanity. No doubt the entire male population of Grand-Pré would have joined forces to throw him into the fire or pitch him over one of their dykes into the water, pelting him with rocks to make sure he drowned.

The Acadians were a chaste and honorable people. They protected their women.

Well, he'd felt a compulsion to protect this Soleil Cyr himself, hadn't he? From every man but Remie Michaud.

There was only one way he could have the girl, and that was with the permission of her parents and the Church.

He wasn't at all certain that he was ready for anything like that. In fact, before the Cyr family had arrived at the dance last night, he would have sworn that any such consideration was years away in his mind.

He liked the life he led. Alone in the woods, trading with the Micmacs or carrying his furs on to Québec City for eventual shipment to France—an infrequent dalliance with some pretty girl from either a French or Indian settlement adding a bit of spice to his life now and then.

Soleil Cyr was not a girl to be dallied with. Not even in the most innocent sense. If he were to see her after today, it would have to be with serious intentions. Intentions that until last night had never entered his mind.

Yet after he'd returned to Uncle Guillaume's house, he'd lain awake for hours on his pallet before the open fire, seeing the girl's face in his memory. Feeling her skin, the soft flesh, wanting so badly to touch the firm young breasts that swelled her bodice, to run a hand over the curve of hip and thigh. Feeling the blood coursing through his veins like the rum the soldiers at Louisbourg drank, heating his body until he'd have welcomed the opportunity to run out into a snow bank to cool off.

There was only one way to quench such a fire, Remie knew. Only he did not know if he was ready to do it.

Perhaps, he thought almost hopefully, she would not be beautiful in the light of day, without the beer. Perhaps he had not noticed that her teeth were bad, or that she had a limp....

No, she had danced as gracefully as the grain waved before a summer breeze. Her teeth had been perfect, and her smile... Even at this time of day his loins grew warm, remembering her smile.

Well, he would soon know. And what would he do then? he wondered, not sure whether the knot in his stomach was from dread or joy.

"He's coming!" Danielle hissed from the doorway. "Soleil, Mama, he's here!"

Soleil quickly ran her hands over her skirt, smoothing it, and twisted a curl to peek provocatively from beneath the white cap. Should she have worn a different dress or made a different kind of cake...?

And then he was there, filling the doorway with a size that would dwarf her father and brothers. So tall he was, and broad through the shoulders, though slim through the waist and hips.

"M. Michaud," Barbe greeted him, neither warmly nor coolly. "What a surprise. Come in, come in."

"Madame Cyr," he greeted her, but his eyes were drawn past her at once toward the girl who stood in the middle of the comfortable room. "My apologies. I would have a word with M. Cyr, if it is not too much trouble. I am told that he is very good at repairing leather work, and I have need of such services."

Did he indeed? Barbe thought, amused at the transparent excuse. Émile *was* an expert with leather, but she doubted his talents were superior to Michaud's own. A man who had spent years in the wilderness was not likely to be inept at seeing to his own needs.

"Soleil, fetch M. Michaud a cool drink. Perhaps some fir beer, *monsieur*?"

"No. No, thank you." Remie had already determined to keep a clear head today. "Though a drink of water wouldn't be amiss."

"Of course," Soleil said at once, and brought the gourd; she could not help wondering if her voice sounded as breathless as she felt.

He took the drink, steadying her hand ever so briefly as he accepted it; he could not tell if the tremor was hers or his or the two combined.

"Thank you, *mam'selle*."

"You're welcome, I'm sure."

"Well," Barbe interjected, afraid if she did not take a hand in the matter they would fall over as they stood staring into each other's eyes, "I'm afraid M. Cyr is in the fields, harvesting the hay, you know. He does not usually return until dusk. But my daughters will be taking food to the men at midday—very shortly, now. Danielle, stir the stew and see if it is nearly ready. Perhaps you wouldn't mind walking out to the fields with them to meet Émile?" As if the two of them hadn't planned it that way, she thought.

"Not at all," Remie assured her quickly.

"Very well. Please, sit down until the food is ready to go. Venison stew, it is. Perhaps you would like some of it? Soleil and Danielle usually eat before they go, rather than carry their own food along."

No one mentioned that normally only one of the girls would have made the journey. Today there would be a chaperon, even if it was only a silly twelve-year-old. Barbe was not truly concerned about Soleil's virtue; she only wanted to maintain the illusion of propriety, and she knew her daughter even if she did not know Remie Michaud; there would be no scrambles in the bushes for Soleil Cyr, ever.

Remie sat across from the women at the table and ate the stew, which was thick with chunks of meat and vegetables. He wondered if Soleil had made it.

The magic had not been in the firelight, in the twilight or the darkness, nor in the fir beer. The girl was still beautiful, so beautiful it made a deep, intense ache in his gut.

Remie was afraid that his days of freedom were drawing to a close, and he did not know if he was more glad or sorry.

6

SOLEIL HAD NO reservations whatever.

She had not known that it was possible to feel such exhilaration as this, walking beside the tall, strong man who carried her basket. Never had she felt so alive, so expectant.

He had come. It meant he was as seriously interested in her as she was in him.

After an envious and admiring glance, Danielle had obeyed her sister's unspoken instruction to move on ahead, though she would take pains to fall back before they came in sight of the fields so that the three of them would appear to have been together all the way from the house.

Soleil had sometimes wished her father and brothers worked closer to home. But today, with Remie beside her, she wouldn't have minded walking all the way to the Minas Basin.

"Is it far?" he asked, as if reading her mind.

"Three miles, perhaps. You are much used to walking."

He looked down at her, shifting the basket to the other arm. "Well used to it," he agreed. "Am I walking too fast for you?"

She glanced up into the sky. "They will not expect us before the sun reaches its peak."

Obediently he slowed his steps. "Then by all means let us not hurry too much. I wasn't sure . . ."

"Sure of what?" she prompted when the silence had drawn out too long.

"That you would be the same when I saw you today. Still beautiful. Still . . . exciting."

Something constricted in her chest. "And . . . am I?"

He grinned. "Only a female who knows the answers full well would dare to ask. I do not think there is much artifice in you, Mlle Soleil."

"I am only a simple country girl. Artifice is for the ladies in Paris, perhaps. Or at least those in the cities . . . such as Louisbourg. How long were you there, *monsieur*?"

"This time, about six months. More time cooped up inside four walls than I have ever spent since I was a child. And four walls colder than those at the fortress are hard to imagine. In fact, the whole of Louisbourg in winter is beyond imagining, far colder than the woods. Even in summer the wind sweeps in off the sea with the chill of winter in it. I've been warmer in a lean-to made of cedar boughs than I was at Louisbourg."

His voice was deep, even, assured. Mature for one of his years. Like Louis's, she thought. He was a man like her oldest brother. The thought gave her confidence. "Why were you there, then, if you liked it better in the woods?"

For a moment he hesitated, then he looked directly at her, forgetting to walk. "I was injured. There is a hospital at the fort, and doctors. I would have preferred a Micmac medicine man, a *puoin*, to the doctors and their leeches. The Micmacs do not believe in bloodletting, and they are excellent healers, as I've reason to know. And," he added wryly, beginning to walk again with shorter strides to match hers, "their lodges are warm."

Her dark eyes were wide. "You must have been very ill to have stayed for six months."

"I would have healed more quickly under the ministrations of the *puoin*. Next time I am mauled by a bear I will try to arrange it nearer an Indian village than a fort," he said.

"Mauled by a bear? Mother of God!"

"On second thought," Remie said, his wide mouth twitching, "perhaps I'll forgo another tussle with a bear. He left a few marks that leave me permanent reminders, and less... attractive."

Soleil felt as if her heart were in her throat. Without conscious thought she put out a hand to touch his sleeve, to cause him to halt so that she might study his face.

Sure enough, there were a few small marks that she had not noticed last night. At the hairline on the left side several tiny scars showed a lighter shade in the bronze skin, and there was another line beneath his chin. Her lips parted and she put out a hand again to trace the scar down to the mat of dark hair visible at the open neck of his shirt.

"It gets worse as you go down," Remie said. His tone was offhand, but there was a tenseness in his eyes.

"Mother of God," Soleil breathed again. She was suddenly aware of the touch of his skin, the coppery scent of him, and she withdrew her hand as if she'd inadvertently touched the handle of a hot skillet.

She was aware, too, of the changes in her own body. Sensations she had never before experienced were coursing through her, in the most private parts of her; her breathing seemed constricted, her blood hot and racing so that the pulses pounded in her ears and in her throat.

As she stared into his eyes, instinct told her that it mattered to him, mattered very much, how she reacted to his disfigurement. He did not want to come to her less than perfect, yet a wild animal had already dulled that perfection given to him by God.

"Sweet Jesus, I thank Him for sparing your life," she said huskily. And then, again on instinct and against all propriety, she lifted her hand and spread the neck of the shirt so that she might see the worst.

Remie stood quite still as she pushed the coarse fabric aside to reveal a mass of scarring amid the chest hair. She winced. The wound was well healed, but the angry color had not entirely faded from the worst of it.

Her fingertips brushed across the marks made by claws and teeth, and by now the fiery liquid in her veins was nearly unbearable. Tears formed in her eyes.

She didn't remember lifting her hands to either side of his face, but she would remember forever when he shifted the basket out of the way and brought up his free hand to cup her cheek in a caress as feather light as her own.

They stood for long seconds, touching, yet with their bodies held apart, eyes locked together in the most intimate communication Soleil had ever known.

She had seen this man for the first time only last night, yet somehow— Oh, Blessed Mother! What magic it was!—she felt as if she had known him forever.

She would not have resisted, no matter what he had chosen to do next. This, then, was what she had dreamed of and waited for: this man, this moment.

Only the moment did not last. Reality intruded. Remie dropped his hand, exhaling a breath as tremulous as her own, and stepped back, glancing up at the sun.

"If we don't deliver the stew soon, they will question how long it took us to bring it," he said. "I've no wish to face an indignant and protective father and six brothers when I ask permission to call upon you."

Sanity reluctantly returned. A shudder ran through her, a belated realization of how near she had come to disgracing herself. What must Remie think of her?

He did not, however, appear to think badly of her, Soleil decided as they moved on with quickened steps. Danielle was nowhere to be seen ahead of them; Soleil wondered, with burning cheeks, whether her sister had looked back during those few crucial minutes, and if so, whether she would report to Mama.

"You've no objection to my calling?" Remie asked, swinging the basket so that it brushed against her skirts.

She felt strangled but managed a coherent reply. "Not at all, *monsieur*. I am sure Papa will give you permission to do so."

"No doubt he has been worried," Remie suggested cheerfully, seemingly recovering more quickly than she, "that he would not be able to marry off such an ugly daughter."

"No doubt," Soleil agreed, and they were both laughing when they overtook Danielle.

Her pretty face was lively and inquisitive. "What have you been doing for so long?"

"It was not long at all," Soleil retorted, and then her eyes met Remie's in a shared understanding such as she had never before known with anyone else.

All the rest of our lives, she thought suddenly, it will be this way. I will look at Remie across a room, and he will look at me, and we will each know what the other is thinking.

"It's late enough so that they will all be starving," Danielle said. Her curiosity was intense and unrewarded, though her imagination raced. "No doubt Papa will want to know what took us so long."

Émile, however, had something far more disturbing to think about than the fact that his midday meal was a few minutes late. Louis had made his announcement.

Émile was thunderstruck, incredulous.

"You cannot be serious! Leave Grand-Pré? Leave your family, and Madeleine's?"

Louis, who had thought out his words ahead of time, even rehearsed them in his mind until his head ached, was certain he had made himself quite clear when the time came to confront his father. He might have known, he thought wearily, that it *would* be a confrontation rather than simply an announcement. Émile would not let the matter go at that.

"I am a grown man, Papa. I have a responsibility to my family to see to their future, and there is no future for any of us here."

"Cyrs have been on this land since 1648 . . . over a hundred years! My grandfather and my father passed it on to me, and I will pass it on to my sons!"

Émile faced his firstborn in desperation; he could have been no more stricken, no more distressed, if he had been bleeding to death. Indeed, to him his children *were* his blood, and the land was second in importance only to his sons.

Louis knew this. His own heart twisted in shared pain, but he had made up his mind and he knew he was right. "I'm sorry, Papa. We go as soon as the hay is in."

If it had been Antoine or François, or even Pierre, Émile might have employed persuasive words. Louis was different. He made his plans without consulting anyone, and once his decision was made, he was immovable. He had been that way from the time he was Marc's age and had refused to eat his boiled cabbage.

Émile's throat worked. The words he would have spoken refused to form.

Louis stared into his father's face, then clamped a hand firmly on the older man's shoulder. "I would go more easily with your blessing, Papa."

Émile's face twisted. "You will always have that, my son," he said.

The moment was broken by Pierre's shout. "Ah, here comes our food! What is it today, Soleil?"

There was a cessation of work as the younger brothers put down their tools and moved toward the approaching trio. Grand-père, who did not ordinarily work in the fields anymore, trailed behind them, still carrying his rake. Émile, feeling as if his heart would burst, swallowed and struggled to pull himself together as he greeted the newcomers.

"Ah, M. Michaud. How convenient that you happened along to carry the heavy basket," he said, striving for an appearance that all was well.

Remie swung the basket upward, demonstrating. "It is indeed very heavy for a woman to carry, M. Cyr." He was smiling. "I didn't mind the walk. The company was most charming."

Gradually the shock was receding and Émile's perceptions of the ordinary returning. One look at his older daughter was enough to convince him that here, too, dramatic change was coming. Soleil was blooming; her eyes sparkled, her lips curved in a smile, and color flooded the perfection of her small face.

She, too, I will lose soon, Émile thought. But at least this one would stay in Grand-Pré; she would not be lost to him forever, as he feared would be the case with Louis and young Marc.

Barbe did not yet know about Louis and Madeleine. When she was told, Émile's own pain would be magnified as he took on his wife's distress as well.

Yet it was the will of God, no doubt, he thought dully. Émile wondered hopelessly what he had done to incur His wrath, but he made no attempt to pray about the situation.

Short of striking the boy with lightning, not even God Himself could sway Louis once his mind was made up. Émile crossed himself and accepted the inevitable.

Soleil knew that Louis had told their father he was leaving. It was clearly written on both their faces for all to read. She was amazed, as she had been many times in the past, that her brothers remained unaware of any crisis.

They gathered around the basket, helping themselves to the stew and the bread, joking, teasing.

She had expected the teasing and tensed herself for it, but Remie Michaud was not easily embarrassed or shaken by their sly glances and provocative gibes.

As last night he had offered to pitch the twins into the fire, today he calmly agreed to a jesting challenge from François to a bit of rough-and-tumble amid the hay that Grand-père and Jacques had raked into windrows behind the others with the scythes.

"Before you eat, or after?" Remie asked.

The others laughed, and François danced out of reach. "On second thought, *monsieur*, I believe your reach is considerably longer than mine, and you outweigh me by too much. Give me a year to gain my full size and then we'll discuss the matter again."

"I'll still be faster," Remie assured him, helping himself to a slab of the hearty bread.

"Eat," Émile said sharply. "And get back to work. There will be time for foolishness when the hay is in."

The twins exchanged glances, their eyes rolling. What was the matter with Papa? He was not usually so short of temper.

Louis said nothing. He would tell the others when Papa had adjusted to the news; when he might be expected to say a word or two on Louis's behalf.

It was a relief to Soleil when the meal was finished, when the crumbs were scattered for the birds and the empty bowls replaced in the basket. She could not wait to get out of sight of the others again and wished for some excuse to send Danielle far ahead.

On the return trip, however, the younger girl was disinclined to leave them alone. She ignored Soleil's smoldering glances and strode along at Remie's other side, chattering away at him like an impudent squirrel.

"What is it like at Louisbourg, *monsieur*?"

"Cold, and crowded," Remie told her. "And foggy. You have never experienced fog until you have spent a winter at Louisbourg."

Danielle's eyes went round in a manner that her sister found extremely irritating. "We have heard tales about the governor's house. It is said it is very large—fifty rooms or more!"

"It is enormous," Remie agreed. He was amused by the girl's innocent coquetry. Given another year or two she would probably be as beautiful as her sister was. "It is also, I understand, just as cold as the rest of the place. Though it is far more elegant than the barracks and the hospital, and since the firewood is cut by the soldiers rather than by the governor, no doubt the fires at his mansion are more generously fed."

"Have you been inside it?" Danielle demanded, ignoring the expression on her sister's face.

"I was never invited to tea, no," he said, laughing when her face fell. "However, I did see in through open doors on several occasions."

Soleil wanted to know these things, too, but she resented Danielle's being the one to put the questions to Remie. "What was it like?" she asked. "Was it very beautiful?"

Remie considered. He was acutely aware of this girl beside him, of the loveliness of her face, of the rise and fall of her bosom beneath the chaste white bodice, of the tendrils of dark hair that escaped from beneath the modest cap. He felt a quickening in his loins as he gazed down upon her.

"It depends on your definition of beauty, I suppose. I saw one room where there was a rug on the floor, cream-colored, with an intricate pattern of flowers in pink and green and a gold design something like a sheaf of ripe wheat. The floors are all waxed and polished so that a man would probably be shot for walking across them in his boots. There were gold hangings at the windows, tied back with gold cords with tassels, and chandeliers overhead so filled with candles and crystals that at night they must have outdone the sun and the stars together."

"And what were the furnishings like?" Danielle pressed, actually leaning into his arm.

"Fragile things not much to *my* liking," Remie told her. "Chairs with such spindly legs that a man would fear to sit on them, with green and gold brocade upholstery too fine to touch, and mirrors everywhere with elaborate gilt frames. Pictures on the walls. Oh, the governor has the best that France could offer."

"And you didn't like it?" Danielle was incredulous. Surely he was making fun of her.

Remie, however, was perfectly serious. He gazed deeply into Soleil's eyes. "My idea of a home is not stone walls that let the cold seep through, and hold the damp, and mildew the bedding. Not a place where no amount of fire can ever warm all the corners, where the ceilings are so high that the heat all rises and there is none left where a man keeps his feet or a baby plays by the hearth."

Soleil's resentment of her sister had faded. Her breast rose and fell more quickly now; he was speaking to *her*, sending her one of those messages that she had already learned to recognize at once.

"One day I'll have a house of my own," Remie continued. "A small, snug house of square-cut logs superbly fitted together to keep out the drafts, warmer than stone, with sturdy chairs and bright quilts and food cooking on the hearth. And a...a wife and babes. A place for comfort, not elegance. A house that will welcome me home after a day in the woods as surely as my wife will welcome me."

He is talking to me, Soleil thought. Her heart swelled within her, and those sensations she had experienced earlier returned. Almost, but not quite, uncomfortable and alarming.

Her lips trembled, then firmed as she spoke. "If one is not a governor, then one must be sensible about such things."

"And you are very sensible," Remie said gravely.

But the humor lurking in his eyes warmed her, and at last she lowered her gaze. "Very sensible," she admitted. About everything, she knew, except this man, this Remie Michaud.

She would probably never ever be sensible as far as Remie was concerned. And, she thought as they walked on and the corners of her mouth involuntarily curled upward, she didn't care.

7

NEVER HAD SOLEIL been so strongly pulled in opposing directions.

Now that Louis's plans had been revealed, Madeleine wept openly. Like everyone else in the family, Soleil often averted her eyes from the young woman's misery, even as her heart ached for her sister-in-law. When she picked up young Marc, Soleil found herself hugging him too hard so that he cried out a protest. How many more times would she be able to hug him at all? Knowing that once he left Grand-Pré she might never see him again, or that if she did he would no longer be this chubby, happy infant, tore at her heart.

It was clear that the others felt the same way. Barbe did not cry, but she hugged Marc more often and made fewer demands on Madeleine. Once Soleil saw her mother's hand stretch out toward her oldest son's shoulder as he sat at the table, then draw back without making contact as Barbe bit her lower lip.

In the stillness of the night the entire household heard Madeleine's muffled sobs, heard Louis's deep murmurings, though they could not make out the words. Each morning ten pairs of brown eyes sought out the faces of the two, hopefully, only to see at once that Louis had not changed his mind. He would go when the harvest was in.

That would be no more than another week at most. There was no singing in the fields, no laughter or horseplay. Only Louis seemed himself: methodical, sober and efficient.

And then there was Remie.

No one could have had the slightest doubt that he was courting Soleil. Least of all, herself.

He came to church with Guillaume and his children on Sunday. Guillaume's wife, Marie, was too close to her confinement to walk to the village for services, so it was Remie who carried the smallest child and wiped his nose and took him outside when he had to relieve himself.

Remie was not totally occupied with his young cousin, however. His eyes met Soleil's boldly across the aisle when she glanced in his direction, causing delicate color to flood her face.

Even when she wasn't looking at him, she could feel his gaze upon her, making her acutely conscious of her appearance. The white cap covered most of her hair, but a curl or two had been allowed to tumble, as if carelessly, onto her forehead. She wore her best skirt, woven in a pattern of brown and tan vertical stripes, and her newest white blouse with a neckerchief that did not quite manage to conceal how her bosom rose and fell more quickly under Remie's gaze.

When she shifted her feet so that her wooden clogs made a slight sound on the church floor, eyes swung in her direction.

As if on cue, Remie rose with the little boy beside him, drawing attention away from Soleil. Unlike most of those in the congregation, Remie wore leather moccasins, not clogs, so his passage was virtually soundless, but by the time he had gone out the door at the rear of the church, everyone had forgotten they had been looking at Soleil.

The sermon this morning seemed endless. Outside it was a perfect autumn day with warm sunshine, a breeze that rustled the trees and held the fragrance of drying hay. Soleil's mind wandered; she wished that she, too, could escape into the open air.

She recognized the restless stirrings around her as first Mathieu Vaudreuil and then her father and several others felt the craving for tobacco begin to take precedence over their interest in the words of the priest.

When first one man, then another and another got up to give in to his weakness, Father Castin's voice rose to cover the surreptitious sounds of moving feet. His face took on that pinched look, which would become more pronounced if the escapees decided to enliven their smoking interlude with a wager or two. Even Barbe, usually the most tolerant of spouses, had had a few sharp words to say about the last episode. There had been a horse race around the church with enough noisy encouragement from the spectators to virtually drown out the sermon; the poor Father had actually lost his train of thought and had to start over again.

There would be no racing or wagering today, Soleil decided. There was laughter, though, drifting in through the open doorway with the scent of good tobacco.

While the priest would remonstrate with the defectors later, and perhaps their wives would also chide them mildly, nothing would change. The men would tolerate as much inactivity and deprivation as they could, then they would walk out of the church for their smokes and their conversations about the crops and the weather.

It would be unheard-of for a female to do the same thing. Soleil sighed and waited for Remie to come back. Perhaps she could invite him to join them for supper later. Her pulses quickened at the thought, and whatever the priest was saying was as lost on her as on the men outside.

There had been times when she had wished that she were a boy, that she could have the same freedom of the woods and the fields as her brothers. The twins, especially, often disappeared for days at a time; they would come home with rabbits or a deer for the stew pot, their skin more deeply bronzed than before, and both sporting an air of satisfaction they didn't get from working the fields. Clearly there was joy to be found simply in escaping the chores and rules at home and roaming the forests.

Today, however, knowing that Remie Michaud was only a few yards away, Soleil was glad that she was female, that every part of her tingled with sensations surely only a female could know.

Not even a glimpse of Madeleine's woebegone face could entirely suppress Soleil's exuberance, though her heart twisted in sympathy.

Still, it was Remie who won out over Madeleine and Father Castin and everything else. Eventually the men returned to their pews. Soleil could no more have resisted meeting Remie's gaze than she could have stopped the hot blood from surging through her veins.

His dark eyes were intense, his lips twitching a little in the faintest of smiles; she felt as if he touched her, and her own smile curled the corners of her mouth before she looked away.

And then at last the service ended. She stood to chant the responses with the others, then moved into the aisle and out of the church into the sunshine.

The parishioners milled about, greeting friends and neighbors, lighting up pipes, and the children ran happily, free after the hours of restraint. With no thought of artifice, Soleil walked directly toward Remie Michaud.

He was waiting for her. Her breath caught in her throat. Dear Mother of God, but he was handsome! Something about him drew her to him as a honey tree drew a bear. She did not so much as notice the astute glances of the villagers she had known all her life, and would not have been put off if she'd done so.

"Impossible!" Remie greeted her.

Confused, Soleil stared up into the face she had memorized the first time she saw it. "I beg your pardon, *monsieur*?"

"At the dance, I thought you were the most beautiful girl I had ever seen." He, too, was oblivious of the crowd around them, of the amused or envious eyes. "I was certain that in the morning, in broad daylight and without benefit of the fir beer, I would find some defect, however small. You were enchanting. And now..."

"And now?" Soleil echoed, sounding slightly breathless.

"Now," he replied, with every evidence of sincerity, "you are exquisite."

She had been told she was beautiful before. Even her brothers admitted that she was pretty. But "enchanting" and "exquisite" were not words in the vocabularies of either her brothers or the other young men in Grand-Pré. And she had never before felt herself drowning—*wanting* to drown—in a pair of dark eyes, in the mere possibility of an embrace.

If he intended to disconcert her, he was successful, at least for a moment. And then her humor and self-possession reasserted themselves, and her dimples flashed.

"You have a way with words, M. Michaud. One wonders how many females you may have practiced speaking them to, to have become so eloquent."

"Oh, many, many females," Remie assured her, and broke into laughter that sparked her own. "I have lived too much in the woods, however, and I'm not sure I know the customs of a proper village. Louisbourg doesn't count. So many people in one place seems to change them from traditional values and customs. Would it be improper of me to ask if I might walk you home from church?"

Ordinarily she would have felt compelled to consult her mother first, but Barbe was already apart from the worshipers, heading for home. Besides, Soleil knew what her reply would be. Was it not Barbe who had been concerned about her failure to find a husband? "No more improper than for me to invite you to supper," Soleil told him.

"I accept," Remie said immediately, and they fell into step at once, following her mother.

Had it not been for Louis and Madeleine's imminent departure the household would have been a merry one, with much teasing and laughter. As it was, the gathering was more subdued than usual. But the food was plentiful, and the hospitality as generous as it always was in Acadian households.

The conversation, however, wandered onto dangerous paths. Inevitably someone made a remark about Louis leaving soon for Île St. Jean, and Remie's attention was instantly held.

"Île St. Jean is very beautiful," he addressed Louis, "though the winters are hard, and the wind is fierce. You think not to go now, though, in the fall? You cannot carry enough provisions for a family through the winter, can you?"

There was a hush over the room.

"You have been there?" Louis asked, leaning forward in his eagerness for firsthand information.

"Once. I went with a Micmac friend, Young Otter. It is much like the area around the Minas Basin, with red sand and high tides."

"There is game, is there not? And fish to be caught, to feed a family. You have survived on such things for many months at a time, have you not?"

"That's true. But I traveled alone, not with a wife and a child." Remie didn't know about the infant that would be born in that faraway place or he'd probably have mentioned that, too, Soleil thought. "If it were me, I'd go in the spring."

Hope sprang into Madeleine's face, though no one noticed it except Soleil and Barbe. All attention was riveted on Remie.

"Spring may be too late," Louis said quietly. "The English grow more tyrannical by the day. I'm convinced they intend to oust the French once and for all, to confiscate the farms that have been in our families for generations. They despise our priests and our leaders, they have contempt for our religion and our language, and they covet our wealth. I love this land as much as anyone could, but I see no future here for my sons, nor even for myself."

Soleil swallowed against the ache in her throat. Why must this talk spoil what might have been such a perfect day?

To her dismay, Remie nodded thoughtfully. "It could be that you are right, *monsieur*. There is much talk in Louisbourg, and during my stay there I had plenty of time to listen when I was unable to do much else. There are those who think the British will make no more demands than they already make, but I have little confidence in those who proclaim this. I do not think the English like having a French stronghold in Louisbourg, so close to their own territory, and though they've forbidden commerce between Louisbourg and Acadia, the smuggling goes on almost as regularly as if we were allowed open trade. I've no doubt there will eventually be another attempt to lay siege to the fort there."

He seemed not to notice that the gathering was unnaturally still or that the lines deepened around Émile's mouth. "I met a traveler from Chibouctou to the south—or Halifax, as the redcoats now call it—who feels the English grow more hostile, more aggressive, all the time. Personally I avoid them like the plague."

He pulled absently at an earlobe. "I'm not sure, though, that if I were to leave this area I would go to Île St. Jean. There is not as much game there as I would like, and the refugees keep coming, so they need more and more meat. It can only be replenished by migration across the winter ice."

Only the crackle of fire on the hearth broke the silence. Soleil saw her father's face and prayed that this tacit agreement with Louis on the matter of seeking a better place to live would not influence Émile against Remie. Holy Mother, she wanted no obstacles to a union with Remie.

"Where, then?" It was Pierre, who almost never said anything since his wife had died. Was it possible that he, too, considered leaving the land on which he had been born? Soleil's apprehensions deepened.

"Across the Chignecto, toward Québec," Remie said at once. "On the mainland, in Canada, there is no restriction of herd movement such as the Northumberland Strait, and there is more game than all of Europe could eat in a hundred years. The French are firmly entrenched in a walled city there, commanding what must be one of the great rivers of the world, and the Indians between here and there are firmly on the side of the French. Over the past year many have left the area around Beaubassin to cross into Canada, to where they're not constantly harassed by the English dogs."

Oblivious of the lines deepening in Émile's face, Remie continued. "The British will not push so far from their supply bases, not through hostile territory. There is much good land in that direction, this side of Québec. Valleys along the St. John where farming can be done, forests full of unlimited game for meat and furs. There is one particular valley, where the Madawaska River flows into the St. John, which would tempt me if I had a mind to settle down instead of roam the woods for furs."

Again Soleil's heart lurched. She had assumed . . . she had assumed too much, she thought, suddenly drenched in cold perspiration. For the most part the Acadians were farmers or fishermen. They seldom even hunted except for meat. Remie was not like the others.

Yet he cared for her. Already it was clear that he cared for her. Might he not be brought to see the advantages of working the land, or even of making a living from the weirs, when the time came to take a wife?

"You have traveled more extensively than I," Louis said, still leaning forward to be closer to their visitor. "You have talked to other people. I would appreciate your opinion, Remie. Do you think the British will ever let us live in peace, without demands that we make promises to sign away our integrity, our religion, our language? Do you think they will allow us to work our lands in peace?''

Once more the silence was weighted with tension. A wreath of smoke encircled Grand-père's head and drifted across the table. Remie sighed and spread his hands in a gesture of helplessness. ''I'm only a trapper. I listen to what I hear from those who have been among them, but I don't pretend to know what the British will do. I only know that I'm happier when I stay away from them, and I don't trust them. Treaty or no treaty, they do as they please. They are afraid of us. The Micmacs are hostile to them and friendly to Acadians, and together we outnumber them. For years now, the infamous Abbé Le Loutre has led his Indian converts against the English, and the raids have hurt them badly, though never badly enough to make them leave.''

Grand-père spoke for the first time, his voice unsteady with age. ''It is not right that a priest should encourage the savages to kill and scalp, even the British. Le Loutre endangers us all by his reckless violence. If it were not for him, the British would have far less reason to fear us, for we are a peaceful people.''

Remie shrugged. ''So says the bishop at Québec, but The Otter sets his own rules. His hatred for all things English leads him to extremes, and the Indians, too, have reason to hate our conquerors. The English would like us all to flee to Canada so that they might take over our lands for their own settlers, except that if we do that we will join forces with the French settlers in Canada and make them stronger, so that is no solution for them, either. Only, perhaps, for us.''

Soleil's gaze slid around the assembled family, seeking to determine their reactions to Remie's speech. Louis and Pierre were intently interested; Émile was enigmatic; Grand-père showed anxiety. Soleil intercepted a look between François and Antoine that she could not quite interpret. Had she not been so concerned with the impression that Remie was making, she might well have been disturbed by the exchange, for their faces were devoid of their usual humor, and the look they shared was secret, private, a silent warning.

It was at that point that Pierre's son Vincent fell against the corner of the table and cried out in pain. Danielle sprang to get a cold cloth to press against the scrape; Barbe patted the boy reassuringly, and Pierre urged the child not to cry, that all would be better in a moment.

The mood was shattered, and none too soon, Soleil thought. Although the rest of the day passed pleasantly enough, it was a long time before her worries subsided, and even then they did not totally go away.

8

THE HOUSE WAS QUIET after Remie Michaud had left. The children had been put to bed after evening prayers; the fire was banked. Pierre had gone out to make a final check on the cattle, and Barbe had set the pot to simmer for the breakfast that would be served at dawn.

Émile sat on one of the benches at the table, his face sagging into lines of sad contemplation as he stared sightlessly into the glowing coals. He stirred when Soleil paused, then knelt before him to rest a hand upon his knee.

"Papa, do you like him?"

Slowly his gaze focused upon her. He had been thinking of Louis, she knew.

"Who? Michaud?" The use of Remie's last name instead of his first was a bad sign, and Soleil's stomach tightened.

Émile reached up to massage a sore muscle in his shoulder. "He seems a nice enough lad. But he's no farmer. And he talks too much about things better left unsaid."

"Louis asked him, and he has been to distant places, listened to many people. How could he not reply as truthfully as he knows how?"

"His saying something does not make it the truth."

Her heart was beating very fast. "He told us his opinion, Papa, and those of others he's heard. That does not make it untrue, either."

Her grip on his knee tightened, and he put his own hand over hers. "He's a good man, Papa," she said softly, pleadingly.

His smile was crooked, lasting only a moment. "You know that already, do you? Well, why not. I knew the minute I laid eyes on your mother that she was the only woman in the world for me, and I was right, was I not? Twenty-seven years we've been wed, and never a harsh word between us."

Barbe was taking off her apron to fold it until morning. At this statement she raised her eyebrows in disbelief but said nothing.

"He wants to call on me, Papa." There was a perceptible tremor in Soleil's voice.

"To call on you?" Émile simulated amazement. "Why, I'd never have guessed! He scarcely noticed you at church this morning... nor at the dance when you met, either... and he preferred to talk politics and eat rather than look in your direction while he spent most of the day here. However, for all that he's not a farmer, he *did* offer to come and help with the haying."

Soleil's eyes widened and happiness tugged at her mouth. "He did?"

"Of course he probably doesn't know a thing about haying—less than Jacques or even Vincent. We'll be tripping over him every time we turn around. If, that is, he can take his eyes off you long enough to swing the scythe in the first place."

"You do like him, don't you, Papa? It's all right if he comes calling?"

Émile gave a snort and looked up at his wife across the wide table. "As anxious as your mother is to marry you off, who would listen if I said no? He could be so ugly you'd have to marry him in the dark, and your mother would give her approval, just to be rid of you."

Now it was Barbe who snorted and swatted at him before turning away to go to bed.

Soleil met her father's gaze, reading the tenderness in it. "Thank you, Papa." She sprang to her feet and gave him an affectionate smile before she, too, went off to bed.

Danielle was already asleep in the curtained cubicle. Soleil undressed quietly and joined her sister, hugging her happiness to herself. Surely, just for tonight, it wasn't selfish of her to revel in that happiness, to refuse to think of the reason for her father's sadness.

She was in love, and the love was returned. For a few moments she had feared her father's reactions, but Émile was a fair man. "Thank you, Blessed Mother," she murmured into the darkness.

Elsewhere in the house, Marc cried out in his sleep, and Madeleine murmured soothingly. Soleil's smile deepened. Perhaps, a year from now, she too might have a child, she thought contentedly.

REMIE WAS THERE at dawn for the haying, and he also brought a message for Barbe. "My aunt says it is her time, Mme Cyr."

Soleil, who was dishing up the morning porridge, paused with a quickening heartbeat. If her mother went to serve as midwife to Marie, there would be no chaperon while Remie was here. And her father and brothers would not share Barbe's rigid attitude on the subject.

Barbe immediately began to untie her apron. "I'll go at once. Is she having pains?"

Remie nodded. "Yes. My uncle says her babes are difficult, and the pains are already strong. I came as quickly as I could."

Barbe swung toward her younger daughter. "Maybe you'd better come too, Danielle. Soleil would be of more help, but she's also better at handling things here at home. The last time it took two days to birth the child, and I can't leave the family without someone to cook for them."

Danielle's fingers twisted in her neckerchief. "I've never attended a birthing." Her expression suggested she didn't want to do it now.

"Well, there's always a first time for everything. Bring a shawl in case it turns cool and we have to walk home at night. Soleil, don't let the fire go out, and if Vincent is still coughing tonight, be sure to put a poultice on him."

Madeleine, looking wan and fragile, appeared in the doorway from the lean-to room she shared with Louis and Marc. "Is there anything I can do, Mama Barbe?"

"No, just help Soleil." In her hurry, Barbe did not even pretend that her daughter-in-law was of any real service. "My basket is ready, let's go."

"I haven't had my breakfast!" Danielle protested.

Barbe gave her a quelling glance. "Take something to eat on the way, then, but hurry up. It's taken M. Michaud half an hour to get here, and it'll take us more than that to reach Marie, for our legs are shorter. Heaven knows what can happen in an hour's time."

She swept up her basket, which had been made ready days earlier, and was out the door before Danielle could snatch a chunk of the heavy bread she had been slicing.

Émile, scratching himself through the tunic shirt he had just pulled on, appeared moments after his wife and daughter had gone. "Mme Trudelle's time has come? Good! Come along, let's eat and get on our way to the fields."

Soleil served the men while Madeleine busied herself with Marc. Remie sat with the others and consumed his share. He said little, but his gaze followed Soleil as she moved between fireplace and table.

When the workers had gone there were dishes to wash and Pierre's children to feed and dress. Soleil went about the customary tasks without conscious thought except for planning what she would feed Remie at noon with the others. For a time she could pretend that this was her own household, that she and Remie lived here together, that the little boys were her children and Remie's.

She felt guilty when she realized she was hoping that Guillaume's wife did not have her baby *too* quickly.

IT WAS EXCITING to have Remie there with her family when she carried out the midday meal. She need not have been concerned about his ability to hold his own with her brothers, for all that he was unfamiliar with the work. He was muscular and strong, and he was determined to impress Émile as well as Émile's daughter.

Soleil found the opportunity she sought after they had finished eating and she was repacking the basket. Émile, never one to waste time, had already taken up the rake to draw the hay into windrows; the younger males were less in a hurry to go back to work but disinclined to hover over their sister and her suitor. Indeed, Louis was stretched flat in the shade at the edge of the meadow, for even a few minutes of sleep would refresh him.

"I'm surprised," Remie said, handing over a bowl, "that anyone who is such an accomplished cook is still unwed at such an advanced age. There is nothing lacking in your looks, so it must be your disposition that makes the men hold back."

"No doubt," Soleil said serenely.

"A man likes a woman with an even temper," Remie added.

"Tempers vary according to circumstances."

"Of course, it doesn't do to choose a wife who is *too* docile."

She placed the last of the bowls in the basket and covered them with a cloth. "You feel that docility is a virtue, *monsieur*?"

"Up to a point. But so are spirit and passion." He sent a look toward Louis and decided he was really sleeping. "The trouble is in determining, before the banns are read, what is temper and what is . . . spirit and passion."

Soleil impaled him with a dark gaze, silent but so eloquent that she heard Remie's indrawn breath. Oh, yes, she could speak to this man without words.

He forgot that her brother was so close at hand. "I would walk out with you, *mademoiselle*, this evening. If you would not object to my returning before dusk."

"It seems a waste of time to walk to Guillaume's and back. There is always plenty to eat in the Cyr household," she said boldly. "Stay for supper, *monsieur*, and there will be more time for walking out. Although," she added in afterthought, "Danielle is not here to act as chaperon, so perhaps I may not be allowed to walk out after all."

"It would be a pity to be deprived of a walk on that account. Perhaps one of your brothers...the little one, Jacques?"

She was unable to suppress her laughter. "I doubt that Mama would consider a ten-year-old an adequate chaperon. But stay, and we'll see."

Beyond them Louis stirred and sat up. "Is it time to go back to work?"

"Come on, come on," François shouted, "let's get the hay in!"

Soleil stood for a moment, watching as they all took up scythes and rakes, inhaling the sweet scent of the sun-warmed hay. Get the work done before the rain comes or the weather turns cold, she thought. And when it was done, Louis would go.

How was it possible for both pain and joy to occupy her heart so completely and at the same time?

She turned and started toward home, not looking back.

MADELEINE APPEARED at her elbow as Soleil began to clear the table after the evening meal. "I'll do this," she murmured, "if you want to walk out with M. Michaud."

Startled, Soleil turned to face her sister-in-law. It was the first such offer Madeleine had made since Louis had broken the unwelcome news to her.

"He went outdoors with the others to smoke and talk," Madeleine said. "It will be dark soon—too soon if you do the washing up." She hesitated, and her eyes blurred with tears. "I know he is the one you want, as I wanted Louis."

Soleil swallowed hard. "I hope you aren't saying you think you made a mistake in choosing Louis."

A tear spilled over, and Madeleine wiped it away with the back of one hand. "No. No, it is still Louis that I love. But loving a man, even one who truly loves you, does not mean that he will not break your heart. Go, before I make a fool of myself in front of a guest."

Soleil needed no more urging. She smoothed her apron over her skirt, adjusted her neckerchief and dodged young Marc on the floor to step outside into the cool evening air.

Remie was leaning against a tree, conversing with Bertin and Jacques, but he straightened immediately and came directly to her.

"There will be no objection if we walk?" he asked.

Émile was nowhere in sight. The twins were crouched over some project at the corner of the house. Pierre squatted beside them, protesting that they were doing it wrong, whatever it was.

Louis, smoking quietly on the bench beside the door, gave the romantic couple a quiet look but made no comment when Soleil replied.

"I don't think so. We won't go far, anyway."

And then, strangely, once they were beyond the hearing of anyone else, Soleil was lost for conversation. What did she, a girl who had never been anywhere beyond her own parish, never lived anywhere except in this house where she'd been born, know to discuss with a man of the world?

Remie, too, was uncharacteristically silent. They walked side by side, together yet apart. Soleil's uneasiness grew; would he think her a simpleton if she didn't speak?

And then, on the edge of the forest, Remie halted and reached out for her hand. His own was calloused and hard; the warmth of it sent heat surging through her.

He was studying her face as if to memorize it. When he finally spoke, his words were soft. "You are different from any girl I've ever met, *mam'selle*."

The discomfiting constriction was back in her chest. "And you've known many girls, M. Michaud." It was not a question. During the weeks he had recuperated at Louisbourg there would have been plenty of females. Yet he had left them all behind, she thought.

"Enough," Remie said, "to know the special one when I meet her. Enough to know the one I would take to wife."

Her heart was now hammering so wildly that she was sure it would tear its way out of her rib cage. She felt as if she were about to float right off the ground in sheer joy.

And then Remie's seriousness made her catch her breath as his thumb began to stroke her palm and he leaned over her. He did not kiss her, however.

"The thing I cannot know, *mam'selle*, is whether *I* am the right husband for *you*. Because I am not a farmer, nor a man content to pull his livelihood from the sea. I am a man of the forests, the woodlands. I must often be from home, following my trap lines. I take the furs to Québec to sell, because that's where I can get the best price, for I refuse to traffic with the English. My woman must either go with me or be self-sufficient enough to remain behind."

Consternation rendered her numb. "But there is plenty of land here at Grand-Pré, and with Louis leaving—"

He released her and cupped her face between his big hands, looking into her eyes with great tenderness. "Ah, would that it were that simple! A man is what he is, *mam'selle*. I would not make a moccasin out of the reeds, and no more would I make a captive of a free heart by tying myself to a land for which I have no feeling. It's not that I do not feel strongly enough about you to do it. But if I did, I would not be the same Remie Michaud. I would not like the man I would become, and most likely you would come to resent him, too. An unhappy husband is worse than no husband at all.''

Perturbed beyond measure, Soleil dredged up the only persuasion she could muster. "With Louis and Madeleine gone, their room will be free—"

Remie's face shifted into planes of regret. "I cannot do it, my love. A woman will keep house and have her little ones wherever she is. But a man dies—at least inside—if he cannot live in the way his heart tells him to do. I would marry you, Mlle Soleil, if you will take me on my terms. I can't offer you any other."

His words were a knife blade in her heart. And then Remie bent to brush her lips with his own, and the white-hot fire raced through her bloodstream; when his hands slid down to her shoulders to draw her into a firm embrace, she was helpless to resist or protest. The feathery kiss became an impassioned one, long and deep. She opened her lips beneath his, and for the moment she was able to put aside his stipulations, to ignore what they must surely mean.

"Will you marry me, Soleil?" he murmured at last.

And even as she heard her own breathy "Yes, I will," she felt the beginnings of the pain that she sensed would remain with her for a long, long time.

9

THE HAYING went too quickly. Soleil was busy enough during the days, for she managed the household virtually alone. Except when something needed to be done for Marc, Madeleine seemed sunk in lethargy and morning sickness that lasted well into the afternoon.

It was the evenings Soleil lived for, however. The evenings when she and Remie could stroll about within sight of the house and the rest of the family—her father was not as permissive as she had expected—and talk. In that, at least, they could be private, for the watchful eyes kept their distance from the lovers.

There were, however, no more embraces. Not with so many observers.

The night of Remie's proposal, Soleil had first cried and then schemed once she was alone. Remie loved her; that was the important thing. Perhaps if he spent some time with the Cyrs he would see that there could be a future for him here at Grand-Pré. A man could learn to love the land, couldn't he?

It didn't take long, however, to disabuse herself of that notion. Remie was not a man to be easily swayed.

When they were together, Soleil was convinced that whatever they did would be wonderful, as long as they did it as man and wife. When Remie was away, however, it was impossible not to imagine what it would be like to be separated from her family, leaving them behind as Louis and Madeleine would soon do, forsaking the security of Grand-Pré, the neighbors and the Church for somewhere new and strange.

In part the idea generated excitement. Had she not wondered about the world beyond her own small part of Acadia? Had she not longed to see other towns, other scenes? And to see them with Remie—what more could she ask? Perhaps, in spite of what he said now, he would one day be content to return to Grand-Pré and settle down here, when the attraction of the forest lost its magic and a desire for his own snug cabin and cozy fireside proved the stronger lure.

After that one brief episode when she had been unable to think of anything to say, it was as if a floodgate had been opened. She discovered that she could say anything to Remie, pour out her innermost thoughts and feelings and in return find interest and understanding.

And always there was the thrill and excitement of being together, of feeling the love grow between them. They made each other laugh; Soleil refused to think about crying and pretended to herself that there were no danger signals, that all would be well.

She was sorry when Barbe and Danielle at last returned home after four days, ending the period of relative freedom she had had with Remie. The two women were exhausted, and Danielle clearly considered the entire matter of giving birth to be disgusting and frightening.

"I spent the entire time calling on the Blessed Virgin to ease her suffering," Danielle declared, dropping her shawl on a bench. "I thought the babe would never be born, and there was so much blood—it's a wonder either of them survived. There was no resting. Even when Mama told me to sleep for a bit, Mme Trudelle cried out so piteously that I could not relax and close my eyes. I want to sleep for a week."

Soleil glanced from one face to the other. "But all is finally well?"

"The Trudelles have another boy, poor little mite. He looks like a fresh-skinned rabbit, only too scrawny for the pot. From his size he ought to have been born much more quickly, Mama says, but he came feetfirst. I'll tell you, the whole thing made me decide I never want to marry and have babes if that's what you have to go through."

"And *madame*?"

Danielle gave a snort of incredulity. "If you can believe it, though she's too weak to move, she is delighted by the whole thing. Thinks her skinny little rabbit is beautiful."

Barbe checked the kettle over the fire, then bent to pick up small Marc from the floor and cuddle him against her breast. "When *you* were born, you, too, looked like a skinned rabbit. And see you now, a fine specimen! How is Grand-maman's big boy, eh? Did you miss me?"

Her smile wavered as she suddenly remembered that there would shortly be considerable missing of family members. "Where is your mama, eh? She's left you to Tante Soleil, has she?"

"She's lying down. She can hardly lift her head without being sick today," Soleil said.

"Well, at least Louis won't set out for Île St. Jean with her in that condition," Danielle surmised. "I'm hungry. Is that stew ready to eat yet?"

"Not for another hour or so," Soleil predicted. "There's hot water for tea, though, if you want some."

She brought out three mugs and set them on the table, both eager and shy about telling them her own news. "I haven't told Papa yet, but Remie has asked me to marry him."

Barbe passed the baby to her younger daughter in order to hug the older one. "Congratulations. He's a very handsome man—not that looks have much to do with a man's qualities as a husband. How did everything go while we were away? Aside from you finding time to spend with M. Michaud."

Hearing their voices, Madeleine appeared, and another cup was added to those to be filled. She was pale but composed, and she'd obviously overheard the conversation. "Louis says the haying will be done by tomorrow. We leave the day after that, and I don't think it will matter how I feel. With Marc, this morning sickness did not last long, and I pray that will be the case this time, too."

"You have reconciled yourself to going, then," Barbe said softly, resting a hand on her daughter-in-law's arm.

Madeleine's smile faltered. "What else can I do? He truly believes there will be no freedom or future for us here. Perhaps—" her voice trembled, and she firmed it "—perhaps one day, if Louis is right, you will all leave here, too. Perhaps—" this time her voice cracked "—we will all be together again one day."

"We will pray to the Blessed Mother that it will be so," Barbe said gently, and the others echoed the words, then drank their tea in silence for a few minutes.

After what she considered a decent interval, Barbe turned to Soleil. "And when your papa has given his permission, the banns will be read for an early wedding?"

Soleil blushed. "We haven't discussed a date. Not until I've told you and Papa."

"Of course. Quite right." Barbe sighed and rose to her feet. "Well, with a wedding to prepare for, there is much to be done."

Soleil rose, too, with a guilty twinge when she saw Madeleine's pale, sad face. Impulsively she bent to hug her sister-in-law. "It will be all right, Madeleine. You know that Louis will take care of you and do what is best."

"Yes," Madeleine agreed, but once more the tears spilled over so that she got up from the bench and walked quickly out of the room.

Barbe's gaze followed the younger woman, her expression one of concern. "Louis is a dependable man, a steady one. He is usually right about things, but I cannot be sure he is right about this. The English have been making their demands for years that our people sign their cursed papers, and nothing has come of it. These are our lands, and your papa is too old to start over somewhere else. Besides that, Madeleine is in no condition to travel very far, or very fast. I shall try again to talk to Louis. He hasn't listened to Papa, but perhaps he will listen to me."

Soleil swallowed painfully, saying nothing. She knew Louis; she knew he would not change his mind. If Madeleine's tears had not moved him, neither would their mother's pleas. Without really thinking about it, Soleil lifted the lid on the simmering kettle and stirred the stew, automatically adding salt. Her stomach was churning. Now that she had broken the news to Mama, she must also tell her father, and she could not be as complacent about his reaction as she had once imagined she would be.

SUPPER WAS a strained meal with less conversation than usual. Even Jacques and Danielle, who ordinarily chattered along steadily unless rebuked for it, were silent. Tension was thick in the air once the news about Marie Trudelle and her new infant had been recounted.

Remie, usually so admirably assured, seemed nervous, which made Soleil nervous, too. What would they do if Papa refused them permission to marry? She kept exchanging long looks with her intended across the big table, but Remie's smile was not as reassuring as it might have been.

It was not until the table was being cleared and the family members began to go about their evening chores that Remie finally cleared his throat and began.

"M. Cyr, we have a matter of importance to discuss with you."

Soleil moved quickly to his side, studying her father's face. Unfortunately it didn't look as if he were going to make this easy for them. He was unduly sober, and she felt a wave of giddiness, of apprehension, though surely the sobriety must be because tomorrow the haying would be done, and Louis would be leaving.

Émile pursed his lips. Where she had anticipated humor, Soleil read only gravity, and it did not appear to be assumed. She, too, cleared her throat.

"Mlle Soleil and I," Remie said, then found it necessary to swallow audibly, "we...we would like your permission, sir, to marry."

There was no perceptible change in Émile's expression. Almost of its own volition Soleil's hand crept out to meet Remie's; they clung to each other in a sort of desperation, both of them rigid.

"And what do you offer my daughter, M. Michaud?" Émile asked heavily.

Remie seemed taken aback by the query. "Why...why... I would marry her, and have a family, *monsieur*. I would take good care of her, I assure you. I have always managed to take care of myself, and I would see that she has the necessities of life. And—and—" For a moment he floundered, for there was no yielding in the older man's face. "And we would, of course, be married in the Church, and obey the edicts of the priests—"

Émile's broad chest rose and fell in a sigh. "And where would you do this, M. Michaud? You have indeed been a help during our harvest, but it is clear you have no bent for farming. Indeed, your talk is all of faraway places—Louisbourg, Annapolis Royal, even Québec City! Is it your intention to take my daughter away from Grand-Pré to live among strangers?"

For long seconds Remie stared at his prospective father-in-law. His hand tightened involuntarily on Soleil's. She thought the bones would be crushed, but she made no move to withdraw from his grip.

"My livelihood is found in the woods, *monsieur*. Trapping for furs is the thing I know best, the thing I love best. It is true I have no bent for working the land, but does that make me less a man? Less worthy as a husband and a father?"

Émile's consideration of this took too long. Soleil clung to Remie as if to a line thrown out from a boat to one fallen overboard.

"No less worthy," Émile said finally, "but perhaps it keeps you from being the best for Soleil. She has been reared in this same village where all her family for a hundred years back has grown up. This land is in her blood, as it is in mine. Her mother and I have always expected that she would marry and settle near us or with us. We have a strong sense of family, *monsieur*. We do not like to break the ties between us.''

And the day after tomorrow my firstborn breaks those ties, and we may never see him again. The words hung unspoken between them, but all were acutely aware of the reality. *I cannot be expected to give up both a son and a daughter all at once.*

''Papa—'' She didn't know what she could say to him, but Soleil knew she must say something. Remie's hand was strong and warm around her own, and her misgivings slid away into the back of her mind. ''I love Remie, and he loves me. This is what we want, to marry. If *you* love me, do not forbid us!''

''Even if it means leaving Grand-Pré?'' Émile asked. ''Leaving your mama and me and all the others?''

The words tore at her throat, but Soleil had to say them. They were all she had left to prevent her future, her love, from slipping through her fingers.

''Yes, Papa. Wherever Remie goes, I want to go.''

Barbe, who had been listening without comment from her stance before the fireplace, tensed and waited expectantly. The fire crackled; there was no other sound except Soleil's ragged breathing.

Émile pursed his lips and heaved himself up from the table so that he looked them more or less in the eye, though Remie was a head taller.

''You are very young,'' he told Soleil softly. ''I do not think this is a matter to be decided in a moment. A few months of consideration may save you both—all of us—years of unhappiness. Marriage is not to be entered into lightly. I'm sure the good Father would agree.''

Overcome by distress, Soleil had trouble finding words. She had suspected her father would have misgivings, that he would have doubts to express. But this sounded as if he were refusing permission altogether, at least for the present! And it was right now that the blood raced hotly through her veins, right now that Remie was here.

Émile correctly read their faces, and his smile was sad. ''I know what you feel. It was a long time ago, but I, too, was once young and hot-blooded. Since that time, however, I have learned much about life. However much the young deny it, wisdom comes with the years, and I have more of them than the two of you put together. I would be failing in my responsibilities as a father if I handed over my daughter to you, *monsieur*. If your love is true—" he lifted a hand to still the protests that trembled on their lips "—it will bear the test of a little time. And if it is not, if parting causes it to falter, why, then it is better to know it now than later. You have mentioned a cache of furs that must be taken to Québec. I suggest that you take them and do your customary trapping through the winter, and that in the spring, if you return and still want to marry my daughter, and she still wants to marry you, her mother and I will then give you permission to do so."

Soleil sagged against Remie with a wordless bleat of anguish. Wait until spring? And was Papa saying that he doubted Remie would even return, doubted that he would still want to marry her by then?

Remie had paled beneath his tan. "Almost you insult me, M. Cyr. I have made an honorable proposal of marriage and you make it sound as if my love for Mlle Soleil is of only passing interest, not strong enough to last through a winter. I assure you—"

Émile lifted a hand to stop the flow of indignation that threatened. "Please. Please do not take offense. I am a simple man, not an eloquent one, and perhaps I have said this badly. I do not mean to imply that you have any shortcomings other than this business of taking my daughter away from everything and everyone she has ever loved. Guillaume testifies to your character, and Soleil believes she loves you. No—" he wagged a hand at her "—do not interrupt! I would have no objection to reading the banns next Sunday if you planned to stay here in Grand-Pré, *monsieur*. My daughter has always been a sensible girl, and I've no desire to deprive her of what she really wants. I must only be certain that this is not a spur-of-the-moment decision stemming from youthful enthusiasm alone. You've known each other only a few weeks. Surely it is not too much to ask to wait and see if her love endures parting and separation for a short time, for that is what she will experience in the marriage, is it not? If your feelings remain the same, then in the spring you will marry with our blessings."

Soleil was stunned. She turned to her mother for support, only to see Barbe's viewpoint reflected on her face. While Barbe was sympathetic, she agreed with Émile.

There would be no banns read, no fall wedding.

Soleil burst into tears and pulled free of Remie's grasp to run to her own curtained bed, trying unsuccessfully to muffle her sobs in her pillow.

Spring was months away, over a lonely and confining winter. She had never dreamed that Papa could be so cruel, that Mama would say not one word in her defense.

Soleil knew she would always love Remie, that no matter what Papa said, her heart was breaking. She wept until she could weep no more.

10

DANIELLE DREW ASIDE the bed curtains and peered uncertainly into the dimness. "Soleil?"

"What?" Her head ached and her nose was stuffed up. She rolled over and looked at her younger sister, barely discernible in the dusk.

Danielle held her candle higher, dangerously close to the curtain. Her whisper could not have carried to anyone else. "He's waiting for you . . . down by the weir."

"Who?" Soleil demanded, but she already knew. Her heart was suddenly thundering in her chest as she scrambled out of bed, trying to smooth her crumpled skirt, straightening her cap.

"Remie. He called out to me when I was coming back from the privy. You'll have to wait a few minutes. Papa hasn't gone to bed yet."

Soleil hesitated. "Let me know when it's safe to go out."

Danielle ducked her head in agreement. "Is it true? Papa said you couldn't marry him?" She sounded incredulous.

"Not until spring. He thinks I'll change my mind between now and then." Her eyelids felt hot and swollen. "I must look a mess. How can I let Remie see me like this? He'll be the one who changes his mind!"

"It'll be dark by then. He won't be able to tell what you look like. Is it because Remie encouraged Louis to leave rather than to stay?"

"That probably didn't help. Danny, bring me a wet cloth so I can bathe my face. And don't let on to anyone that you've talked to Remie."

Danielle nodded again and withdrew with the candle, leaving the room virtually dark, for there was only one small window.

I hate Papa, Soleil thought. And I hate Louis. If he had not decided to go away, Papa would not have been so upset at the thought of *my* leaving. He can't bear to lose both of us.

And then the unfairness of her resentment surfaced and she was swept by guilt. Papa loved them, her and Louis both, and that was why he felt the way he did. But everybody said it was past time she married, and now that she had met Remie she knew there could never be anyone else. She would rather he'd settle down here at Grand-Pré, but if he could not, why, then she must go with him, wherever he went. Even to the distant walled city of Québec, far from the tyrannical British governor and his soldiers.

Papa was old. He had forgotten what it was like to be young and in love, with yearnings and needs that would not be denied. Besides, no one had opposed him and Mama; they, too, had fallen in love at first sight and had had the banns said over them within a matter of weeks; they were married as soon as was decently possible after that. The only difference was that Mama had come from a neighboring village and had not had to go far from home.

When Danielle returned with a cloth and a basin of water, Soleil mopped at her face, pressing the cool compress against her burning eyelids until she imagined that the swelling had gone down a little, though they still felt thick and unpleasant.

It was at least half an hour before Danielle rejoined her. "Mama and Papa have gone to bed," she reported. "Madeleine is still up. Marc has a cough and she's making him a poultice, but she won't tell on you. It's safe to go now."

Moments later, after exchanging a mute glance with her brother's wife, Soleil slipped quietly out of the house.

It was almost totally black, but she knew the way. She had been walking this path from the time she could stand.

She moved quickly, hoping that Remie might have crept closer to the house as time went by, praying that he would not have given up and gone back to his uncle's place. Surely he would wait for her, even if it took all night, for he knew it would be difficult for her to leave undetected.

The night air was cool with the hint of impending autumn, and she had forgotten her shawl. It didn't matter; it wasn't worth the risk of going back. When she reached Remie he would keep her warm. She felt warmer already, just thinking about it.

There was no moon, only a sprinkling of stars that grew brighter as she moved along the edge of the clearing toward the bay.

For well over a century Acadians had lived here on the edge of the Minas Basin. The British considered them lazy because they did not clear the land of forest. Instead they reclaimed the land from the sea; they had built an intricate system of dykes in the manner of the Dutch, and year by year had gained more arable acres to grow their hay and grain. There was no other way of stopping the sea; indeed, the tides on the Minas Basin were the highest known in the entire world, rising and falling more than fifty feet at a rate of a foot a minute, turning every six hours, day and night.

Undaunted, the Acadians used the tides to their own advantage. At a season of low tides, they built staunch dykes of heavy sod along the edge of the marshlands, sometimes with a core of upright tree trunks reinforced with hard-packed clay. They left sluice gates that swung in only one direction, outward to drain into the basin. The water from the marshes flowed out through the gates, which then closed tightly against the pressure from the sea, preventing it from flooding behind the dykes.

Slowly, then, over the following year or so, the rain would wash the salt from the soil behind the dykes, making the land sweet enough to raise crops. Gradually dykes would be constructed farther and farther out into the water; now there were more than thirteen thousand acres of reclaimed farmland, flat and easily worked. The British who thought building dykes was easier than cutting down trees were idiots, Émile said. It was one of the reasons he ignored them.

Even in the dark Soleil could find the pathway along the top of the dyke. She could have found the weir in her sleep. She had helped her brothers build this one when she was only seven or eight years old and had been tending it ever since: a trap of poles, brush and netting snared the fish as they came upstream, confining them when the tide fell so that they could be easily harvested.

She heard the lap of the water, and somewhere nearby an owl hooted mournfully. A stick cracked even closer, and Soleil spun eagerly.

"Remie?"

A moment later she was drawn into a strong embrace. Remie's mouth was pressed into her hair, touched her forehead, found her mouth. For long moments there was nothing else but his lean body against hers, and the depth of their kiss. Then he straightened and said, "I was afraid you wouldn't be able to get out of the house."

After all the effort she'd made to take the swelling out of her eyelids, now she was weeping again. "Oh, Remie, I was afraid you'd already gone!"

"Not without seeing you one more time," he said. "It's not the end of the world, my love. Until spring, your father said. That's not so far away. And I do have a trap line to run. It may be best this way, with you safe and warm at home rather than trekking through the snow with me, sleeping out in makeshift shelters, foraging for food."

She sniffed, determined to control herself. "You've never gone hungry. Nor should I. The woods are full of game, you said so."

He drew her again to his chest, cradling her there, his lips moving against the hair just above her ear. "I've been hungry, though never for long. And cold, and wet. You're not used to the woods. It would be better to introduce you to them in spring, when it's warm even if there is no shelter."

"I've used snowshoes since I was a little girl," Soleil protested. "I could keep up, and we would sleep together—"

She felt his reaction to this and was distracted by the distinctly pleasurable realization of her power over this man.

He laughed, however. "Yes, there would be advantages to taking you with me now. I will think about you often in the months and miles between here and Québec. But I'll be glad you are safe and comfortable until I come for you. I *will* come, Soleil. Only promise that you will be waiting, that you will not cry the banns with anyone else before I come—"

She hugged him tightly. "Never! There will never be anyone else!"

"Good. I've had time for nothing but thinking since your papa made his conditions. I'm disappointed, for a time I was nearly out of my mind, but sitting here in the dark, listening to the night birds and the fish leaping in the weir, I had nothing to do but think. A man alone learns to use his imagination, and I've often gained advantage by being able to put myself into another man's position. If I had a daughter like you—" he sighed, stirring her hair so that her scalp prickled "—I would not want another man to take her away, either."

Soleil did not want to admit that Émile had any reason on his side. "But it is my future, my life! I want to be where you are, and spring is so far away!"

His voice was husky. "Very far," he agreed. "If I allow myself to dwell on it, I, too, will weep." His thumb found the path of her tears and gently wiped them away. "I leave at dawn—"

Her cry was that of a wounded animal. "Tomorrow!"

"The sooner I go, the sooner I will be back. And in the meantime, before I go, there is tonight. Will they miss you and come looking for you if you do not return at once?"

"I don't care," Soleil told him recklessly. "I want to be with you as long as possible—"

His response was another lengthy embrace and a kiss even more passionate than before.

It was Remie who broke the spell. "You're so intoxicating that if we continue to stand this way I'll feel drunk, as if I've had too much fir beer, and we'll fall off the dyke into the water. You know the way better than I—where can we go instead of balancing here like a pair of herons?"

There was no hesitation. Her hand sought his, and she drew him along. "Down the path and into the field. There is hay waiting to be loaded onto the cart in the morning—"

Once she stumbled and he caught her, an arm around her waist so that for a moment she was pressed close to him. Then they went on, hesitated at a sluice gate and slithered down the embankment into the field.

At once they were out of the breeze off the water, and when they sank into a mound of hay they found that it held the warmth of the sun beneath its top layer.

It was too dark to see Remie's face as it hovered above hers, but that didn't matter. His hands were practiced and knowing, his mouth eager and her own quick to learn. Her breath came in gasps, and when his fingers sought her fastenings, Soleil made no protest. He was her husband, in heart and intent if not by the blessings of the Church, and she had no mind to deny him—or herself—anything.

For a matter of seconds the evening air was cool on her exposed skin. Then Remie lowered his head to seek out previously unawakened nipples, and her entire body was bathed in spreading heat and sensation that overwhelmed inhibitions and timidity.

This is my wedding night, Soleil thought, amazed, and parted her lips for his kiss.

11

"MY LOVE," Remie whispered into her ear, and Soleil stirred, curling closer to his warmth until he traced her face with one finger, awakening her fully. "'Tis time to go home. It won't do to have your father know you've spent the night in a pile of hay with the man he forbade you to wed."

"I don't care," Soleil said, but she was waking up. The air had grown chill, though Remie had drawn the hay over and around them. She wished she could stay forever, pressed against him this way, but he was urging her up.

"*He* will care," Remie stated. "And if he learns about tonight, he may come after me with murder in his eye."

"Not Papa," she said, still drowsy. "Papa does not believe in violence."

"That's because no one has ever seduced his beautiful daughter before. Come on, on your feet! That's the way."

"You didn't seduce me," Soleil replied. Once out of the hay she began to shiver, and she fumbled with the fastenings on her clothes. "I wanted you to make love to me."

Remie chuckled as his fingers closed over hers and he took over the task. "Here, let me. You'll still be here at daylight at this rate. I didn't mean to sleep so long. There's already a hint of gray in the eastern sky. You'll have to hurry."

"I don't want to go home." Soleil slid her hands under his shirt, exulting in the texture of his skin, in the rippling muscles. "I want to stay with you. Remie, take me with you."

"I can't. My love, you know I can't. Wait for me! I'll be back in the spring, and then we can be married the way we'd like, with your family and the whole village celebrating. You know that's the kind of wedding you've dreamed of, not running off like a thief in the night."

She swallowed audibly, knowing he was right even as she sought for words to persuade him otherwise. But then, if her body had not already persuaded him, what could she do with mere words?

He bent his head to kiss her, then eased her away from him. "Goodbye, Mlle Soleil," he said softly, and was gone before she could utter a protest.

It was cold without Remie. There was no frost yet, but they'd gotten the hay in only just in time, she thought numbly. Already the sounds of his footfalls had died away; he walked with the easy agility of a man of the forests, disturbing nothing, frightening neither birds nor animals at his approach.

She felt like crying again, but she did not. Nor did she feel any guilt. She had spent the night in Remie's arms, had learned the secrets of his lean, powerful body and learned a good deal about her own body as well. It didn't matter that there was lingering tenderness—which, Remie had promised her, would quickly diminish—nor that she had disobeyed her father in this matter. Many a couple conceived a child without disgrace before their banns were cried, for marriage was sure to follow; there was no trifling among the Acadians, for all their hot blood.

A child! Soleil stopped along the unseen path, catching her breath. What if their initial lying together produced a child?

Well, she thought, striding out again quickly as the darkness became less absolute, if that happened, so be it. She wanted nothing more than to have Remie's child, except to call the father husband. And he would return before a babe could be born. In a country where priests were few and far between, there were many couples who had two or three little ones before the union could be officially blessed by the Church, though that wasn't often the case here at Grand-Pré, where there was almost always a priest in residence.

She moved rapidly, almost running now; the first light of dawn usually brought her father awake, and for all her brave words she didn't want to meet him this way, coming in with hay clinging to her hair and clothes. No, not yet. She didn't want Émile's wrath—or pain—to spoil this most perfect of nights.

She felt a thrill of alarm when she smelled wood smoke as she approached the house. Was someone already up? Feeding the fire to begin the new day?

Cautiously Soleil eased open the door, which was never bolted, and crept silently through the passageway. The inner door into the kitchen gave way beneath her hand without a sound, and to her vast relief she heard her father's snoring.

The embers glowed on the hearth; the kettle gave off the delicate aroma of cooking porridge. No one was as yet astir.

She carried her clogs across the main room, past the pallets where Jacques and Bertin slept on the far side, and moved noiselessly into the room beyond. The curtains on her brothers' beds were undisturbed, and she slipped between those on her own.

Danielle was immediately awake. "Where have you been all this time?" she hissed, and Soleil clamped a hand over the younger girl's mouth. Her own whisper came only an inch from Danielle's ear.

"Where do you think I've been, you idiot? Be still or you'll wake someone!"

"Were you with Remie all this time?" At least Danielle had moderated her voice, though Soleil would have preferred that she kept silent altogether.

"Yes, of course. Be quiet! I'll talk to you later!"

Soleil squirmed out of her clothes, then burrowed into the welcome warmth of the bed, grateful that for once her sister obeyed her.

She had no time to fall asleep, however. Only moments later the household began to rouse. There were muttered curses, feet thumping on the floor, the sounds of coughing and scratching.

Soleil lay in the near blackness of her curtained cubicle, drawing a sigh of relief.

"Thank you, Blessed Mother," she mouthed, and then it was time to get up.

BARBE'S GAZE was a sharp one, but she was too busy to study her older daughter that morning. If she had, she might have detected a subtle change in Soleil beyond what one might expect from a young girl who had been proposed to, had had an immediate wedding forbidden and lost her suitor for at least six months, all within a matter of hours.

Soleil did her best to stay out of her mother's way. Madeleine was too busy with her own packing and silent weeping to pay her any attention. It was only Danielle who was devoured by curiosity, finally finding an opportunity to ask the question that had been burning her tongue for so long when they were both sent for water from the stream to do the laundry.

"Where did you spend the night?" she demanded as soon as they were out of Barbe's hearing.

"In the hay field," Soleil said defiantly. "Though if you ever expect another favor of me, you'll keep it to yourself."

"Did you..." Danielle sought a delicate way to put it. "Did Remie...make love to you?"

"There are some things a person doesn't talk about," Soleil told her with a lofty tilt of the head.

"He did, didn't he? I can tell by the way you look, that little secret, satisfied smile! Soleil, what was it like? Tell me. It'll be years before I know, if Mama keeps telling me what a baby I am!"

"You are a baby. Too young to know about such things."

"Oh, you're mean! You're hateful!" Danielle stopped on the pathway. "You're walking as if...does it hurt?"

Soleil tried to walk normally, which was difficult because she *was* sore. Good grief, would everyone be able to tell just by watching her walk? "A little. But it will quickly go away," she stated, hoping she was right about that.

Danielle's brown eyes were wide. "Did it hurt terribly when . . . when you did it?"

Soleil was torn between keeping this most private thing entirely private and wanting to share her elation. She also was not desirous of alienating her younger sister. Danielle did have her uses if she felt cooperative.

"A bit," she admitted finally.

"Did you bleed? Was it like having a baby?"

"Since I've never had a baby, how could I know? I shouldn't think so, though. Certainly I didn't want it to stop. Look, if you keep staring at me that way the whole family is going to know, and it's better if they don't. In fact, once we've carried the water and put it on the fire, I'm going to tell Mama I need to go visit Céleste Dubay. It's only natural I'd want to tell my best friend that I am betrothed, even if the banns can't be read until spring. And if you say one word to make her suspicious, I'll strangle you."

"I wouldn't do that," Danielle said with reproach. "Only it's hard when everyone treats you like a baby."

Soleil strode on ahead, moving so swiftly in spite of her discomfort that it was impossible to carry on further conversation. To her relief, Danielle fell into a disappointed silence.

Barbe made no objection to Soleil walking over to the Dubay place, other than to observe that it was Madeleine's last day with them.

"Louis says they will leave at dawn tomorrow," she reminded.

"I know. But she's busy now, and so upset she isn't really talking to anyone anyway. I'll be back to help with supper," Soleil said, and fled before her mother had time to probe any more deeply into her own motives.

Céleste was busy in the kitchen and greeted her with delighted surprise. "Come in, I'll fix you a cup of tea. Mama's gone over to visit Mme Trudelle and see the new baby. Have you seen him yet?"

"No." Soleil sank onto a stool and accepted the hot tea sweetened with honey, the way she liked it. She wondered how to begin, but in the end there was no need to bring up the subject. Céleste did it for her.

"I heard that Remie Michaud helped out with your haying, and that he even slept in the barn rather than walk back and forth to the Trudelles' morning and night. Did that give you time together?" Her eyes were bright with interest.

"Yes. He's asked me to marry him."

Céleste gave a squeal and dropped the knife she was using to chop vegetables. She gave her friend a hug. "Soleil! So soon! I knew he was smitten. I could tell by the way he singled you out at the dance!"

"Yes, well," Soleil said, sipping at the tea, "Papa was not smitten with *him*. He says we cannot marry until spring."

Céleste was aghast. "Why ever not? Oh, Soleil, what a pity! How did Remie take it?"

"He said that Papa was no doubt right, and that he would be back in the spring. He left early this morning." She said it bravely enough, but her lip quavered.

Céleste forgot what she was supposed to be cooking and sank onto a bench where she could reach out and take the other girl's hands in her own. "He's gone? Already? Oh, Soleil, is your heart breaking?"

"I feel more anger than anything else," Soleil confessed. "Against Papa. Remie is not a farmer, he said, or a fisherman. He traps for furs, and he goes to distant places. If he'd agreed to join Papa in farming, we'd have been allowed to marry right away."

Céleste was mystified. "But why must you wait until spring? Your father hasn't forbidden you ever to marry."

"He thinks I'll change my mind if we're separated that long. I suppose he hopes someone else will come along who will take Remie's place, someone who'll stay at Grand-Pré so I won't have to go away! But that won't happen," Soleil declared staunchly. "There will never be anyone else! I feel as if I'm married to him now!"

Céleste's expression shifted perceptibly. "Have you—did you…?" Unlike Danielle, she didn't quite put the question into words. But with Céleste, Soleil was somewhat less inhibited.

She trusted her friend more than her sister to keep what she knew to herself.

"Yes," Soleil confessed softly, caught between joy and tears. "You must swear not to tell. We spent the night together, and it was wonderful." She decided there was nothing to be gained by admitting to the soreness that had made the walk there less comfortable than usual. That would sound so prosaic, so . . . common. "And when he returns in the spring, we'll ask Father Castin to marry us as soon as the banns will allow."

Céleste was gazing at her with parted lips. "Oh, it's so romantic, and so sad! But he will come back, won't he? He's promised to come back?"

"Yes, of course." She felt quite certain of that. "He said he loves me, and he knows I love him."

At that point Georges Dubay entered the house, annoyed to find his daughter visiting rather than preparing his supper, though all he wanted at the moment was something to tide him over for a few more hours.

"Is the haying done, Papa?" Céleste asked, hurriedly preparing him a bit to eat.

"If it were done, your brothers would be here, too," Georges said, though his temper eased as she poured him tea to go with the thick slab of bread and the slice of beef she put on the plate beside it. And then, striving for courtesy, he questioned their guest, "And how goes it at your place, *mademoiselle*?"

"Papa expects to finish today. Then it's only a matter of getting it all into the barn before it rains. They have all but the last field in now."

Georges was older and wearier than Émile Cyr. His muscular shoulders sagged with the weight of his years and responsibilities. His five sons were good workers, but they were all married, and there were many mouths to feed. "And then Louis will go. What a pity it is, for he is Émile's right hand."

"Yes," Soleil murmured.

"I cannot believe that Louis is right in thinking the English will drive us from our lands. They have been at this absurdity about signing the pledge for many years and it's never come to anything more than harassment. The soldiers at the blockhouse in Grand-Pré are arrogant and foolish, but they do not truly threaten us." He sighed and ate his lunch while Soleil sat silently and Céleste prepared the rest of her vegetables to go into the pot.

Only when Georges had left the house could they return to their private conversation, and Remie was not mentioned again. Instead, Céleste asked about Antoine. "He'll be at the next dance, won't he?"

Soleil drew herself out of her own private world to smile a little. "So it's Antoine, is it? You've decided between them?"

"Well, I don't know. They're as alike as two grains of barley, so there's naught to choose between them for looks. But Antoine is always thinking of something funny, or exciting. And I think perhaps he has an eye for me, too." She hesitated, then asked, "Do you think so?"

"I don't know. With the twins it's hard to say. They're so seldom serious. But now that the harvest is in, there'll be more time for social affairs. And I don't think either of them has formed an attachment for anyone else."

They chatted for a while longer, then Soleil rose to go. "I'll have to help with supper. It will be special, because it's Madeleine and Louis's last night. I'm afraid we'll all take it hard, losing them. Especially since Remie will be gone for months, too." Her eyes prickled as she moved toward the doorway. "I'll see you at the next dance, anyway."

After Remie, it would be difficult to go back to dancing with her brothers and the young men she'd known all her life, she thought.

The winter, not yet here, stretched ahead of her, intolerably cold and long and lonely.

12

ATTEMPTS TO MAKE the meal a cheerful one fell flat.

Madeleine made a valiant effort not to cry, and the twins tried to maintain their reputation as jokers, but since everyone except baby Marc was aware of the reason for the special cake and the wine that was not homemade but had come from France at considerable expense, the results were doleful.

Louis and his family would leave at dawn, and because Madeleine's own parents had begged them to do so, they were spending their last night with the Bouchards. Therefore the Cyr clan went down on their knees together before the first step of the journey had begun, and Émile led them all in prayers for the small family's safety and well-being.

For once, no one thought his prayers overlong or tedious. Each of them echoed the entreaties silently and fervently. Émile concluded, "And we ask Thy blessings and protection as well upon young Remie Michaud as he travels through the wilderness. In Thy Holy Name, amen."

This was totally unexpected, and Soleil felt her throat close painfully with emotion. Her eyes blurred as she rose to her feet to take her turn hugging and kissing the trio who were leaving.

When the final goodbyes had been said and the door closed after those who had departed, the house was unbearably quiet.

Pierre ruffled the hair of his young sons and left them to Danielle to put to bed. "I'll check the stock," he said gruffly, but it was well over an hour before he returned.

The twins and Bertin also disappeared outside, without specifying where they were going. Jacques was sent off to bed with the little boys, even though it was not yet his usual time. He went without protest, already both missing his oldest brother and envying him for setting out on such an adventure.

Soleil and Danielle went to bed early, too. There was nothing to be said, though Soleil almost wished she could thank her father for adding Remie to the petition for protection. Why, though, could he not have agreed to an official betrothal?

She was still awake when she heard her brothers return and retire. And though she was here, at home, in the bed in which she'd slept ever since she was out of the cradle, her heart was out along a woodland trail somewhere to the north, with Remie.

THERE WAS A FROST that night.

Barbe looked out at the white ground sparkling in the morning sun. "I didn't expect it to freeze quite so early. I hope that doesn't mean a long, hard winter. It will be more difficult for Marc and Madeleine if it's cold every night," she said, and turned away from the window with a sigh.

Although there were still a dozen people in the household, their numbers seemed vastly diminished. Fewer plates and cups were set out on the plank table, and there were leftovers at the bottom of the pot. The older boys might have taken over the room Louis and Madeleine had shared, but they did not; it was left empty, unvisited after the girls had replaced Madeleine's bedding with sheets and quilts belonging to Barbe.

Often in the days that followed, Soleil saw her mother standing at the doorway, looking out, noting the changes in the weather. The leaves turned yellow and scarlet, then fluttered free with every gust of wind until all the maples and birches were etched nakedly against the sky. Only the firs, pines and spruce trees retained their deep green color.

Barbe seldom mentioned her son and daughter-in-law, but Soleil knew she was thinking about them. Once Barbe found a wooden boat Louis had carved for Marc, and another time came across a tiny sock that had gotten wedged into a corner. When Soleil saw her tears, Barbe smiled crookedly and said simply, "I miss him so."

Every night at evening prayers, Émile called upon the Almighty to protect their loved ones away from home. And he continued to mention Remie Michaud, as well. So he knows, Soleil thought, how much Remie means to me. Why, then, did he insist on separating us? Despite the prayers, she could not quite let her bitterness die.

Yet she could not go on resenting her father to the point of disliking him, for his sincerity was apparent. Gradually her anger against him subsided, while her longing for Remie grew stronger.

A few weeks after the harvest had been completed, the twins announced casually that they were going off on an excursion of their own. "We'll go over to the Micmac village with some of the red cloth that was smuggled in from Louisbourg," Antoine said, "and see if we can trade for something. Anybody want anything special?"

Danielle and Soleil spoke up in chorus. "Embroidered material for a skirt!" "A pair of moccasins!"

Barbe looked up from the wool she was carding. "On your way home, shoot something large enough to keep the pot filled for a few days. No rabbit. I've had my fill of rabbit for a bit."

Soleil followed them to the doorway. She had seen them off this way many times before, yet somehow this time seemed different. "Be careful," she said.

François made a face of mock dismay. "Who, us? You know our reputation! The wild Cyr twins, always joking, never serious! If there is real danger, you won't find us within miles of it!"

"Good," Émile grunted. "Stay away from the British. There was an incident in Grand-Pré only last week when some children foolishly provoked the soldiers at the blockhouse and were threatened by a bayonet. The youngest Blanchard boy actually caught the tip of it across his cheek. He could have lost an eye."

"Charles? But he's only seven!" Barbe exclaimed, forgetting the wool that would make warm stockings to see them all through the winter ahead. "The British are brave, indeed, to make war against mere children!"

"The children must learn that it is dangerous to tweak the lion's tail," Émile said heavily. "The best way to get along with the English is to ignore them and everything they stand for."

Behind his back the twins exchanged a look that carried no humor whatever, but no one noticed it.

On impulse, Soleil reached up to hug first François, then Antoine. "Take care," she cautioned once more, and then, to make her words seem less urgent, she asked lightly, "Have either of you a message for Céleste?"

"Céleste who?" Antoine asked, swinging the pack onto his shoulders and securing it.

At the same time François gave a knowing grin and remarked, "It's not us she's worried about, it's Remie, only he's not here to hug."

Soleil punched each of them on the arm, knowing that what François said was true. The twins had been going off on jaunts of their own for years, and she'd never worried about them before. It was only her love and concern for Remie that heightened her perceptions of everything and everyone else.

"Céleste will miss you at the dance tomorrow night," she persisted out of loyalty for her friend, who would be crushed when the twins didn't show up.

"We've done nothing but work, and work hard, for the past month. We need a change," Antoine asserted. He bent to kiss his mother. "Keep a fire under the kettle, Mama, and we'll fill it up for you when we return. Goodbye, Grand-père. We'll bring you a new supply of tobacco."

The old man grinned, exposing gaps between his teeth. "Good! Good!"

Émile, too, seemed less casual than in the past about letting them go. No doubt the loss of Louis had changed his perceptions, too, Soleil thought.

"Get the tobacco and the fancy embroidered cloth and whatever else you like. But stay away from British patrols. They have set severe penalties for smuggling, and they're not noted for their fair trials."

"Don't worry, Papa. Two Frenchmen can outwit an entire battalion of Englishmen," François said.

"And outshoot them, as well," Antoine added.

Émile refused to be drawn into laughter by their banter. He gave them a level look and spoke soberly. "Don't put it to the test," he warned.

And then the twins were gone, and the house was emptier than ever.

A few days later on a deceptively summery day, which was to prove the last such weather of the season, Soleil's monthly show of blood came; she stood in the woods behind the outhouse and wept a little.

She had not really wanted to confess to her parents that she had lain with Remie, that she was carrying his child when there could be no wedding until spring. Yet there had been a part of her that hoped the child was there in her belly, that she had indeed conceived Remie's son or daughter on that memorable night.

Soleil moved mechanically through the following days, days that grew increasingly colder, with frost more nights than not. She did her usual tasks of cooking and cleaning, and now that there was no garden to tend nor harvest to preserve, she and her mother and sister took up the winter tasks of weaving, spinning and sewing. Her fingers worked of their own accord, needing little help from her brain; her mind was filled with Remie, wondering where he was, how far along on the trail between Grand-Pré and the walled city of Québec. She wondered if she would accompany him to that distant and mystical city after they were married, and she tried to imagine the stone walls of the fortifications and the security of French soldiers guarding them, rather than the red-coated English who dampened everyone's spirits here in Grand-Pré.

The twins were gone for nearly three weeks, returning as abruptly as they had left. They carried tobacco and scarlet cloth with the intricate and beautiful embroidery of the Micmacs that would be incorporated into dresses for every female in the household. The girls exclaimed over the fur-lined moccasins that laced up well above their ankles for protection during the cold winter months, and Barbe was pleased with baskets that would be used to carry and store foodstuffs.

And there was meat aplenty for the pot, for François had brought down a cow moose so that their own stock could be left for breeding and enlarging their herds rather than eaten. Because it was far too much for the twins to transport through the forest, they had shared it with their Micmac neighbors. A haunch of it was immediately set to roasting on the spit, while the remainder was hung outside, out of reach of predators, where it would stay cold until they needed it.

Except that Louis and his family were missing, the night of the twins' return was like the old days, with food and drink and laughter and talk as Antoine and François amused the others with tales of their exploits among the Indians who had welcomed them.

Remie, too, would be spending time with the Micmacs, Soleil thought. She imagined him in their villages, snug inside a birchbark wigwam, being waited upon by dark-eyed, slender maidens. Though he had not said so, she was certain there was one in the place where he often cached his furs who was—or had been—special to him. Soleil put down the twinge of jealousy that thought inspired and told herself it would be different now that he had promised himself to *her*.

One morning in early November, they woke to Henri's excited shouting. "Snow, Grand-maman, snow!" he cried.

The clearing before the house was blanketed in white, with more of the fluffy stuff continuing to fall. After breakfast, Danielle and Soleil went outside with the children to play in it for a time before duty and warmth called them back to the fireside. The snow, like everything else, made Soleil think of

Remie. How far had he gone by this time? Was he comfortably holed up in a wigwam with the Indians, or alone on the trail, cold and hungry? Her heart ached with yearning for him.

ONCE A WEEK the Cyrs got together with their neighbors to dance. Soleil spun around the floor with the village men, feeling no more at their touch than she did with one of her brothers. She watched a ripening romance between Antoine and Céleste and wondered wistfully if they would be allowed to marry at once when they decided they wanted to. She noted, as well, and with a twinge of uneasiness, that François scarcely took his eyes off the couple, his usually vibrant face oddly still. Did he, too, have tender feelings for her friend? Soleil hoped not, for she did not want to see François hurt over such a matter.

It was Barbe who decided that, when their turn came to host the dance, they could open their house to more people if they pushed the table and benches against the walls and opened up the room that had belonged to Louis and Madeleine. The stomping feet, the friendly voices that grew louder as the level in the barrel of fir or spruce beer dropped, the fiddles that played such rollicking tunes did nothing to brighten Soleil's life, though she tried to pretend they did.

She imagined Remie walking briskly through the woods while the snow fell silently around him, or moving upstream in a canoe, camping at night in the open under the stars, or improvising a shelter with fir boughs, eating his solitary meals as he squatted by a small fire. How she wished that she were with him!

Did he think of her as often as she thought of him?

Soleil prayed that he did.

She missed Louis and Madeleine and Marc, too. There was, of course, no word of them. Once or twice a year the village priest might come across a newspaper from the Old World, and he would relate to them some of the things that were happening in France, although the events had taken place many months earlier. News from Halifax, Annapolis Royal or Beaubassin came only by word of mouth from the infrequent traveler.

Few in Grand-Pré could have read a paper or a letter if it had been available, except for old M. Gagnon, a contemporary of Grand-père's, and one or two others. If by some chance Remie found a way to send her a letter, she would take it to M. Gagnon rather than to Father Castin to read it to her, she thought. She blushed, thinking what Remie might write, for *he* had once gone to school, and could pen more than his name if he needed to.

Remie's life had been different from her own. He barely remembered his parents. His father had been lost at sea when Remie was only a small boy. His mother took a chill that same winter and died shortly thereafter. There had been a younger sister, but she had lived less than a year, so Remie had had no one.

He had spent his life from the age of five onward with various families, including that of his Uncle Guillaume. At one point he had spent two years with the priests in Annapolis Royal, where he had learned about reading and writing; he had been on his own since the age of twelve.

Remie had never known the love and support of a big family such as hers. He had never had a home of his own, but he knew what he wanted. During the night they had spent in each other's arms they had talked about the cabin he would build, how snug and warm it would be, and how, God willing, they would fill it with sons and daughters.

How quickly he had filled the void in her life! It was impossible not to cry sometimes, missing him. Barbe and Émile never asked her why her eyes were red; they knew. She wanted them to know, for this heartache could have been avoided if her father had given them permission to marry.

Winter was in earnest now. Temperatures seldom rose above freezing. The wind howled around the eaves, and the fireplace had an insatiable hunger for the wood the males in the family had been cutting all summer. One wall of the entry hall was stacked with it from floor to ceiling, narrowing the passageway by half, and whatever wood was used during the day was replaced as soon as possible from the supply outside.

In the bedrooms the water froze in the basins and the chamber pots. Quilts and fur robes were piled so heavily on the beds that it was difficult for a sleeper to turn over. A drift of snow that blew in under the door did not melt in the outer end of the passage. Danielle, busy with the spinning wheel or the loom, complained that she couldn't work when her fingers were stiff and blue with the cold, though she was no more than a few yards from the hearth.

The men were in the house more than usual. They still had stock to care for, and chopping wood was an unending chore, yet they were inside enough so that they became restless. Barbe would flap her apron and shout at them.

"Go on, get out the snowshoes and go hunt up enough rabbits or a young buck for stew! And stop teasing the children! Take them outside to play!"

Émile was quieter than Soleil could ever remember from earlier winters. He mended and repaired tools, made leather footwear or carved out wooden clogs, but with few of his usual good-humored remarks to cheer those around him. There was no doubt that he thought of Louis, and worried about him.

The twins tried to liven things up with their customary banter. Antoine had finally realized that Céleste had taken a fancy to him. Far from entertaining thoughts of marriage, he regarded the entire business as a great joke. He and François were perpetually plotting some hoax—often involving Céleste's inability to tell them apart—to play upon the poor girl, though it seemed to Soleil that François was sometimes halfhearted about it. Surely, though, he would not have indulged in such foolishness, she told herself, if he himself harbored tender feelings for Céleste.

Under other circumstances Soleil might have been amused. As it was, she barely noticed their antics. She was engrossed in stitching linens for the home she intended to share with Remie, in mending or making new garments, in preparing for the new life that would begin with Remie's return.

Fast days came and went; feasts were celebrated, but with less exuberance than in the past. Long before spring they all yearned for an end to the cold, bitter weather.

In early January, M. Gagnon suddenly appeared on their doorstep, bundled to the eyebrows in heavy woolens and furs. When Soleil opened the door at his pounding, the brilliance of the sun reflecting off a mantle of snow was so dazzling that she was momentarily blinded after she had closed the door.

"Come in, *monsieur*, come in!" she greeted him warmly. "Sit by the fire with Grand-père and have some tea, and I've just made a cake, too, full of raisins and spices!"

Émile, who had been carving a small wooden shoe, moved from his own place at the hearth. "Tea and be damned, girl, a man who's walked all the way from the village in freezing cold needs more than tea! I've just the thing, monsieur, just the thing! A good brandy, come all the way from France, that I've been saving for such a moment!"

Grand-père grinned and removed his pipe from his mouth as their old neighbor allowed himself to be helped from his outer wrappings and held out blue-veined hands to the welcome flames. "Ah, brandy is it! I'll not turn that down, my friend!"

It was not until M. Gagnon had drained the brandy and taken a second serving that he spoke of his reason for coming.

"We had a visitor at Grand-Pré a few days ago, from Beaubassin, on his way to Annapolis Royal. I tried to find someone to send with a message at once, but no one was coming this way, and it was not until today that I felt up to coming myself."

He drained his cup and didn't hesitate to extend it once more when Émile lifted the bottle, suggesting a third tot. Grand-père, too, held a cup to be refilled, for the brandy was a cut above what was usually poured around the fire during an evening.

"Excellent, *monsieur*, excellent! I don't know when I've had anything of this quality! Well, yes. The traveler had news for the Cyrs, he said."

Soleil went very still, her heart racing. Remie? She was torn between excitement and dread.

"I'm an old man, and memory does not serve me as well as it used to, but I believe I can remember it all. Young Louis wanted him to send you word that they had reached Beaubassin, where he and his family spent a few weeks until his wife was better able to travel. They were fine and were preparing to depart for Île St. Jean with two other families, traveling in canoes. There were fourteen in all, including the children."

Not Remie, but Louis and Madeleine, and they were all right. Soleil released the breath that had made her chest ache.

"Other families! Thanks be to God," Barbe said, her hands clasped in an attitude of prayer. "At least Madeleine has other women and is not at the mercy of mere man when her time comes!''

"Her time doesn't come for months," Émile told her shortly.

"Ah, who knows about such things? At any rate, she'll feel better for the female company! You understand, *monsieur*, my son is an unexceptional husband, but he is still a man, and what do men know of such things?" Her expression included her own husband in this blanket indictment. "Did the traveler have anything to say about our grandson, young Marc?"

M. Gagnon shook his head. "Only that they were all well. I am glad the news I bring of Louis is good news, for there is much that is bad, I fear."

"And how is that, *monsieur*?" Émile asked, sipping at his own warming draught.

"The English again grow restive. They are not satisfied that we live peacefully, for the most part, minding our own fields and boats and our own business." Worry lines furrowed M. Gagnon's brow. "The Indians and a handful of our more impetuous young men continue to harass their soldiers. There was another incident involving young children at the blockhouse last week. Stones were thrown, and there was an ugly scene. A soldier had a bloody nose, and another a cut lip. They caught the boys and detained them overnight for questioning as to who put them up to their mischief. Their parents were frantic, of course."

Émile drained his cup. "Perhaps they'll learn not to tease the soldiers, then. It is a foolish pastime, and as unproductive as a sheep taunting a wolf."

Both Grand-père and M. Gagnon nodded.

"It is the young men who run the real risks, however. Those who join forces with the Indians and raid British farms and villages, burning and pillaging."

"And bringing the wrath of the British down on us all," Émile agreed, sighing. "What further news of Beaubassin, then? There hasn't been another attempt by Colonel Lawrence to take that town and Fort Beauséjour? My son was in no danger there?"

M. Gagnon shook his head. Between the fire and the brandy he was feeling quite comfortable after his strenuous walk. "No, though the people continue to fear it. Of course it was not

Lawrence who burned the church there, it was a band of Indians under the command of the Abbé Le Loutre."

"A disgraceful act," Émile said after a moment of silence unbroken except by the crackle of the fire, "to drive out our own settlers, to force them behind the battle lines into Canada. Le Loutre is a priest and a Frenchman, yet sometimes he behaves as badly as the enemy. Some of the refugees have returned, however, have they not?"

The old man nodded. "Yes. But Colonel Lawrence has declared that any settler who leaves his land to assist the enemy, as they designate our own people in Canada, is refuting the oath of allegiance and therefore sacrifices his right to the lands. It is a difficult position for a man who wishes to keep his family safe yet fears for the land he has worked for years."

"Many things are difficult these days," Émile said. "We must keep our heads and leave the British alone. Then they'll leave us alone."

Soleil, listening, prayed that he was right. But she was afraid he was mistaken.

13

IF ANYTHING either ominous or exciting happened that winter, Soleil was unaware of it. There was always work to do, and her hands were busy, even if her heart and mind seemed disconnected from them.

Danielle had finally attracted the attention of Basile Lizotte and lived for the dances, where they could be together. Her constant chatter and speculation about a future with Basile might otherwise have driven Soleil mad had she not been too wrapped in her own dreams to listen to much of it.

At least once a week, aside from the times when neighbors gathered to dance, drink and enjoy one another's company, Soleil and Céleste managed to get together for an afternoon. Talking in private was difficult to do inside, for both their families would usually be gathered around the fire, working on various projects. That meant they often bundled themselves well against the cold and walked along the tops of the dykes where no one could approach within miles without being detected. There they shared confidences and dreams until the cold finally drove them inside, wondering if they had frostbitten toes and fingers.

Céleste despaired of bringing Antoine to the point of proposing.

"Sometimes he's so sweet. He tells me I'm pretty, and he likes my apple pie better than anyone's, and he says I'm the best dancer, too. And then," Céleste said indignantly, her words issuing on a puff of white in the frigid air, "he and François trick me into kissing François!"

She gave her friend an imploring look. "Would a man do that if he truly cared about a girl?"

"I don't know. The twins are so immature in many ways," Soleil responded. She stepped onto an icy spot and heard as well as felt it give beneath her feet. "For instance, today they are off playing games, sliding on the ice as if they were Jacques's age, or even Henri's. Like children."

"I'm nearly sixteen now. Everyone I know was at least betrothed by the time they were sixteen."

"Even me," Soleil said, laughing.

"Even you," Céleste echoed. "Mama is becoming impatient with me and says I waste my time on the Cyrs, especially when there are always two of them. She says I'd be better off to find a man who wants to see me by himself."

She kicked at a knob of ice that had formed around a clump of reeds and sent it skittering down the side of the dyke, her pretty face rebellious. "I don't want another man. I want Antoine. Sometimes I think he wants me, and then he goes off for days at a time without any explanation, not even saying goodbye. When he comes home it's passed over as if it should be of no concern to me."

A gust of wind whipped her long brown hair out from under her cap and the scarf she had tied over it, so that she put up both mittened hands to secure the dark locks better. She was extraordinarily pretty, Soleil thought, and wondered why Antoine didn't propose to her friend. At the dances he seldom paid attention to anyone else anymore.

"How did you decide it was Antoine you wanted, rather than François?" she asked gently, unable to find anything truthfully reassuring to say.

"Oh, he's the most fun! He's the one who leads—it's always François who follows. Have you noticed that?"

"Yes. They've always been that way."

Céleste lifted her head, staring out across the deep red sands of the mud flats left exposed by the outgoing tide, though it was clear that she didn't see them. "Well, your brother Antoine is taking me for granted, while making no commitment on his own part, and he may soon find that he has some competition!"

Soleil's eyes widened. "Oh? Who? François, after all?"

"No, silly. François is simply Antoine's shadow, and even more a foolish boy than his twin. No." A defiant note crept into her voice. "One of the soldiers at the blockhouse has been paying attention to me lately. Whenever I walk by, he makes an excuse to talk to me. Only this past week he said I was the prettiest girl he'd ever seen."

Shock made Soleil rigid. "A soldier! An Englishman! Céleste, you can't be serious!"

"No doubt that's what my family would say, too, if they knew. But he's a nice young man, Soleil, he really is! His name is Tommy Sharp—you know the one, so tall and blond, and very attractive. He wants a girl to talk to, anybody to talk to, other than the soldiers. All they do is drink and gamble, and they hate us. Papa says it's because they're afraid of us, that we'll rise up in rebellion against what the British are doing to us with all their restrictions and penalties, and there are more of us than of them."

Soleil could scarcely credit what her friend was saying. "But a redcoat, Céleste! Everyone in Grand-Pré hates them! Everyone in Acadia!"

"I know. I hate them, too, mostly. But Tommy is not like Colonel Lawrence. He's only doing his job, and he's across an ocean from everyone he loves, his parents and brothers and sisters. I don't think he's ever even had an attachment for a girl before. He's just eighteen and he's been away from home for a year and a half. He wants to talk, like any ordinary young man, and he's lonely."

"You wouldn't seriously consider him as a suitor, surely!"

Céleste's full mouth twisted unhappily. "I don't know. I *like* him. I *more* than like Antoine, but what good is it doing me?

And every day Mama keeps making remarks about being stuck with an old maid who is too fussy for her own good—'' Tears glistened in her eyes.

Soleil's own emotions were always close to the surface, and her eyes prickled, too, as she gave her friend an impulsive hug. "Oh, Céleste! I'm sorry! But the answer is not a British soldier! Your parents would never let you marry him, and what would happen if you did? Where would you live? You'd be an outcast from all your own people!''

Céleste groped for a handkerchief and blew her nose. "I know. I've thought of all those things. But I'm tempted to let your inconsiderate brother *think* I'm seriously drawn to Tommy.''

"Just don't let anyone else think so," Soleil said soberly. "It could be dangerous. And it's not fair to Tommy, either, is it? To let him think you might be serious about him when you know you can't be?''

By the time she had walked home through the afternoon winter dusk, Soleil had made up her mind to confront Antoine for a serious talk.

But it was too late, at least for now. The twins, irresponsible as ever, had suddenly taken off again. Sometimes she wondered why Céleste cared one way or the other about a man who insisted upon remaining a boy and thought of no one but himself.

THE WORLD WAS HELD in an icy grip that lasted for weeks. The snow was heavy and deep; except for the necessities of tending stock and refueling the fires, few ventured outside.

In the Micmac village of Angry Waters, Remie Michaud holed up until the worst of the storm was over.

He had spent many nights in the wigwam of Angry Waters. He spoke the language fluently, and the Indians also spoke French, so there was no difficulty in communicating. The men ate and smoked around the fires, talking endlessly of the hated British who burned Acadian villages and drove helpless women and children out into the elements to perish of the cold and starvation.

Angry Waters also spoke, with a satisfaction that Remie found mildly disquieting, of the raids his people made upon the enemy. "Take many scalps," he asserted, and puffed on his long-stemmed pipe.

Remie kept his voice neutral. "You don't think the raids inflame the English? Drive them to more cruelty against us all?"

The Indian's face was impassive. "The redcoats have always been cruel, both to Indians and Frenchmen. They have many soldiers to the south, in the colonies with the strange names. They wish to drive out all Indians and Frenchmen so that they can bring English settlers on their ships with the tall sails. As long as their settlers are not safe in our lands, fewer of them will come, perhaps."

During one of the long afternoons when the wind howled around the big wigwam and the smoke from the fire was driven back from the vent above so that they viewed one another through a perpetual haze, one of Angry Waters's sons made a remark that brought Remie out of the semistupor induced by inactivity and too much good food. He and Young Otter had been friends for years, though since Remie's arrival in the village this time he had sensed a constraint that had not existed between them before.

There was some good-natured teasing because of the Micmac's name. The Abbé Jean-Louis Le Loutre was known as The Otter; every soul in Acadia and Canada had reason to know the priest's name, as did those in the British colonies to the south, because of the bloodthirsty raids The Otter and his young braves made against their settlers.

Young Otter approved the raids as a necessary fact of life as he saw his homeland shrinking under British rule. He did not, however, care for Abbé Le Loutre.

"He is a madman, I think," Young Otter stated. And then, slanting a glance toward their guest that might have held a touch of malice, he added, "Of course, most white men are mad."

When that elicited no reaction from the only white man present, Young Otter amplified this statement. "Especially Frenchmen."

Remie grinned. "Especially Frenchmen," he affirmed.

The Indian launched into a terse account of one such raid against the distant farms outside of Halifax some months previously, when houses and barns had been razed and considerable slaughter had taken place.

"Many dead," Young Otter stated. "We lost none, had not even one injured."

Remie lay back contentedly, enjoying the warmth of the lodge and company, having nothing in particular to do until a change in the weather made it possible to go on. And then he stiffened as his friend continued.

"The French are brave, but they are even more crazy. Two of them, who looked as alike as two scales on a salmon, were everywhere at once. None of us could tell them apart, but it didn't matter, because they were both mad. They took chances no sane man would take, and they came away unscathed. Fire, arrows, muskets—nothing could stop them. They ran, they shouted, they lighted roofs with their torches. Perhaps it is true that the white man's God protects those who are mad, like the abbé. He is—" Young Otter searched for the right word "—obsessed with killing Englishmen. It is good, and right, to drive the redcoats from our lands. But the abbé—" He shook his head. "I will not go again under the leadership of one who is not sane. One day his God will be looking the other direction and we will all be killed. I am not afraid to die, but I do not wish to die senselessly."

Remie, who had been reclining on a pile of fur robes, sat up. His heart was beating so loudly he could hear it, but he kept his voice offhand.

"Who were they, these mad Frenchmen who looked alike?"

Young Otter made a gesture of indifference. "What does it matter? I never heard their names and would not have remembered if I had. The French have absurd names."

Young Otter lied. He never forgot names, whether Micmac, French, English or Abenaki. It disturbed Remie that his friend's attitude toward him had perceptibly altered since they had last met, but he was more perturbed by Young Otter's description of two of the participants in that raid.

"Were they from Grand-Pré, do you know? Were they dark, good-looking?"

"They looked like Frenchmen," Young Otter said flatly.

"Ugly," Remie suggested, forcing a smile that went no further than his lips.

"Yes, ugly," Young Otter agreed.

There was a round of laughter, and another of the young men rose to leave the gathering. The conversation was ended, and the Micmacs began to disperse to their own wigwams in anticipation of the meals the squaws would be cooking.

Only Angry Waters and Remie were left in the lodge. The older man puffed silently for a few minutes on his pipe, then asked quietly, "There is trouble between you and my son, my friend?"

So he hadn't imagined that cutting, hostile edge in Young Otter's words. "If so, I don't know about it," Remie said evenly. "Young Otter has saved my life, and I his. He is my brother."

Angry Waters grunted an acknowledgement and no more was said, but Remie determined to get to the bottom of the apparent estrangement.

Enlightenment came later that evening when Running Fawn appeared in the wigwam with a birchbark container of water for the guest's use; he had seen little of the girl since his arrival, and not only because the weather had brought most communal activities to a halt.

She was, he thought, quite beautiful as she knelt in the firelight, with her dusky skin and dark eyes. She wore an exquisitely embroidered blue tunic made from French goods—or perhaps it had been stolen from the English—over red leggings also decorated with moose-hair embroidery, and Remie thought for a moment how striking the outfit would be on Soleil.

Even now, knowing that he did not love this girl as he loved Soleil, he felt a quickening of pure desire.

"Thank you, Running Fawn," he said, taking the water basket.

She smiled shyly, hesitated, then spoke in a soft voice that everyone pretended did not carry to Angry Waters, who lay stretched out on his robes. "You have not approached me on this visit, Remie Michaud. Are we no longer friends?"

"We'll always be friends," Remie told her. "But we cannot be the same as . . . before. I have found a woman, an Acadian girl, and we are betrothed. We will be married when I return to Grand-Pré in the spring."

For a moment something flickered in her dark eyes, he thought. Or was it only the shadows cast by the fire?

Her sigh was almost inaudible over the moan of the wind. "So. It is as my mother says. You will not wed a Micmac girl."

"There are many braves who will seek your hand," Remie told her. "You have only to choose between them."

"I could not choose," Running Fawn told him, not meeting his eyes, "until you returned. Until I knew...how you felt about me."

Remie sat very still. "You have already been asked, then?"

A faint smile hovered at the corners of her mouth. "It is true."

"And there is one you favor?"

She looked at him then, and this time he had no doubt what her answer would have been had *he* been the one to ask for her hand. There was no mistaking the pain in her eyes, but she would not embarrass him by putting her feelings into words. "There is one," she acknowledged, without stating that the "one" would be her second choice.

And suddenly Remie knew the reason for his friend's resentment. How stupid that he hadn't realized it sooner. "Young Otter," he said, and saw her nod.

"He has waited for me to give him an answer, but I could not until I saw you. And now...now I can accept him."

"Young Otter is a very lucky man," Remie said sincerely. "I shall tell him so, after you've talked to him yourself."

Running Fawn rose gracefully to her feet. "I will tell him tonight," she said. A moment later she was gone.

Remie did not speak to Angry Waters when the girl had left them alone. It was only common courtesy to carry out the charade that the older man had not heard any of Remie's conversation with Running Fawn. They both knew now why Young Otter had spoken with such a barbed tongue.

Remie had been inactive for days, and he could not immediately fall asleep when he pulled the fur robe over him and closed his eyes. Desire had risen quickly and would subside much more slowly. Perhaps not for days, he thought in bittersweet amusement, if he lay there this way, thinking about Soleil.

He remembered every detail about her, from the way her dark hair tumbled down when he had removed her cap, to the swell of her exquisite breasts, the curve of her hip, the incredible sweetness of her lips.

He wondered if Soleil, too, lay awake, thinking of him. Wanting him. The wanting was a painful ache, not only in his groin but in his heart.

Spring was such a long way off.

14

IT WAS NOT until spring that news filtered through to the settlers around Grand-Pré. The reports made even Émile uneasy, though he spoke reassuringly to his family.

"There have always been those who make difficulties," he said. "The English are impossible to live with. The best policy is to ignore them."

The English commander, Charles Lawrence, had grown more aggressive over the winter, however, and the reports that gradually drifted into Grand-Pré were unnerving. There were those who said that the British demands were becoming impossible to meet, no matter how passively the Acadians sought to comply.

With the grip of winter broken so that travelers might once again move about from one community to another, the trickle of information became a torrent; though it was impossible to sort out speculation from fact, it seemed clear to all but the most optimistic that the situation between the Acadians and their British rulers was worsening.

Lawrence, they learned, had arrested the priests and taken prisoner many of their followers from the area around Beaubassin. In some places the settlers had been deprived of their boats and their weapons, presumably for fear that they would use them in an uprising against their British masters. How could men hunt for food or protect their stock against wild beasts without guns? the Acadians asked in dismay. How could they make a living from the sea without their boats?

The twins muttered angrily under their breath at such news, and even Pierre was roused out of his customary lethargy to hold his young sons against his knees and speak in anger. "No one will deprive me of weapons to feed and protect my children," he stated.

Émile waved a hand, indicating much flap about nothing. "They have been through it all before, the British idiots. If the hotheads don't get carried away, the tumult will die down. It always has."

A delegation of men, who had been sent earlier to Halifax to protest Lawrence's actions, was thrown into prison when they refused to take an unconditional oath of allegiance on the spot. Those few who returned home were shaken, bewildered and angry.

"The tyranny of the British increases every day," they protested, and cast black looks at the English soldiers stationed in their midst, though few of them took any overt action. They had no desire for war or rebellion, only wanting to be allowed to farm or to fish in peace. Surely, the elders counseled, this latest uproar would blow over eventually, as it had always done in the past.

But the younger men of the villages were not all reassured by their elders. Some of them spoke impulsively and with anger; some simply packed up their belongings and left, heading north to Île St. Jean or across the isthmus into French territory.

The Acadians around Beaubassin were accused of taking food to the hostile forces gathered by the Abbé Le Loutre. This, Colonel Lawrence made angrily clear, would not be tolerated. Those who fled their lands to keep their families safe when they feared battles between the abbé and the British forces would be considered to give aid to the enemy; if the settlers withdrew to avoid being caught between two lines of fire, they would be fleeing from their oaths of allegiance to the British conquerors. The hundreds who feared for their lives and crossed over into French territory sacrificed their rights to return to their lands when the battling was done.

News traveled slowly, but it continued to trickle in. There were few who could fail to be alarmed at the tactics Colonel Lawrence was using to oust Acadian settlers from lands they had worked for many years.

The twins and Pierre began to talk more openly about their apprehensions, but Émile crushed their conversations as soon as they had begun.

"When you ask for trouble, you are almost certain to find it," he stated.

Antoine gave him an uncharacteristically sullen look. "And when you ignore the trouble under your nose, Papa, it can only grow worse. Already it stinks like a dead cow left lying in the sun."

"Enough. I'll have no more such talk. We've lived under British rule for years, and if we keep our heads and mind our own business, we'll go on doing it for many more."

The twins exchanged speaking glances, which Soleil, at least, found vastly disturbing. She prayed that it was her father, and not her increasingly volatile brothers, who was right.

Mostly she prayed for Remie's return. It was such a long way to where he gathered his furs, and the winter had been a hard one. When could she expect Remie back in Grand-Pré? It was a matter of more immediate concern than what went on in Halifax, on the far side of the country, or in Beaubassin, also miles away. Somehow, she felt, once Remie was with her she would feel safe again, and happy.

When that moment came, however, all was not to be as fair sailing as she'd hoped.

IT WAS AN UNSEASONABLY warm day, and the door had been left open at the back of the church. Henri and Vincent squirmed more than usual, and Barbe had reprimanded them twice already. A bee, looking for the sweetness of an early-spring blossom, had made its way inside, and the little boys delightedly watched its progress as it hovered over the back of M. Diotte's neck just ahead of them. If it decided to sting, it would liven up the services a bit.

Soleil's eyes were unfocused; she noticed neither the bee nor her nephews, and she did not hear Father Castin's sermon, either. It was so warm today, almost truly spring, and surely Remie would be coming soon, though she knew there would be snow remaining in the woods for weeks yet. Remie was used to snow and long treks across unsettled country, and he had friends among the Indians who would speed him on his way. Her heart quickened, just thinking about him.

If her father had thought she would forget Remie over the long winter, he would soon see that he had been mistaken. And perhaps—just perhaps—Remie might be persuaded to become a farmer or a fisherman and settle down in Grand-Pré, where she had lived all her life.

The bee settled tentatively on M. Diotte's ear. The little boys stifled their amusement as that gentleman batted at it, no doubt believing it to be a harmless fly. Any moment now, surely it would sting.

And then there was a disturbance at the rear of the church. It was not loud, and no voices were raised, but heads began to turn. M. Diotte turned, too, and the bee flew away, disappointing the small watchers who had been certain that it would create an amusing lump on the thick red neck.

Brought out of her reverie by the slight commotion, Soleil turned her head. Even the priest faltered over the closing benediction, for he had lost the attention of everyone in the congregation to the newcomer.

Soleil made a strangled sound of joy and started to rise before recollecting where she was and sinking down again. Her prayers had been answered; Remie had safely returned!

After a moment of uncertainty Father Castin completed the benediction, crossed himself and lowered his upheld hands. "Welcome, M. Michaud. Do you have news for us?"

Remie strode down the aisle, looking more Indian than Acadian in attire. He was taller than Soleil remembered, and more heavily developed through the chest and shoulders, the lower part of his face obscured by a heavy growth of dark beard.

"Your pardon, Father, but there are things that all of Grand-Pré should know, yes."

The priest beckoned the younger man forward. "What news do you bring, then, *monsieur*?"

Soleil was so glad to see him that for a moment his words did not quite register. And then she saw the countenances turned toward Remie, her father's face among them, and heard the words that sobered them all.

"Many have believed for years that the British Colonel Lawrence seeks to drive out all Acadians from the Fundy basin," Remie was saying. "Now he's brought in two thousand troops from Boston to Chignecto to accomplish it."

There was a hush throughout the congregation, and Soleil's fingers curled tightly around the edge of her seat as the breath caught painfully in her chest.

"Food shipments across the bay are henceforth prohibited and will be confiscated if they're intercepted. Lawrence's soldiers besiege Fort Beauséjour, and since he's already deprived many of the settlers of their weapons, the outcome is hardly in doubt. 'Tis said he intends to drive all the Acadians from their lands so that the British may take what our fathers have worked for since before any of us were born. Any who feed or otherwise offer aid to those who oppose Lawrence—including the Indians—will be considered an enemy and driven off their lands. And any who flee to avoid the battleground are considered to have abandoned them to the British. They will not be allowed to return."

Remie's words were level enough, and he did not have the bearing of a man who was afraid. Yet he struck deeply into their hearts. Could what happened in Chignecto happen here, in Grand-Pré? Was it true that the British would deprive them of their lands, their livelihood?

The chill of the stone church soaked into the men and women of Grand-Pré, most of whom had been on this land all their lives. Beyond the open door there was warmth and sunshine; within, there was a rush of fear and despair that was almost tangible.

Old Broulet's voice was ragged with emotion when he spoke across the aisle from Soleil. "My lands have belonged in my family for over a hundred years. Where is an old man without living sons to go, then?"

Behind and around him there was a murmur, which grew to a rumble as more voices joined in.

"The land is ours, and we'll not be run off by the British!"

"That bunch at Chignecto have always been troublemakers. No wonder the British have decided to put an end to their mischief."

"Mischief?" someone asked irately. "To try to protect their own lands? Their own boats? What mischief is that, to try to hold on to a man's livelihood?"

"We cause no trouble here," another asserted. "Why should we fear like treatment? We are peaceful farmers and fishermen. We threaten no one."

Remie raised his voice to carry over the mutterings. "The British do fear us. They say that troublemakers are everywhere among us. The wise man will prepare for the day when the British will tolerate Frenchmen no longer upon this soil, and make his plans accordingly. Or go now, before the redcoats with their bayonets drive us out and burn our homes as they have done elsewhere."

In the silence the bee buzzed once more around M. Diotte's neck, but this time not even the children were watching it. They did not understand the import of Remie's words, but they could tell from the faces and voices around them that something was severely amiss.

"It must be that you are mistaken, *monsieur*." The speaker was Réné Grégoire, a burly man with eleven sons who helped him work his fields. "No doubt a few foolish young men have joined with the Indians to harass the British, but we are a peaceful people. Surely the British will not punish us all so severely for the poor judgment of a scattered few."

"I've just come from Chignecto," Remie stated flatly. "And I assure you that matters there are exactly as I have described. The 'foolish young men' you refer to may indeed be few in number, but the damage they have inflicted on the British included deaths of both soldiers and settlers as well as the destruction of their homes and barns. The English do not take such things lightly. My own advice, *monsieur*, would be to remove your family to Canada, where the governor still offers some protection to Frenchmen."

M. Grégoire was pale with agitation. "And leave my lands? You are a single man without fields of your own, and you give advice lightly, young sir! You do not realize what you suggest!"

Remie didn't back down. "It's true I'm young, and for the moment without a family or lands of my own, but I assure you, sir, that had I a family I would give up the lands in order to assure their survival."

There was a muttering of denial, of refusal to believe that matters were as bad as he described. People began to rise from their seats to make their way out the door at the rear of the church, angry and agitated bursts of speech breaking out among them.

The Cyrs rose, too, and Soleil bit her lip when she saw her father's face as he approached Remie.

"You have certainly caused an uproar, M. Michaud," Émile greeted him stiffly. "I do not think you will be a popular man in Grand-Pré today."

It was a bad sign that he had addressed Remie so formally, Soleil thought anxiously. Without realizing it, she had stopped so that she blocked the exit of family members behind her. Much of her initial joy upon seeing Remie had already faded into apprehension, for it was obvious that his words had created a major controversy among the villagers.

A touch of color showed through the tanned skin above his dark beard, but Remie held his ground at the side of the aisle.

"What would you have me do, M. Cyr? Fail to relay the news of what happens to our countrymen in Chignecto? Those who refuse to believe it can also happen here are at liberty to follow their own counsel. But there are some, I think, who may choose to remove their families while there is still time to do it without loss of life, and take their livestock with them. If the British come here to remove Acadians forcibly, that may not be possible."

It was difficult to tell whether Émile's emotion was anger at Remie for giving his opinion or dismay at the cloud over Acadian futures. For a moment the two men, young and old, stared at each other. Then Émile shouldered his way past, and the rest of the family followed, except for Soleil.

She stood to one side, scarcely aware of being jostled by other parishioners eager to debate the issue in the churchyard.

Remie put out an arm to encircle her waist, drawing her aside when she might have been trampled, protecting her with his own body. When he looked down into her face and smiled, Soleil felt the warmth flood through her and knew that no matter what else was happening, all was right between her and Remie.

"I thought I must have imagined it, how beautiful you are," he said, in spite of the fact that the Widow La Rochelle gave them a sharply inquiring look as she squeezed past them, "but it's true. You are exactly the way you have appeared in my dreams since I last saw you."

He glanced back to where Father Castin was approaching them from the direction of the sacristy. "Dare we ask him now to announce the banns next Sabbath? Or must we confirm the matter with your father?"

Soleil's heart leaped, but she did not dare say the words she wanted to say. "Perhaps we'd better talk to Papa first," she managed reluctantly. His arm was still around her waist, and his nearness made her dizzy with joy, though she was not unmindful of potential pitfalls on the road to betrothal and marriage.

Remie sighed. "He acted almost as if I'd deliberately brought bad news. I hope he can despise the message without despising the messenger, for that's all I am. A messenger." It was possible to see from his expression when his thoughts shifted from Émile to Soleil. "And I have months' worth of things saved up to convey to Mlle Soleil Cyr. Do I dare to hope that I can begin by walking you home without a chaperon within hearing distance?"

Soleil's dimples appeared in both cheeks, and her dark eyes took on a sparkle they had seldom had since his departure nearly half a year earlier.

For answer, she started along the aisle, tucking her hand through Remie's arm as he fell into step beside her.

"I promise it," she said. "Papa's going to be arguing out there for an hour, more than likely, and Mama is too sensible to do anything to prevent a spinster daughter from making a proper match."

Yet when they emerged into the unseasonable sunshiny warmth, she saw the faces of the men around Émile and her chest grew tight with uneasiness. Only Remie's touch enabled her to keep smiling as they left the churchyard and started the long walk home.

15

BARBE STOOD on the edge of the crowd, talking to Marie Tru-delle and several other women, her attention more on her husband than on the conversation. Remie's news had had a terrible effect on Émile, and she was concerned for him. He was getting old, she realized with a pang. She'd never thought that before, not even when Louis went away. He hadn't looked then the way he looked now.

Louis had been right to leave, she decided numbly. She prayed that her firstborn was safely on Île St. Jean, that he and his small family had weathered the winter, that nothing had made them return to Beaubassin before the English, with their terrible guns and their ruthless intentions, swept over the isthmus that joined Acadia to Canada.

But Émile would never leave his land. The idea was appalling to Barbe as well, though she didn't place the land ahead of their lives. She was afraid that her husband might.

"Mama, Remie is going to walk me home."

Barbe hadn't even seen them coming. She looked into the young faces, hopeful, expectant, full of the tentative joy they were not yet sure they had securely grasped. For a moment the pain she felt for them—and for herself—was almost more than she could bear. And then she forced a smile.

"Take Danielle with you, then. I'm going to wait for your father."

"He'll be hours," Soleil predicted, the dimples showing briefly.

"No doubt," Barbe agreed. "I could wish your news had been better, Remie."

But she didn't hold him responsible for it being bad, Soleil thought, and was grateful that her mother, at least, seemed to be in their corner.

"I wish it could have been better, too, Mme Cyr." Remie hadn't missed the fact that she'd used his first name. "It's a matter of grave concern."

Barbe sighed inaudibly. "Yes. Yes, it is. Go on along, then, and we'll be there eventually. Take Henri and Vincent, too, and see they're fed. Heaven knows when Papa and I will get to eat."

And so they went, the little boys running ahead or darting off to the sides of the path to discover small treasures or simply let free the energy that had built up during the long church service. Danielle was kept too busy pursuing them to stay close enough to listen to the pair who wanted privacy.

There was so much to say between themselves. To speak of the long winter, of their loneliness, of how they had missed each other. To make their plans.

"You don't think there's a chance that your papa will take back his word to let us cry the banns now, do you?" Remie spoke quietly enough, yet with an underlying urgency that was unmistakable.

Soleil gave him a quick look, eager yet oddly shy now that the waiting was over and the words she had imagined could be said. "He promised. In the spring, he said, if I hadn't changed my mind."

"You haven't, have you?" Remie stopped walking and reached for her hands.

She felt breathless, as if she'd been running instead of walking as slowly as possible. "No," she said softly. "I haven't changed my mind."

Danielle glanced back to see her sister being soundly kissed, and her heart swelled with longing and envy.

"It was so long," Remie whispered as Soleil slid her arms around him, returning the embrace with no shyness whatsoever once they had touched. All those sensations she had experienced the night they'd spent together were returning; not imagined any longer, but real, wonderful, exciting. She felt as if she might fly apart in all directions from the sheer joy of it.

"Now stay on the path," Danielle called to her small charges more loudly than was necessary.

Reluctantly, smiling, the couple drew apart and fell into step behind their chaperon. "Should I approach your papa at once, or do you think I should wait a day or so?" Remie asked. "Give him a chance to settle down?"

"He always settles down," Soleil said, content to hold hands as they walked. "He's incapable of staying angry or upset for long. Much as I'd like to have it resolved tonight, so that you could speak to Father Castin at once, perhaps it would be better to wait until tomorrow."

"And not see him in the meantime," Remie added dryly. "Well, you know him better than I." He hesitated before adding, "He looks ... older than when I left last fall."

Soleil hadn't noticed. "Do you think so? Well, of course, he misses Louis. They've never been apart before, not in twenty-six years." The question had been hanging over her all those cold months and could wait no longer to be put to him. "Will ... will you be staying on in Grand-Pré when we're married? Or will we ... have to leave, too?"

"I'd thought to leave at once," Remie said without hesitation, so she knew he'd made up his mind a long time ago. "I've looked at the place where we'll build our cabin, up the St. John in Madawaska territory. From there I can carry my furs to the St. Lawrence and on into Québec, and you'll be safe there when the time comes that I must leave you behind. There's a Micmac village near the falls, and they're good friends. You wouldn't be completely alone."

Fear wriggled through her like a serpent. "We've hardly come together again, and already you speak of leaving me alone."

"No. I've just told you. Running Fawn and Young Otter and Angry Waters are as close as any family I can remember. They would protect you as I would myself. Not that there's any danger there. The redcoats don't dare come so far upstream, not with the woods full of Indians eager for their scalps."

This talk of scalps was unsettling, though Soleil had no worries for her own safety among the Micmacs. "I know little of their language," she murmured uncertainly. She had always had Barbe to advise and instruct and support her; what would she do without her mother?

"They speak excellent French," Remie said easily, "for the good fathers have brought them all to faith in Christ. Are you afraid, Soleil, to go with me?"

Her mouth was dry. For a moment she could not speak. Remie drew her once more into his arms, ignoring Danielle up ahead. He was strong and warm, and within his embrace the world around them seemed to recede, yet she could not be entirely reassured. "A little afraid," she confessed.

"There is no need to be. Wherever we go, I will see that you're taken care of, kept safe," Remie promised. "And I'll bring you back here in the fall to see your family again."

She clung to that promise as she clung to his hand when they walked on, but she could not entirely put down the tumult within her.

Now she knew how Madeleine had felt when Louis told her he was taking her away from her family and friends to a distant, unknown shore.

But the thought of living on in Grand-Pré without Remie was unbearable. Soleil held her tongue.

It was, indeed, late when the others returned home. The children had been fed; Vincent was taking a nap, and Henri had been set to carrying wood from the shed to the kitchen to keep his hands from mischief.

Wrapped in her own concerns, Soleil barely noted how quiet her mother was. As Barbe dished up meat and vegetables from the pot for those who had belatedly taken their places at the table, Soleil spoke softly and with a compulsion she could not repress.

"Mama, would you speak to Papa about Remie and me? May we have the banns read next Sunday?"

"We'll see," was the unsatisfactory reply. "Right now your father has much on his mind. Here, slice some more bread and set out the butter."

The conversation—or perhaps it might better have been described as an argument—that had been going on all the way home continued at the table as they ate hungrily, unaware of the taste of the food, only easing the discomfort in their bellies.

At least, Soleil thought gratefully, her father no longer sounded as if the news were Remie's fault. Émile and her brothers all had opinions, which they had already made known, but since they did not agree with one another, they went on to express their viewpoints again, this time with increasing forcefulness.

"Never," Émile stated emphatically, "will I abandon my home and my fields to the British. I've worked for them all my life, as did my father and grandfather before me, and they are my sons' inheritance, and my grandsons'."

"We will fight for what is ours," Antoine said at once.

Pierre gave him a withering glance. "What do you know of fighting? A tussle with François is a far cry from meeting red-coats with bayonets on their muskets. You speak like a boy who does not yet have a beard to prove his manhood."

The twins exchanged guarded glances. "The land is ours," Antoine insisted. "I agree with Papa. We should fight for it, if it comes to that."

"I said nothing of fighting," Émile interjected. He sounded weary but calmer. "It is all the young can think of—to fight, even when fighting is foolish. I said I would not run away and abandon what is mine. For more years than I can remember, the English and the French have fought over who will rule Acadia, but the land has been ours. Now it seems the British rule, once and for all, but nothing else has really changed. The land is still ours. We earn our living from it, as we always have. As we always will."

"But if the soldiers come, as they came to Chignecto—" François began.

"The soldiers have been here for years in their blockhouse, seeing that nothing happens," Émile pointed out. "There is no reason to think they will burn fields and houses here. We are a peaceful people. We do not raid the British forts, steal their supplies, kill their settlers. They have no reason to fear us."

"But we have reason to fear *them*, Papa!" Antoine said, leaning forward across the table in his earnestness. "What they have done in other places they may well do in Grand-Pré sooner or later!"

"They never have in over forty years," Émile said in the voice that had so often silenced his offspring in the past.

Grand-père removed his pipe and cleared his throat, appeared about to speak, then decided not to. Antoine spoke in his stead.

"That's not strictly true, Papa. I was only a little boy in 1746, but I remember how François and I hid under the covers, hoping that the British would not come and find us to murder us in our bed after their own men were massacred in Grand-Pré by our neighbors."

Émile gave him an angry look. "It was a foolish act by foolish young men." He put a slight emphasis on the second "foolish." "It is true that no Acadian was happy to have six hundred Englishmen quartered here in our own houses, but it was insane to think the British could be driven out by surprising them in the middle of the night with guns and axes. We only endanger ourselves by giving them another excuse to retaliate."

"Retaliate, Papa?" François was so intent that his voice squeaked slightly, something it had not done since he was Jacques's age. "But it is the English who encroach on our lands, our rights! It is we who should think of retaliation—"

"You speak with the ignorance of the very young," Émile said sternly. "No Cyr took part in that violence, and I pray to God that no member of this family will ever chop through a barred door in the middle of the night and murder a man in his bed, not even if the man is a British soldier! The treaties have been signed, we live now under the rule of foreigners, but there is no reason to endanger our lands or our lives by reckless violence. If every soldier in Acadia were to be killed, it would not be the end of the situation. More soldiers would eventually come from England, and with fear and hatred that would cost us dear. We were fortunate that the British commander extracted no penalty from the Acadians as a whole for that disgraceful episode but was content to punish only those who were responsible. That kind of disregard for the law of the land can only endanger all the rest of us, and I swear that my own family will not participate in any such thing!"

At that point Pierre the Silent, as the twins irreverently referred to him, expressed what Barbe had been thinking all afternoon. "Louis saw this coming. He escaped while there was time to do it."

"Nothing has come yet," Émile remarked, scowling.

"When it does, it will be too late," Pierre countered, almost as if to himself.

"It would be cowardly to run without putting up a fight," Antoine said, his meal forgotten.

"Nobody is going to run, and nobody is going to fight," Émile told them. He did not remember when he had ever been so tired. "Enough now, you are spoiling the meal the good God has provided—as He will continue to provide, as He has always provided. Be done with the matter and eat."

The discussion subsided at last, though it was clear from Pierre's thoughtful expression and the twins' ferocious ones that Émile had convinced no one.

Soleil longed to broach the subject nearest her heart, but this did not seem a propitious time to do so. She was glad she had sent Remie away before the others returned home. She did not want him to be a further part of the controversy.

As she bided her time until her mother had had the chance to prepare the way for her, she prayed most fervently that her father was right and that nothing more would come of the fears Remie had generated.

The dissension in the midst of her family and the warming weather that drew the men out of the house served the purpose over the following days of taking everyone's mind—except Soleil's, of course—away from the situation with Remie.

If Barbe suspected Soleil was meeting him in the woods during her afternoon walks, she was less concerned about that than about Émile. He was very quiet and his shoulders had taken on a perceptible sag. He made his plans for the usual plowing and planting, the mending of the weir and the fences, and consulted with the other elders in the village about the lands that would be planted and harvested as a community.

His sons talked of the political situation among themselves but under Barbe's quelling glances refrained from further discussion with Émile. She was seriously concerned about her husband, and spent many hours praying for him.

Soleil and Remie took advantage of her preoccupation. It wasn't easy to restrain themselves, but now that it was almost time to announce a formal betrothal, with a wedding to follow as quickly as possible, Soleil set the ground rules.

"I know we—" she blushed under Remie's smoldering dark gaze as they walked through the woods "—we made love before. But I think . . . now, perhaps, it would be best to . . ."

"To wait," Remie prompted. "Until we've taken our vows." He didn't sound as if he were enthused about the idea, but at least he understood.

"Yes."

"Then we'd better speak to your father tomorrow night. He must have recovered as much as he's going to from his anger with me."

"It isn't you he's upset about," Soleil protested, though she was not absolutely certain of that. "All right. I'll talk to Mama again. And then come for supper tomorrow." She hesitated before she added, "And could you try not to talk politics? Or to mention anything about . . . going away?"

Remie agreed, and from then until the following evening when he showed up at suppertime, Soleil felt as if her stomach were full of butterflies that not even her prayers could calm.

16

ÉMILE had been working hard all day alongside his sons, repairing the dykes after the ravages of the winter sea. He hesitated perceptibly on his own threshold when he saw Remie, then nodded shortly and entered the house. "Evening, Michaud."

Soleil's heart, already pounding, sank to her stomach and sat there, heavy, uncomfortable. Oh, Papa, she thought, why couldn't you call him Remie? Why couldn't you at least do that much?

Émile was dripping, and he complained to his wife, "There's no towel above the washbasin."

Barbe clucked, producing the towel for him to dry himself, then handed the rectangle of coarse linen to Jacques. "Here, put this outside for your brothers before they decide not to wash tonight. And fetch Vincent back. He's escaped because the door was open." She had refrained from stating the obvious, that Émile was the one who had left it open; this was no time to irritate him.

"Hurry along to the table before everything gets cold," Barbe said, raising her voice to carry to her sons still clustered around the washbasin on the bench beside the door.

There was the usual confusion as the family members took their places. Soleil, who was helping to dish up, was the last to sit down, and she slid along the bench next to Remie. Through the fabric of her skirt she felt the pressure of his thigh against hers, and after a moment the warmth came through, too, exciting images perhaps best left alone until the coming ordeal was past.

It *was* going to be an ordeal, she had already decided. Papa didn't look angry, only rather grim. Did that mean he intended to forbid the banns, the wedding? Panic almost suffocated her; her appetite was gone completely.

To Soleil's surprised relief, supper—except for the fact that she scarcely ate a bite—went smoothly enough. Émile and the boys discussed what they had accomplished that day on the dykes and what they would do tomorrow. Remie made no offer to help them this time; in fact, he was virtually silent throughout the meal. Having been warned not to discuss politics or his own future plans, he was left with about as many conversational possibilities as a stump.

For once, Émile made no effort to engage a guest in polite chatter. The stone in Soleil's midsection grew heavier, until she wondered if she might be sick. Papa had promised that if she still wanted Remie in the spring they could be wed. What would she do if he changed his mind now?

She slid a glance at the man beside her and knew the answer. Acadian daughters were trained to be obedient, and she always had been. But in this matter she would defy her father. If the only way to be with Remie was to run away with him, that was what she would do. It wasn't what she wanted, however. She wanted the thrill of hearing the banns from the pulpit, of preparing for her wedding, of hearing the priest's words over the two of them and of reveling in the festivities that would then follow. A girl dreamed all the time she was growing up of the feasting and toasting and dancing, and of retiring at last with the embarrassed groom.

Only this prospective groom didn't seem embarrassed, only uncharacteristically silent, and she didn't even know if they were going to get to the festivities. Her eyelids burned with resentful tears as she watched her father finish mopping his plate with a piece of bread to get up all the gravy.

Danielle and Barbe rose to clear the table. The boys scrambled off the benches and made for the door, except for Pierre, who settled beside the fire to mend a moccasin, and Grandpère, who lighted his pipe. Émile and Remie and Soleil stayed where they were.

"Well," Émile said finally, when the silence had become strained to the breaking point. "I assume since you're here,

Remie Michaud, it's with the purpose of renewing your offer for my daughter.'' Soleil supposed she ought to be grateful that he hadn't been more heavy-handed, pretending he didn't know why Remie had come and making him spell out the whole thing from the beginning. She couldn't keep still any longer.

"You promised, Papa, that if we still wanted to marry when Remie came back, we could do so.'' She couldn't help the aggressive note in her voice, nor the tremor.

Émile's face was tired and sad, but there was no animosity in it. "So I did. I take it you're both of the same mind?''

"Yes, sir,'' Remie answered, at the same time Soleil said, "Yes, Papa.''

She braced herself for the question, "And what are your plans after the wedding?'' It didn't come.

Émile put his hands flat on the table and stood up. "Very well, then. Tell the good Father to tie the knot. God bless you both.''

He didn't wait for their stammered replies but strode out of the house.

Soleil was stunned. She had prepared for battle, and there was none. She turned to Remie and found him grinning at her. Her own smile was tremulous. "The banns on Sunday?''

"I'll talk to Father Castin tonight,'' Remie promised. "And the wedding two weeks hence, if that's agreeable.'' Since Émile had left the house, he turned to Barbe.

She was smiling. "There'll be a lot to do between now and then. I suggest you stay out of the way, my son, so that we may get on with it.''

Remie almost overturned the bench when he rose. "I'd better head for the village at once so that I don't have to call Father Castin from his bed to discuss it with him.''

"I'll walk with you a short way,'' Soleil offered quickly, glancing at her mother for permission to do so.

Barbe nodded. "Come right back, though. The sooner we begin to make plans, the faster they'll be carried through. Danielle, go with your sister. I'll finish up here.''

Excitement sparkled in the younger girl's eyes as she followed them out into the dusk. Now that Soleil was betrothed, or as good as, her turn would be next. She was nearly thirteen and many village girls were wed by fourteen. Basile Lizotte would be eighteen by midsummer, of an age to take a wife; Danielle wondered if her parents would allow her to marry then if he should propose before fall.

Soleil dismissed her sister's chaperonage from mind as she accepted Remie's hand to walk along the path toward Grand-Pré. "I didn't think it would be so easy," she confessed. "I was afraid he was going to say we should wait until the political unrest had been resolved, or something equally impossible."

"We'll be lucky if the political unrest is ever resolved," Remie remarked. "I'd like to linger longer, but I think it best to hurry back to the church. And—" in the dimness she saw the grin split his face "—to report to Uncle Guillaume. He's asked for the first dance with the bride, after the one we have together."

They were far enough from the house that they were unlikely to be seen. Remie stopped, bent his head and kissed her so that she melted against him, wanting to stay in his embrace forever.

Danielle, observing, shivered with delight.

And then Remie was gone, and Soleil's heart sang as the two girls returned slowly to the house.

In only a matter of weeks she would be Madame Remie Michaud, she thought, and wondered how long it would take for her fluttering insides to return to normal.

NEVER HAD TWO WEEKS been packed with so many things to do. Never had time flown so swiftly. Sheets were hemmed. Blankets and quilts were added to the pile, along with feather pillows, until Soleil wondered how they would remove these things from the house when the time came. Wedding finery was stitched with painstaking care. Remie had brought a gift of strips of red cloth, exquisitely embroidered in moosehair in a pattern of flowers and leaves by the women of some Micmac village; these were incorporated into the bride's dress. There were red ribbons from France, produced by the twins, who blithely admitted they were smuggled in from Louisbourg past the British soldiers who sought to prevent such illegal trade. Remie had brought another gift, as well: Indian-made moccasins, which would be more comfortable for long-distance walking than her customary clogs. They were lined with soft, dark fur and were also intricately embroidered, quite the most beautiful and luxurious footwear Soleil had ever owned.

The bedchamber vacated by Louis and Madeleine was aired and cleaned and made ready. In fact, the entire house was swept and tidied, and during the last few days was nearly always vacated by the men, who sought to escape the frenetic activity of the women. Even Grand-père, who usually toasted his old bones near the hearth, withdrew to the bench outside the door and hoped the sun would shine.

The cooking went on day and night. Cakes and pastries were baked. Kettles simmered constantly over the fire, meat was roasted, and French wine and brandy appeared in vast quantities with no one inquiring as to its source. Émile's determination to avoid conflict with the British authorities did not extend to depriving himself of the excellent spirits he was used to.

Soleil emerged from the house with a rug to be pounded clean by Bertin and Jacques and found her father sampling the latest bottle. He appeared so somber that her heart twisted within her. She looked at him more closely than she was wont to do and felt a stirring of dismay.

She handed the rugs over to Bertin and approached Émile. "Papa?" she said tentatively.

He turned, summoning a smile that had none of the heartiness she remembered from all the years before. "Here, take a sip of this. Let no one say that Émile Cyr married off his daughter with nothing better than fir beer."

She accepted the mug but didn't drink. "Papa, please be happy for me. I want very much to marry Remie, but it hurts to see that you are not happy for us." She looked at him beseechingly.

Émile met her gaze directly, then pulled her into his arms for a bear hug of the sort he had not given her since she was a very small child. "Of course I'm happy for you, girl. It's only that I never thought to lose Louis and Madeleine and little Marc, and I'd always expected that when you married you would stay here in Grand-Pré. You don't intend to do that, do you?"

There. It had finally been said. "I think...I think Remie wants to take me to Canada. But we'll be back, Papa. He's promised that as long as it's safe to do so, he'll bring me back to see you in the fall.''

Émile released her with a rueful smile. ''Ah, that's the question, isn't it? Whether or not we are safe here. I pray your young man is mistaken, Soleil. I cannot believe that after all these years the British intend to make war on innocent citizens. We didn't want them for rulers, but we've been loyal to their government, the most of us. They've no reason to wish us ill.''

That wasn't what Remie said, and she knew now that her brothers didn't believe it, any of them, though Bertin and Jacques wanted to. It was, however, the only time during the wedding preparations that the political situation was discussed in Soleil's hearing, and since nobody talked about it, she was able to put it out of her mind.

The night before the ceremony she thought she would never be able to sleep.

There had been so many last-minute preparations in the kitchen and with the sewing that there had been no time for Remie. He had stood hopefully in the kitchen doorway for a time, then given up. ''Tomorrow, tomorrow,'' Barbe told him impatiently. ''There is still too much to do, with the house to be readied for guests tomorrow! Soleil cannot go on a romantic walk through the woods even if there were anyone free to chaperon!'' She flapped her apron at him and Remie laughingly withdrew.

That night Soleil lay in bed beside her sister for the last time. Had they accomplished everything that was necessary? There was enough food for an army. There would be three fiddlers besides Émile, for the music would continue far into the night. There was a supply of fir beer for the younger celebrants, and enough of the smuggled spirits, Barbe said dryly, to make half of Grand-Pré unfit for work for the rest of the week.

Those things, of course, were only the incidentals to Soleil. Beside her, Danielle's breathing was soft and regular. Tomorrow night it would be Remie whose body warmed hers; they would sleep in each other's arms from that night onward for the rest of their lives.

Imagination had kept her going throughout the winter, and she had been grateful for that night spent with Remie, because she knew now what to look forward to. Strong arms, eager lips, exploring and caressing hands. And those fiery explosions in blood and body that only Remie could arouse, the sensations she would never tire of for as long as she lived.

Imagination kept her awake for a long time. She could hear her father snore in the distance, Jacques cry out in the throes of a nightmare, to be quieted by Bertin before he woke the others, and Grand-père's coughing spell. Tomorrow would be a long day, the most important one in her life, and she wanted it to be absolutely perfect.

She did not even realize that she was allowing herself to imagine only her wedding day and the night to follow. That was as far as her plans went, though she would have denied that she was afraid to think beyond the coming day.

And at last she slept.

17

MORNING DAWNED bright and cold with a touch of late frost in the open places. As family members went to and from the privy, their breath issued in steamy tendrils on the still air.

Soleil couldn't remember whether or not she ate that morning. Danielle fussed with her sister's hair before Soleil donned the new cap her mother had stitched for the occasion; Barbe was everywhere, giving orders, making last-minute decisions, overseeing Soleil's wedding costume.

And at last it was time to go. Émile appeared, scrubbed and smiling, though his smile held a trace of reserve. "Well," he said, "are you ready?"

Through the blood thundering in her ears, Soleil heard her own muted reply: "I'm ready."

He stood for a moment gazing into her face, then nodded. "My little girl is a woman today. May God bless you, child. Today and forever."

"Thank you, Papa." Her eyes misted, and she kissed him on a weathered cheek.

The walk to the church seemed both longer and shorter than usual. They were there almost before she was ready to be there, yet she had had time to think so many thoughts on the way.

People spoke to her, and most of the time she answered, though she could not have said what her response had been. Mostly she moved as if wrapped in a cocoon that insulated her from the reality around her.

Friends and neighbors turned expectant faces toward the Cyrs as they approached the churchyard. They were happy for her, Soleil knew, except for a few of the young men who would have liked to be the one meeting her at the altar. And even they were only wistful rather than resentful of Remie's good fortune.

She caught a glimpse of Céleste's face; her friend appeared thrilled for her, yet her expression held a slight longing on her own behalf. Céleste was like a sister to Soleil, closer than her real sister, actually, and Soleil had a moment to wish that Céleste might be next, that Antoine would see the girl as she saw him. It would be lovely to have her best friend as a sister-in-law.

And then, at last, there was Remie.

He, too, was dressed in wedding finery, and he had neatly trimmed his beard. He stood at the front of the church, towering over everyone else there, waiting to claim her for his wife.

For a moment the church seemed chill and too dim after the brightness of the sunlight. And then Soleil's vision adjusted as she moved toward the man she had chosen from among all the others.

She had anticipated memorizing every moment of this ceremony, every word spoken over them by the priest, every vow taken by Remie and herself. Yet she was still in the cocoon and everything around her seemed at a great distance. Afterward she remembered almost nothing except for Remie's dear face and his dark eyes holding hers, promising without words.

And then it was over. Father Castin was smiling, lifting his hands in benediction, and Remie was guiding her up the aisle between the rows of happy faces, and they emerged into sunshine and hugs and kisses and congratulations.

Guillaume enveloped her in a bear hug, murmuring, "He's a good boy, Remie is." Marie patted moist eyes and added, "May you have a marriage as good as ours has been, you two, with as many children to comfort you in your old age."

There was a ripple of laughter among the well-wishers, for Marie was obviously pregnant yet again. The Trudelles stepped aside, and their places were taken by other villagers, all eager to offer their congratulations and blessings and to join in the festivities that would follow.

Céleste, eyes brimming, hugged Soleil, too, no doubt dreaming of her own wedding day and praying that it would be in the near future.

The procession was formed spontaneously, Émile leading the way with shouts of encouragement and promises. "By the good Christ, this will be a wedding supper to remember!" he cried.

His misgivings about this union had been either forgotten or repressed. There was nothing in his manner to cause Soleil distress; all she could see was his obvious love for her.

As they wound through the village they passed the block-house where the English soldiers stood guard. The redcoats with their muskets watched impassively or with curiosity, according to their temperaments. Most of them were very young, sent out from their homeland to this distant place where the natives refused to speak their language and ignored their existence. Soleil felt a moment's disquietude; Céleste had said nothing more about making Antoine jealous by allowing him to think she was interested in the young soldier named Tommy Sharp, but Soleil knew which one he was. The village girls *looked* at the Englishmen, even though they cultivated the art of pretending to be unaware of them.

And then they were past the blockhouse, surrounded only by happy chatter. Remie's hand, warm and strong, encircled her own. Céleste was walking between Antoine and François and did not so much as glance at the soldiers or the blockhouse.

Soleil began to feel the cocoon melting away, like the mist over the water as the sun warms it. Her senses heightened. The stirrings began deep within her, needs not to be fulfilled at once but soon, soon. And happiness flooded her mind and soul as well as her body.

The rest of the day passed in a dreamlike haze, shot through with moments of startling clarity. After days of a stomach too unsettled to encourage eating, Soleil was ravenous. She filled a plate and sat with Remie on one of the benches that had been carried out of the house to make room for dancing later.

Remie murmured approvingly over the brandy— "As good as any I ever tasted in Louisbourg or Québec," he pronounced to a smiling Émile—and urged her to try a little, but she was cautious with it. She knew it was potent, and she had no wish to be swirly headed. She was already drunk enough with sheer happiness.

The fiddlers had never played with more enthusiasm, nor the dancers stomped and swayed with more gusto. Truly everyone in the village of Grand-Pré would remember the wedding of Soleil Cyr and Remie Michaud!

Some of the celebrants went home before dark, but most stayed on. The fiddlers continued to play, their dexterity only quickened by the copious flow of brandy. There was still plenty of food on the low table against the kitchen wall. Infants and small children were put to bed behind the curtains or in corners where their mothers hoped they wouldn't be trampled by the dancers.

At last it was midnight, and the bride and groom would be allowed to retire. Remie's gaze met Soleil's with the unspoken message, and her pulse once more quickened without regard for the music. She looked toward her mother and saw Barbe's nod. A moment later Émile signaled for the last tune.

The ribald remarks at its finish brought a blush to Soleil, a grin to Remie. At least, she thought gratefully, there would be no shivaree, that abominable custom of subjecting the newlyweds to an infernal racket that reduced them to such a state of exhaustion that making love was beyond them for that first night. Soleil had consulted her parents on that subject days earlier.

"No, no," Barbe had reassured her. "That is only for those who do not observe the proprieties, who remarry too soon after the death of a spouse, or when an old man inappropriately weds a young girl. That is not the case here."

Nevertheless, Soleil did not quite dare to relax until she and Remie had taken their leave and were closeted alone in the room where Louis and Madeleine had also spent their wedding night. There was still laughter and loud conversation beyond their door, but there was no banging of pots and pans and hooting such as would happen during a shivaree.

Remie drew her into his arms as soon as he had put down their candle. "I've been waiting a long time for this," he told her softly.

"It's been a long day," Soleil murmured, welcoming the strength of his arms, the nearness of him.

"Are you too tired?" There was concern for her in his tone, but an underlying anxiety on his own behalf, too.

Soleil leaned back against his arms, smiling up at him. "Not *too* tired," she assured him.

The laughter was back in his eyes as he bent to extinguish the candle. "Good," he said, and he sounded so smugly content that she laughed aloud.

Her amusement faded away to tenderness, then to anticipation, as his fingers sought out her fastenings in the dark. First the cap was laid aside, next her bodice.

Soleil summoned her courage and with somewhat timid fingers began to perform a similar service for him. Suddenly she was crushed in an embrace that made it difficult to breathe.

"Dear God, but I love you!" Remie said huskily. His mouth claimed hers until she felt as if she were swooning, and then his hands busied themselves again, divesting them both of their remaining garments. "My wife," Remie said with satisfaction as he carried her to the bed.

There was a moment of anticlimax when he became entangled in the bed curtains. He could not find the opening, and Soleil began to giggle. "Here, set me on my feet and I'll find it." The excitement of bare flesh upon bare flesh was beyond anything she had experienced before; she was as eager as he to be closeted behind those hangings. Yet he was unwilling to put her down, and for a few moments more they struggled to find the way in until they finally fell through the opening amid Remie's curses and her smothered laughter.

Immediately, as she lay beneath him on the bed, her hilarity evaporated, as did his exasperation. She had thought the night together in the pile of hay below the dyke to be the ultimate union, but she was suddenly aware that she had only begun to taste the delights of lovemaking. This time there were no garments to hinder, no guilt to inhibit, no haste whatever.

His skin was warm and tasted of salt. His breath stirred the hair loosened from her cap, and his lips traced temple and cheek and throat, then moved slowly downward.

She murmured his name and gave herself over to incredible sensation, wondering how much she would be able to bear without splintering into a million pieces, more than willing to die that way if necessary. His tantalizing hands and lips were far more expert than her own, but she was eager to learn.

And when at last their bodies were joined, the rhythm came to her readily. The responses were instinctive—she need not have worried about them, after all—and Soleil felt drowned in the wonder and ecstasy of it. She knew that Remie felt the same way, that they were truly one in body, heart and spirit.

She had been right to marry Remie, and it no longer mattered that her father had kept them apart for so long.

This was what she had been waiting for all her life.

The following morning, Remie announced they were leaving at once for the Madawaska Valley.

18

SOLEIL SUSPECTED immediately from the way her parents reacted to the news of her departure that Remie had already discussed the matter with them.

There were no attempts to dissuade the newlyweds, as there had been when Louis made his announcement the previous fall. This time there was only quiet acceptance.

Barbe had made a few small parcels of salt and foodstuffs. "You won't be able to carry much more than this," she said regretfully, looking at the quantity of food that remained from the wedding feast. "How many blankets can you manage? The nights are still so cold." For a moment it seemed that tears shimmered in her eyes, then she was brisk and practical again, so that Soleil thought she might only have imagined them. "I'd be happy to let you take that small kettle."

"I have a pot," Remie told her, resting a hand on Soleil's shoulder so that his warmth and strength flowed through to her. "Two blankets, no more. We'll stay warm enough."

He grinned and turned toward Émile, who was extending a knife in a scabbard. "What's this, Papa?"

"A wedding present. I've been working on it all winter. What other kind of gift can one make for a man who is determined not to stay in one place? The blade is of the finest steel I could obtain."

"Smuggled out of French territory, no doubt." Remie took the knife, examining it carefully. "The English have nothing to equal it. Thank you, Papa."

Soleil was staring at Émile. "All winter you worked on it, while you let me worry about whether or not I'd be allowed to marry Remie, come spring?"

"I knew you'd have him whether I gave my blessing or not," Émile said gruffly. "If a man is going to provide for my daughter, I want him to have the best tools to do the job."

"I'll take good care of her," Remie assured him. He hoisted his own pack onto his shoulders and secured it, then lifted the other one and fitted it on Soleil. She had never worn one before, and it felt strange and unnatural, though it was not excessively heavy.

"There," he pronounced. "We're ready to go."

Ready to go. Was she? Soleil fought down a momentary panic. She had never been away from home and family in all her sixteen years. But then she met Remie's encouraging smile and was able to return it, albeit unsteadily. "I'm ready," she said.

ALL OF THAT and the hugs and kisses and blessings had been hours ago. The sun was now directly overhead, and there was no remaining hint of frost. A trickle of perspiration dampened Soleil's bodice. The pack felt a bit heavier, and though she was used to walking considerable distances, she hoped that Remie would soon call a halt for a rest. Only the thought of Madeleine, pregnant and caring for a small child, walking much farther than she had gone so far, kept her silent. She would not have her new husband think the less of her so early on.

Remie led the way, stepping along at a brisk pace, and there was little breath for conversation. Soleil didn't mind. She had her wedding day to think about, taking out the memories and examining them one by one, as well as her wedding night.

Remembering had the power to make her feel very warm. Surely not all men had the ability to make love in such a satisfying manner, she thought. Guiltily she tried to imagine Mama and Papa doing the things together that she and Remie had done, and she could not. It was a little easier with Louis and

Madeleine, though it did not seem to her that anyone else could have experienced quite what she and Remie had. How, if that were the case, could they keep from talking about it?

She felt a rush of need to see Madeleine again. It would be wonderful to be able to speak frankly with another female. But Madeleine was far away to the north, while she and Remie would be turning west once they'd reached the isthmus.

That, however, was far away, on the other side of the Minas Basin. They were headed now for Cape Blomidon, where they would make their way across the water toward Chignecto. Madeleine had walked this distance, Soleil reminded herself as her legs grew more tired, in the fall, with winter rapidly approaching. At least she had summer to look forward to.

Ahead of her, Remie came to a sudden halt. "Are you getting hungry?"

She had been thinking so much about protesting legs that hunger had been pushed to the back of her mind. Now that food was mentioned, her mouth watered. "Starved," she admitted.

"We might as well eat what your mama provided," he said, easing off his pack. He gestured for her to turn around, and removed her pack, as well. "Then we won't have to carry it. Tonight we should be able to have fresh fish."

She was realizing that there were many matters she had never considered when it came to walking several hundred miles. "What if you don't catch any fish?"

He laughed. "I've seldom gone hungry, wherever I've been. If there are no fish, there will be rabbits, or deer. I've no wish to shoot a deer at the beginning of a journey, however. It's wasteful to leave what we can't eat, and too much work to carry it. Here, let me look at you. How are you holding up?"

"As you see me," she said impudently, not wanting him to know how pleased she was that they'd paused, however briefly.

Remie considered. "Maybe I'll make love to you instead of eating."

She glanced around the small clearing—at the birches just sending out their first tentative buds and the cedars that still sheltered small amounts of snow beneath their protective boughs.

"Here? In broad daylight?" Surely he was joking, but even the joke made her nervous.

"Here, or anywhere. In broad daylight or in the dark. Whether I'm full or famished." He was warming to the idea and reached for her. "On the ground or up a tree."

"Up a tree?" She tried to pull free but could not. "I had no idea I was marrying an idiot!"

"What's idiotic about that? Only a comfortable tree, of course, with broad branches and perhaps some moss for padding. I don't see one that answers the purpose at the moment, but what about over there? There's a sunny hollow that's full of last year's leaves . . . soft and comfortable."

"But you promised me something to eat!" Soleil objected, beginning now to believe that he was serious. "We're on a well-traveled path; there might be someone along to see us!"

"First we make love," Remie announced, "then we see what your mama has packed for us to eat."

With that he swept her off her feet and carried her, protesting, toward the sunny hollow. Her struggle continued until he had pinned her down against the damp leaves and his mouth covered hers in a long, deep kiss.

"It's not fair," she gasped when they finally came up for air.

"That's why men are stronger than women," Remie informed her gleefully, "so that we can bend you to our will."

"I wasn't referring to your muscles," Soleil said. "It's the things you do...kissing, touching me that way...I can't think when you do it."

His exaggerated leer was ludicrous, and she laughed in spite of having been more or less serious. "Let's see if I can reduce you to complete mindlessness," he suggested, and proceeded to do so with quite satisfactory results.

It seemed indecent to behave this way, Soleil thought a short time later as she rearranged her clothes and turned her pink cheeks away while Remie set out their bread and meat. Yet she had to admit that after the first few minutes, she had not really tried to stop him.

She had only been married one day, and already she was learning that marriage was not quite as she had imagined it. She was certain that her parents made love only at night, behind the drawn curtains of their own bed. What would her mother say about this daytime frolic in the open air? The very idea made her cheeks hotter than ever.

Yet there was no denying that Remie's touch was magical. It was extraordinary what even his glance could do to her, reducing her bones to jelly, her mind to mush, and her flesh . . . well, she decided, best not to dwell on that. She took the slab of bread Remie handed her and bit into it hungrily.

The respite was all she needed to keep her going again for the rest of the afternoon. She was glad that walking was a normal part of her usual day; otherwise she might have collapsed on the trail. She wondered guiltily how her sister-in-law had managed, for Madeleine had not walked at all except to church and to visit her family. In truth, had Soleil not experienced again that discomfort induced by unaccustomed lovemaking, she could have walked the entire day without any distress whatever.

The path widened perceptibly, so that they were able to walk side by side. When Soleil commented on this, Remie nodded.

"More traffic here. We're close to a small settlement, and two trails cross a few miles ahead. We may even meet other travelers."

Soleil stopped with an exclamation of dismay. "And yet we . . . we . . . !" She spluttered, unable to speak the words. "Someone might have seen us!" The very idea made her face hot.

"No one did, did they? Besides, I would have heard anyone coming." He was laughing at her.

"I wouldn't have heard anything," she said truthfully. The way the blood had been rushing through her ears, a troop of British soldiers could have walked up on them, unheard.

"That's why you have me," Remie said, touching her arm to start her moving again.

Her reply had a waspy tinge. "If it weren't for you, I wouldn't need to worry about it."

He had a full-throated laugh that sent shivers through her even when she was trying to be angry with him. "Do you know your eyes fairly snap when you're annoyed? Oh, I can see that life with you is going to be interesting."

Obediently Soleil began to walk again. She was not sure that *interesting* was quite the word she'd have chosen for her married life so far, and she had a moment's uneasiness about whatever else was in store.

They did meet a few other travelers, who were civil enough whether they were Micmac or French settlers. One Acadian couple who looked as if they'd been on the trail overlong, paused to exchange a few words.

They were an older couple, in their forties, and the woman was limping. She had, she explained, injured her ankle earlier in the day, and walking was painful. Grateful for the pause, however brief, she sat on a fallen log and took off a clog to examine the swollen, purplish ankle. Since there was little to be done about it, she sighed and replaced the footwear, then inspected Soleil's young face.

"Newly married?" she asked, smiling.

Soleil blushed. How did the woman know? Was it so obvious by the way she walked, or was there some new expression on her face? "Yesterday," she confessed.

The woman nodded. "I thought so. You have that look about you. As if the sun shines out through your countenance. You have a good man, I think, if the look of him is anything to go by."

Pride swelled within her. "Yes," Soleil agreed.

She became aware then of what the woman's husband was saying. "I'd avoid Beaubassin if I were you. It's a bad situation there. We've seen three battles in only the last six months, and when our house was burned to the ground...well, it didn't seem worth it to stay."

Remie's jaw bunched grimly. "The British burned your house?"

"No, no, not the soldiers. The Indians. Not our local Micmacs, but a strange tribe out of Canada. They say 'twas led by The Otter himself, though you couldn't prove that by me, but 'tis likely. Le Loutre seeks to drive us all into Canada. He'll be the end of all of us in order to be rid of the British, and what good will that do us? The man is like a wounded animal, snarling and biting even at friendly hands!"

"And you don't think it's safe to take the usual trail across Chignecto, then?"

"I wouldn't if I were you. Not with a young bride."

Soleil wondered how long it would be before the most casual stranger stopped guessing at once that she was a new bride. It was as if her inexperience—and her recent limited experience—were branded on her forehead for all to see.

"Well, I thank you for the information," Remie said. "We must be on our way."

They exchanged good wishes and blessings and parted company. Soleil hesitated, staring after them. It must be dreadful to have your house burned, with all your belongings, especially when you were no longer young. She wondered where they were going to start over.

Remie was having similar speculations. "If it were me, I'd have gone into Canada, even if it was what Le Loutre wanted to force me to do," he said. "It won't be any better in this direction than it was around Beaubassin, for the British are apparently determined to be rid of Acadians. I wish your father could be persuaded to leave. He's the only one holding your brothers there, and they'd be safer elsewhere."

"Papa will never go," Soleil said automatically. "And they'll look after him. All any of them wants is to be left in peace, to farm their land."

He gave her an odd look, one she couldn't interpret. "They're not all as passive as you think," he muttered, then looked sorry for having spoken the words.

"What do you mean by that?"

"Nothing. Come on, let's get moving to make up for the time we've lost."

Soleil fell into step beside him, but she was troubled and could not let the matter drop. "What do you mean about not being passive? Pierre is as unaggressive as a man could be. He was always quiet and never stirred up any trouble. And since Aurore died, he scarcely talks at all."

"He'd go," Remie said with conviction, "if it wouldn't mean leaving his sons behind. They're too young to be without a mother—or a grandmother—to care for them. But even if it means leaving your parents to fend for themselves, eventually he'll go. He's quiet, but he's not stupid. He can see what's coming with the British."

Was he right? Had Pierre said something to Remie he had not said to her? It didn't seem likely. She'd known Pierre all her life, and he had never been one to rock the boat. Yet Remie's words made her uneasy.

"The twins won't leave," she asserted. "All they think about is having a good time, but they work hard. They'll support Papa in whatever he does."

Again his expression held something strange, and her uneasiness deepened. "You don't know them very well, either," Remie told her, "if you believe they have no serious thoughts of their own beyond having a good time. You were there when Antoine said they would fight for the land, and it may well come to that if they stay."

"Antoine is a boy," Soleil said, dismissing her brother, "and he speaks of things he knows nothing of. His idea of fighting is a wrestling match with François."

Remie didn't look at her this time, and his grunt could have meant anything between assent and disagreement. He must be mistaken, she thought; she knew her brothers far better than he could on such limited acquaintance. She plodded along in silence for a while, because talking took too much additional breath.

She was weary when Remie finally called a halt for the night. The temperature had dropped sharply, and the fire he built was more than welcome. They did, indeed, have fish for supper, which Remie helped himself to from a weir he said belonged to some settlers a short distance upstream. No one in Acadia would have considered this theft, for it was only good manners to offer food to a traveler, and there were plenty of fish; had the owner of the weir been present, he would probably have cooked it for his guests, as well.

They ate the fish with more of Barbe's good bread and licked their fingers clean before they scoured off the remaining sticky juices with the wet red sand exposed along the streambed by the falling tides. And then, as darkness fell in earnest, they went to bed sheltered by a stand of small cedars.

It was different here, alone under the stars, than it had been at home in Louis and Madeleine's curtained bed. It was cold, and Soleil snuggled tightly against Remie to draw warmth from him. He kissed her and stroked her deliciously, but they had not undressed except for their footwear, and they did not make love again. She was torn between wondering if Remie had already grown tired of lovemaking or if he knew she was tender from their earlier efforts and was allowing her time to heal.

Soleil had a few moments of homesickness—wondering what it was like at home now that she, too, was gone, missing even Danielle's scatterbrained chatter about that idiotic Lizotte boy—and then the long day caught up with her. She fell asleep in Remie's arms, secure and happy.

19

EVERY HOUR BROUGHT new scenes, new places and, occasionally, new people.

There were not quite as many people as Soleil would have liked—Remie did not seek out settlements, for the most part—but she was content with only her husband for companionship, although she did miss her family. It was strange not to be able to talk to them, to exchange ideas, to share her travel experiences.

Remie was not as talkative on the trail as he had been in Grand-Pré, but that didn't bother her. Theirs was a companionable silence. When she exclaimed over something or asked questions, he was always responsive, eager to share with her his own knowledge, which was considerable.

She was always tired by the time Remie called a halt, but it did not take long to become accustomed to walking all day. She enjoyed it and found it far less monotonous than keeping house. Around every turn or on every rise there was something new to see, and even this early in the spring, all of it was beautiful.

She had never lived anywhere except on the edge of the Minas Basin; she was accustomed to the rise and fall of the water. But living behind the dykes was a different matter from standing high on a bluff and watching the wall of water created by the incoming tide as it met the water trying to flow out of the basin. A tidal bore could be dangerous as well as impressive in its force, and she put a hand on Remie's arm for reassurance.

"How are we going to cross?" she asked faintly.

She had yet to see Remie disconcerted. He sat down and pulled off his moccasins, wriggling his toes in the grass. "When the tide begins to drop, we'll go. There is a canoe near the base of the cliff—securely above high tide—and when the tide ebbs, there is no time to waste." He reached up for her hand and pulled her reluctantly to her knees beside him, for she was mesmerized by the red water so far below. "We won't go before morning. Until then, we rest."

"What if we don't make it to the far side before the tide comes in again?"

Their destination looked far away, though Remie had told her this was the narrowest part of the watery span.

He grinned. "We will. We'll paddle like fury, as if the devil himself is behind us."

She was learning that Remie often made such irreverent remarks, and she crossed herself and shivered. "And we'll pray," she stated quietly.

He caught her hand and pulled her toward him. "And we'll pray," he agreed before he kissed her.

She struggled a moment longer against succumbing to his touch. "How will we know when it's time to go? It's hard to see from up here."

"We'll start down the trail. When we see wet red rock instead of dry red rock just below us, we'll know the tide is dropping."

"And what if it carries us out to sea instead of allowing us to go straight across?"

His face was only inches from hers. "I can see you're going to be a joy to travel with," he told her, amused. "You will worry about everything, so there will be no need for *me* to worry. Of course the tide will carry us toward the sea, but that's all right. It's a long way to the west before the channel widens, and then it is only into the main channel, miles and miles from the Bay of Fundy. I've done it many times, my love. I won't fail now that I've the most important reason in my entire life to succeed. Come on, prove to me that it's all worthwhile."

She wondered if she would ever get used to making love, let alone under the open sky and in daylight. Yet all he had to do was kiss her . . . hold her down, if necessary, but kiss her, and she was lost. She could only pray that no one else would come along and see them.

And later, while Remie slept with one arm protectively around her, the heat of his body warming her back, she prayed for a safe crossing of the Minas Channel.

BEING ON THE WATER was even more alarming than looking out over it from the top of the bluff.

The canoe was so fragile. From the water the distance appeared greater than it had from above, and she felt totally helpless. A desperate litany ran through her mind. *Please, Blessed Mother, keep us safe.*

Remie had said she needn't paddle unless she chose to; he was used to doing it alone. But fear wouldn't allow her to sit with white-knuckled fingers gripping the sides of the canoe. Though her effort was small compared to Remie's, it might make them travel a little faster, a little more directly. At least the bore had subsided with the turn of the tide; they wouldn't be caught in its turbulence and dragged down in the swirling waters.

It was impossible to tell the depth of the water; she knew that in some places it was very deep even during an ebb tide. Since the force of the water enabled it to pick up sand, looking down at it was like peering through red mud. Soleil imagined falling into it and sinking like a stone, for she could not swim.

When she glanced behind at the cliff, she could tell that the water had already dropped dramatically. A foot a minute, she remembered, heart hammering. It rose a foot a minute and fell at the same rate. And once it had fallen as far as it was going to, it would come in again just as quickly, re-creating the bore that could swallow up a canoe and two people as easily as the sea devoured the beaches, over and over again, every day, every night.

There was no way to measure time. Remie paddled tirelessly, in a perfect, steady rhythm. Occasionally, when she looked back, he would glance at her pale face with a reassuring grin, which didn't really help very much. Dear God, how she loved him! How terrible it would be to lose him—to be lost herself—when they'd had so little time together.

And Mama and Papa would never know, she thought dismally. There would be no trace of them in the red sea. Perhaps their bodies—or what was left of them—would eventually be found somewhere along the Bay of Fundy, but no one would recognize them by then. No one would take the sad message to Grand-Pré.

There was too much time to think. Even if they survived this crossing there would be other dangers ahead, and it would be months before they returned, before she would see her family again. She had been prepared for homesickness—it was inevitable—but she had not expected it to be so severe so soon.

She would think happier thoughts. She would imagine the Madawaska Valley Remie had described. She would picture the cabin they would build there, the family they would have, their lives together, on into old age.

Her shoulders began to ache from the unaccustomed use of the paddle. She had to rest for a moment; her muscles were screaming. They seemed no nearer the far shore than they had the last time she'd looked. She closed her eyes and prayed silently, then thrust the paddle once more into the water.

After a time she turned to glance back, and to her moderate relief they *did* seem farther away from that shore. The dark stain on the cliff was enormous now. Fifty feet high? She couldn't judge; she only knew that in a short time the tide would turn, and that they must reach shore ahead of the bore.

She wept a little, silently, ashamed of her weakness but unable to help it, hoping Remie would not see what a coward she was. Her arms and shoulders burned with an unremitting fire that no longer subsided when she paused for a few minutes, so she forced herself to keep on. She stopped watching either shore, it was too discouraging, so she stared into the water or at the packs in the bottom of the canoe and the musket that pressed against the side of her foot through one of the new embroidered moccasins.

As if he sensed her need for distraction, Remie suddenly lifted an arm and pointed east. "Over there are the Five Islands," he told her. "The legend has it that they were created by Glooscap centuries ago when he threw five clods of mud at Beaver, who had unwisely become impudent with Glooscap's people. At extreme low tide it is sometimes possible to wade across to one of them, but it's a good idea not to loiter. An unwary man can be swept away if he's trapped against the bottom of a cliff he can't climb."

Soleil stifled a sound that was half sob, half laughter. Did he think to cheer her up with tales of unclimbable cliffs when the ones both ahead and behind seemed impassable? But of course they had come down the one to the south, and Remie had been this way before. He would know how to find a way up the cliff ahead; they were in no danger of being trapped on the beach as it was eaten away to nothing.

She knew the legends of Glooscap, the man-god of the Micmacs who lived in harmony with both man and animals. When she was a little girl, a traveler had displayed for her some of the glowing jewels said to have been scattered along the shore for Glooscap's grandmother, Nogami, and Soleil had longed to have one for her own, for she had never seen anything like them.

Jasper, agate, onyx and amethyst, they had glistened and sparkled in the traveler's bronze hand; his big finger had pointed out a pale lavender one, the most beautiful of them all, and he'd said, "This one is Glooscap's eye." She had taken his words literally until the twins hooted with laughter, and she had subsided in embarrassment.

She missed her brothers' teasing and their antics, though she knew she would not trade Remie for this. She only wished it were possible to have them all, Remie and her family.

Remie's voice broke the silence so abruptly that she jerked and sent the canoe tilting a bit. "We're almost there! I told you there was nothing to worry about!"

She could have wept again in sheer relief. She let the paddle lie across her lap and crossed herself. "Thank you, dear God! Thank you!" she said, and did not know she had spoken aloud until Remie answered.

"I don't mind giving credit where credit is due, but thank your husband a little, too, my love. Here we go, tuck your paddle securely in the bottom for the next fellow!"

It was over. They had not drowned, after all. Her legs were cramped from being immobilized for so long, and they shook when she stood up and accepted Remie's hand to help her out. The canoe was hauled above the reach of the next tide, and Remie swept up the packs to reposition them on their backs and slung the musket over his shoulder.

When he saw her face, with its traces of tears, he ran a thumb gently under each eye, then kissed her the way her father had done when she was a very small girl. "That's my good wife," he told her lovingly. "Now, let's be on our way. We've a good way to go before dark." At least he hadn't ridiculed her fear, she thought gratefully, the way the twins would have done.

And so, on legs barely able to hold her up, Soleil once more fell into place behind him and they started up the path to the top of the red cliff.

THEY SLEPT that night in a Micmac wigwam.

Remie had said nothing to her of their specific destination, so she was amazed when they walked into the cluster of Indian lodges shortly before dusk. Obviously the inhabitants knew Remie; they greeted him first in their own tongue, then, upon learning that Soleil understood only a few words, in French.

Dark-skinned women saw to her comfort. They brought furs to sit upon, and food in birchbark containers. There was a bowl of steaming soup filled with chunks of moosemeat, and some kind of roasted fowl that was so delicious and so welcome that Soleil had no problem using her fingers the same way as the others. She smiled her gratitude, then asked Remie, "What is their word for thank you?"

When Remie told her, and she spoke it awkwardly to their hosts, the Indians smiled their appreciation for her attempt.

She was so tired that she could not quite keep her eyes open as Remie talked to a quartet of the Micmac men. Later she was aware of being eased into a more comfortable position lying down, and instead of blankets she was covered with a fur robe that smelled a bit strong yet was wonderfully warm. Drowsily she tried to say her evening prayers, but she didn't stay awake long enough.

She was not even aware when Remie, smiling in the darkness of the wigwam, slid under the robe beside her, though she murmured his name in her sleep.

At dawn Remie shook her awake and the Indian women came again with food, which they ate quickly and with little conversation. Shortly thereafter they had refitted their packs and were walking once more along the Maccan River valley toward the Chignecto isthmus, where they would cross out of British territory into Canada.

20

EVERY DAY Soleil felt herself toughening up, gaining energy. Every day the sun seemed a little warmer, the birds sang, and her happiness grew to a crescendo that culminated in Remie's arms, in Remie's bed.

He seldom had to shorten his stride to keep from leaving her behind. The Minas Basin and its terrors were behind them; there was no more water to cross except ordinary rivers. When they could, they traveled north by canoe; the lightweight birchbark vessels were readily available, either traded for or borrowed from the local Indians. They ate off the land, for there was plenty of game and more fish than they knew what to do with. Once they were invited in by settlers in the valley for a good meal and to spend the night before their fire. Nights were still cold, though it was June now; tiny wildflowers appeared in the meadows, and there was fresh green grass beneath them rather than last fall's dead leaves.

Soleil enjoyed the infrequent nights spent indoors, but in truth she liked it better the way Remie did: by themselves under the stars. Even when it rained and they had to build a canopy of thick spruce boughs, and Remie spread over them a deerskin he had bartered for from the Micmacs, they were comfortable and warm.

The first time he insisted they sleep naked so that their damp clothes would not chill them through the night, Soleil was both horrified and fascinated. Her mama would never approve, she was sure, but the texture of Remie's skin against her own was exciting; the weight of his hand on her hip was far more stimulating than when there had been garments between them. His now familiar hand tended to rove more, too, she thought as it slid over her hip, her waist, and then cupped a breast while he nuzzled her ear.

"We'll never get any sleep this way," she told him, then turned to face him to make it easier for him to kiss her.

"Who cares?" Remie murmured. "We'll have the rest of our lives for sleeping."

Not if they crawled under their robes without clothes, she thought, amused, and parted willing lips beneath his insistent ones.

THEY SAW THE SMOKE long before they reached Fort Beauséjour.

Too much smoke to be rising from chimneys. Even without noting Remie's wariness, Soleil would have known that.

"A house burning?" she asked, unable to speculate in silence.

"Many houses, I'd say." He lifted his head, sniffing, and by then she, too, could smell the smoke as well as see it, for the wind blew toward them. "The man we met on the trail was right about avoiding Beaubassin, at least until I've had a chance to reconnoiter."

Soleil felt her heart rate increase and she was filled with a growing dread. She had looked forward to Beaubassin, hoping someone there could give her news of Louis and Madeleine. "The British, do you think?"

"The British," Remie confirmed, still staring at the smoke that marred the blue perfection of the sky, "or Le Loutre and his savages. Either way, I've no wish to encounter them. There's a settler, name of Breslay, half an hour ahead. He may be able to tell us something."

They went on without talking for some time. The smell of smoke grew stronger, until it began to sting their eyes and throats. Soleil hardly realized that she had begun to pray inwardly, the same plea over and over again. *Blessed Mother, keep us safe.* Le Loutre was French, and a priest, but she was as much afraid of him as of the British. Everyone said he was not quite sane, and he was constantly being admonished by the bishop at Québec. The Otter cared no more for the bishop's wishes than for those of the settlers he kept trying to drive out of their homes or of the British he hated.

"You'll like Mme Breslay," Remie said, though she could tell his mind was not really on the settlers. "They have several small children, and his old father lives with them, too. They're right through that grove of trees...."

His voice trailed off, and when Soleil stepped up beside him she saw why, and felt sick.

The cabin had been burned to the ground, only the chimney and fireplace remaining amid the charred timbers.

Remie strode ahead into the clearing. He kicked at one of the timbers and it fell with a crash, crumbling. His oath was eloquent. "It's cold. This happened days ago."

Soleil saw a carved wooden doll, one arm broken off as if it had been crushed under a careless heel, lying on the ground beside a stump still embedded with an ax. No man would have left the ax so exposed to the elements, not if he could help it. Her stomach churned. "Do you think...they were all... killed?"

"There's no sign of bodies. With any luck they weren't in the house," Remie said after a moment. "If they got away, they're hiding in the woods, I suppose."

She imagined being in the woods—especially at night, when it got cold—with small children. And if their house had burned, they might not even have blankets or food. She looked around fearfully, as if the enemy who had done this thing might even now be watching.

Someone was watching, all right. After the first startled moment, however, she realized it was neither one of Le Loutre's Indians nor a red-coated soldier. "Remie..."

He turned and saw the old man at the edge of the woods. "M. Breslay," he said, and the poor fellow tottered forward uncertainly. "What took place here? Where are the others?"

He reminded her of Grand-père, except that he was emaciated and had fewer teeth. He gestured with a withered hand.

"Gone. They've all gone, to Île St. Jean, though the devils will no doubt pursue them there, too."

"The Otter?" Remie guessed, but the old man shook his head and spat into the bushes.

"The redcoats. You haven't heard? But no, you be coming from the south."

"We saw the smoke. We've spoken to no one."

The old man spat again. "The fort's fallen. Surrounded for weeks, starving in there, and the British all around. Hundreds of them. They said the settlers were supplying help to the enemy, and The Otter and his men almost as much our enemies as theirs, but then there's never been any talking sense to that Lawrence. And now he's in control of Beaubassin and Fort Beauséjour, and everybody who can has taken off for safer places." He paused to consider, then added, "If there are any."

"And what about you, *monsieur*? Why were you left behind?"

M. Breslay shook his head. "I'm too old to keep up their pace, and they had to go quickly or risk being overtaken. God knows what the soldiers are doing when they round up our settlers, but we see them no more. My son did not want to leave me, you understand, *monsieur*, but I insisted. My days are numbered in any case, and I would not extend them at the cost of theirs. I have a bad leg and many infirmities, and I have no wish to make a long trek and then cross the water to a foreign place to end my days. I'd rather do it here, on my own soil."

"You have enough to eat?" Remie asked. "We can spare a little . . ."

The old man shook his head. "No, *monsieur*, though I thank you. It doesn't take much to feed an old man who no longer works. Even with the British cutting off all outside supplies, a man can still find enough fish, a rabbit or two." He jerked a thumb toward the woods behind him. "I have a shelter of sorts. I have to move once in a while, build a new one, when the patrols come too close." His wry smile revealed numerous gaps in his teeth. "Fortunately the good God provides many spruce boughs."

Remie hesitated, then nodded. "If there is nothing we can do for you, M. Breslay, we will move on. Good luck to you."

"Stay away from the town and the fort," the old man advised. "The smoke has been rising for the past four days, and I do not think any Frenchman is safe. God bless you, young sir and *madame*."

"God bless you," they murmured in return, and did not look back as they left the clearing behind them.

They walked in silence for some minutes, then Soleil said softly, "He reminds me of Grand-père."

Remie nodded. "There will be many such, no doubt. We'll have to move off the trodden path or we'll walk right into the middle of the soldiers. It will be harder going, and we should try to move quietly. If there is a patrol, we'll be safer if we don't talk or crash through the brush.''

Her mind was still on the old man. "I suppose he daren't even have a fire to keep himself warm.'' Grand-père often complained of his cold, old bones, which necessitated toasting himself before the fire. "He won't survive a winter in the woods when it comes, will he?''

"Probably not,'' Remie agreed distractedly. "I'll lead the way. Try to step where I step. Don't break any twigs if you can help it, though it's damp enough they probably won't snap too loudly. We'll play it as safe as we can.''

The smell of smoke grew stronger as they walked. Soleil felt as if her heart were in her throat, though they saw no one; heard nothing. They were in deep forest now, and it was cooler than it had been in the sunshine. Cold, almost. Or was that chill generated from within? She didn't know. She thought longingly of home, where at this time she'd be preparing to take a midday meal to her father and brothers in the fields. A hot stew, full of tender chunks of moose or venison, with fresh bread thickly spread with butter, she thought; and her mouth watered.

She was truly hungry now, and the sun directly overhead, filtering through the leaves of a stand of birches, signaled as clearly as her stomach that it was time to eat. But Remie did not stop, and she said nothing to him. She knew he wanted to circle the soldiers and move beyond the danger zone before they paused.

An hour later they heard a musket shot.

Soleil stumbled and would have tripped if Remie hadn't reached out to steady her. A soldier? A refugee from the village or the fort, shooting game?

They had no way of knowing, and there were no shouts, no further shots. They kept going.

Her own limbs began to ache, but Remie, as always, seemed tireless. The sun lay to the left of them and had dropped notably when Remie finally called a halt.

"Hungry?'' he asked, pulling off his pack. "We'll take time to have a bit of cold meat before we go on.''

He kept his voice low, and she knew they were not out of danger. Dear God, would they ever be out of danger? She could not put the question into words. She chewed methodically, scarcely tasting the jerky they had brought from the last Indian encampment. Their rest was not long, and soon they were moving again through the silent green forest.

She no longer smelled smoke, and when she looked back she couldn't tell if there was still a column of it, for the trees were too thick and too tall. She plodded on after Remie, trying to watch where she put her feet down so as to minimize the sounds.

And then, suddenly, they were on a path again. Remie grinned back at her. "We'll make better time now," he said, and set off at a brisk pace.

Beaubassin was behind them. There would be no chance to ask any of the villagers if they remembered Louis and Madeleine. She thought of old M. Breslay and Grand-père, and her own bones seemed cold, although the day had now grown fairly warm.

When they finally made camp for the night—off the trail, in case anyone came along, and without a fire, for the same reason—she finally had the courage to put into words what she had been thinking all day.

"Will it be like this all the way to Québec? Hiding, having to be quiet?"

Remie was much more relaxed now than he had been since they'd first seen the smoke. "No. As far as I know, the British aren't burning anything to the west of here. By tomorrow night we'll dare a fire, I think."

Soleil had trouble falling asleep that night, for all that Remie thought they were past the danger point. Not even the night before they'd crossed the Minas Channel had she been so apprehensive. The sea was awesome in its power and impersonal in its threat; the British soldiers were a different matter, since they clearly hated Acadian settlers and sought to be rid of them by whatever means came to hand, including muskets and torches. She had no idea what the soldiers would do if they discovered a pair of travelers, and she was afraid to ask Remie's opinion.

They had, however, no further difficulties. They kept to visible trails, which made walking faster and easier, and the weather grew better. Had it not been for the settlers they encountered who had fled before Colonel Lawrence's forces, Soleil would have found it easier to slip back into the carefree mood they had experienced at the beginning of their trek.

The refugees were sobering, however, and each small, ragged band of them reminded her painfully of her brother and sister-in-law. What had *they* suffered on their journey? How were they now?

The tales of woe they heard were all similar. The settlers had fled their homes before the onslaught of the British, many of them looking back to see their houses and barns in flames. None carried more than the barest of essentials, and some had escaped with only the clothes on their backs. There was game in the woods and fish to be caught, but the refugees all had a lean and hungry look. The women and small children were the most pathetic. There were very few old people, and Soleil wondered if they had been left behind, like M. Breslay, to shift for themselves.

Only the nights in Remie's arms made her own discomfort and homesickness bearable.

21

AT GRAND-PRÉ, except for the fact that they missed the members of their family who had gone away, the Cyrs went about their lives as usual.

There were fields, dykes and the weir to tend, as well as the livestock. The household chores went on—cooking, baking, cleaning, soap and candle making and gardening.

Several times during that summer the twins slipped off on their excursions. The second time they were gone longer than usual, and when they returned, Antoine limped on a bandaged foot.

"What happened this time?" Barbe asked, not unduly concerned. The twins had a nineteen-year history of mishaps.

François grinned. "He pretended to be a bear and stepped into a trap."

"I was careless," Antoine admitted, after punching his twin on the shoulder hard enough to send him careening into a wall. "It heals. It's nothing to worry about."

He was careful not to expose the foot when he had to change the bandage, not wanting to reveal that the "trap" injury looked suspiciously like the wound from a musket ball. He had to sit out the dances for a few weeks, but Céleste Dubay proved an attentive companion, willing to observe from the sidelines for a short time.

Danielle was deliriously happy at the attentions of Basile Lizotte whenever they attended the dances. He had as yet made no mention of marriage, but she went so far as to sound out her mother on the subject. "You weren't much older when you married Papa," she pointed out.

Barbe gave her a scathing glance as she kneaded her bread. "I was far more mature than you when I met your Papa. I was used to keeping house, and I was a good cook and seamstress. I didn't plot and scheme to avoid work. Speaking of which, have you weeded the garden yet today?"

Whenever the villagers assembled together, news and rumors were exchanged. Rumor abounded, and increasingly Émile found it difficult to keep his sons from repeating it.

It was unquestionably true that Lawrence's force of several thousand men had subdued Fort Beauséjour and imprisoned hundreds of settlers. Even the priests had been arrested. The fate of these people was a matter for much speculation, all of it fearful. The farmers around Beaubassin had been unable to work their fields, and their livestock and families were starving. The fishermen there had had their boats confiscated or burned on the grounds that they were aiding "the enemy." They, too, were hungry, and their fellow countrymen were forbidden to ship them food; should any be intercepted, it would be confiscated by the British as contraband.

Émile and Barbe could only pray that Remie and Soleil had crossed the Chignecto before the reported capture of the fort had taken place and that they were safely beyond all danger. There was no way to find out.

At the same time, Le Loutre and his savages were reported in far distant parts, bent on exterminating the English conquerors. Mysterious raids were made on English settlers, sometimes by Indians or men dressed and painted to appear to be Indians. The British were reportedly enraged and vindictive, and there were villagers who passed the blockhouse in Grand-

Pré with caution in case the soldiers there had new orders that might cause them harm.

Émile forbade the discussion of such hearsay at the supper table, but it was impossible to keep his sons from talking among themselves at other times or to other men in the village. Though on the surface he was for the most part unruffled, inwardly he found it more and more difficult to dismiss every bit of information as rumor rather than fact.

He didn't even notice that his wife fussed at him less than usual. He didn't see that she tried to shield him from even the minor unpleasantnesses of life, and he didn't notice the concern in her eyes when she watched him.

Émile had aged ten years, she thought, since Louis and now Soleil had gone. He was more disturbed by the news from the surrounding area than he was willing to admit. She prayed more diligently than ever, and she had always been a woman who spent much time speaking to God and the Holy Son and the Blessed Mother. She asked for the flourishing of her garden and the rising of her bread, and now, much more earnestly, she sought blessings on her loved ones.

The time had come and gone for Madeleine to have her baby, and there was no way of knowing whether this one had lived or not, or even if Madeleine herself survived. Yet Barbe daily asked for heavenly intervention on behalf of her daughter-in-law and the new babe, even as she wondered if it were another boy or her first granddaughter. She tried not to think of it as it might be—in a tiny grave on a distant shore.

And Soleil...her most yearned-for child, a daughter after all those sons, her heart's companion, second only to Émile in her affections, though she would never have admitted to the partiality. Soleil and her handsome Remie: was the girl pregnant by now, perhaps with that longed-for granddaughter? The child that Barbe might never see, nor even know about?

When her thoughts grew too much for her, Barbe would retreat to kneel beside her own bed, her head bowed in fervent supplication.

The worst of it was not knowing whether or not her prayers were answered.

SOLEIL, in fact, was not pregnant. She had had one show of blood since her marriage, a situation that caused her to bite her lip until Remie asked what was the matter.

"I had hoped . . . perhaps . . . Is it possible that all this walking every day, all day, makes a difference? I had thought that something might be . . . different by now."

"It's probably just as well if nothing happens too soon," he told her. "We have a long way to go, and some women don't travel well when they are in the family way."

That was true; she remembered Madeleine, who had not managed anything well during her pregnancies. Still, she couldn't help worrying a little.

"You don't think there's anything wrong, do you?"

"With you? Never! You are perfect," Remie said, giving her a robust kiss. "Don't worry. In due time, it will happen."

"But we . . ." She still colored when she tried to speak of their lovemaking, though she ought to be getting used to such things by now, she thought. "We make love almost every night—"

"And sometimes in the morning," Remie agreed happily. "I never tire of it. One of these times we'll get it exactly right, and then you'll see. We only need to keep practicing until we get it *just right*—"

They had stopped for a midday meal in a small clearing where a tiny creek trickled across the path, providing cool water to drink and bathe their hands and faces in. Remie turned to her with that smile of anticipation she had come to know so well. "The more we practice, the sooner it will happen," he said teasingly, reaching for her.

Soleil loved being touched, being kissed, being loved. Never had she been so happy with anyone; knowing that she carried Remie's child was the only thing that could have added to their relationship. She was still too shy to initiate lovemaking, but that didn't matter. Remie was not shy in the slightest. All she had to do was close her eyes and let him take over.

Yet she could not help worrying a little. Madeleine had gotten with child on her wedding night. So had lots of other people, for one could count out the precise nine months from the date the knot had been tied, and there were many who kept track of such things. It was always a matter of whispered discussion when the first babe came a few days early. Had the parents been a bit hasty and indiscreet, or was it only a vagary of nature that brought the birth before a full nine months had passed?

No one will be suspicious of *me*, she thought, then wondered if anyone who had been at her wedding would even know the exact time of her child's birth.

It was impossible not to think about those at home: Mama and Papa and the others, and Céleste—had she won Antoine yet?—and Louis and Madeleine. There would be a new baby by now, if her sister-in-law had carried it safely; Madeleine might even be pregnant again by this time.

Yet Soleil was determined not to allow herself to be melancholy about things she could not control. And it was easy to be happy, because of Remie.

Once they had gone beyond Beaubassin and the fort, they encountered little to dismay them, except for a few dispirited fellow travelers.

Soleil had always wanted to see the world—or at least a slightly larger part of it—and now she was doing so. Remie had seen it all before, and he took pleasure in showing it to her.

At the northern end of Chignecto Bay they took once more to a canoe.

There was a high tide and a bore here, too, but this time the expanse of water that faced them was narrower, and they crossed without incident, heading northwest up the broad Petitcodiac River into the interior. Paddling was easier for Soleil now, though she still would have preferred walking, and for days they saw no one except each other; although they worked hard, all day, every day, life took on a dreamlike quality that made Soleil almost euphoric.

One evening when they cooked their meal over the open fire, Remie looked at her and grinned. "We are now, Mme Michaud, in Canada."

"Out of reach of the British?" she asked eagerly.

"Well, they have a tendency to overreach themselves. If they can push back the boundaries of the French, they'll do so. But they know this is hostile territory. The Otter and his savages are too dangerous for the English to attack when they already have their hands full elsewhere. They have all they can do to control the territory that is legally theirs. Let's celebrate having come this far."

There was no mistaking his meaning. And she had no objection to celebrating, Remie-style. She had begun to wonder, since Remie was so insatiable and she herself was not at all reluctant, how long this peak of excitement could last. Was it possible that even a couple as old as her parents still felt this way? But no, she decided. Passion was for the young. She would surely have sensed it if Barbe and Émile had retained such fires. Yet she hoped her own and Remie's would go on forever, for she had never been so happy.

They continued toward the walled city of Québec. Soleil had worn out the beautiful moccasins that had been Remie's wedding gift to her, and she was not consoled by the barter for a replacement at a small Indian village.

"These were so beautifully embroidered," she murmured, eyes blurring when she discovered the soles had worn through.

"I know someone who can repair them," Remie said. "Stick them in your pack until we get there. Running Fawn is very clever."

There was no particular inflection in his voice, and he was already moving again, but something quickened within her. Running Fawn? He had not spoken the name before, yet there was something now that suggested Running Fawn was a friend of long standing.

Or more than a friend?

She knew there had been women in Remie's life before he met *her*. How could there not have been? He was twenty years old when they met, and handsome enough to send any female into palpitations.

Jealousy was an insidious worm in her heart, and she did not have the courage to ask him more about Running Fawn. She put on the new moccasins and they set out again.

At the place where the river made a sharp bend to the west, they would stop for the night and do a little trading, Remie told her. The place had been called Le Coude—the elbow—but since a small church had been built there for the benefit of surrounding settlers, it was now referred to as La Chapelle.

"A church? Is there a priest there, too?"

"I don't know about that." Remie's paddle dipped smoothly into the water in that seemingly tireless rhythm. At night her own shoulders still ached, though not as badly, but Remie never gave any sign that the day's paddling took a toll on him. "There was no priest the last time I was here. Those who travel from one community to another sometimes only get back to a particular parish once every year or two. But I thought you'd like to see the church."

"Yes," Soleil agreed, "I would."

It turned out to be very tiny, but it *was* a church. She walked there through the twilight, her heart racing, while Remie sought out a local trader.

She said her prayers every morning as soon as she awoke—not always on her knees, but snuggled against her husband's warmth—and again before she went to sleep. Besides that, as they glided up the Petitcodiac, she spoke often to God of her concerns for her family and her gratitude for His blessings on Remie and herself. But it was not the same as kneeling in a proper church, and this was the first one she'd seen since she'd left Grand-Pré.

Her prayers began with thanksgiving for their safety and a request for their continued protection on the trip to Québec. After that, until her knees began to feel the almost-forgotten pressure of a wooden floor, she prayed for all the people she loved, wiping away tears she could not hold back as she remembered them one by one. And finally, not as an afterthought but because she had saved the important prayer for last so as to devote her full attention to it without distraction, she asked that the good God would bless her with a child.

That night when they made love, Remie seemed to read her mind. "Tonight," he told her, his lips close to her throat, "I think we may have done it just right. It could not have been more perfect." He laid a hand on her belly. "Tonight, I think, we have made our child."

Soleil prayed with all her heart that he was right, and that the first child would be a son. Wistfully she added a plea that her child—Remie's child—could be safely delivered in Grand-Pré, with her mother in attendance.

And, all the prayers done, she slept.

22

SOLEIL KNEW that her presence slowed Remie down. On his own he would have traveled more than twice as fast, by either foot or canoe, pausing only to sleep and to eat, and often even eating was done on the move.

"When it's necessary," Remie told her, "a man can move from Québec to Annapolis Royal in a matter of days. It'll be faster going the other way, of course, when we don't have to paddle against the current." His grin warmed her, as it always did. "And you'll be tougher."

She already felt tougher. She didn't expect she'd ever be able to walk or paddle steadily for long periods as Remie did, but she knew she wasn't holding him back the way she had on the initial leg of their journey.

Had it not been for concern about her family, she would have been blissfully content during those early-summer days as they went first along the Kennebecasis and then up the St. John River. She was a little disappointed that she did not get to see the reversing falls at the mouth of the St. John, for Remie had told her about them, but there was no time to spare. Québec City was still a long way off, and they wanted to reach there and return before the winter set in. Remie didn't mind traveling in the winter, but he didn't plan that Soleil should do so.

"'Tis true the river actually runs backward, *up* the rapids?" Soleil pressed him, suspecting at first that he was having fun at her expense.

"Every day," Remie confirmed as they paddled steadily up a stretch of river so wide it seemed more like a lake. The water was a milky blue, and placid, and the dark trees marked its boundaries on both sides. "When the tide comes in, it pushes back the waters flowing downstream to the Bay of Fundy. It's the same thing as the bores you saw, except that at the mouth of the St. John there is a small waterfall, and the tide rises above it. Someday I'll show it to you. Look!" He paused, crystal drops of water dripping from the paddle suddenly stilled in midair, and pointed toward shore.

A cow moose and her ungainly calf were drinking at the water's edge, unperturbed by their passage.

After a moment Remie's paddle returned to its work, rising, falling, rising, falling, as it did for hours.

Soleil welcomed the occasional breaks from that routine when they found it easier to walk beside the river, pulling the canoe, than to fight the current. Once or twice Remie had pulled the craft while she rested, but she really preferred walking to sitting motionless in the canoe.

Remie regarded her thoughtfully the second time she elected to walk. "If you aren't going to rest anyway, it would help if we had a second canoe. We'll need it before we gather up all the furs. Do you think you could handle a canoe by yourself?"

"I can't paddle as strongly as you do. But if you don't go off and leave me behind, I think I could." It made her feel good to think there was something she could do for him, when he worked so hard at taking care of *her*. "Where will we get another canoe?"

The availability of canoes, she was rapidly learning, was no problem at all. They were constructed of lightweight birch-bark and could be traded for at virtually every Indian encampment. Remie had left canoes at various points where a portage had been necessary, and most of them were still there, though some gave evidence of having been borrowed by other travelers.

So, from that time on, Soleil paddled a canoe of her own as the bundles of furs Remie had cached grew at each stop. It meant they traveled farther apart, for she invariably fell behind, and there was less conversation, but Remie in the woods was not the talker he had been in Grand-Pré, anyway. And there was time for talking around the camp fire or after they had made their bed each night.

By now Remie shed his shirt once the sun was up, and he was as bronze as the Micmacs they met in scattered villages. Soleil, too, had tanned nicely. She had no mirror, but sometimes when the water was especially calm she saw her own reflection and was pleased at the way she looked. Even without that improvised looking glass, however, she would have known from the appreciation in Remie's eyes that she had never been prettier.

"Tonight," Remie told her during one golden afternoon when they had made very good time on another lakelike segment of the river, "we'll be at the village of my friends Angry

Waters and Young Otter. We'll spend a day visiting and feasting with them, resting up for the next leg of the journey. That's where the last of the furs are."

Soleil's stomach muscles tightened involuntarily. "It'll be harder from now on?"

"Oh, we have a major portage around the Great Falls, but there is considerable river to travel yet before we go across country to reach the St. Lawrence and head upstream to Québec." His grin, as always, was reassuring. "It's only that when friends have done you the favors that Angry Waters and Young Otter have done for me, you pay your respects when you visit. You show your appreciation."

"How?" Soleil asked bluntly, wondering what her part in this appreciation might be.

"By listening to their stories, even if you've heard them before. By sharing their pipes and their food and their wigwams. And by giving them gifts of friendship."

"You've brought gifts for the whole village?"

"Only for those who are closest to me. For Angry Waters and his son, Young Otter. And," Remie added as an afterthought, "for Running Fawn."

Was that why she had tensed? Had instinct warned her? Running Fawn. There was something special about Running Fawn, though she could not have said how she knew this.

Soleil kept her tone carefully neutral, concentrating on paddling strongly enough to keep her own canoe close to Remie's. "What sort of gifts do you bring?"

"A pipe for my Indian father, a knife for my brother, Young Otter. And a pewter spoon for Running Fawn."

He had not specified his relationship with the girl, Soleil noted. She dug the paddle into the surface of the river with such force that her canoe brushed against Remie's. Her heart thudded as she concentrated on paddling properly. What a mess if she dumped them both—along with their cargo of furs—into the river! Remie would never forgive her.

She cleared her throat. "Where did you come by a pewter spoon? They're rather rare." She might have added "and valuable." It would most likely have come from France and had undoubtedly been smuggled past the British at considerable risk.

"I got it in Louisbourg," Remie said. "Look up around the next bend, see the smoke from the village? We're nearly there."

In Louisbourg, he said. But he had been here once already since he'd left Louisbourg last spring, she thought. Why hadn't he given the spoon to Running Fawn then? Or did he only mean that it had come from the French settlement, not that he'd carried it from there himself?

She couldn't quite bring herself to ask, but her heart continued to pound uncomfortably.

They reached the village in late afternoon, and at once there were cries of welcome, first from the children, then from the adults who moved to meet them.

Even here, many miles from the nearest French settlement, the Micmacs wore garments made of European or Acadian fabrics, traded for with the white men. They had decorated their tunics and leggings in their own fashion with quills, beads and moosehair dyed in vivid colors, and they also incorporated French-made ribbon and braid into the designs.

After weeks on the trail, Soleil felt eclipsed in her simple and practical skirt and blouse. She had abandoned the traditional Acadian apron and cap—keeping them white in the wilderness was impossible—and she did not even have a red ribbon in her hair.

The greetings of the Indians who came to meet them made it clear that Remie was a welcome visitor. He had been teaching her Micmac words, but when they were spoken so rapidly she had difficulty making out even those she was familiar with.

Almost at once, however, the Indians switched to quite passable French when they understood that Soleil did not speak their own language.

Angry Waters was an imposing man of middle years with strong, regular features. His dark eyes were perceptive and intelligent and, she thought, approving as he acknowledged her presence, though he spoke no more than a few words to her. It was the way of men to be more interested in one another than in one another's wives.

The smaller children peeked at them from behind their mothers' legs, and the women stared openly at Remie's wife from a respectful distance, assessing both her features and her clothes.

Which one was Running Fawn, Soleil wondered? The special maiden for whom Remie had brought the treasured pewter spoon. The one about whom Soleil knew almost nothing except that she would be able to repair her own valued moccasins.

And there she was. Soleil knew at once, though no introduction had been made, because this girl's face was different. The English found the Indians impassive, incomprehensible, but there was no mistaking Running Fawn's interest in Remie Michaud and his bride, quite apart from the general curiosity of the others.

She's in love with Remie, Soleil thought, and felt suddenly bruised by the conviction. *She knows she's lost him, but she wanted him, and even knowing she has lost, she loves him still.*

She could not have said how she could be so sure of all this, but she was. She looked into the other girl's beautiful face and read it there, along with Running Fawn's appraisal of herself.

Soleil felt a tightness in her chest. It was easy to see how Remie might have felt something special for this girl. She was very lovely, and she had been here during the winter when Remie brought his furs for safekeeping.

Something very like physical pain swept through Soleil as she fought back the inevitable question. Had Remie made love to Running Fawn? Had he once thought to take her for his wife, before he had met Soleil? Had he still been tempted by her this past winter when he had holed up in this village during a blizzard, even though he had asked Soleil to marry him?

She knew suddenly that if Remie had ever touched the other girl, she did not want to know about it. The hurt would be too great to bear, and she was so convinced that she saw such a depth of emotion in Running Fawn's great dark eyes that she could not hate her. She could only envy the other girl for having known Remie first.

And then the expression was wiped from Running Fawn's countenance so quickly, so completely, that Soleil wondered if she had really seen it there, after all.

The reason for this change was immediately made clear by the approach of a tall and handsome man who came from the river behind them, causing everyone to turn and face him. Even before Remie spoke his name, Soleil knew this was Young Ot-

ter. He stood taller than his father and was every bit as imposing. And though he said nothing to Running Fawn, nor she to
him, Soleil knew intuitively that he took a proprietary interest
in the Micmac girl, and that it was from him that she shielded
her emotions.

Young Otter's assessment of Soleil was considerably length-
ier than his father's had been. She hoped her tan covered her
blush as she lifted her chin a bit defensively and returned his
gaze.

She could not tell what he thought of her. He was not as
transparent as Running Fawn had been for those critical few
moments. Yet Soleil was sure that he, too, felt more than a
passing interest in Remie's bride, though for a different reason.

When Young Otter swung his attention back to Remie, his
wide mouth relaxed in a smile. "Welcome, my brother," he said
in Micmac, then repeated the words in French. "You are always welcome in the wigwam of the Micmacs."

There was general movement then, as everyone made their
way toward the cooking fires. Children and dogs milled around,
and the women returned to tending their kettles. Remie gave
Soleil a warm smile before he left her with the women to join
the men, and for a moment she felt totally bereft.

The women were kind, however. Smiling, they led her to a
place where she could sit in the shade and offered her a drink
of cold, clear water. She sipped at it, feeling out of place and
awkward, though she had never felt that way in other Indian
encampments.

The reason, of course, was Running Fawn. Did they all know
she had loved Remie, or was it a secret between the two of
them? No, she amended at once, knowing the answer to her
own unvoiced question; Young Otter had known, and Young
Otter had wanted Running Fawn for himself. Seeing Remie's
wife had caused an eroded friendship to begin to mend. As for
Angry Waters, though he spoke little, Soleil was certain he saw
everything.

She was amazed at how clear all of this was to her. Ever since
her marriage, she had marveled at how much her sensitivity had
been heightened, not only to the beauty around her and to her
own awakened body, but to other people, as well.

Even if Remie had never spoken of his intimate relationships with these people, she thought, she would have known about Running Fawn and Young Otter.

As Remie had anticipated, they were treated to a feast when at last the women began to dish up the food. Moose, bear and venison, fish, fowl, smoked eel and strawberries were brought forth to honor their visitors.

After the feasting and the smoking and talking came to an end, Soleil was grateful to retire to the wigwam that had been turned over to them. A light rain had begun to fall, and she found herself thinking of their usual starry canopy of open sky, which she had come to enjoy. Then her thoughts drifted to Running Fawn and Young Otter. They were married now. Had Running Fawn made her decision after learning that no marriage would be forthcoming with Remie? Soleil wondered. Their union had not yet been blessed by a priest, because there had not been one in their village in many moons, but not even the Acadians waited for a priest to sanctify their living together in a land where they might not see one of the Fathers for years at a time.

Soleil wasn't sure how she felt, knowing Remie could have had the Micmac girl if he'd wanted her. Instead, he had chosen Soleil. There were many marriages between the French and the Micmacs; this strengthened the friendship ties between them. Would Remie have gone to live with the Indians if he had married Running Fawn?

Beside her, Remie stirred, running a hand over her hip, sending tendrils of excitement through her. But he was asleep, not making a familiar advance, and Soleil smiled, covering his hand with her own.

She thanked the Blessed Mother that it was she, not Running Fawn, who lay beside Remie now. In the morning they would leave the Micmac village behind. And within a few days, perhaps, she would know whether or not she carried Remie's child.

She curled against him and prayed that it would be so.

23

THE FOLLOWING DAY they set off again, their canoes gliding silently upriver between thick stands of fragrant balsam fir, spruce, cedar and pine. An occasional maple, birch or beech, lighter shades of green than the more numerous evergreens, promised a glorious show of color by fall.

Frequently they saw deer, squirrels and porcupines, and an occasional raccoon or muskrat. When they needed food, Remie was adept at shooting or snaring it; there were no weirs here, but the fish were plentiful and Remie was equally as skilled at spearing the succulent salmon as the Indians who lived around the river.

Remie could paddle for hours without conversation, and for once Soleil was almost as quiet as he was. She told herself that what Remie had done before he met her was of no consequence, but it was impossible to put Running Fawn out of her mind.

The Indian girl was very lovely. She had been no more forward than any of the other Micmac women in serving the visitors, but her face had revealed much in those first few moments after Remie appeared in the encampment with his bride.

Remie had had no private opportunity—nor sought one—to present Running Fawn with the pewter spoon. He had handed it over casually, saying that it and the knife for Young Otter were wedding gifts in the custom of the white man. The girl's face was lighted from within as if by a dozen candles; her strong brown fingers explored the smooth, silvery surface of the spoon with obvious delight, and her smile transformed her otherwise solemn face.

Soleil, with her newfound perceptiveness, saw that Young Otter watched his mate closely, and that Running Fawn quickly tempered her pleasure, thanking Remie in a formal manner before withdrawing, as if he were little more than a stranger.

Soleil's own convictions were strengthened by the brief interplay. She wondered if Young Otter knew that he had been second choice, and decided that he did, and that he would be very angry if any intimate feelings lingered between his friend and his woman. Soleil wondered if he would even allow her to keep the spoon once Remie had gone; she wasn't sure how *she* felt about the situation. She was sorry for Running Fawn, for it was easy to imagine herself in the other girl's position. Yet the spoon was a very special gift, of considerable value among the Micmacs, and the fact that Remie had not mentioned it until shortly before he presented it to the other girl seemed to give the act more significance than it might otherwise have had.

It would be a long time before Soleil forgot about the spoon, the gift her husband had carried so far for another woman.

Yet Remie was the same as ever: tender, loving, amusing. And he *could* have had Running Fawn if he had wanted her, before or after his meeting with Soleil.

It was impossible to brood about the matter on such a fine day, with the forest and the river vibrant about them, and the wonder of her future with Remie.

Gradually she came out of her reverie, her paddle suddenly motionless in her hands as she realized that she had been hearing a sound, soft at first, now rapidly growing louder. "What is it?" she called out.

Remie cast a glance over his shoulder, still paddling. "The Great Falls. We'll portage around them and camp above them tonight."

Since it was not yet nearly late enough to be halting for the night, she assumed from his reply that the portage would be a strenuous one, and she was right.

It was actually some time before they reached the gorge, which was impassable. The thunder of the water grew louder and louder, and gradually the turbulence of the river grew as well, until Soleil began to feel apprehensive about how close to the falls they could get before they risked being caught in a whirlpool or overturned in the rapids.

She began to flinch at the roar of falling water before Remie finally swung toward the bank and gestured for her to follow. Speech was impossible over the sound of the falls; even a shout would not have carried far. She had a gut-wrenching moment when her canoe was caught and thrown sideways, and then she was beyond the most forceful part of the current and Remie was hauling her canoe ashore.

Only then did she stare upstream into the gorge through which spilled the incredible wall of water, boiling with froth and spray that drifted to them some distance away.

By gestures and mouthed words, Remie managed to convey that they would abandon the canoes here for use on their way home. Other canoes would be available above the rapids and the falls; it would be easier simply to portage with their bundles of furs and supplies than to attempt carrying the canoes, as well.

She soon realized why it would be necessary to camp above the falls. It was going to take them several trips to transport their goods, and the path was very steep and the walk quite a distance to where the river was again navigable.

This portage was the hardest thing she had ever done—harder, even, than learning to walk all day or paddle constantly for hours at a stretch—and by the end of the first trip, Soleil's legs were trembling with fatigue. Coming back down the trail was even more difficult than going up had been, in spite of having no burdening pack, because of the steepness of the incline. The deafening roar of the cataract made her head ache, as well.

Remie had gone ahead of her down the path so he could break her fall if she slipped. When she came down the last few yards in a rush he caught her in his arms, giving her what was intended to be a quick hug but turned into a more prolonged embrace. Her tremors were communicated to him as their bodies met full length.

"Are you all right?" He put his mouth close to her ear and shouted to be heard.

She was short of breath. "Yes, I think so. I will be in a minute, anyway. Do we have time to . . . rest a moment?" She was reluctant to ask, but she feared she might actually collapse before she reached the top again.

Remie evaluated her rapid respiration. "Yes, of course. I'll tell you what. You sit here while I make the next trip, and then you can go with me on the last one. I'll get us a salmon for supper, and you can cook it while I'm gone. There are some wild chives over there to give it flavor."

She nodded gratefully and went to gather sticks for a fire, knowing her throat would be raw from shouting if they tried to communicate further.

It felt strange to be alone here in the wilderness after Remie had gone. Once she turned sharply, sensing someone watching her, only to discover a bull moose come to drink. His gaze met hers before he ambled off into the forest, leaving her mildly shaken. She was not as well prepared to survive alone as she had imagined she might be; she hoped Remie would hurry back.

There was nothing to be afraid of, she told herself, adding a few twigs to the fire. The Indians were friendly, and even a bear should not bother her at this time of year, for there were plenty of fish, easily caught, to feast upon. Yet she stayed on the riverbank, out in the open as much as possible, until Remie returned.

When the time came to make the final ascent, she had recovered enough to reach the top without her legs refusing to function.

In the places where the path led to the lip of the gorge, she stared down at the roaring water, watching it carry great logs and branches large and small, smashing them against the rocky walls; anything in the river's path would fall nearly a hundred feet before finding an end in the turbulence below. She shivered and moved back from the brink.

It was not until they finally finished off their salmon at dusk, well above the falls where it was again feasible to carry on a conversation, that she gathered her courage to ask the question that had been on her mind ever since she'd first been aware of this gorge and its tremendous force of water.

"Are there any more like this we must go around?"

Remie reached for the last of what had been a sizable salmon. "There remains the Little Falls of the Madawaska, but that is nothing compared to the Great Falls. Have you heard the legend connected with this waterfall?"

Soleil shook her head. She was very tired, but content to be sprawling beside him on a low, mossy rock. She was even proud of herself for having made it this far, and it helped to know there was no worse ahead of them.

Remie swallowed the last of the fish—it was so tender that chewing was scarcely necessary—and lay back beside her, gazing up at the darkening sky where the stars were beginning to appear far above them. "Angry Waters told it to Young Otter and me when we were little more than boys, but not before warning us that we were not to act the story out, as we had done with some others. Supposedly it took place nearly five hundred years ago, long before any white men had come to these shores."

He reached out his hand to take hers, his callused thumb caressing her palm without thought. "There was a Maliseet village a short way upriver from here. The Indians called the river Wigoudi. Sacobie and his daughter Malabeam were on an island in midstream when they were surprised by a large party of warring Mohawks, the sworn enemies of the Maliseets and all the Micmacs, and the man was killed."

It was easy to imagine this as they lay here in the darkening forest, listening to the now distant rumble of the water as it forced its way through the gorge. Soleil curled her own fingers around Remie's, thinking of that girl left defenseless after her father's murder.

"The Mohawks took Malabeam prisoner. Of course she thought she would be killed as well, when the men were through with her, but she held her head high, too proud to weep or beg for mercy. Their leader then said to her that if she would guide them to her father's village, her life would be spared. She was even promised the honor of being married to a Mohawk brave."

The rock, despite its mossy covering, was hard, and Remie shifted to a more comfortable position, bringing him into greater contact with Soleil. He put an arm across her and drew her closer to the full length of his own body.

"But she didn't agree to do it," Soleil guessed. "She would not betray the rest of her people."

She sensed rather than saw Remie's smile. "She spoke boldly for a maiden confronted with three hundred enemy braves. She pretended to consider her fate, and then to submit. 'Very well,' she told them. 'Keep all your canoes together, and I will lead you to my village, if you will spare my life.' And so they began their journey downstream. It was a black night, and they heard the roar of the river as it tumbled through the gorge, and they became alarmed. But Malabeam reassured them, saying it was only a waterfall that joined the Wigoudi just below them. And then she cried out triumphantly as she led them over the Great Falls to their deaths far below."

Having just seen the power of the river, the menacing rock walls of the gorge, Soleil could imagine the plunge over the falls, the warriors falling out of the canoes and being battered against the rocks.

"The bodies of the Mohawks were found the following day, every one of them dead. Malabeam's body was never found, and there are those who believe she ascended directly into heaven as a reward for saving her village from the massacre that would have taken place had the Mohawks found it."

For a few minutes after Remie had finished, they lay together in silence. It was almost fully dark now, and growing cool. At last Soleil sat up, pushing back her dark hair. "I don't think I would have had the courage to do that. She must have been terrified."

"Anyone who had ever seen the falls would be terrified," Remie agreed. "But there are many such tales of bravery, not only among the Indians but among our own people. Anyone who truly loves another will sacrifice for them." He sat up, too, and drew her face close to his so that she felt his breath meet her own. "As I would die for you, if the need arose."

She hugged him fiercely, crying out in protest, "No, no, don't speak of such things! We've only begun our lives together! I don't want to think about dying!"

Yet, as they rose to spread their robes upon the ground for sleeping, she was thoughtful. Was it true that anyone, even an ordinary person, would die willingly to save a loved one? She thought of Barbe and Émile and decided that quite possibly they would give their own lives for their children. And Madeleine—yes, she would die in order to save Marc and the new baby she must surely have had by this time.

Her hand brushed Remie's casually as they smoothed out the robe stretched between them. And yes, she thought with a lump in her throat, if it came to that, she would sacrifice herself for Remie. She loved him more than life itself, and she swore that she would so do forever.

THEY COULD SEE the legendary city of Québec for a full day before they reached it.

The journey had been arduous, but they were young, and the fatigue of each day was washed away by a night's sleep; every morning found Soleil as eager as Remie to push onward.

Her first glimpse of the St. Lawrence was dismaying. She had expected another such river as the St. John, yet this was an inland sea, so wide that the far bank was merely a narrow blue smudge on the horizon.

She said nothing, but Remie heard her indrawn breath and hastened to reassure her. His tone was cheerful. "If you saw it from the Gaspé, you would truly think it a sea, for there one cannot see across it. While the tide does push the river back, it has no tidal bore, and no fifty-odd-foot rises."

"But the city is on the far side?" Soleil asked faintly.

"The river narrows considerably before we have to cross it. See, there, a ship from France!" He pointed out across the shimmering, milky blue water toward a handsome vessel under full sail. "You'll see no cursed British ships in these waters! If they ever again should venture up the St. Lawrence, no doubt they'd get the same response they got sixty or seventy years ago when Sir William Phipps laid siege to the city. The governor of Québec vowed to reply through the mouths of his cannons. And it's cannons the British will get if they ever return."

He gave her a sly look, which she had come to know would precede a provocative remark. "'Tis said that when Champlain first explored this area a hundred and fifty years ago, he was amazed to find Algonquin women dancing in the nude. It was, I'm told, an astonishing entertainment."

Soleil stared at him. "I don't believe you."

"I swear it! Ask anyone in Québec City!"

She sniffed, not totally convinced that he was telling the truth, yet sure of one thing. "I hardly think I'll ask anyone," she said, sending him into a gale of laughter.

"Well, you and I cavorted on a sandbar without clothes," he reminded her. "And most pleasant it was."

She flushed, remembering. "We weren't dancing! And that was different. We washed all our clothes because it was such a good place to do it, and we have so few..." She stopped, realizing she was using the very arguments with which he had persuaded her to take off her clothes in the first place. Had the water not been so cold, she would have remained submerged in the river until their garments dried; even so, she had put on her undergarments while they were still damp, for all Remie's assurances that no one was the least likely to come along and observe them.

She suddenly remembered those times when her father would make some under-the-breath remark and her mother would slap only half seriously at him. Had it been because of just such a gibe as Remie's? That seemed unlikely, yet she had always been curious about those private exchanges between her parents. These days she was considering them in a different light than when she had been a child.

As they made their way along the banks of the St. Lawrence she saw that Remie had spoken the truth about the river, at least; gradually the far shore came into sharper focus, the blue haze softening to green until finally it was possible to make out vegetation across the water.

"In the winter we could cross on the ice," Remie told her. "Tomorrow we can cross easily in our own canoes."

Excitement rose within her. Grand-Pré, for all its hundreds of houses, was only a village compared to Québec. Tomorrow she would see the magnificent city with Remie, who would explain it all to her as they explored together.

How wonderful it would be when she returned to Grand-Pré and she could tell Céleste and her family about this grand adventure. She tugged on the rope of the canoe that she was pulling along the riverfront and stepped out briskly after her husband.

24

FOR THE FIRST FEW DAYS, Soleil was delighted and bewildered by the great walled city. Even from a distance it was easy to see why the French had been able to repulse an attack by the English; while there were some buildings on the open plain along the bank of the St. Lawrence, most of Québec was encircled by a stone wall that protected its citizens.

There were more people than Soleil had dreamed could assemble in one place. Remie had shrugged off her query as to their numbers. "I don't know. Five or six thousand, I suppose. At least as many as Louisbourg, probably." Mere numbers of people did not excite him; he preferred the sparsely populated wilderness.

The room they took at an inn was modest enough, though it felt strange to be in a proper bed after weeks of sleeping in the open or in Micmac wigwams. The inn's stone walls had not the coziness of the log houses she was accustomed to, but since they spent little time there, it didn't matter.

Remie had business to attend to with the fur merchants on the Place Royale, leaving Soleil to her own devices for most of each day. There were no chores to do, not even meals to prepare, since they ate in the public room of the inn.

At first she was afraid to venture far from the hostelry for fear she would get lost. The Place Royale was densely populated, and while she heard frequent greetings called out between acquaintances, their faces were all unfamiliar to her. No one paid her any attention except for occasional admiring male glances that were more unnerving than gratifying.

Yet the lure of the populace and the big stone buildings was irresistible. The houses and stores and warehouses were nearly as fascinating as the people in their varied garments, because they were so different from anything she had ever seen before. Some of the ladies surely wore the latest fashions from France, she thought, storing away details of their gowns to describe to those at home, or perhaps even for a gown of her own some day. She longed to peek through an open doorway into one of the multistoried mansions where those elegantly gowned ladies lived, as Remie had peered into the governor's mansion at Louisbourg.

Yet even without that privilege, there was much of interest to see. Houses taller than the spire of the church at home, with many windows, many chimneys, and virtually all built of stone to last hundreds of years. Indeed, some of them had already stood since the early 1600s.

And there were churches. Many churches. Soleil sought them out eagerly, venturing farther and farther from the Lower Town to the Upper Town, where the more important people lived in their amazing mansions. The terms Upper and Lower were accurate, for most of the business section of Québec lay on the river plain, and a steep set of steps must be climbed to reach the exclusive residential area on the top of the bluff.

At every church, whether small like the one at Grand-Pré or enormous like the Notre-Dame-des-Victoires, Soleil went inside, holding her breath for fear someone would challenge her right to be there. But no one ever did. She knelt at each altar and lighted a candle, praying for those she missed so much, as well as for Remie and the child they both wanted. The bishop of the whole of the New World was here in Québec—his grand residence up on the hill had been pointed out to her—and she wished she might catch a glimpse of him so that she could impress the whole village when she returned home by having been close to such an eminent authority.

The climb to Upper Town was enough to deprive her of wind but was worth the effort, for the view from the top was magnificent. She could see out over the broad river with its ships and small boats and canoes to the wooded shores of the Île d'Orléans.

It was the houses that fascinated her the most, however. No one seemed to care if she wandered the streets admiring all those grand edifices with their steep roofs to shed the snow and their thick walls, which seemed almost as fortresslike as the walls about the city.

And everywhere there was bustle and commerce. Trappers and traders brought in their goods, carried away other goods and supplies. Ships from France were unloaded—foodstuffs, wines and brandies, materials to make the clothes she saw everywhere, leathers for shoes and garments, glass for windows, all manner of goods to be sold. No sooner were their holds emptied than the ships were reloaded with furs and hides and casks of salted fish to be carried back to France.

The ships also brought newspapers. She saw a few of them and wished she knew how to read the words printed there. Remie could read, but he declined to purchase a paper. "The news is all about the troubles between France and England," he told her. "We can do nothing about any of it. If they insist on fighting each other, let them do it. They have always warred."

"How do you know what the news is if you will not buy a paper?" Soleil asked.

"The same way everyone in Grand-Pré knows the news, of course. A messenger brings it, and everyone talks about it." He sobered. "There is news from Acadia, to the effect that Colonel Lawrence is now firmly entrenched in the area around Beaubassin. 'Tis said he plans a similar fate for the rest of the colony, that he's again demanding that all Acadians sign his damned oath of allegiance to England without the provision that we be spared from fighting either the Indians or our own French relatives. Why can't they be satisfied with that, that we will agree simply not to take up arms against the British?"

She was always uneasy when the talk took such a turn. "Papa says they've been making that demand for years, and nothing ever comes of it."

Remie's expressive lips were pursed. "There are those who don't agree with your papa, I'm afraid."

She wanted to ask if he were one of them but feared the answer. She deliberately turned the subject aside, which was not difficult since Remie did not want to talk about the English demands, either.

Eventually it occurred to Soleil that if she became lost while exploring the city, she had only to walk straight in any direction until she encountered one of the outer walls, and then follow it around—again in either direction—until she came to a street that was familiar. After that she was braver, probing into every corner, every alleyway, making mental notes to share with those who would never see these places.

Walking on streets of stone or brick was harder on her footwear than the forest paths, and she realized ruefully that these moccasins, too, were going to need replacing soon. That reminded her that Running Fawn was repairing the ones she had gotten for a wedding present; each time she thought about the Indian girl she was uncomfortable.

If Running Fawn had been no more than a friend, why did Remie not talk about her as openly as he did about Young Otter?

Yet it was not Running Fawn but she herself who was here in Québec with Remie. She must remember to give thanks for that blessing the next time she entered one of the city's churches.

Remie did not seem to share her love for the places of worship. She did persuade him to attend mass with her once or twice, but after that he rolled his eyes. "You go ahead."

"But we won't be here long, you said so, and there are so few churches between here and home—"

"I don't need a church in which to say my prayers," Remie informed her. "The good God made the forest and the sky, too, did He not? Nature's cathedral offers me more of His own works than stone and colored glass." How casually he dismissed the leaded windows of stained glass, brought all the way across the ocean to grace their churches, to bring glory to God!

When she voiced that idea, Remie grinned. "Glory to the men that build them, more like! How would you like to go shopping tomorrow? By then I will have collected all that is owed to me, I trust, so if you want to buy gifts for your family, that will be the time to do it. Small things, not too bulky or heavy," he added, "since you'll probably wind up carrying them over three hundred miles."

She did not want to be diverted from the matter of church attendance, but this was a new and exciting prospect. "Gifts?"

"I saw a shop up the street that has a wide selection of fabrics. You'll want something for a special gown for yourself, too, no doubt. And there is jewelry—have you ventured into that alley just to the west of us? It's a tiny shop, but the goods M. Hébert displays might take your fancy. Walk over today and have a look. Tomorrow, when there are francs to spend, I'll go with you."

The subject of church was allowed to die, though Soleil continued to attend services whenever it was possible. She felt as if her prayers conveyed more urgency when they were made on her knees before an altar in one of the handsome stone churches.

She was, in fact, feeling an overwhelming homesickness. She missed her family almost desperately in spite of her happiness with Remie. She missed having Céleste, and even Danielle, to tell things to. She wondered again, as she had so many times already, if Antoine had ever gotten around to proposing to Céleste. Why, her friend might already be pregnant with another Cyr grandchild!

She herself was not yet in a family way. It wasn't as if she weren't perfectly happy with just Remie, at least for now, but the fact that her monthly show had not ceased caused her increasing uneasiness. Almost everyone she knew had conceived within a month or two of marriage, and it would be a terrible fate to fail to produce a family. Remie might even be sorry he had married her, which was the most dreadful thought of all.

When she voiced her concern, Remie only laughed. "You say you have faith in God. Do you not think He knows what He is doing? When the time is right, it will happen. I told you, we need only practice until we do it right."

She stared at him with a hint of resentment. "You make a joke of everything."

"Of course. Life is the biggest joke of all. Don't you think God has a sense of humor? He must, or he would have devised a less amusing way of creating a child."

"It isn't supposed to be amusing," she remonstrated, only to evoke more laughter.

"But it's great fun, is it not?" He kissed her, a noisy, boisterous smack. "If you are so worried, perhaps we should try again right now, before I go off to collect my francs."

She shoved against his chest with both hands. "Stop being so foolish!"

"What's foolish about a man wanting to make love to his wife, to make babies? That is what the good God intends, is it not? That a man and his wife make babies?"

She met his laughing gaze with coolness. "For a man who talks about what God intends for us, you seem strangely reluctant to attend mass and hear His words."

Remie dismissed her remark with a wave of one bronze hand. "Ah, I went to mass every day when I lived with Father de Laval in Annapolis Royal. I heard enough sermons to last me a lifetime."

She was genuinely shocked. "How can you say such a thing!"

"My memory is excellent. I remember every one of them. I got to hear them at least twice, you see. First when Father de Laval practiced them at home, and later again at mass. I expect over those two years I was warned against every evil a man could know. So I no longer worry about it. I am very comfortable in my relationship with God."

Soleil was *not* comfortable with such an attitude. It went against what she had been taught, and she said so.

"Well, that's the difference, you see. Father de Laval was one of those priests who was quite certain of *his* relationship with God, and he conveyed this to me. I've never been one of those who believes he can do whatever he likes because going to confession will wipe the slate clean. I try to follow my conscience all the time. And I have no guilt whatever about enjoying making love to my wife."

He dragged her toward the bed in an exaggerated fashion. "And as a dutiful wife, you must respond in kind."

"No such thing!" Soleil denied, struggling, but she started to giggle, and as usual, Remie won out in a most satisfying manner.

IN A MATTER of a few weeks, even the magical city of Québec lost much of its hold upon Soleil. She had visited all the shops and delightedly purchased trinkets for everyone, even Louis and Madeleine and their family. She had stared in awe at every impressive building, but the novelty had worn off.

She was so homesick that sometimes at night, after Remie had fallen asleep, she cried for her mother and the other members of her family. And the stone walls were confining; she longed for open skies and wooded paths, for the dark red sands of the Minas Basin with its spectacular tides, the smell of fresh-cut hay, and the aromas of supper cooking over her own fireside.

Her heart leaped with joy the evening that Remie returned to their room with the news that his business was completed. "We can leave in the morning," he said.

Impulsively she flung her arms around his neck. "And go back to Grand-Pré?"

"And go back to Grand-Pré," he confirmed. As she leaned back against his encircling arms to look up at him, he put on his most lascivious leer. "And I intend to deliver you to your mother in a properly expectant state, so let's give Québec City its last chance to be the site of the conception of our son."

They tumbled onto the bed, mouths meeting joyously, eagerly, and all cares melted away from them. Tomorrow they would head for home.

25

THOUGH SOLEIL KNEW the return journey went more quickly, since they paddled downstream instead of going against the current, paradoxically time seemed to have slowed. Perhaps it was only that she was so homesick to see her family and friends that she could not bear the waiting, now that they were on their way back to Grand-Pré.

"It may be," she said eagerly to Remie, "that there will even be news of Louis and Madeleine."

Remie poked another stick into the fire that was cooking their supper. He grunted in a noncommittal way.

"They could even have come home," she added. Her own longing for the family heightened her understanding of her sister-in-law's plight on her trek to Île St. Jean, and she wondered how Louis could remain so unyielding to his wife, who had left behind not one but two families she loved.

"It's not likely, love," Remie said.

She felt as if he'd scooped up a handful of the icy river water and thrown it in her face. "Why not?"

"Because the situation he fled from hasn't changed, except to grow worse. Your father may still believe that poor relations with the British will blow over, but there are many who don't think that way. There will never be any help for Acadians from France, now. There wasn't very much, ever, but since the Treaty of Utrecht, France has abandoned us once and for all. And the British want only to deprive Acadians of their lands so that their own settlers can claim them. I'm glad I have no attachment to a particular section of land. They can't take what I don't have."

She sat back on her heels, gazing at him through a blur of tears. "There have been Cyrs on our land for several hundred years. Don't you want a home of your own, Remie?"

"My home is where you are," he said, and expertly flipped the trout in the pan.

"But when we have a family we'll want a home. A snug cabin with a fireplace and our own garden—"

"It might be safer, for a time, to settle for a way of life like that of Angry Waters and his people. To have a lodge that can be taken down and moved, ahead of the British if necessary.

Don't worry about it, love. No Englishman is going to get the best of me in the woods on my own territory, surrounded by friendly Indians. I'll take care of you," he promised.

She believed that, yet his words caused a pain in her heart, for he could not also be responsible for those she loved. Every night and many times during the days as they traveled first overland and then down the length of Lac Temiscouata, she prayed that all would be safe and well at Grand-Pré.

It was full summer now. The sun was hot on their backs and heads, sinking behind them this time rather than directly before them. When they stopped long enough, Soleil picked berries to supplement their meat-and-fish diet, wistfully hungering for some of the bread she or her mother would have baked at home. There were wild chives and onions to add flavor to their food, and they never went hungry; except for her eagerness to get home and her anxiety about her family, Soleil could have been supremely happy.

They came again to the Madawaska River, flowing from the lower end of Lac Temiscouata, and along the valley where Remie had said he would like one day to live. It *was* a lovely, tranquil place, with thick dark trees rich with wildlife, and one special grassy expanse of plain where they camped for two days while Remie replenished their supply of fresh meat. Soleil washed their clothes and dried them in the hot sunshine. It was a welcome respite, yet she could hardly wait to go on again, for every hour on the trail brought them closer to home.

They lay that night under the stars and a sliver of pale new moon, entwined in each other's arms. For once Remie did not roll over and fall asleep at once after lovemaking but continued to hold her as they talked about what it would be like to live here.

"We'll come back here in the fall," he said dreamily, "and build our cabin before winter. Tight and snug, a single room to begin with, and we'll add on to it next spring. Eventually others will come, too—maybe some of those who are being driven out of the Chignecto region will settle here, so we'll have neighbors."

A twinge of that earlier uneasiness surfaced when Soleil thought about living here with a child. "If only it weren't so far from Mama! But she'll never leave Grand-Pré, for Papa won't go, no matter what happens."

His hand, resting on her breast, slid down to her smooth, flat stomach, making it quiver. "You know what? I think tonight was perfect, the night when, on the site of our home some day, we have finally done it right and conceived a baby. When our son is old enough to understand, we'll tell him that this is where it all began."

"We will not," Soleil contradicted. "We'll not talk of where he began at all, nor how."

Even when she was annoyed with him, she loved his low, rich chuckle. "By that time he'll probably be old enough to understand the *how* of it," he predicted.

Feeling perverse, Soleil made her own prediction. "Besides, the first one, I think, is going to be a girl."

"Fine. Then the second one will be a boy. Or the third. Or the f—"

Her hand had closed over his mouth, stopping the words. He reached for her wrist to pull it away, then kissed her palm. "I love you," he said.

As was often the case, she remained awake after he had fallen asleep. She prayed most earnestly that he was right, that the seed had been planted within her, that when they reached her own village she could make the happy announcement that she was with child.

THE PORTAGE around the Great Falls was easier this time, for they carried no heavy bundles of furs, only the smaller packets of trading goods Remie had bought in Québec. And Soleil was buoyed by the knowledge that every step carried her closer to home.

The St. John hurled itself with enthusiasm into the gorge, boiling and roaring, carrying with it everything it touched. Soleil could not help recalling the story of the Indian maiden, Malabeam. Could an ordinary person show that much bravery, she wondered, on behalf of others?

As she stood on a projecting rock and stared down into the maelstrom, she was glad she had never been put to such a test.

Below the falls they took to a single canoe again, which made it easier to communicate. Not that they talked much while they were paddling; Soleil dealt with her own thoughts and wondered what occupied Remie all those hours on the river, for he was content with silence. Even when he spotted a moose or a deer along the shore, which he always noticed before she did, he only broke the rhythm of his paddling and pointed, not speaking.

As they neared the spot where Angry Waters had his village, Soleil realized she was growing tense. She told herself she was a fool, for if Remie had wanted the Indian girl he could have had her, though not without rupturing his long friendship with Young Otter. But there had always been such rivalries, and she could not seriously believe Remie would have backed off for that reason.

She dreaded meeting Running Fawn again, yet she knew that Remie would not be content to pass by the village without halting, no matter what time of day they reached it. She could only pray that they would spend no more than one night there and be gone.

She was not unprepared then, in midafternoon, when the birchbark wigwams came into view at the edge of the woods and Remie dug in with the paddle, sending them shoreward.

A shout went up, and those who were not out hunting or fishing came to meet the newcomers. A few dogs barked in desultory fashion, wagging their tails to show that this was a greeting rather than a warning.

In spite of herself, Soleil searched the gathering women and children for Running Fawn. She came with a lithe stride, carrying herself proudly, and at once Soleil knew there was something different about the girl.

For a moment she could not identify it, and then she knew. Running Fawn was pregnant.

It had only been a little over a month since they'd seen her, but she had changed almost imperceptibly. There was a new fullness in her face, in her bosom, and though her stomach was still flat, the real difference was in her eyes. Happiness lent a glow to her coppery skin, and because Soleil herself knew the satisfaction of loving and being loved, she believed she recognized that in the other girl. Although Running Fawn smiled and welcomed them as before, Soleil guessed that her feelings for

Remie had altered. Running Fawn no longer yearned for him but was content with her own man.

Remie appeared to notice none of this. He was striding up the bank toward Angry Waters, who had acquired a limp since they had last been here.

"My friend, the bear, objected to my intrusion on his territory," he said in excellent French when Remie asked about it. "It heals, but not as quickly as when I was a young man. Come, let us smoke together."

Once more Soleil was left to the ministrations of the women. Several little girls gathered around to finger her garments and examine the shining gold cross Remie had bought for her at the little shop in Québec City.

Running Fawn was friendly, not at all reserved this time. She brought forth the mended moccasins, the original elaborate embroidery intact, the soles brand-new, and handed them over. She also presented Soleil with a gift: a cap like the ones the Micmac women wore, made of scarlet wool trimmed in strips of silk ribbon appliquéd in a pattern of scallops and bands.

It obviously represented many hours of work and had been done for Remie's bride. Soleil accepted the present with profuse thanks—to have done otherwise would have been insulting—and mixed feelings. She did not want to be indebted to this girl, which meant that she must produce a gift in return.

She chose a packet of bright ribbons that had been chosen for Danielle, and saw that the Indian girl was as delighted as the intended recipient would have been.

As she had expected, they stayed the night, and again there was smoking and feasting as well as music and dancing. Had it not been for Running Fawn, Soleil thought she would have enjoyed their stay far more than she did, and she was glad when Remie made it clear they would be leaving at dawn.

Somehow, after they had left the Micmac village behind them, the journey went more quickly. More often now they encountered fellow travelers, and their news increased Soleil's concern for her family.

"I don't like it," Remie told her after one such meeting. "The British took prisoners at Fort Beauséjour, including the priests, and carried them away on ships. No one knows exactly where they were taken, and conditions have deteriorated everywhere. Trading is prohibited between various settlements, and there are those who grow hungry because of it. If the good God had not provided bountifully of game and fish, the hunger would be starvation.''

They saw several new homesteads along the river since their earlier passage. Raw new cabins stood in recently cleared meadows; cows grazed where before there had been nothing but the animals of the forest.

''And damned lucky we are to have the cattle,'' one transplanted farmer told them angrily. ''Not that we didn't lose over half of them. The British were determined we would not escape with them, but we took to the woods with everything we could manage. At least we have a few left to start over with. Of course we have no bull, but two of these will freshen in the spring. We may have to interbreed them with their own offspring if we can't locate a bull by then.''

''You came from Chignecto?'' Remie asked quietly, while Soleil stood tense and apprehensive beside him.

''That we did. Born and grew up there. Had a house and a barn and a goodly number of acres,'' the farmer asserted. ''The British said if we left it we were guilty of abandoning the land to the enemy, by which they meant our own people who resisted them! Damn them to hell!'' The man spat for emphasis. Then he added stiffly, ''We saw the smoke behind us for two days, where they burned the house and the barn.''

He was not the only one who spoke in this way, although very few had been as lucky as his family, who had at least gotten away with some of the cattle and chickens and a few sheep, and most of their household goods. For many, they arrived at their destinations along the St. John with no more than the clothes they wore and perhaps a blanket or two and a cooking pot.

Almost always, however, before the conversation was concluded, the farmer would add, ''We give thanks to the good God that we escaped with our lives.'' Sometimes, however, the sentence would end with something like ''Except for Pierre, who died of fever along the way, when there was no shelter and the weather was so bad.'' Or it was Marguerite or Grand-maman or Agnès or Bernard.

Soleil listened with growing anxiety, but so far there had been no mention of trouble at Grand-Pré. Please, Blessed Mother, she murmured inwardly, and then wondered why the Blessed Mother should be any more protective of the Acadians at her own village than of any of these other people, who also regularly knelt in their devotions.

"Perhaps we would be better off to cross the Bay of Fundy than to go back the way we came," Remie speculated as they neared the lower end of the valley. "It sounds as if even game might be hard to come by, with so many British soldiers quartered on the Chignecto."

The settler to whom he spoke aloud his thoughts shook his head. He was a man of middle years, with a half-dozen sons and nearly as many daughters and another infant on the way, if Soleil judged correctly the condition of his wife.

"My own guess, *monsieur*, is that you'd be safer taking to the woods than the water. The British ships are all over the place, intercepting so-called illegal cargoes, confiscating boats. They do not want our people to cross the water, and the patrols have increased fourfold in the past weeks."

"We carry no contraband," Remie protested.

The older man glanced shrewdly at the bundles in the canoe Remie was about to launch. "Nothing from Québec, *monsieur*? Or from the Indians to the west? If there's a taint of the French on it, or anything from the Indians, be assured it will be considered contraband. And the penalties for smuggling are very high." His faded gaze slid toward Soleil. "I would not want to risk it, with a woman to be left alone if I guessed wrong."

Soleil's heart beat heavily. Neither route seemed to offer safety. She was mildly relieved, however, when Remie decided to retrace their original route. The idea of crossing the Bay of Fundy reminded her of the Minas Channel, chilling her even in the summer sunshine.

"Stick to the woods, well clear of the settlements," the farmer advised. "Travelers come through nearly every day who have managed it, if they were careful."

"All right. Thank you for the meal, and the advice." Remie gestured toward Soleil to get into the canoe so that he could push off. "May God bless you, my friend."

The words of the farmer drifted toward them across the narrow expanse of water as they set off again. "God's blessing on you, too, *monsieur*, *madame*."

And they went on toward home.

26

A BURNED CABIN stood in the clearing where they crossed the Petitcodiac. They could smell it for half an hour before they reached it, and Remie moved cautiously ahead, musket ready to fire, should that be necessary.

He paused when he arrived at the edge of the woods, surveying the damage. There was an additional stench now, and Soleil stiffened, trying not to breathe through her nose, fighting nausea.

"A dog," Remie said. "Looks like they bayoneted it."

He moved forward and she followed, praying there would be no more than the unfortunate dog. The clearing was hot and silent. Everyone had fled at least a few days earlier, yet Soleil kept forgetting to draw in air, dreading an encounter with a soldier who might have stayed behind.

Even in the woods beyond the ruined cabin she felt as if there were eyes and ears marking their progress, lying in wait for them.

However, nothing happened. Remie walked so quietly that no one could have heard him coming, but Soleil had not yet entirely mastered that feat. Whenever a twig snapped under her foot she expected a shot in the back; her chest began to ache with the tension.

After the third such charred homestead in less than two days, Remie decided to give up following established trails. They would be safer in the woods.

The only sign of strain was that he was even less talkative than usual. They no longer dared build a cooking fire, for fear it would be seen by the soldiers, and Soleil realized why he had traded with the Micmacs for jerky and smoked fish when they could easily have provided food for themselves in the forest. Remie had known they would have to do without fires.

Apprehension was a constant companion. Soleil felt as if her stomach would never settle down. She no longer slept well, waking at every sound in the darkness, and sometimes she knew that Remie, too, had awakened, though he didn't usually speak.

In the middle of the afternoon, three days' east of the first of the ruined cabins, an apparition stepped suddenly out of a heavy grove of beeches. Soleil thought her blood had congealed in her veins. She came to a halt and stretched out a hand to steady herself against one of the big trees.

In a matter of seconds she realized this was no British soldier, but the trembling went on, and she felt sick to her stomach. How long could she live this way, constantly fighting fear?

"Greetings, friend," Remie said. He, too, had stopped, though he carried his musket as casually as ever.

Now that her initial panic had passed, Soleil could see that the man was old and feeble. His garments hung in shreds on an emaciated frame, exposing grimy hide through the rents in the fabric. He spoke in a raspy voice that suggested he had grown unused to conversation.

"Greetings," he echoed.

Remie stared past him, as if looking for companions. "Are you alone, *monsieur*?"

"Alone," the old man confirmed. "Everybody else is dead."

A shudder ran through Soleil. She wanted to touch Remie, but he was not quite near enough.

The man carried nothing—no weapon, no food. Indeed, he appeared not only unwashed but long unfed, so it wasn't surprising that Remie reached for his pack. "Are you hungry, *monsieur*? We were about to pause for a bite to eat."

"Could you share it, I'd be obliged," the old man conceded with a dignity that was touching, considering his condition. "Though my teeth don't allow me to chew jerky very well."

"We've smoked salmon," Remie said, and proceeded to take out a packet of it. He squatted on the ground, back against a tree, and motioned Soleil down, too, without looking at her. After a moment their guest also sat, cross-legged; saliva glistened at the corners of his mouth at the aroma of the smoked fish.

They shared the simple meal, and the old man gave them their first news report in a week. Soleil, though hungry, decided she couldn't eat and listen to this at the same time.

The old man, whose name was Olivier Gaudet, had lived with his grandson and his wife and their three small children. He gestured vaguely to indicate the location of their cabin. The soldiers had come in their scarlet coats with their muskets and bayonets. His grandson, Germain, had reached for his own firearm and been shot down.

"Like a dog," M. Gaudet related. "He bled to death on his own doorstep. The others tried to flee to the woods, and the English killed them all, even the youngest, who was only five years old, *monsieur*. The British pigs killed the little ones while their mother screamed and tried to protect them. They would have killed me, as well, no doubt, had I not been hidden in the outhouse. I grieve that I was too cowardly to come out until they had gone, and then I wished I had allowed them to find me. They took all the flour, the peas, everything. The chickens and the cow. All gone to feed their troops."

He ate the salmon greedily, licking his fingers when it was gone, then wiping them on what remained of his trousers.

"You are brave—" or foolish, his tone suggested "—to take your lady through this country. There are few Acadians left free; they took most of them away on the ships."

"To where?" Remie asked quietly.

M. Gaudet shrugged bony shoulders. "Who knows, *monsieur*? They have not been seen since."

Soleil's indignation finally overcame her fear. "And the settlers, they do nothing? Nothing to protect themselves?"

M. Gaudet spread his hands in a gesture of helplessness. "What can they do, *madame*? Each man has one musket against dozens. Many abandoned their farms and I do not know what has happened to them. My grandson swore he would never give up his land."

Like Émile, Soleil thought numbly. Her father, too, insisted he would not give up his land.

M. Gaudet returned his attention to Remie. "You have heard that the soldiers have given a new name to the fort? It is now Fort Cumberland." The English pronunciation was awkward on his French tongue. "The redcoats are everywhere. They take every morsel of food, every head of livestock. They burn the houses and the crops in the fields. They even put the torch to our churches. On one such occasion the farmers tried to beat them back with hammers, hoes and axes, and they left twenty-nine of the British dead. But more soldiers came, the church and the rest of the houses were razed, and what had they accomplished? Nothing, *monsieur*. We are too few against too many, and they cut off our food supplies.''

In the silence a bird twittered from the beech tree overhead. The old man sighed and began to pull himself stiffly to his feet. ''I am most grateful for the food, *monsieur*. I wish you and your lady a safe journey.''

A moment later he vanished into the woods.

Remie turned to her with a faint smile. ''Well, the sooner we go on and get away from here, the better off we'll be.'' The smile faded. ''You didn't eat much.''

''I'm not hungry. It makes me ill to think of those poor people. Slaughtered, as if they were no more than animals. Even helpless women and children.''

''It's bad,'' Remie admitted, putting an arm around her, holding her to his side for a comforting moment. ''But that will not happen to us. Keep the fish out and try to eat it. You can't travel without food.''

She did not talk about her fear for her family as they went on, but it was there, deep and disturbing.

Within another day they had seemingly passed through the dangerous area where the British were exercising their brutality. Though settlers were wary, there were no more burned-out farms, yet food remained scarce.

''Flour's in short supply,'' they were told. ''And peas— damned English won't let a ship touch shore with supplies. Not much gets through from Louisbourg, either. They've increased the patrols from Halifax.''

Just saying the names the English had given to formerly Acadian towns left a bad taste in the mouth.

Still, except for the embargo on food and other goods, no one here was suffering, and Remie and Soleil headed south at last toward the Minas Basin, hope building that they would find all as they had left it months earlier.

They moved more quickly on established trails; they cooked over open fires; they slept more easily, though a deer crashing through the brush brought them awake in a hurry, and the musket was never far from Remie's hand.

A day's walk from the Minas Basin, Soleil began to dwell inwardly on the crossing that would soon have to be made. She was now a far more seasoned traveler and more expert paddler and would help Remie make the journey across the channel more quickly, but she remembered the threat of the bore and wished they did not have to face it again. The only alternative was taking the long way around the eastern end of the basin, many miles and many days farther, however, and she did not want to delay their homecoming even if Remie would have considered such a thing.

The blackberries were ripe, and they stopped for the night early enough so that Soleil could pick a batch for supper. She ate of them ravenously, promising that when she had a kitchen, she would bake some in a pie.

"Only a few days more, now," Remie said, sounding more relaxed than she had heard him in a long time.

She woke the next morning to the smell of smoke and frying fish. Remie squatted beside the fire, grinning when she lifted her head. "Come on, sleepyhead. Tonight we should camp on the bluff over the basin, if we get an early start."

Groggily Soleil crawled out and staggered into the nearby brush to relieve herself. Strangely enough, the customarily appetizing aroma of food held no appeal as she headed back for the camp fire. In fact, before she reached it she was stricken with a wave of violent nausea that ended with her retching into a bush. She was weak and trembling when she finally emerged beside the fire.

Remie looked up and saw her, pale beneath her tan. "Something wrong?" he asked, rising to his full height and taking a few steps toward her.

"I feel . . . terrible," she said, leaning against him, though already the nausea was subsiding.

He hugged her, thinking. "How long is it, my love, since your last bloody show? More than a month, surely?"

She drew back from him, astonished, for during the frightening time of crossing the Chignecto isthmus, avoiding the

British soldiers, she had given little thought to the matter. "Remie . . . do you think that's it? Oh . . ." She calculated rapidly, then joyously. "Oh, Remie! A baby! Are we going to have a baby?"

He was laughing, hugging her again. "I'd say there's a good chance, unless you got a bad fish yesterday, and it didn't make *me* sick! I told you the Madawaska Valley would be lucky for us!"

Her indisposition was rapidly fading. They kissed and hugged again, and then he swung her off her feet and danced around the fire. "Our first son," he said, and she countered with "Our first daughter," as they dissolved in happy laughter.

There was no time to dwell on the prospect of parenthood, of course. Not when they had to pack up and get moving. But when Remie turned to offer her a hand to get over a tree trunk that had fallen across the path, or when he simply glanced over his shoulder to see how she was doing, there was a renewed gentleness in his touch, a new tenderness in his smile.

Soleil had plenty of time to reflect on the business of pregnancy, however. Occasionally she would look down with wonder at her flat stomach, touching it almost reverently, praying that it was so, that she carried Remie's child.

The joy of it carried her through the rest of the journey. Even crossing the Minas Channel was not as daunting because of her exultant imaginings, except that she realized that if the canoe were to be caught in the bore and sucked down into the swirling red waters, the child would die with her.

"Nothing will happen to the babe, nor to you," Remie told her as they pushed off, as if he read her thoughts, and she chose to believe him.

The red cliffs drew nearer, the bore was safely bypassed, and they climbed the path to the top of the bluff, spirits rising with every step. For from here on the route was familiar even to Soleil.

They reached Grand-Pré with its multitude of houses inhabited by people she had known her entire life; they were greeted with surprise and pleasure on all sides.

Some new soldiers were among those garrisoned at the fort, but there did not seem to be many more than usual. Though the redcoats stared at them coldly, they were not challenged in any way as they walked past the blockhouse.

And finally they were on the path to the Cyr place, footsteps quickening—Soleil would have run if Remie had not held her back. Every leaf, every tree, seemed beloved, welcoming her home. She had left a mere girl, a bride, and she returned a mature woman, soon to be a mother.

When they came into the final clearing, she pulled free from Remie's hand. She dashed the final hundred yards to the doorway where she could hear the blessing being asked over the evening meal in her father's measured tones.

"Mama, Papa," she cried, "we're home! We're home!"

27

FOR THE FIRST TIME Soleil could remember, Émile interrupted a prayer, leaping to his feet. "Soleil! Barbe, it is our daughter, returned to us by the grace of God!"

He reached for Soleil, hugging her until she was nearly crushed, then released her to look down into her eyes, tears in his own. "You have changed! You used to be a soft little girl, and now you are stronger, harder, a woman! And Remie— welcome, my son, welcome! You have taken good care of our girl!"

Remie was grinning, lowering his pack into a corner behind the door. "I told you I would, Papa. How goes it here?"

There was a babble of voices as the meal was forgotten, everyone rising from the table to greet the newcomers. Soleil thought her heart would burst with joy.

Her family was the same, yet each one a little different, too. In the flurry of hugging and kissing and asking questions that were not immediately answered, it was some time before the subtle changes began to register with her.

Barbe wept openly with joy; she and Soleil clung together fiercely, letting their tears mingle on their cheeks. And when Barbe at last stepped back, remembering that the family had been about to eat, Soleil feasted her gaze upon her mother.

"No, no!" Barbe protested when Soleil prepared to help with the dishing up. "You are guests tonight, at least! Danielle, two more plates, if you please! Make room there on the end, François! Sit down, you two, before the food grows entirely cold!''

Had her mother had that much gray in her hair before they went away? Soleil wondered with a pang. Yet, except for her hair, she looked the same as always. Soleil accepted the filled plate and began to eat hungrily, but she was almost as starved for these familiar faces and voices.

Émile was grinning broadly, happily. It was not until some of the tumult of the family welcome had died down and his face fell into repose that the difference in him became apparent. The lines were deeper around his eyes and mouth, and his wide shoulders sagged perceptibly, as if he'd grown older and wearier while she was away.

Danielle, Soleil saw with amusement, had finally achieved a respectable bosom. And judging by the younger girl's pretty face, along with the developing figure, she was probably no longer regarded by the young men as a child. At thirteen she approached womanhood, and she had more than likely chosen the man to make that transformation complete. Was it still Basile Lizotte, or had some other youth supplanted her first love?

Soleil's gaze moved around the table as she ate. Henri and Vincent had grown incredibly over the summer, though Vincent retained his baby fat while Henri was simply taller. Grand-père was nodding and smiling; *he* was exactly the same.

Pierre's slow smile seemed unchanged at first, and then she thought she detected a difference even in him. A woman, Soleil surmised, and smiled back at him. Pierre had met someone who would perhaps take the place of his Aurore. Since he was seated across the table, she leaned forward to speak directly to him over the chatter among the others. ''Who is she, Pierre?''

For a moment he hesitated, and then the smile deepened. ''Cécile Meignaux,'' he admitted, torn between pride and sheepishness.

Soleil hid her surprise. Cécile was only Danielle's age, or perhaps a year older. Pierre was nearly twenty-five, and he had two young sons to raise.

''Have the banns been read?'' she asked, under cover of a burst of general hilarity over something Remie had said.

"Not yet. But soon, I think." Understanding passed between them, and for a moment they were very close.

Antoine's voice cut through the laughter. "What news do you bring, Remie? Passed you by Fort Beauséjour? We don't like what we hear from there."

"Nor do I," Remie said, sobering, as the others around the table fell silent. "The English have left little but charred remains on most of the farms, and they've renamed the fort. We talked to many who were driven west, their lands confiscated, to start over in the wilderness."

Émile lifted a commanding hand. "No, not tonight! Tonight we do not talk tragedy or politics! We celebrate! Bertin, bring out the wine, that we may all drink a toast to Soleil and Remie, safely returned home!"

Jacques, who had also added an inch or so to his height during their absence, piped up for the first time. "Can I have some wine, too, Papa?"

"Why not?" Émile said in a burst of generosity. "Even your mama must admit that this is a special night, and everyone must celebrate!"

Henri, who had often admired the ruby color of the wine, made his own timid request. "And I, Grand-papa? May I taste it, too?"

"No, no," Barbe protested, "you are still only a baby!"

Before the little boy's face could pucker up with disappointment at being excluded, however, Émile overruled his wife. "A tiny sip won't hurt him. Here you are, lad, see how you like the best French wine ever to slip past the British patrols!"

They all waited with interest for the child to take a sip. Henri swallowed a mouthful with a gulp, as if it were fresh milk from the cow, then choked and stared at the others around the table in horrified astonishment. "It's poison!" he cried, to the laughter of everyone except his grandmother.

"I told you he was too young," Barbe said, wiping Henri's chin with a corner of her apron.

"Yes," Émile agreed, "but now *he* believes that. How about you, Vincent? Do you want a taste, too?"

The youngest member of the assembly, big-eyed at his brother's reaction, shook his head emphatically. "No, thank you, Grand-papa." There were more hoots of amusement as Émile began to pour the wine for the others.

When they had all been served, Remie sent Soleil a questioning glance, then, interpreting her smile, he proposed a toast. "To the next Cyr grandchild, and the first son of Remie and Soleil Michaud, to put in his appearance about the end of next April!"

That announcement set off a new round of enthused congratulations, with both Barbe and Danielle rising from the benches to hug Soleil tightly.

Only when the hubbub had died down could Soleil ask the question that had remained uppermost in her mind. "Is there any word of Louis and Madeleine?"

Immediately the room quieted. "No," Émile said, subdued. "We have heard nothing. We can only pray that they had departed from the mainland before the British reached Beaubassin."

"Word would surely have reached you by now if that were not the case," Remie assured them. "There are still many travelers on the trails to carry news."

They drank the wine, and Bertin was dispatched for more, which they finished, as well. Before they all retired for the night, Émile led them in family prayer, kneeling before the benches that flanked the long table, giving thanks for the safe return of the travelers, asking His blessings upon those who were absent.

Tired and pleasantly relaxed from the unaccustomed consumption of the wine, Soleil and Remie retired to the room where they had spent their wedding night. That seemed much longer ago than it had actually been.

"Pierre and the little boys have been sleeping here," Soleil said, feeling slightly guilty for dispossessing them. "I suspect that he is expecting to bring Cécile here as his bride before long."

Remie grinned, snuffing the candle. "It's a good bed for a newly married couple. It got us off to an excellent start, didn't it? Rather different from a moose hide spread on the ground."

"I never minded sleeping on the ground," Soleil said truthfully.

"As long as I'm sleeping with you, it doesn't matter where."
Remie reached for her in the darkness. "Let's see if the magic
is still here, before you grow round and fat and have to be
helped to your feet when you get down on the ground."

"I've never been so happy in my entire life," Soleil murmured contentedly, before the words were cut off by Remie's
mouth on hers.

Now she had everything she'd ever wanted, except the baby,
and for a moment she pressed a hand against her belly where
that last wonderful wish was being fulfilled. Life, she thought
gratefully, could not be more wonderful.

BY MIDMORNING of the following day, however, reality began
to intrude upon Soleil's euphoric state.

The first thing she noticed was Remie and the twins in earnest consultation in the yard outside. There was, she saw with
a twinge of apprehension, nothing boyish about either of her
brothers as they spoke to her husband. Nor was there humor in
any of their faces when he responded.

As she wiped the last breakfast dish—they had sat overlong
at the meal, something that had never happened before in the
Cyr household—Soleil paused to stare out the window. The
prickle along her spine made her press a hand for a moment
against the belly that protected her babe. She wanted so much
for this child! Please, God, let him be born into a life as content and as safe as her own had been!

"How are things, really, Mama?" she asked quietly.

Somehow she expected Barbe to smile and reassure her. To
her dismay, her mother was slow in replying, and then there was
strain in both words and voice. "Not good, I'm afraid."

Danielle, stirring the kettle where the noon meal already
simmered aromatically, swung around to face her sister.
"You've heard no news from Grand-Pré?"

"No. We met no travelers going north from here." Her scalp
seemed to tighten with sudden tension.

"The British grow more hostile by the day," Barbe said
alarmingly. "Even your father must admit that they are no
longer to be trusted." She hesitated before elaborating in a
rush. "In early June, troops came from Fort Edward, pretending to be on a fishing trip. No one thought anything of their

asking to be given quarters in various houses rather than sleeping in barns, as they have done in the past. Our neighbors took them in, fed them, treated them with the utmost civility, and they laughed and drank Acadian wines, as if they were our friends."

Her throat worked, and Danielle, her face stormy, interjected angrily, "They waited until everyone had gone to sleep, and then they rose in the middle of the night and confiscated all the guns and the ammunition! Like thieves, no longer laughing or friendly! They put the guns on a boat and sent them off to Pisiquid, saying that the authorities had need of them!"

" 'Tis true," Barbe said wearily when Soleil turned to her in distress for confirmation. "Georges Dubay and his sons lost all but one musket the soldiers didn't find. So did many others."

"No one stopped them? No one stood up to them?" Soleil heard her own words and realized how much her views on such matters had changed over the past few months. There had been something in seeing the burned cabins, the destroyed crops, the ragged refugees that had perceptibly altered her concept of the British soldiers to whom she had previously given little thought.

"In the middle of the night?" Barbe asked quietly. "Wakened from a sound sleep, reaching for weapons that were no longer readily at hand but aimed at themselves? No, no one stopped them. Thank the good God that none of them were quartered here. As it is, there has been much anger. The Blanchards lost several sheep to the wolves, and so did Guillaume Trudelle, because they had no weapons to protect their stock. The twins brought a dozen muskets from Louisbourg only a week ago, but at such a risk! I beg the Blessed Mother to protect them, but I fear for them so!"

The tears in her mother's eyes made Soleil reach for her, and they stood for a few moments in each other's arms.

When she had released Barbe, Soleil was unable to conceal her astonishment. "Papa knows they're smuggling? And he doesn't object?"

Barbe's mouth twisted in a wry parody of humor. "If there were not someone smuggling, I fear we'd all be the worse for it. The British blockades prevent our getting anything we haven't grown ourselves. Yes, Papa knows. He, too, is afraid, but they have persuaded him they are more clever than the soldiers. I pray they are right about that."

So Remie had been correct about the twins; they were not the carefree boys she had thought them. Soleil felt chilled, though the day was warm. "Surely," she said slowly, more to convince herself than the others, "the soldiers will not do here what they have done at Beaubassin."

"Why not?" Danielle demanded. "What's to stop them? Basile says they've taken away the boats of the fishermen in other villages, though not yet here, and Céleste was frightened half out of her wits only last week when one of the soldiers she thought was friendly to her challenged her right to wear a dress trimmed in French braid! She thinks she persuaded him that it came through trading with the Micmacs, though it was actually Antoine who brought it to her, and she was afraid they might throw him into jail, or worse, if they knew the truth!"

Soleil would have allowed herself to be sidetracked from the disturbing political issues to hear about her friend and Antoine, but Barbe went on.

"The Micmacs are withdrawing by the hundreds. Bertin went over only a few weeks ago to the village of Iron Eagle to trade for tobacco, and the entire encampment was gone. Vanished, overnight! Eventually Bertin found someone who knew about them, and 'tis said they've gone to Canada to avoid the British." She hesitated, then spoke with deep regret. "I fear your father may be wrong in thinking that things will go on as they have done for so many years under English rule. Their colonies to the south continue to grow, and they draw upon them for additional soldiers to enforce their cruel restrictions."

"A delegation was sent to Colonel Lawrence at Halifax to protest the taking of arms and boats," Danielle said, replacing the lid on the kettle without remembering to add the herbs she'd had ready. "They tried to explain to him that we must have arms to protect our families and our livestock. Since so many of the Indians have departed, the wild animals have increased, and they attack our cattle and even lone travelers! Pierre says the petition they presented pointed out that taking away our weapons would not increase our faithfulness to the government, only deprive us of the means to protect ourselves, but do you know what the Halifax council replied?"

She seemed to swell with indignation, and Soleil saw that in Danielle, too, the child was mostly gone.

"They decided, unanimously, that the petition that was so well reasoned out—and Pierre and Papa were consulted about it, so you know what it would have been like—! They decided it was highly arrogant and insidious and deserved the highest resentment! Can you imagine? They take our boats and our weapons, yet it is *we* who are arrogant! No wonder those who carried the petition refused to take the oath of allegiance immediately!"

It sounded worse with every word. Soleil moistened her lips. "What happened?"

"M. Grégoire pleaded that they be allowed to return home to consult with the others who helped draw up the petition," Barbe said quietly, dropping onto a bench as if her legs were too tired to hold her any longer. Her fingers restlessly folded and refolded a crease in her striped skirt. "Our entire delegation was imprisoned at once on George Island in Halifax Harbor. Except for M. Grégoire himself, who was freed when he was taken ill and barely made it home, they are still there. Not even his son was allowed to accompany him to look after him."

The chill had become an icy rock in Soleil's stomach. "Dear God," she breathed, in little more than a whisper. "What is to become of us?"

"What, indeed?" Barbe echoed, and never had Soleil heard such bitterness, such helplessness, in her mother's voice.

Her fingers trembled as she folded the dish towel and hung it to dry, and it was some time before she could even ask about her friend Céleste and the others.

Surely even Papa could see now that matters were not going to blow over easily. And if that were the case, what would they do?

What would the British *allow* them to do?

28

EXCEPT FOR THE PRIESTS, who because of their French ancestry and their Catholic convictions were regarded by the British as mortal enemies, the Acadians had no one in a position of leadership or authority to speak on their behalf.

There were no magistrates, for there was virtually no crime. Smuggling was considered a criminal activity only by the British conquerors; to the Acadians, it was simply a survival tactic to which they had been driven by the irrationality of those in power over them. When a dispute arose between any two citizens, either the pair worked it out themselves or the matter was submitted to arbitration by their neighbors.

In a question of civil disagreement, such as land boundaries, the official government declined to rule. The more cynical among the Acadians suggested this might be, in fact, a refusal to set a legal precedent acknowledging that the Acadians had rights of any kind to the land the British now wanted for their own settlers.

As the only educated individuals among the French-speaking people, the priests were of necessity the ones who wrote out the petitions and protests against increasingly punitive British regulations. But everyone agreed it was pointless to depend on the priests to take their own articulate arguments to their rulers. The mere sight of a cleric's garb was enough to send Colonel Lawrence and his adjutants into a rage, it was said, for they blamed the priests for inciting the populace against them.

In some measure this was unfair, for it was primarily the renegade Abbé Le Loutre who actively led the savages against the British settlers. For the most part, the rest of the priests only counseled, according to their concern and their consciences, that their flocks refuse to submit to the demanded oath until the paragraph was inserted into it exempting them from fighting either their own people or the Indians who had befriended them.

Émile had sincerely believed that because the situation had existed for so long without bloodshed—or nearly so—it would eventually be resolved. Other than a few hotheads, the Acadians could hardly have been a less aggressive people. They didn't care who ruled them, as long as they were left to their own pastoral lives. Anyone with an ounce of intellect, he thought, would see that signing the oath would not guarantee that there would never be an uprising of the Acadians against the British; only trust could do that, and the British were making it harder and harder to trust *them* in any regard whatever. On the other hand, the Acadians themselves were completely trust-worthy; they took their oaths seriously and would feel bound to the death by whatever they were forced to sign, which was why they refused to make the promise that might pit them against their own.

It was clear to both Soleil and Remie that during the months they had been gone, Émile had suffered a great disillusion-ment about the basic integrity of the British. He no longer protested, or only feebly, against dinner-table talk of anger and frustration, though he still made at least token protest against proposed armed rebellion.

"Breaking the law will never help us," he said, his words quickly buried like the red mud in the tides by the vehement words of his sons.

It was no longer just the twins who were angry. Pierre, though he was still thoughtful and considered his opinions be-fore he voiced them, had grave doubts about remaining in Grand-Pré. He said little at table—"Because it upsets Papa," he explained—but was quite frank in speaking to his sister and brother-in-law.

"If it weren't for Papa, and Mama, too, I would follow Louis's course. Not to Île St. Jean necessarily. I hope the re-ports of food shortages there are exaggerated, but I would not risk taking my children there, or a bride." Faint color touched his tanned face at the oblique mention of Cécile Meignaux. "But there is a vast continent to the west with much land as yet unclaimed by anyone. The British surely don't need it all. There must be a place for a man to raise his family in safety and plenty, perhaps up that St. John you've spoken about, Remie."

"It's safer than here," Remie agreed, while Soleil shivered beside him. "Have you tried to talk your papa into leaving while there is still time? What happened on the Chignecto may well happen here sooner or later."

"Will it be sooner, do you think?" Pierre ran an agitated hand through his crisp dark curls. "Or do we have at least un-til the spring to decide? Papa is weakening, I believe. At least he listens to us now, which is more than he's done in the past, though he still tries to convince himself the British will even-tually settle down and leave us to our own devices. I can no longer believe that way. Given a winter to persuade him . . . do we have until spring, do you think? The summer is nearly gone now, and he'd never walk away and leave the hay in the fields, the garden unharvested."

Remie shifted his weight uneasily. "I don't know, Pierre. I hope so. The British had to draw on troops from Boston to reinforce their local ones in order to sweep over Fort Beauséjour. I shouldn't think they'd have time to make another major effort before winter."

Pierre silently assessed this information, then sighed. "And you, Remie? What do you plan?"

"To return to the Madawaska Valley before the snow falls," Remie said at once, "and build a cabin to winter in. In the spring, after the baby comes and I've taken my furs to Québec, I'll clear enough land to keep a few cattle and sheep, and perhaps enlarge the cabin. There's plenty of land available for all of you if you choose to join us. I know Soleil would be thrilled if Mama Barbe could be there for her confinement, though that would mean traveling before the frost goes out of the ground."

Pierre leaned back against a beech tree, drawing up a knee to rest the sole of one foot on the trunk behind him. "How do they seem to you, Mama and Papa?"

"Older," Soleil said softly. "But they're still well, aren't they?"

"Yes. So far. But this damned political situation takes its toll. One thing I can tell you—it may be possible to lead Papa, but it's not possible to push him. He must be convinced that leaving Grand-Pré is the best thing to do, and there are times I wish I could punch the twins in the mouth and make them keep still, because I almost believe Papa would come around better if they backed off a bit! I've tried to tell them that, but they're as irrepressible as the tides!"

"Maybe I can talk to them," Remie said thoughtfully. "And I'll remember not to pressure Papa. Only, perhaps, to lure him to a safer place. With subtlety, of course."

Please God, Soleil prayed, let the two of them succeed. The thought of delivering her first baby so far away, without Mama, frightened her a little. How wonderful it would be if the entire family—maybe even Louis and Madeleine, too—could congregate in the Madawaska Valley, far from the British they all hated and feared!

SOLEIL'S MORNING SICKNESS quickly dissipated. She had never felt better in her life. Her appetite was enormous, so that Remie teasingly proposed sleeping in the barn because there would soon be no room in the bed for both of them.

"Go ahead," Soleil agreed pertly. "No doubt the babe will sleep better, too, without his father snoring beside me."

Remie immediately retracted his idea. "He will sleep best if his father's arm is around his mother and he is kept safe. Very well, I'll allow myself to become accustomed to a wife who is shaped like an apple rather than a reed."

In truth her clothes had not even grown tight on her, though that surely would happen before much longer. And as long as she didn't show, she could enjoy the music and the dancing and renewing her friendships.

Each new social encounter led to speculative glances at her waistline, with most women deducing at once that she was pregnant. When they guessed aloud, Soleil blushingly admitted it was true, and thanked the Blessed Mother that she had not returned home this long after her wedding day having failed to conceive.

Danielle confessed that Basile Lizotte had not yet proposed, but it was obvious that she had no worries that he would. "In the spring, no doubt," she said with a complacency that struck her sister as comical, coming from one so young. "He mentioned ever so casually that he and his father are going to build an addition on their house as soon as the hay is in."

"And you're certain it's for you and Basile," Soleil said, amused.

"Why else would they need it? All his sisters are married and have homes of their own, and his brother and sister-in-law have a room of their own. I should be rather embarrassed to have to sleep in a corner of the kitchen, the way Pierre and Aurore did, with no privacy whatever. I suppose it's different when you've been married for a time, but it would be dreadful to spend one's wedding night in the kitchen where anyone might walk through on the way to the outhouse."

"No one would do that," Soleil assured her. "Not the first night, anyway. Would Mama mind if I walked over to see Céleste right away, do you think? I can't wait to see her!"

Barbe entered the kitchen at that point, carrying the side of pork to be put on the spit for the evening meal. "Go! Go! I remember what it was like to be a young bride, eager to tell my best friend all my secrets!" She was smiling, happy, yet the smile did not completely erase the new lines in her face, Soleil noted with a pang of regret. Her parents had both aged far more than they should have in the few months she had been away from them.

It was easy to put her worries into the back of her mind, however, when she reached the Dubay house. Céleste flew into her arms, and for a few moments they laughed and cried together. "Mama," Céleste called over her shoulder, "I'll be back in a little while, but we must have an hour or so to talk first, all right? Come on, Soleil, let's walk on the dyke!"

Soleil could hardly wait to be out of hearing of the Dubays before putting to Céleste the question that had been tormenting her. "How is it between you and Antoine?"

Céleste's brown hair blew around her face in spite of the cap that should have contained it. Her smile was rueful. "I think it's never been better, but he's afraid to commit himself to a wedding while affairs are in such a state. He says he may have to fight—he's determined no one shall ever confiscate his musket as the English did ours—and that it wouldn't be fair to me to be his wife if he's going to get into trouble."

"It's true, then. The British *did* take your arms."

"All but the musket Papa had left in the barn, hidden under the hay."

Soleil's dark eyes were round. "He expected some such treachery?"

"No, not really. He'd simply left it out there because twice he's seen wolves when he was milking, and he wanted the musket handy. He had a pail in each hand when he came to the house so he left the gun there, and the hay fell over. He hadn't actually tried to conceal it. Of course he was very bitter and wished he'd hidden them all."

"I don't know what Papa would do if they took his weapons," Soleil murmured, once more deeply concerned.

"They came as friendly as anything," Céleste told her, ignoring her skirts which whipped in the wind. "Going fishing in the morning, made arrangements for Mama and me to feed them at dawn and promised to bring us fish for supper! They played cards and sang in the evening, and two of them flirted with me, laughing and asking why I didn't settle for a good Englishman who would one day take me back to a civilized country! And all the time they were planning to rise up at midnight and frighten us all to death and point our own muskets at us!"

"Remie is worried about what they're going to do," Soleil said slowly. "Even Pierre thinks everyone should leave before the British take a notion to punish the innocent along with the guilty."

"And Antoine is one of the guilty, did you know that?" Warm color suffused Céleste's face. "When I finally became suspicious of his mysterious trips off into the forests and accused him, he admitted it! He and François and the Lizotte brothers—"

"Basile?" Soleil demanded, feeling a rush of sympathy for her sister.

"Hah! Basile hasn't the courage of a rabbit. No, it's Claude and Alain, would you ever have guessed it? Claude has always been an idiot, but Alain? And they have been going off to raid the British settlements as well as to trade with Louisbourg for years, since they were little more than children! And no one else ever knew it!"

So Remie had been right. The twins were in deeper than she had ever dreamed, and the idea chilled her. Soleil turned her face to the sun, but its warmth failed to penetrate.

"What's to become of us all?" she wondered aloud.

"I don't know, I'm sure. But I've told Antoine that I want to be married, even if there is some risk in it. There's no less risk to him, staying single, and perhaps if we were married I could talk some sense into him—"

Céleste stopped, her eyes welling with tears. "And that's a dream, isn't it? I'll never be able to change him. Antoine is Antoine. And as long as Acadians are persecuted by the British, he'll find a way to fight them."

Without weapons? Soleil wondered. Oh, the Cyrs still had their muskets, but for how long? If only Remie and Pierre could persuade her parents to leave here for a safer place.

She stood looking out over the fields that had been so pains-takingly reclaimed from the sea, and then at the red waters that lapped at the other side of the dykes, until everything blurred through her own tears.

She, too, loved this place where she had grown up. For all that she knew the dangers of the sea, she loved it. That was one thing that was missing far up that Canadian river where Remie wanted to build a cabin: the sea, with its compelling tides and red sands.

Perhaps, she thought, some miracle would happen, and the Cyrs could continue to live here, and some day she and Remie could return as well.

Or was that, like Céleste's desire to settle Antoine down, no more than a dream?

For a few minutes the girls stood, holding hands, trying to draw courage and strength from each other. And then they turned and walked back toward the Dubay house, feeling as subdued as they were happy to be together again.

29

EVEN CHURCH SERVICES, which Soleil had dreamed of during her entire journey to Québec and back, were not the same.

Oh, Father Castin was there, and Father Chauvreulx, and though the sermon preached by the latter was familiar in its warning against sin, there were additional warnings, too, of a more secular nature.

The priests were grave, and so were the parishioners. There were fewer who rose during the service to have a smoke in the churchyard. And when they all filed out after the final bene-diction into the summer sunshine, there was more sober talk than friendly greetings.

It was true that Soleil and Remie were at once surrounded by old acquaintances who welcomed them back. And the women were, indeed, congratulatory about her pregnancy. However, even among the women, politics quickly crept into the conversations.

Having only just come from the Chignecto a few days earlier, Remie had more recent news than anyone else, and he was quickly surrounded by a sea of eager, anxious faces.

Soleil drew back with Céleste and Danielle and a few others, allowing the men their access to the newcomer. Soleil did not want to hear any of it again. In the few days since her return, she had heard the same stories repeated endlessly over the table at home and spilling out into the hay fields or along the dykes and every time two or more males of the family gathered in the yard.

She wanted to talk about babies and families and happy times ahead. Yet it was impossible not to be aware when Father Chauvreulx came through the crowd and spoke to her husband, impossible not to listen.

"Remie Michaud," the good Father said, his trained voice carrying over the others, so that everyone turned to face him. "I have only recently returned from Annapolis Royal, and I bring a message to be delivered to you upon your arrival."

Soleil's throat tightened with pride and love as her gaze settled on Remie. He was the handsomest of the lot with his thick dark hair and bronze skin.

"For me? From Annapolis Royal?"

"I spent some time there and visited with Father de Laval."

Immediately Remie's face changed. It was Father de Laval who had taught him to read and write, whose sermons Remie had known almost as well as the priest himself. "How is he, Father? He must be getting on for seventy years by now."

"Seventy-one," the priest confirmed. "His health is failing, I fear, as it must with us all, eventually. But his mind remains clear, and he remembers you with fondness. When I told him you had married a Grand-Pré girl, he expressed his good wishes for a long and happy marriage." Then, the conventional taken care of, Father Chauvreulx became serious. "He obviously looks upon you very nearly as a son. He is dying, Remie. His days are numbered, and his pain is considerable. He seemed to rally when I visited, as if simply talking of old times eased his discomfort, and when he asked me to, I agreed that I would urge you to visit him if you can. I know—as does he—that it is a lot to ask, for the journey is not an easy one in these uncertain times. Yet it would mean much to him if you could do it.''

Then, his message delivered, the priest smiled and reached out to pat the head of a small girl standing near his elbow. ''And how is that foot healing, eh, Claudette?''

Conversations were taken up again, yet Soleil did not hear any of them. She was watching Remie. She knew he felt he owed much to the old priest who had taken him in when no one else wanted him, who had trained and cared for him. Would he want to go to Annapolis Royal?

Had they returned home under any other circumstances, she would have anticipated that he would go at once, if the old priest was dying. Yet things were different now, weren't they? Remie was married, *she* was going to have a baby, and political unrest made hazardous many things that had previously been taken for granted.

She didn't have an opportunity to talk to Remie in private about the matter until long after they'd left the town and walked home. Dinner was a noisy meal; Céleste had been invited, as had Cécile Meignaux, and there was much laughter and teasing.

All of that was a relief after the tension in the churchyard; Soleil was glad to fall back into the old ways of enjoying her family after months away from them. She saw no signs of strain in Antoine or François, who were as outrageously amusing as ever, and it was obvious that Antoine and Céleste were mutually taken with each other.

It was harder to adjust to the idea of Pierre and Cécile as a couple. Cécile was a pretty little thing, but such a child. Though a little older than Danielle, she seemed younger. She said almost nothing, smiling shyly when addressed, and gazed at Pierre with worshipful eyes.

Was he in love with her, or did he merely feel the need of a wife and consider her the most easily available female? Soleil would have wagered that the girl knew little of the physical side of marriage, and hoped that she was not too much an infant to satisfy Pierre's desires.

It was not until late afternoon, when the older members of the family were half dozing and the youngest were playing quietly in the dirt outside the door, that Soleil brought up the subject of the priest. She and Remie had wandered toward the water, ostensibly to check the weir.

"Will you go? To Annapolis Royal?"

"To see Father de Laval?" He kicked a rock out of his path. "I'd like to. He's a grand old man, and I owe him a lot. He told me once that the only thing he regretted in becoming a priest was that it meant giving up having a family. He came from a large one, had twelve brothers and six sisters, and they were very close when he was a small child. He said he'd convinced himself that all his parishioners were his children, but it wasn't until he found me in rags and half starved and took me in that he truly felt he'd found a son." He laughed. "He took seriously the biblical admonition about sparing the rod. No father could have been more diligent about keeping me on the straight and narrow. Yet he never used the cane on me unfairly."

Something tightened in Soleil's chest. "So you'll go?"

Remie stopped and put his hands on her shoulders. "Would you mind very much if I did? I wouldn't be gone long. It's only a couple of days' journey each way if I travel alone, and you'd be with your family."

Why did she feel this inner tremor of dismay? Soleil tried to suppress it. "We've never been apart since we were married," she said softly.

"No. But it'll only be for a short time. He did so much for me, and I never really did anything for him."

"Except to be the nearest thing he ever had to a son."

"Yes," Remie agreed. "He made it clear that I was a trial to him, so it wasn't wholly a blessing. Just like real parents, I suppose. I've a lot to learn about being a father, since I never had a real one that I remember."

"You'll be a wonderful father," Soleil told him, and lifted her face for his kiss.

He was right to go to the old priest, she knew. Yet already, before he had even left, she felt an ache deep inside that was not eased even when they made love that night.

THOUGH ANNAPOLIS ROYAL had grown considerably, Father de Laval's house looked the same as it had years ago when Remie had gone there as a young boy. It was near dusk when he walked up the path and knocked on the stout wooden door.

He could smell the sea in the distance and the woodsy tang of cedars and firs, and over it all the fragrance of roasting meat, which set his mouth watering.

He had been away for a long time. Memories of his initial encounter with the priest came flooding back. Near starving, Remie had sought to snatch a pastry just transferred from oven to table in the kitchen, the compelling aroma luring him over the threshold when the priest's back was turned.

Remie had not been as agile in those days as he subsequently became. Though his clogs had worn out and he traveled barefoot, his desperation made him incautious, and Father de Laval turned and cornered him when the pastry proved too hot to handle.

Remie's howl of dismay—both at burning his hands and seeing the precious food dumped upon the wooden floor—turned to terror when the black-clad cleric fastened bony fingers on his ear and squeezed, holding him fast.

"What have we here, a thief?"

The voice was stern, the priest very tall.

Remie's wail died away; he was sure that he had only a few moments left to live.

"A novice thief," Father de Laval decided, maneuvering Remie by his ear over to the door, where he could get a better look at him. "You don't know the rules, boy. First of all, never attempt to steal from a priest. We don't have much to surrender. Besides that, we are willing to share freely what we *do* have. You've only to ask. Secondly, never steal anything that is too hot to touch." He squinted a little. "I don't know you, do I? You're not from my parish?"

Stricken mute, Remie made no reply.

"No. I've never seen you before. Where are you from?"

He didn't wait for a reply, however. He let go of Remie's ear, which continued to sting, but he remained blocking the doorway, so there was no escape. "I think we might rescue the pie. Fetch me that plate, and we'll see."

Not knowing what else to do, Remie complied. To his astonishment, when the pastry had been transferred from the floor to the plate, he was instructed to take a seat on the bench and given a fork and half of the pie. He might have fled while the priest said the brief blessing, but he was too befuddled to think of escape, and besides, there was the food in front of him.

When he stared in uncertainty at the old man—even then, the priest had been old—Father de Laval had picked up his own utensil. "Eat. You're hungry, aren't you, boy?"

Remie ate. He burned his mouth on the first few bites, but the pie cooled rapidly after having been broken into pieces, and it was ambrosia on his tongue. Chunks of meat and vegetables, and the pastry itself . . . Once urged, he wasted no time in cleaning his plate, swiping up the last of the gravy with a thick slab of bread.

"Now, tell me. Why did you attempt to steal my supper?" the priest asked when they had both finished. "Aside from being hungry, of course. Don't you have a home?"

Remie's story had emerged haltingly. He spoke about his uncle, Guillaume, and his aunt, Marie, and all their children. How they had taken him in, but in those days scarcely had enough food to go around for their own brood, and how Guillaume had flogged him for eating what was to have been a meal for the lot of them.

"So I thought . . . they didn't really want me," Remie concluded. "And I decided to fend for myself."

"And a fine job you've done of it, too, from the look of you," the old man said in that dry, acerbic way that Remie would soon become accustomed to. "Well, it just happens that I've need of a boy to run errands for me. I hurt my leg, you see, and I'm not walking as well as I'd like. So it is your duty to serve me until it is well."

Remie licked his lips. He had never met anyone like Father de Laval. His gaze flickered to the half loaf left in the middle of the table, and his voice was husky. "Does that mean I would eat with you, too?"

"Whatever I have, I will share," the priest promised readily. "That includes my house, but not my bed. You look as if you have lice. There is water in the bowl beside the door. Clean yourself, and I will find other garments for you to put on. The ones you wear can best be burned. Then I will find a pallet for you for the corner of this room. You do not snore, I trust?"

"N-no, sir," Remie responded. "I don't think so."

"Well, I've been told that *I* do. If it bothers you, don't mention it, for no doubt it is the Lord's will. Give me your garments and I will dispose of them."

Since no replacements had yet been produced, it seemed to Remie that this was getting the cart before the horse, but he handed over what was left of his shirt and trousers anyway. When he had scrubbed himself, he was again subjected to close scrutiny at the doorway, where the light was better.

"You call that clean?" Father de Laval asked caustically. "I've seen cleaner pigs. Let me show you what I mean by clean."

By the time Remie was allowed to retire for the night on the straw pallet, his skin tingled and stung from his scalp to the soles of his feet. But his belly was full, there was the promise of another meal the next morning, and some of his apprehension had abated.

He had lived with Father de Laval for nearly two years.

He hadn't thought of that first meeting for a long time. Remie was smiling when the door opened inward after his second knock.

The man who stood there was in clerical garb, but he was nothing like Father de Laval, being short and plump and at least thirty years younger. "Yes?" he asked in a neutral tone.

"I've come to see Father de Laval. My name is Remie Michaud—I lived with him for a time, years ago—and I was told that he is ill, that he asked for me." For a moment he feared from the expression of the younger priest that it was too late. And then the man stepped backward, pulling the door with him and allowing Remie to enter.

"I am Father Dubois," he said, his voice oddly high-pitched for one of his bulk. "Father de Laval is indeed most ill. I will take you to him, but only for a short time. He is very weak, and talking tires him."

The house was as Remie remembered it. Dim, smoky in the candlelight, with the remains of a meal on the rough-hewn table. They walked through the kitchen and into a room furnished only with a narrow bed and three pegs on the wall where a few garments hung.

Remie had prepared himself for the worst, he thought, but seeing his old friend was a shock, nevertheless.

Father de Laval turned his head as they entered, the younger priest leading and holding high a candle that cast its light over the old man's face. Pale and cadaverous, it was, with the dark eyes sunken deeply into the skull.

Yet there was intelligence in those eyes, and after a few seconds recognition came.

"Remie? Remie Michaud, who would have stolen my pastry?"

Father Dubois gave him a startled glance, but neither Remie nor Father de Laval noticed. Remie fell to his knees beside the bed, reaching out for the papery, blue-veined hand nearest him.

"One and the same," Remie told him, forcing a heartiness he did not feel. The old man's flesh was nearly gone, the bones sharply defined between Remie's fingers. "I had hoped to find you in better shape than Father Chauvreulx reported."

There was only the faintest pressure from the old hand he held, and the words were spoken with an effort, but there was no distress in them.

"Ah, my son, it is a great pleasure—no doubt the last I shall know!—to see you again. I have thought about you much these past few weeks." Amusement twitched at the bloodless lips. "You provided me with much entertainment when you came here all those years ago."

"I thought I provided mostly exercise for your arm, with the switch, and a sounding board for your sermons."

"Indeed. Both services of which I was in need. And now you are a married man, with a wife who is chaste and beautiful?"

"Chaste and beautiful," Remie agreed, unconsciously lowering his voice to the level of the old man's. "And pregnant, as well. In the spring we will have our first son."

Father de Laval nodded almost imperceptibly. "It would give me great pleasure to be the one to christen him. However, that is not to be. No, don't look that way, my boy. Did you learn nothing from me, after all? I have no fear of joining my Heavenly Father. He only calls me home, and it is time. My bones are old and tired, and I am ready. I will go more easily now that you have come to say goodbye."

"We need not say it quite yet, surely," Remie said, glancing up at the other priest. "I've no lice this time, Father. Perhaps there is still a pallet so that I might spend the night and in the morning talk with you again?''

"Of course. Father Dubois will see to it. And—'' amazingly, the dying man chuckled in a dry fashion ''—see to it, as well, Father, that M. Michaud is fed. He always had a good appetite. We'll talk again in the morning, as you say.''

But in the morning while the old priest still slept, there came a peremptory banging on the door. Before Father Dubois could waddle across the room to answer it, the door was kicked open and two soldiers entered the house.

Remie, who was finishing his morning meal, rose slowly to his feet, the beginnings of a frown on his face.

"This is the house of the priest, André de Laval,'' the taller of the soldiers said in a flat, hostile voice. He was not asking a question in his execrable French but stating a fact. His red coat was notably soiled, and he had not shaved as yet this day.

"Father de Laval is ill,'' Father Dubois stated, falling back before the pair as they advanced into the room. "What do you require of him?''

"We've come to place him under arrest,'' the soldier stated. "Direct us to him, if you please.''

There was a moment of thunderstruck silence, and then Remie burst into protest. "He's ill! He's not been out of bed in weeks!''

The gaze that raked him was contemptuous. "Our orders are that he is to be taken into custody.''

"But why?'' Father Dubois asked, squeaking like a frightened mouse. "What has he done, a man on his deathbed?''

"He is accused of sedition against the crown'' was the reply. "He will have his day in court when the time comes, no doubt.''

"But he's near death!'' Remie insisted, stalking forward to tower over the smaller pair. "You can't move him now!''

The slovenly soldier in charge jerked a thumb at his companion. "Call in the others. Devise a stretcher if need be. Get him out of here!''

The other soldier moved with alacrity; four more were called inside and disappeared into Father de Laval's tiny cubicle.

Remie watched, stunned. "This is insane! He can't possibly go anywhere, there's no need to arrest him! Leave him here where he can be cared for during the little time he has left!''

A great glob of spittle landed on the floor in front of Remie's feet. "Get out of the way," the soldier in charge commanded.

Rage boiled up through Remie, overwhelming his sense of caution where the British were concerned. "I'll be damned if I will," he said through his teeth. "Not until I've talked to your commanding officer. He can't be aware of Father de Laval's state of health or he'd never insist on arresting him!"

A malicious grin spread slowly over the English face. "You want to talk to my commanding officer, do you, Frenchman? Very well, you shall have the opportunity! Bolt, Seaton, put this man in chains! He shall travel to prison with his friend, the traitorous priest!"

And only then, as three muskets with bayonets closed in on him, did Remie realize what his outburst would cost him.

30

FOR THE FIRST FEW DAYS after Remie left, Soleil was too busy to miss him much during the day. She and Barbe and Danielle could not stop talking and laughing. Her mother and sister were eager to hear all about her journey to Québec, and especially about the famed walled city. On her part, Soleil could not get enough details of their lives—and those of their friends and neighbors—while she had been away.

The talk went on as they cooked and cleaned and worked in the garden, and it continued in the evenings when the family sat in the candlelight mending or knitting or repairing clogs, endless tasks that kept their hands as busy as their tongues.

It was only at night that Soleil grew lonesome. The bed was large and empty. There was no muscular masculine arm thrown over her, no delicious skin-to-skin contact, no soft breathing to stir the hair over her ear as Remie snuggled closer in his sleep.

Still, though she longed for him to return, she didn't worry about her husband. Confidently she prayed for him. A safe journey, a safe return. Had not the good God protected them so far?

Ten days had passed before she began to experience uneasiness. Annapolis Royal was not so far away; Remie could have been there and back by now, and she knew he would be missing her as much as she was missing him.

"No doubt the priest is dying, as Father Chauvreulx said," Barbe soothed her. "He would not want to go off and leave his friend—his father, almost—before the end."

Of course, that must be it, Soleil agreed.

Yet, as the hot days of summer slipped past one by one, her disquietude increased. Why did he not return? Her eyes grew strained watching the path for him, and her sleep was restless, too.

And then, on the first day of August, Father Chauvreulx from their own church in Grand-Pré was arrested and taken away. No one knew where; they could only speculate as to why.

Danielle brought the news. She had made the excuse of an errand in the village to create an opportunity to see Basile, who was working with his father and brothers on one of the dykes. But when she heard about the priest, she fairly flew home with the tale, even seeking out the men in the fields to tell them.

It was sobering, shocking. Their own priest was in prison somewhere, perhaps in Halifax, and Father Castin had disappeared as well—in hiding, Danielle's informant hinted, though there was no assurance of that.

Soleil listened, feeling as if the icy waters of a winter stream flowed through her veins. Remie was visiting a priest in Annapolis Royal, and clearly priests were being targeted by the British for persecution. The litany became almost continuous in her mind: Please, God, keep him safe!

VIOLENCE ERUPTED when a trio of small boys, no more than six or seven, commenced to throw rocks at a pair of the patrolling redcoats. A year ago, even six months earlier, the episode would have quickly ended when the children were scolded and taken home by their parents. Now they were not let off so easily.

"They arrested them—little children!" Bertin reported with indignation. "All their parents had to go to the blockhouse and speak with the commandant—or listen to him speak, rather! Guillaume says they were all lectured and threatened and told that next time such an incident takes place the boys will spend the night in prison! Imagine, boys as young as Guillaume's Jean!"

The community shared Bertin's indignation, but they contained their anger. They were not prepared to provoke the armed soldiers to further hostilities, for all that their own fury smoldered just beneath the surface.

More days passed, and still Remie did not come.

Fear was now a mantle over Soleil's heart. She continued to pray but with less conviction that God or the Blessed Mother was listening. At last she said the words aloud: "If Remie were all right, surely he would have returned by this time."

There was a moment of silence, and her fear intensified. It was obvious that the others, too, had come to that conclusion.

"It may be that he's having to come home by way of the woods," Pierre finally offered, "the long way, to avoid British patrols. They accuse everyone of smuggling these days, even when nothing of the sort is happening."

Émile roused himself from his own apprehensions to try to comfort his daughter. "Your Remie is a man of intelligence, well at home in the woods and the town alike. He can take care of himself."

Yet his primary job was to take care of *her*, and he did not return. All words of reassurance sounded false to Soleil. She cried herself to sleep that night and worried that her own state might somehow communicate itself harmfully to her baby.

Despite the general unrest, however, life went on. The hay was ready for harvesting; carrots and turnips and cabbages were packed into root cellars; those with sugar to spare made jams and jellies of the late-summer berries; and everyone watched the apple trees for the right time to pick them. Henri and Vincent decided the apples were ready, and the women were up that night dealing with their resulting bellyaches.

Movement throughout Acadia was curtailed because of British activity, and news came slowly, if at all. Under ordinary circumstances the inhabitants of Grand-Pré would have learned much earlier than they did about the events taking place to the north of them. As it was, they remained for too long in a hesitant, half-fearful, half-hopeful state.

In late August in the village of Chipoudy, which was situated below the mouth of the Petitcodiac River, to the west of what had once been called Fort Beauséjour, the English set fire to the church. They then burned a large number of houses, as well, and marched to do the same to more houses and several flax and wheat storage barns along the river, determined to make it impossible for the settlers to remain in that area.

However, before they could succeed in putting the torch to the latter buildings, they were surprised by the French commandant from Miramichi with his men and a band of Indians. A fierce battle ensued, with the English finally retreating after losing fifty men and sustaining another sixty casualties. During the fighting the residents fled to the woods to the west, knowing that they could never return to their homes but grateful for their lives.

None of them carried the news to the south, to Grand-Pré. There the people balanced on a tightrope of insecurity, continuing to hope that as in the past, all would eventually settle back into the uneasy peace they had had with the British for so many years.

And Soleil's personal anxiety reached a nerve-racking pitch. So quickly Remie had become the largest part of her life! She felt as if she had been married to him forever, and her emotional dependency on him was even greater than her physical dependency.

One morning, after a nearly sleepless night, she stared at her mother with reddened eyes and asked tremulously, "What will I do if he doesn't come back?"

Barbe did not make light of her fears. "You will do what women have always done. You'll make the best of it. But it's much too soon to give up on him, Soleil. Your Remie is a resourceful man, well accustomed to taking care of himself. Even if he is in trouble, be sure his mind is working furiously to get himself out of it."

And what if he were already dead? Soleil wondered despairingly. She could not tempt fate by putting that terrible thought into words, but it remained like an icy lump in her chest, a pressure that would not go away.

Barbe seemed almost to read her mind. "There is no reason to think any harm has come to him. When he can, he'll return home. Remember how many times the twins have stayed away overlong, so that we began to worry about them? And they always turned up, though sometimes a bit the worse for wear, with their jokes and their smuggled presents."

Soleil knew, now, that Antoine and François had not always been on such innocent excursions as a simple bit of illegal trading with Louisbourg. They had risked their lives in retaliating attacks on the British settlements. She wasn't sure her mother was aware of that, and Soleil didn't mention it now.

Yet Remie was not on a mission that should have been dangerous. He only went to visit a dying priest. Surely not even the British would find that reason to harm him.

Barbe had given her an idea, however. It made her tremble to think about it, because she didn't want anything to happen to the twins, but her concern for Remie was greater.

She approached them that evening after supper when they sat smoking and talking in the yard. She had chosen a time when no one else was around. Her heart was beating very rapidly, and her palms were wet.

"Antoine," she addressed her brother, "you have been to Annapolis Royal, haven't you?"

She knew from his immediate alertness that he had grasped her intent at once. "Several times," he agreed.

Her eyes filled with tears she could not hold back. "Would— would you go again? To find Remie? I cannot bear this any longer, not knowing if he is alive or—"

Antoine looked at his brother. "To find Remie," he said quietly.

"It's harvest time. Papa will not want us to go," François observed, though not in a manner suggesting this made the proposed idea impractical. From the time they were young boys they had worked around Papa when necessary.

"No," Antoine agreed. "Which means we shall have to do what we usually do."

"We shall have to go without telling him ahead of time," François agreed with a faint grin.

Soleil's heart leaped in both hope and fear. "I would not forgive myself—nor would Mama and Papa!—if anything happened to you, too! I would go myself if there were any way to do it, but—"

"We wouldn't have you go," François assured her, knocking out his pipe on the side of one clog. "And nothing is likely to happen to two of us. We're more than a match for a troop of redcoats."

Consternation surged through her. "I don't want you to confront the British! I only want you to see if you can discover what has happened to Remie, why he hasn't come back! It will do no one any good if you allow yourselves to be thrown into prison!"

"Or shot," Antoine said cheerfully. "No, of course not. Do you think we've survived this long by being foolish? Ah, don't cry again, for heaven's sake! What are brothers for, if not to rescue a brother-in-law from his own folly?"

"Remie wouldn't have done anything foolish! That's why I'm so worried about him! Oh, God forgive me for asking you, but I don't know what else to do!"

"You've come to the right parties," Antoine told her, squeezing her hands. "We'll leave in the morning."

"Or perhaps," François said thoughtfully, "it would be better to leave tonight. After everyone else is asleep, of course. You can tell the others in the morning where we've gone."

Soleil shuddered. "Papa will be . . . annoyed."

"Papa is often annoyed. He always gets over it. And it's for a good cause."

"How—how long will it take? To go there and back?"

The twins exchanged glances, then shrugged in unison, mirror images of each other. "A week," they said, also in unison. And then Antoine added, "If we don't get caught up in extricating your wayward husband from some disagreeable situation. No doubt we will find him simply dallying with some buxom blond maiden."

"No doubt you will not," Soleil said indignantly, but she was able to produce a slight smile. The smile faded almost at once. "I'll pray for you every moment you're away."

"Good," Antoine said. "Tell Pierre first, after we've gone. Let him handle Papa. He's almost as good at it as Louis was."

She dared not subject herself to close scrutiny by her parents, Soleil thought when the twins had ambled casually away to make their preparations for departure. They would know at once, simply by looking at her face, that something was up. And if they knew what it was, Papa might be able to stop the twins from going to Annapolis Royal.

She was afraid for Antoine and François, but she was more afraid for Remie.

31

To Soleil's surprise, neither Émile nor Barbe made any re-monstration when Pierre announced that Antoine and François would be away for a few days. He did not even have to tell them where the twins had gone.

Barbe glanced up from the soup she was preparing, her movements suspended. Émile looked toward Soleil, and she read the concern in his eyes. "They have gone to look for Remie," he said softly.

It seemed to her that she was always on the verge of tears these days. She stared at her father through a blur. "I have to know," she said, swallowing hard, and did not have to add "whether he is alive or dead."

Émile rested a hand on her shoulder. "Of course you do," he agreed, and that was all that was said. Except that from then on, when he led the family prayers, he asked for blessings on the twins as well as on Remie.

Soleil had always taken considerable solace in those pray-ers. Yet now she had doubts; her faith wavered. If God were truly looking after Remie, why had he not returned to Grand-Pré by this time? She wept and made her own prayers every night in her lonely bed. It was unthinkable that her brothers should return without Remie, yet she could not stop imagining just that. Her family refused to allow her to voice her fear.

"You have sent Antoine and François to fetch your hus-band home, so have faith that they will do it," Barbe scolded gently. "They are quick, and clever. If anyone can bring Remie home, it will be the twins. Pray for them."

August gave way to September. Émile and Pierre, Bertin and Jacques and even Grand-père went every morning to the hay fields, returning at dusk to report on their progress. They missed the help of the twins, though no one complained at their absence. Only Émile glanced worriedly at the maples begin-ning to show their scarlet leaves and said, "I'm afraid it's going to be an early winter. I hope we can get all the hay in before the rains come."

When the knock on the door sounded on the evening of September second, Soleil dropped the wooden plate she was holding, letting it clatter across the floor. Remie? The twins? Or news of them?

It was not Remie or the twins, of course. They wouldn't have knocked. When Pierre opened the inner door it was only Basile Lizotte, and Soleil felt her stomach twist in actual pain at the disappointment.

Danielle, up to her elbows in dishwater, turned from the table with an eager expression until she saw Basile's face. He had clearly not come on an amorous errand.

"Pa sent me to tell you the latest news," he said to Émile, and from his puffing it was plain that he had run part of the way. "Colonel Winslow has made a proclamation to all citizens of Grand-Pré and the surrounding area."

Émile rose slowly, putting aside the knife he had been sharpening. The others, seated around the table with their various evening tasks, fell silent and motionless.

"Yes? What do the British demand of us now?" Émile asked heavily.

"All men of this district, including old men and boys down to the age of ten, are instructed to come to hear a communication from his Excellency, the Governor." Basile's delivery suggested he had given the speech several times already. He seemed to have memorized it, for he was not used to speaking in public.

"Oh?" Émile brightened. "Are we at last to hear some good news? That the clause barring us from fighting either our countrymen or the Indians has finally been inserted into that damned oath they insist we sign?"

Danielle had passed Basile a gourd of water, and he drank thirstily before he replied. "I don't know, sir. All males are ordered to report at the church in Grand-Pré on this coming Friday, the fifth, at three of the clock in the afternoon, so that Colonel Winslow may make an announcement."

A frown was beginning to form on Émile's face. "During haying season we are to take an afternoon off? Does the man know nothing of farming?"

"They said," Basile continued with the rest of the message, "that no excuse whatever will be accepted for failure to appear, on pain of forfeiting goods and chattels, in default of real estate." The youth stopped, regarding the Cyrs with a certain amount of apprehension. This was obviously not the first time his speech had been ill received and he himself made the target of someone's anger because of it.

Pierre's jaw sagged. "Forfeiture of . . . what is all this? How important can it be?"

Basile licked his lips nervously. "Papa says it must be important. He doesn't like Colonel Winslow any better than anyone else does, but it seems wise to follow his orders."

"If it's about the oath, if they've finally given in to reason," Émile said hopefully, "they would want everyone to know about it."

Pierre was more cynical. "With such good news, all they would have to do is tell one individual, and within hours it would be known from Beaubassin to Halifax. I don't like the sound of it—a meeting we must all attend or be subject to such heavy penalties. Why threaten us if the news is good?"

"Your father and your brothers will go," Émile said to the Lizotte boy, not asking a question.

"Yes, sir. Everyone is prepared to go. Down to the age of ten," he said, glancing at Jacques.

Henri, who was standing beside his father, plucked at Pierre's sleeve. "May I go, too, Papa?" he asked.

Pierre gave him a rueful smile. "You are only four, my son."

"Four and a half," Henri corrected seriously.

"Well, we'll see. It's a long way to the village for such short legs."

"But I go for the dances," Henri pointed out. "My legs are long enough for that."

There was a ripple of laughter, and the matter was left open. But Basile's news left them uneasy for the rest of the week. It hung in the backs of their minds that they had not been requested but commanded to appear at the church. Father Chauvreulx had been arrested and taken away on a British ship. Were they now to witness the humiliation of Father Castin, as well, in a similar move?

The priest was added to the list of those mentioned in their daily prayers. While the Acadians tended to depend as much on their own consciences as on the teachings of the Church, they valued the guidance of their priests.

Friday came, hot and smelling of autumn. There was a haze in the air as the men, who had for once come to the house for their midday meal, prepared to leave for the village. Barbe's forehead was settled into worry lines that Soleil thought were becoming permanent.

"All that insistence on *everyone* being there," she said uncertainly. "No excuse whatever for not attending. And the British commandant surely knows we have more sons than those who are going."

Émile kept his voice level, though he, too, had been concerned about the matter. "Antoine and François have been gone for a week, and they have no way of knowing about the proclamation. We are not magicians and cannot be, no matter what Colonel Winslow orders. Surely even the British can see that a man must know about the order before he can obey it."

Barbe bit her lip, glancing toward Grand-père, who was making sure he had enough tobacco to last him until he returned at evening. "I hate to see him go. He hasn't even been attending the dances these last few months. It's too far for an old man to walk."

"Tell that to the British," Émile said dryly. "Don't worry about your father, we'll see to him." He reached for the musket that leaned against the wall beside the door. "Keep an eye on the pigs. That wolf pack is getting too brave again. It's time we shot a few more of them."

"Am I to go, Papa?" Henri's small voice piped in the silence. "Please, Papa?"

Pierre hesitated, then relented. "Well, why not? Just don't expect me to carry you home, boy. You're too big for that these days."

"Me too, Papa?" Vincent demanded, but Barbe scooped him up before Pierre could speak.

"No, no, not this time. You will stay home with Grand-maman and help watch for the wolves that come to steal the pigs."

"I will shoot the wolves," Vincent said, easily diverted. "Bang! Bang!"

Soleil watched her father and brothers leave with misgivings she did not voice. God grant that nobody would have to shoot at anything this day, she thought, and wished she felt more confident that God was paying attention.

JACQUES STRODE along with the others, his shorter legs breaking into an occasional trot to keep pace. At least he didn't have to run part of the time, like Henri.

It was a rather boring walk. If the twins had been there, Jacques reflected, they would have turned it into a game. He glanced toward Bertin, but *that* brother was of no use. Bertin seldom talked, let alone made jokes. He did engage in a playful tussle once in a while, but again that was only when the twins were present.

As they neared Grand-Pré they began to encounter neighbors on the same mission. Georges Dubay and his sons, M. Diotte with his, old M. Gagnon on the edge of the village. None of them knew what to think about the peremptory summons to the church on a Friday afternoon.

"Why couldn't it have waited until Sunday?" Georges grumbled. "We'll all be at the church then, anyway."

"Perhaps Father Castin objected to the use of his pulpit for a communication from the British," Émile suggested.

Georges made a sour face. "Do you think Winslow would care one grain of barley for what a priest thinks?" he asked, and Émile, discouraged, made no reply.

Grand-père had fallen behind, and they paused to let him catch up. Jacques used the time to race ahead a bit, stopping momentarily to gaze out over the harbor. "Look! There are three ships!"

He liked being out on the water, though he had never been on any such vessel as these, with their great tall masts and rope ladders over the sides to reach the decks. Jacques harbored a secret longing to be a fisherman rather than a farmer, and he wondered what his father would say of such a thing, should he ever voice that desire.

No one paid any attention to his remark. Jacques was used to that. No doubt the ships had brought soldiers to garrison the blockhouse during the coming winter, replacements perhaps, for those who had already been here for a year or two. Everyone was aware that the redcoats did not relish this duty on foreign soil among citizens who resented them and refused, for the most part, to make any attempt to learn their language.

A novelty had been added to the church since the last time he had been there, Jacques noted. When he remarked on it, the men, who had been conversing in low tones, came to a halt and paid him heed.

"Why have they built a stockade around the church?" he asked.

"To protect our priests from the soldiers," one wag blurted, but there was no laughter. It was not an amusing situation.

"No," said old M. Gagnon, who lived closer to the village than any of the others and often picked up gossip more quickly than those from outlying farms. "Colonel Winslow has quartered himself and his officers in the presbytery for the winter. See, the new soldiers have set up tents in the open square, and I've heard there are arms stored in the sanctuary."

There was a rumble of resentment among the men as they joined the several hundred citizens already ahead of them. "To desecrate a church by their unholy guns!" someone muttered. "And what of Father Castin?"

Guillaume Trudelle fell into step with those in Émile's party. "He's gone."

"Arrested?" Pierre asked sharply.

"No, no. I didn't see him go, of course, but 'tis said he took to the woods, hoping to make his way to Louisbourg. May God grant him speed and the cleverness of a fox in getting past the patrols."

Jacques could see that these things were very upsetting to his father, though Émile made no comment as they trudged on toward the gathering place.

"Next thing you know," Guillaume said, "they'll have their soldiers quartered in the church itself. They are complete asses if they think those tents will see them through an Acadian winter!"

"Let them freeze their asses, and maybe they'll go back to England where they belong," Georges proposed, and a few people laughed.

What faint humor there was evaporated, however, when they had joined their fellow citizens tramping through the new stockade to the church door and were met by soldiers who stood, bayonets fixed, awaiting them.

They were addressed by a Lieutenant Farnsworth, who spoke passable French because, as everyone knew, he had been trying to romance the Widow d'Aulnay. Afraid of being outcast by her neighbors, she would have none of him, but somehow the man had picked up a fair amount of her language.

"You will leave your arms here, and take seats in the church," he instructed.

Those at the head of the line came to a halt. Hands toughened by hard work tightened on the barrels of a dozen muskets.

"Leave our guns? Why should we do that?" M. Mauger demanded.

"Why should you need them in a church?" Lt. Farnsworth countered smoothly. "They will go nowhere. They will be right here when you come out. And during the meeting there will be no accidents because of careless handling of your muskets."

Resistance rippled through those close enough to have heard. Leave their guns? Because of the possibility of an accident? The muskets were with them at all times, even when they were in their fields or on their dykes or boats. Hadn't the British confiscated most of their guns already, anyway?

Yet the officer was firm, and the soldiers perceptibly shifted the position of their bayonets. First one man, then another, put down his weapon as ordered.

Beside him, Jacques sensed Pierre's rigidity. What would happen if his brother refused? Would one of those bayonets be brought forcefully to bear? Jacques felt his heart begin to hammer in his thin chest.

The men behind them did not yet realize what was happening. Some of those ahead had disappeared inside, a few continued to hesitate. Émile was now face-to-face with Lt. Farnsworth, who greeted him by name.

"M. Cyr. I am glad to have a man of good sense to lead the way. Assure your countrymen that there is nothing to be lost by leaving their weapons for a short time." The pale eyes flickered over those around Émile. "Your other sons have not come with you as ordered?"

"François and Antoine have gone to Annapolis Royal, days before the orders came," Émile said flatly. "I will be certain to give them your message when they return."

Something flickered in the Englishman's eyes, and the soldiers beside him did not waver with their bayoneted muskets. Jacques shivered. Yet Farnsworth's words were not particularly intimidating.

"Very well. I will relay that to Colonel Winslow. Now, if you will put down your arms with the others and enter the church so that we may begin as soon as the colonel arrives."

Émile's hesitation was brief, then he did as commanded, with a quelling glance at Pierre. After a moment Pierre followed suit, though with obvious reluctance, and Grand-père and Bertin did the same. Jacques brought up the rear, refusing to meet the eyes of the soldiers whose bayonets were held only inches from him as he passed between them.

It was cool inside the stone church. Jacques squirmed between two large bodies—M. Picot and M. Thibault—to regain his connection with his own family, slipping into a seat between Bertin and Pierre. The latter held Henri on his knee until someone moved along to make more room for them, then the little boy was wedged between Pierre and Émile, where he looked about with big dark eyes. Ordinarily Jacques would have taken some action to entertain his young nephew, as he did during services when his mother didn't notice. Today he was too uneasy to think of anything amusing. Not when all the faces around him were so sober, so angry, so frustrated.

Under cover of the sounds of men taking their places, their clogs noisy on the stone floor, Pierre spoke out of the corner of his mouth, leaning over Henri toward Émile. "It's a good thing the twins weren't here. They'd never have handed over their muskets. Never!"

"Nor should we have," Georges Dubay said from the row ahead of them, turning to glance backward. "I don't like it, damn it."

Pierre's face told Jacques that *he* didn't like it, either, that he was wishing he'd refused.

Though he was clearly as upset as everyone else, Émile remained under better control. "You're right about the twins, they would have caused trouble. And what good would a bayonet in the belly have done any of us? Eh? Sit quietly until we see what they want.''

They were not long in finding out.

The church must have held over four hundred men and boys, their body heat already causing the temperature under the vaulted ceiling to rise notably when the local British commandant strode down the aisle and climbed into the spot where the priests usually stood. Anyone looking at the faces of these men would have known how much they resented such an action.

Colonel Winslow wore his scarlet coat, dripping with gold braid and bright buttons, with pride. If Jacques hadn't hated the soldiers so much he would have envied the uniform and the elegantly curled white wig.

Since the Englishman did not speak French, M. Deschamps from Pisiquid served as interpreter. When the officer read from the paper he held, M. Deschamps repeated his words in the language the Acadians understood.

Jacques was studying their faces—the disdainful Winslow, the perspiring M. Deschamps, Pierre's grim visage, Émile's expressionless one—and the words Deschamps spoke did not impress themselves upon him until he saw first indignation and then shock registering on every Acadian face within his line of vision.

''Gentlemen, I have received from His Excellency Governor Lawrence the king's instructions, which I have in my hand. By his orders you are called together to hear His Majesty's final resolution concerning the French—Acadian—inhabitants of the Province of Nova Scotia, who for more than half a century have had more indulgence granted to them than any of his subjects in any part of his dominions. What use you have made of it, you yourselves know best.'' M. Deschamps swallowed and wiped at his brow with his handkerchief, not unaware that his listeners, though still in their seats, were taking exception to this proclamation of how they had been indulged by their conquerors. The paper from which he read wavered unsteadily in his hand.

Pierre swore under his breath, and even Émile had curled his hands into fists on his sturdy knees. Jacques felt Bertin's thigh against his own, a fine tremor in it, and listened intently, for this was clearly of great importance.

M. Deschamps went on. "The duty I am now upon, though necessary, is very disagreeable to my natural make and temper, as I know it must be grievous to you, who are of the same species. But it is not my business to animadvert on the orders I have received but to obey them."

There was nothing in Colonel Winslow's countenance to suggest that he had just—Jacques thought—expressed an apology of some sort. Jacques didn't know the word *animadvert* but he certainly understood as well as anyone the gist of the words that followed in M. Deschamps's cracking voice.

"Therefore, without hesitation, I shall deliver to you His Majesty's instructions and commands, which are, that your lands and tenements and cattle and livestock of all kinds are forfeited to the crown, with all your other effects, except money and household goods, and that you yourselves are to be removed from this province."

Never had the church been so silent. Every eye was fixed on the speaker and the gaudily uniformed man beside him, each man unwilling and unable to believe what he was hearing. Even Henri did not squirm, frightened by the rigidity of the men on either side of him.

"Forfeited" echoed in Jacques's mind. Taken away? Was the man saying that everything they owned would be taken away? How could that be?

A glance at his brothers and his father was not reassuring. They were stunned, incredulous, like their neighbors.

Colonel Winslow read again from his paper, unintelligible English words, looking no more concerned than if he were reading a six-month-old newspaper from London, and this time M. Deschamps had to swallow twice before he could continue to translate.

"The peremptory orders of His Majesty are that all the French inhabitants of these districts be removed, and, through His Majesty's goodness, I am directed to allow you your money and as many of your household goods as you can take without overloading the vessels you go in. I shall do everything in my power that all these goods be secured to you, and that you not be molested in carrying them away, and also that whole families shall go in the same vessel, so that this removal, which I am sensible must give you a great deal of trouble, may be made as easy as His Majesty's service will admit; and I hope that in whatever part of the world your lot may fall, you may be faithful subjects, and a peaceable and happy people."

There was still not a sound from his audience. Indeed, to Jacques it seemed that they had all been stricken dumb. Émile's fists had gone slack in his disbelief.

And there was more to come.

"I must also inform you that it is His Majesty's pleasure that you remain in security under the inspection and direction of the troops that I have the honor to command." Having concluded, M. Deschamps wiped one final time at his sweating face and took a step backward.

Pierre's words were little more than a whisper, but there was not a soul in the church who did not hear them.

"By the good Christ, we have been betrayed!"

A murmur began to run through those gathered in the church—at first a strangled sound of outrage, then a rush of protesting pain, and finally a roar of searing agony. A few men rose and started toward the rear of the building, and when Jacques was brave enough to twist about and see, he understood why they had come to a halt.

The red-coated soldiers blocked the exit, their faces immobile, bayonets at the ready. And at last it was clear to the assemblage what had happened: the British had disarmed them and held them all prisoner; every man had been given what amounted to a death sentence, and there was no hope of a reprieve.

32

THE MEN HAD NOT returned by dusk. Barbe stood in the outer doorway, straining to see the path where it led into the trees at the edge of the clearing, but she could detect no movement. No hail of greeting. Nothing whatever except silence.

Soleil watched her mother with misgiving as Barbe came back into the kitchen. "Maybe I should walk toward town to meet them," Soleil proposed.

"No, no. If they've been delayed there's no reason to think you could do any good by showing up. In fact, they'd probably be annoyed. Well, Vincent must be fed, so I suppose the rest of us might as well eat, too. I hope everything isn't cooked to mush by the time they get here."

They ate mostly in silence, for their concern rose with each passing moment. Émile was a man who liked his meals on time. This fact, along with the ambiguity of the summons to the church, led to only one conclusion: something was seriously amiss.

"Even if something went wrong," Danielle suggested, breaking the silence, "if Grand-père fell or was too tired to walk home, or something like that, why would they *all* stay with him? Surely Bertin and Jacques would be of no use. *They* could have come home and told us."

Barbe said nothing, which was in itself a measure of deepening concern. And Soleil, who was already almost frantic over Remie, felt the tension build within her until she thought she would scream.

They finished their simple meal and cleaned up. It was dark now, and Vincent was put to bed, yet still no one came.

At last Soleil stood up resolutely and reached for her shawl. "I'm going to walk toward town. We'll never sleep tonight if they don't come, anyway."

Danielle was already moving toward the door. "I'm going with you," she asserted. "Anything's better than simply sitting here worrying."

Soleil expected Barbe to protest, but she did not, though she, too, rose to her feet. "I'd come with you if it weren't for Vincent, but he's too heavy to carry. I don't know what's wrong, but approach the village cautiously, just in case."

She didn't specify in case of what, and the girls didn't pursue the matter. They kissed her goodbye and set out through the darkness.

There was no moon, only starlight. They had been walking this path all their lives, however, often at night coming home from dances, and they knew the way.

"It's different when there are only the two of us," Danielle said, clutching her shawl at her breast. "I never thought I was afraid of the dark before."

"There's nothing to be afraid of because of the dark," Soleil stated. "When I was very small, the twins told me some terrible tale about monsters that came out of the sea at night looking for little girls to eat, and after I'd had nightmares for three nights Mama finally got to the bottom of things and put a stop to the stories. I hated to go to the outhouse alone for the rest of that summer, but I finally got over it.'' She was silent for a moment, then added, ''I wish now we'd left earlier. Something has to be dreadfully wrong. Papa would never have stayed away so late without sending one of the boys with a message.''

They walked without speaking for some time, their eyes gradually adjusting to the dimness. As they approached the Dubay farm they saw a flicker of light between the trees and heard a dog barking.

Soleil veered impulsively in that direction. ''I'm going to stop and see if they've heard anything. Maybe Papa and the others paused here for a drink or something, with Georges, after the meeting.''

It wasn't likely that the lot of them would have stayed this long, but Danielle said eagerly. ''That's probably it. If the British announcement was something that angered or excited them, you know how they love to talk things over.''

The dogs rushed toward them, wagging their tails and barking only halfheartedly once they realized who the late-night visitors were. The door opened, and Mme Dubay stood silhouetted in the candlelight. ''Who is it?'' she called out apprehensively.

''It's Soleil and Danielle Cyr, *madame*,'' Soleil sang out. ''Papa and the boys have not come home yet. Have you seen anything of them?''

''No.'' The woman stepped backward, inviting them inside. ''Céleste and I have been sitting here worrying—what can possibly have kept them all this time?''

Since there was no answer to that, Soleil didn't attempt to guess. She swallowed against her disappointment that there was no news here. ''We're going to town to find out,'' she said. ''Do you want to go with us?''

Céleste had risen from a stool near the hearth where she was mending a sock. ''I'll go, Mama. Anything's better than sitting here any longer.''

"Yes, go," Mme Dubay said, sounding relieved that it was possible to take some action. "And when you find Papa, come back at once and tell me what's happened."

"Bring a shawl," Soleil cautioned, "it's rather cool."

Once again they hurried forward along the path until finally they could see the pale, lighted windows of Grand-Pré.

Soleil came to an abrupt halt. "Listen!"

There were raucous male voices, too loud for this time of night.

"Soldiers," Danielle said at once. "They're speaking English."

They stood, hearts pounding, unable to understand the words in the hated foreign language. And then came a voice, raised above the others and not far away, in barely intelligible French.

"Ah, *mademoiselle*, why not be nice to me? You will be grateful for a friend among us before this affair is over, I think."

"When I am grateful for pigs" came the immediate response in a frightened yet defiant female voice. "Get out of my way and let me go home! Be assured that I will report you to your commanding officer for this conduct!"

There was a burst of laughter from the men. Three or four of them, at least, Soleil thought. Yet her own reaction came at once, without time for considering their own situation.

"Huguette, is that you?" she cried loudly.

The laughter ceased at once, and the girl replied with obvious relief. "Yes! It is Huguette! Who is that?"

"Soleil Cyr, and my sister Danielle, and Céleste Dubay." Soleil led the way toward the small group in the middle of the road, able to discern which of the shadowy figures was Huguette by her smaller stature. Four men, Soleil noted, and hoped they could not hear her heart pounding with fear. Four British soldiers to four women. The smell of whiskey was detectable from several yards away. "Come, we'll walk you home," she said firmly, and reached out to touch the other girl's arm.

Huguette was trembling, but she, too, spoke strongly. "Yes, thank you. Let's go."

Soleil waited for the intervening hand, the arrogant challenge that would stop them from leaving, but nothing happened. The soldiers allowed them to depart.

She tightened her grip on the other girl's arm, hoping Huguette wouldn't collapse in her fright, for she was shaking now like the last leaf on a maple tree in an October wind.

"What happened? What's going on?" Soleil demanded as soon as they were some twenty yards away from the soldiers.

"Oh, thank you! Dear God, I prayed for deliverance, and then I heard your voice out of the night! Oh, Soleil, it is so terrible! What are we going to do?"

"Do about what?" Céleste demanded in an almost angry whisper. "What's happened? What are you doing out this time of night?"

"The same as you, no doubt," Huguette responded, trying to regain control of herself. "We waited and waited for Papa and the boys to come home, and they didn't, so Mama sent me to look for them. Oh, dear God, what are we going to do?"

"Stop," Soleil said, giving the other girl a shake when it appeared that she would dissolve in tears. "Tell us what's happened? Where are the men?"

"Locked in the church," Huguette choked. "No one has come out to tell us anything, but they all went in at three o'clock as ordered and left their muskets outside, and they've never come out! The muskets were taken away by the soldiers, and there are guards on the stockade around the church, and they've not been taken food or anything!"

The four of them, too shocked to move, came to a halt in the middle of the street as the girl continued. "I met Mme Latour, who lives just across the road from the church, and she talked to one of the soldiers, one of those who speaks a little French. He says our men are under arrest and that all our possessions are to be taken from us and we are to be loaded on those ships in the harbor and sent away somewhere, forever!"

It seemed to Soleil that the darkness around them grew lighter, gray and fuzzy, and for a moment she clung to her sister, afraid that she was about to lose consciousness. "That can't be true," she said. "Not even the British could be so cruel."

Yet she knew it *was* true. It was the only explanation for the failure of Papa and the boys—for every man in the village—to fail to return home: they had been taken prisoner.

And if the soldiers would burn and kill at Beaubassin, why would they hesitate to take similar measures at Grand-Pré? It was as Remie and Louis had feared. The English were determined to have the land for their own people, and they cared not what means they used to accomplish their goal.

Oh, God, she thought in anguish. Where was Remie? Had the same thing happened in Annapolis Royal as here? Was that why Remie had not returned? And what of the twins?

Her throat closed and she swayed so that Danielle had to support her. Her head, and her thoughts, were swirling.

What if she never saw any of them again?

IT WAS AN UNCOMFORTABLE night in the church.

There was barely room for the men and boys to stretch out on the pews and in the aisles to sleep. Though there were elbows and knees poking into one another, no one complained about it.

Indeed, after the initial howls of protest, there was little complaint of any kind. Most of the men were in a state of shock, unable to believe what they had been told. The lands that had been in their families for nearly a hundred and fifty years were to be taken away from them, along with their horses, cattle, chickens, sheep and pigs. They themselves were to be exported, like livestock, to strange places to begin all over again with nothing.

"Where?" Pierre asked of one of the guards who spoke a little French. "Where are we to be sent?"

The soldier spat on the stone floor, shrugging. "Wherever the ship you are put on is going. To Boston, perhaps. Or the Carolinas. Who knows?"

"But they don't even speak French in those places, and they hate us there!" Pierre protested.

"Maybe they will send you back to France," the soldier said indifferently. "One of the ships, I understand, is going to France."

"*Back* to France? But none of us has ever been to France! The priests who come directly from there do not even speak the same language as the rest of us until they've been here for a year or more! We are not *French*, we are Acadian!''

The man's reply was callous in the extreme. "No doubt, wherever you are sent you will adjust." He might as well have added, *or die.* Obviously it did not matter which, as far as he was concerned.

Georges Dubay, who was standing behind Pierre, had listened to this exchange. "France is not our homeland," he put in. "You cannot do this monstrous thing, *monsieur*!''

"It's not I who does it. I only carry out my orders. And you are of French descent, are you not? Even if what you speak is a bastard French, it is not English, is it?''

"The French have never done anything for us," Georges said angrily. "The English sent ships to invade our shores, and the French sent nothing to repel them. They provided no money or supplies or soldiers to help us. Instead, they dispatched men from Québec to attack the people in the English colonies to the south, and *they* in turn retaliate by attacking *us*! The French!'' He too would have spat if he had not remembered just in time that he was in church. "We owe them nothing! We want nothing to do with them!''

For the most part, however, there were no words between the captives and the soldiers left to guard them, beyond the essential ones.

"Are we not to be fed, then?" M. Meignaux demanded when his stomach began to rumble with emptiness.

"A night of fasting should be good for your Catholic souls" was the reply.

"Surely, though, we are to be allowed outside to relieve ourselves," M. Gagnon proposed.

Uncertainty flickered in the soldier's eyes. "I was given no orders concerning that. I was told only that you are to remain here, under guard." He gestured toward the baptismal font. "Use that for your chamber pot, why don't you?''

He would never have admitted it, but the looks that remark earned him sent prickles over his scalp. For a moment he feared that, bayonets and fellow guards or not, the captives would rush him.

And then the moment subsided, and a rational voice took up the demand. "You must send someone to your commander if you cannot make the decision on your own, but we will not desecrate our church, and we must relieve ourselves.''

The soldier hesitated, then spoke in his own language to one of the men beside him, who then left the church. Still, it was nearly an hour before he returned with the information that the captives would be allowed into the courtyard, inside the stockade, in groups of twenty for a period of five minutes each.

Émile did not rise for his turn until Pierre prodded him. ''Come, Papa.''

Even then, though his need was as great as anyone's, Émile scarcely thought of what he was doing when he went out into the darkness.

Louis had been right, he thought numbly. Louis had urged him to go a whole year back. And young Michaud had also pointed out the dangers, and François and Antoine— His eyes smarted and he rubbed at them. Where were those sons tonight? Was there any possibility that they would escape the British net? And if they did, then what? They would never be allowed to return to their farm. They might only live as fugitives in the forest, and for how long, before they were eventually caught?

As he trudged back inside, propelled by the threat of those bayonets and the unsympathetic faces of their captors, Émile turned his thoughts toward home. Dear heaven, what must Barbe be thinking by this time? Half out of her mind with worry, she would be. And the girls, and little Vincent, what of them?

Winslow had said they would be rejoined with their families when they were loaded onto the ships. He tried to console himself with that thought. Though the land was lost to him—a crushing reality that had not yet completely penetrated—he would still have his wife and his family, or part of it. He must take what solace he could from that.

As he sank back onto the pew, beneath which his frightened youngest son and oldest grandson had been installed to sleep if they could, tears rolled unashamedly down Émile's weathered face and he wondered if there would ever be happiness in his life again.

THE FULL HORROR of their situation came with daylight the following morning.

In the entire community, scarcely a male over the age of ten—with the exception of a few of the aged who had been too infirm to go to the church—remained free.

The women rose bleary-eyed with fatigue after a sleepless night to face the chores normally done by husbands, fathers and sons.

At the Cyr house, the three women had by unspoken agreement crawled into the same bed when the girls returned from the village with their terrible news.

Soleil had burst into the house ahead of Danielle, knowing her sister should not be the one to impart the bad news. Barbe was waiting for them, her hands knotted at her bosom. She had known from their faces, streaked with tears, that the situation was very bad.

She listened without response until Soleil had finished speaking. Then, her lips scarcely moving, she said, "It cannot be true that they intend to dispossess us of everything that we own," but it was obvious she did not believe her own words. The reality of more than four hundred men and boys locked in the church, guarded by soldiers, gave credence to the full enormity of the British mandate.

Having held Danielle's hand all the way home as they sobbed and stumbled through the darkness, Soleil expected her mother to collapse upon learning the facts. Though she turned very white and had to sit down, Barbe did not cry. Her shock seemed too great for tears. Later, when all three had retired to the canopied bed Barbe had shared with Émile for so many years, it was Barbe who held them, offering what comfort she could, not with words but with her loving arms.

Soleil found herself unable even to pray. For the first time in her life she had been dealt a blow of such proportions that her faith was shaken to its roots.

How could God allow something like this to happen?

When she spoke the words aloud in the morning, her mother remonstrated gently, "No, child. Don't blame God. This is no doing of His. Put the blame for wickedness where it belongs, on the British soldiers, or their evil king who commanded this obscene thing. Come, we'll pray together.''

But though Soleil bowed her head obediently, this time there was no sense of relief at the thought that God heard and would answer their prayers.

The people on the Chignecto had prayed, too, and God had turned a deaf ear. Their homes had been destroyed, along with their crops, and their children went hungry while their elderly died because there was no way to care for them.

What had the Acadians done that God should so abandon them?

And if that were true, if the Lord no longer listened, what about Remie? The tears Soleil had thought exhausted were renewed, sliding down her face in a constant trickle.

There was no time to sit and brood, however. Already the cows were bawling to be milked. Barbe gathered herself together to make decisions. ''We must eat—no, no, I understand that the thought of food makes you ill, but we must have strength to withstand whatever it is that will happen. We will have our usual breakfast after the cows have been taken care of. Danielle, see to that first. Then turn them out to graze. Soleil, we must have food to take to the church. They will all be hungry by the time we get there, for I cannot believe the English will cook for hundreds of them. And we must take blankets, though perhaps they will not be held through another night—''

Soleil was reminded of the nightmares she had had as a little girl, when the vaguely pictured monsters had threatened her. She now felt the same terrified apprehension of impending doom from which she was powerless to run. Only this time she was awake, and the monster was real.

She did not understand how her mother could think of such mundane things as bringing in wood to keep the cooking fire going, or stirring the kettle, or counting out quilts and blankets for each of those imprisoned. Soleil felt as if a sharp blade had been thrust into her heart, allowing her to bleed to death. Surely dying could be no more agonizing than this. How did her mother continue to function?

In fact, Barbe knew that if she did not find things to do, she would lose her mind. She clung to her thoughts of Émile, the man who had been her husband for twenty-eight years, who had cared for her and loved her, and now she must do what she could for him.

She feared mightily for his mental condition. Émile loved the land as if it were a living thing, second only to her and the children, and now he was helpless to save either the land or his family. She prayed earnestly as her hands selected the folded bedding to be carried to town that Émile's great, generous heart would not burst and allow him to die before she saw him again.

Her concern for Émile was the only thing that tempered her own excruciating torment. He had never let her down, and now it was her turn. She must be there for him, be strong for him, so that her own weakness did not contribute to his.

THE WOMEN OF GRAND-PRÉ converged on the church in long lines. Their weeping was silent, for the most part, as they carried food and blankets to their men.

A few of the prisoners had been allowed into the stockade, but the posts were too close together for anyone to tell who they were. The soldiers met the women with uncaring eyes, except for a few like Tommy Sharp, who spoke a little French and had been friendly with some of the Acadian girls. These men looked uncomfortably away from the wan, hopeless faces of the women.

No one was permitted actual contact with the men locked inside. The provisions the women had brought were taken away, and there was no way of knowing whether or not they were delivered to the proper men. The best they could hope for was that everyone would be fed and provided with a blanket apiece.

Barbe attempted to talk with the soldier at the main gate, for the first time wishing that the Acadians had not remained so stubbornly adamant in refusing to learn the language of their conquerors. "My grandson is in there," she said, "Henri Cyr, and he is only four years old. Surely you do not need to keep him prisoner, as well. Let him go home with us."

The soldier, young enough to be one of her sons, stared at her without interest. "I have no authority to release any of the prisoners," he said in a flat tone.

"Then I will speak to your commanding officer," Barbe returned in a voice that brought a spot of red to each of the man's cheeks, but still he did not relent.

"Good luck to you there," he said with sarcasm. "You can fall in line behind two hundred other old biddies wanting something, and it ain't likely the colonel will listen to any o' ye."

It didn't take long for Barbe to decide that the soldier was right. There was a long line of anxious or determined women to see Colonel Winslow, and obviously none of them was receiving any satisfaction whatever. "All he'll say," Mme Blanchard reported, "is that when the rest of the ships arrive, we'll all be put aboard and shipped out, and we can be together then. I told him my father is old and ill, but they don't care if he dies. It will make one more space on the ships."

Soleil touched her mother's arm, assessing the length of the line and the countenances of those who were being turned away. "Let him be, Mama. He's with Pierre and Papa, after all. It may give them something useful to do, to look after Henri."

Barbe hesitated, then gave a resigned sigh. "Perhaps you're right," she said.

Some of the women stood around in small groups, commiserating with one another, most of them drained of tears by this time. After a few words with Marie Trudelle and Antoinette Dubay, however, Barbe did not linger.

"We can do nothing for them out here," she said, "and there is much to be done at home."

With scarcely a word exchanged among them, they made their way back to the Cyr homestead.

ON SUNDAY, the seventh of September, 1755, five more ships arrived in the harbor at Grand-Pré, making a total of eight.

Colonel Winslow was heard to express his fear that eight ships were not enough to carry all of the prisoners. Any faint hope among the prisoners that the British would not really carry out their monstrous plan died. It was actually going to happen. The Acadians were going to be put forcibly on the English vessels and carried away to unknown destinations.

The women of Grand-Pré were swamped in a desperate misery, each responding to it in her own way. Barbe's way was to keep busy, even with such things as harvesting the hay that had already been cut, though Danielle protested the uselessness of such activity.

"What is the point, Mama? They've said they are confiscating all our cattle! Let the British worry about feeding them this winter!"

Barbe gave her a level, compassionate look. "Must even the cattle suffer because of the wickedness of the British? Besides, my love, it is better to stay busy. Otherwise—" for a moment her composure faltered "—otherwise we will fall apart, and we cannot let your father and your brothers down by doing that."

"Maybe when the twins come back, they can figure out some way to help Papa and the others escape," Danielle said.

"All by themselves?" Soleil asked bitterly. "Even if they bring Remie with them, what can three men do against an army?"

Danielle bit her lip. "I cannot understand why they laid down their muskets outside the church! I cannot think why they allowed this to happen!"

Barbe's voice was low. "Your father is an honorable man, a man of peace. He could not believe such treachery, such evil, among fellow human beings. He had tried for so long to smooth things out between them and us, and he had no understanding of the depths to which the British would go to gain our lands for themselves."

Danielle's dark eyes, red rimmed and angry, seemed to shoot off sparks. "The twins were right! We should have taken up arms against them, joined with the Indians and run them back to England where they belong!"

Neither Barbe nor Soleil replied to that. They had not fought, and now it was too late.

HAD IT NOT BEEN for the babe she carried, Soleil would have wished herself dead. Her body ached with the unaccustomed strain of hauling in hay and tending the stock, yet the pain was nothing compared to what she felt in her heart.

The tears had long since dried up, and she had not even the comfort of prayer. Unlike Barbe, who insisted upon maintaining the pretense that God still watched over them, Soleil stubbornly hardened her heart against Him during the morning and evening worship that Barbe conducted in her husband's stead. Remie was gone, the twins were gone, and soon all those remaining would be stripped of their possessions and deported to some unknown shore. Soleil refused to mouth the words "Oh, merciful God," for where was the mercy?

IT WAS late afternoon when Soleil staggered toward the house under the weight of two heavy buckets of water. Mama was becoming unhinged by the tragedy, she thought, for she insisted that in the morning they would wash all their clothes and sheets so that they would be ready to leave when the rest of the required ships arrived.

"No doubt," Barbe had said, "there will be no facilities for washing aboard ship. We can at least be clean when we begin."

Soleil emptied her pails into the big kettle in the yard, over the fire already started to be kept going through the night. They might as well forget about bed, she thought with resentment, for none of them was sleeping enough to make it worthwhile to get out of their clothes. Instinct, rather than sound, brought her swinging wildly around, heart suddenly pounding.

Someone was coming out of the forest on the path from the village.

"Pierre? Oh, dear God, Pierre! Mama! Danielle! It's Pierre!"

She fairly flew toward her brother, flinging herself into his arms. She could hear his heartbeat against her own for a few seconds, and then he set her aside and peered into her face.

"How goes it here?" he asked.

Barbe and Danielle, Vincent in tow, came running out of the house. Pierre swung his son into the air and hugged him. For a few moments their babble prevented him from speaking. It was not until Barbe peered eagerly over his shoulder to ask "Your father? The others?" that Pierre finally spoke the grave words.

"They're still detained. We're being permitted, one man to a family, to return home long enough to make arrangements. You've heard by this time, I take it. We are to be stripped of our belongings and deported as soon as there are enough ships to carry us. Eleven in all are expected. The British have obviously been planning this for some time."

Disappointment twisted Barbe's face, and she swallowed painfully. "Your father? How is he?"

Pierre didn't meet her eyes. "He does as well as can be expected. He sees to Grand-père and to Henri. He sends his love and his prayers for you all."

"Grand-père? He is ill?"

"No, but it is hard on him, of course. There is no fire for toasting his cold bones, and except for the food you bring, there is nothing to eat, and all of it cold. He longs for a warming cup of brandy, I think, but the spirits that are brought are confiscated by the soldiers, so there's no point in carrying any to town. I think they'll let me take him some tobacco. That will give him some comfort, perhaps."

His gaze drifted past the three women. "There is no word from the twins? Or Remie?"

"None," Soleil told him. Her eyes prickled, though she had thought herself drained of tears.

Pierre sighed. He had a thick stubble of beard, and he seemed thinner. Certainly he had had no opportunity to wash or change his clothes. "Well, perhaps it's for the best. They may be skulking in the woods, awaiting their opportunity."

"To free the prisoners?" Danielle asked eagerly.

Pierre shook his head. "There's no chance of it. If we had refused to lay down our arms, if we had refused to respond to their summons, we might have resisted them. Now, with nothing but our bare hands against British muskets and bayonets—" He left the sentence unfinished. "We were duped. I knew I was a fool to give up my gun, but Papa thought we should go along with them, see what they wanted—" Again he did not complete the thought in words.

"Surely if you are being allowed to go home, someone will do something," Danielle insisted.

Pierre's dark eyes smoldered. "Twenty of us may go at a time. When we return, twenty more will go, until each family has been contacted. But we have been warned—if any fails to return, retaliation will be made against the man's nearest of kin, or failing of kin, against his neighbors. Few will risk having their wives and children, or even their neighbor's wives and children, shot."

There was a chilled silence. Finally Soleil asked softly, "Then there is no hope? No hope at all?"

Pierre's mute face was an eloquent answer.

It was Barbe who first pulled herself out of a mental agony so great that it made a physical ache in her limbs and her body. "Tell us, then, what we are to do," she said, "and we will kneel together and ask God's help that we may accomplish it."

Soleil's eyes were dry, her voice stony. "When God restores my husband to me," she stated, "I will believe that He still cares about Acadians."

Barbe stared into her daughter's face, her own contorted with the effort of withholding her grief.

"He cares," she said. "And we will thank Him now, that He has sent Pierre to us with news."

She sank to her knees on the ground, and after a moment Danielle and Pierre joined her. But Soleil stood without speaking until the prayer had ended.

34

"I MUST GO BACK QUICKLY," Pierre told them, scooping up his son in a fierce embrace, "so that others may take their turns. Papa told me what to tell you about the stock, the house..."

His voice trailed off and he stood looking toward the house where he had been born, where both his sons had been born, where Aurore had died. The beloved home he did not ever expect to see again. Soleil saw him swallow hard before he went on.

"We have been told we may travel with our household goods. Clothes, bedding, kitchen things for cooking and eating." He glanced at his mother, then looked away. "I don't know what they'll actually allow us to take on board. Papa fears they will confiscate cash, for they tell us to take it. Others are afraid, too, and most agree it would be safer to bury it until such time as it may be possible to return." His eyes revealed how little he thought of the chances of that. "Just prepare what you can, have it ready when the word comes."

"When?" Barbe asked, the single syllable cracking with tension.

"We don't know. When the rest of the ships come, I suppose. A few days, a week. Apparently the British aren't certain, either."

Barbe stood rigidly straight. "A week. And no way to let Louis know where we have gone. He will never know what has happened to us, nor we know of him."

"He'll know," Pierre said. "Word of this infamy will travel to Île St. Jean and beyond."

"But he'll never find us again."

Pierre had no response to that, for how could he refute her words? Vincent was wriggling in his arms, bored with the sober talk, and Pierre set him on his feet. The child raced across the yard, then paused to shout over his shoulder, "Where is Henri? Why didn't you bring Henri home?"

Pierre's words were wooden. "I couldn't bring him this time, but he sends his love to you. And to Grand-maman and all of you." He turned to the women again. "We may take flour and pork enough to last us for several weeks. Pray God that will be enough to see us to our destination."

"And where will that be?" Barbe sounded almost calm, except for the slight quaver in her voice.

"They've not told us. Bertin and Jacques have picked up a little English, and they say there is mention of various British colonies to the south—Massachusetts, Rhode Island, the Carolinas."

"They speak no French in those places," Danielle protested, her dark eyes huge in a pale face. "How will we live in a strange place with only those people around us? They will not give us land to replace our own?"

Again Pierre's silence was reply enough for them to know that no such largess could be expected. "Come," he addressed his mother, "let me tell you what Papa says must be done."

"If I were a man," Soleil said, looking after them as they headed for the barn, "I would shoot the British down, as many as I could get before they killed me. There is still one musket left, and when the twins come there will be two more, and Remie's—" She choked.

"But if Pierre does not return, the soldiers will punish those who remain captive," Danielle reminded her. "Or us. They will come after us."

"Would it matter?" Soleil asked bleakly. "Perhaps it would be better to shed our blood here on Acadian soil than to be trussed like chickens and taken off to some distant place. Do you think the English will make us any more welcome in the colonies than they have done here, which was our land in the first place?''

"Surely," Danielle said in desperation, "God will not allow this wickedness! He will do something to save us!''

Soleil, who had no such conviction, did not reply.

EVERY DAY Danielle and Soleil walked to the village church with food and tobacco. Every day they encountered friends and neighbors on similar errands. Each time they hoped to catch a glimpse of their own loved ones, and each time they were disappointed.

Even Barbe gave up the pretense that there was anything to be gained by getting in the hay or harvesting the produce from the orchard or garden beyond their immediate needs. Soleil stared at the growing mound of belongings piled at one end of the kitchen, ready to be transported to the ships when the word came. They would never be allowed to take so much, she thought, even though it was little enough to enable such a large family to start over somewhere else.

She felt as if she, too, were imprisoned. There was no longer any joy in walking along the dykes, in strolling through the woods to meet Céleste. There were no men to cook for, no plans to make for the future. There was only dread.

Sometimes, from force of habit, she found herself mouthing the familiar words that had sustained her all her life, words that still seemed to bring some comfort to her mother. "Please, God, help keep us safe!''

And then she would remember that God had abandoned the Acadians, and she wondered as well about the Blessed Mother and Jesus Christ Himself, and she wept, because if Remie was dead she would not even know where he had been buried. And she had sent her brothers out to an unknown fate, as well.

After the first terrible night when the men had been locked in the church, Soleil had returned to her own bed, leaving Danielle and Barbe together. Sometimes she heard their two voices murmuring after the candles had been put out. She felt apart from them, from their prayers, from their gestures of affection. Not that she was excluded from them, except by her own choice. Barbe did not chastise her for refusing to join them on their knees, morning and evening. In a way Soleil wished that her mother were not so kind; at least then, she would have had justification for screaming and raging against the God who was allowing these things to happen.

It was only early September and the days were golden and warm with the lingering caress of summer. Yet Soleil was encased in an icy shell, a shell that froze her tears and bottled her anguish. Only once in a while, in the dark of the night when the others had fallen silent, did a crack appear in the shell, when her bitter weeping must be stifled in her pillow, when she cried out to God, ironically in the very words of Christ Himself, "Why have you forsaken me? Why do you allow this to happen to us, who are innocent of any wrongdoing, who have always been devout in our lives and our worship?"

She felt both guilt and a small measure of satisfaction at her own outburst, as well as a sliver of fear, should she eventually have to contend with the Lord's wrath because of it.

One night Barbe stood in the open doorway for a moment before locking up, something they had not considered necessary before Émile and the others had been imprisoned. It was no doubt foolish now, for if the British came, they would not be stopped by a bar across the door.

She sniffed the air. "I'll not be surprised if it frosts soon. The night has the smell of it," she said, and closed the door.

Frost, ice, blizzards...a rain of hellfire, Soleil thought. What difference did it make? *Life* was hell now. She did not understand why God had allowed them to be born in the first place if this was all their lives were to come to.

The fire had been banked. Dried peas simmered in the kettle—it was so hard to remember to reduce the amount of such things, Barbe said, after so many years of feeding a small army—and the kitchen was warm and snug in the candlelight. Soleil felt the familiar ache in her throat as she turned away and went to her bed.

She was unable to sleep. For a time she lay flat on her back, touching her stomach, trying to feel the babe that grew there. Her belly felt no different than it had ever done. She remembered Remie's big hand stroking her, and his promise to tell this child where, and how, it had been conceived, in the valley where they would one day build their own home.

It was as if God had suddenly stopped the sun from rising, plunging the world into permanent darkness. Without Remie, there was nothing left to hope for.

When the sounds came, she thought for a moment she had drifted into sleep and dreamed them. And then they were repeated—someone was at the door, the door Barbe had barred less than an hour earlier.

Soleil swung her feet over the edge of the bed, pushing aside the curtain, listening. Yes, someone was there.

For a moment, fear of the British rendered her still, then reason reasserted itself. The British would pound on the door, demanding entrance, or shoot through it.

She stubbed her toe in her dash across the dark room but scarcely felt the pain. Once she'd entered the kitchen there was enough glow from the fireplace to light her way to the door. Heart hammering, she hesitated and asked in little more than a whisper, "Who is it?"

"Soleil? Let us in, for the love of God!"

"Antoine? Oh, Blessed Mother, it's Antoine!" Her fingers fumbled with the bar, then threw the door open. "Oh, François! You've come home! You're all right!"

"More or less," François said, limping in to the warm kitchen and heading for the hearth. "I hope there's something to eat. We haven't dared to shoot anything for fear the bloody British would hear us!"

He had lifted the lid, sniffing. "We're starved. Is there bread? We've not had bread for days."

"Of course. The peas were only just put on, though, they'll be hard as rocks." She felt as if she were swelling, filling with both laughter and tears. "Here's bread, and there's cold mutton—I must call Mama and Danielle! We'd given up, we thought you were dead—"

She stopped, staring at her raggedly unkempt brothers, who were unburdening themselves of muskets and packs, then back at the door they had left standing open. "Remie?" The name was a fearful whisper. "Did you find Remie?"

Please, God, let them have found him, she thought, forgetting that she no longer believed in God's mercies.

"He's alive," Antoine said, lowering himself onto Grand-père's stool and bending over to loosen his leggings and footwear. "But he's in prison, and we couldn't get him out."

Alive. Remie was alive.

Soleil nearly collapsed with relief. "Oh, God, thank you! Blessed Mother, thank you!"

Barbe suddenly appeared in the doorway in her nightgown, Danielle right behind her. "Antoine! François! Oh, my sons, I knew you would be given back to us!"

For an instant there was a flash of the old Antoine as he grinned and said, "That's more than we knew, I swear. Soleil, is there hot water? That foot took a musket ball, and it needs to be soaked." Already the grin was gone.

The three of them scurried around, finding a container in which to soak François's foot, helping him ease off his bloody rags, preparing cold food and hot tea. Only when they had begun to satisfy their hunger did Antoine glance around the room.

"Where is everyone else? Where's Papa?"

The fire, which had flared up when Danielle added new fuel to it, snapped in the silence and lent a rosy tint to their faces.

Barbe told them all that had happened. They did not interrupt.

"The same as in Pisiquid," Antoine said wearily when she had finished. "Damn their British souls to hell! We nearly got caught in that one ourselves. It was the same—all males told to report to the church, then deprived of their weapons and put under arrest. We wouldn't have reported, of course, but twice we came within an inch of being discovered by patrols. And what happens now?"

"Now we wait to be deported to some distant place," Barbe told them. "We don't know where."

"How could they have been so stupid? Handing over their muskets, like sheep!" Antoine gave his brother a fierce look. "If we'd been here, there is no way they'd have parted us from our muskets!"

"And you'd have been shot," Barbe told them gently. "No, it's better this way. Better to lose the land than our sons."

"Does Papa feel that way, too? He's clung to this land as if it were his life's blood, and this is what it's come down to."

"We should have fought them openly," François said, his voice heavy with emotion. "Instead of running away to Île St. Jean or Québec, those with courage should have banded together, armed themselves and taken back the land from the British!"

"But there was the treaty by which the land was given to the British by the French—" Barbe began.

"The hell with the French and their treaty, giving away *our* land!" François broke in, outraged. "What did the French ever do for us? They never protected us, never supplied us with guns or soldiers, only gained by their trade with us! We owed nothing to the French, and we owe nothing to the English, certainly not allegiance!"

"Pierre says there is nothing we can do," Barbe told them. "Right after he was here, a few young men escaped into the woods when they were allowed to go home to see to their families, but they returned when that Colonel Winslow made it clear that their families would be punished. What else is there to do, except as they say?"

Antoine was massaging his tired feet, and François bent nearer the fire to examine a long gash across the back of one hand. They both looked at their mother.

"Not give up and turn ourselves in," François said, and his brother nodded.

"If Papa couldn't mold us into proper sheep in twenty years," Antoine declared, "the English aren't going to do it now. We'll take to the woods, harass them at every opportunity."

Barbe made a protesting sound. "No! No, my son, that's not the answer! They have promised to transport us to some different place where we can at least start over. Better that, than that any of us should die over the matter!"

"And what's the worth of an English promise?" Antoine asked wryly. "Not much, I'd say. No more than the worth of their word that the muskets be returned after the meeting in the church. They profane our churches with their very presence."

Soleil could bear it no longer. "What about Remie?" she demanded. "Why is he in prison? Is he hurt? Did you speak to him?"

The twins exchanged a glance and, in that silent way they had, decided Antoine would be the initial spokesman.

"He protested their taking his friend, the dying priest, from his own bed to prison, it seems. So they arrested them both, and the old priest died anyway, of course. We didn't see Remie, but we talked to a man who did. He says he's well enough, as well as a man could be on the slop the British feed their prisoners. An Acadian would do better by the pigs. We got a message to him, that we were there, that you were well, and we hung around for a bit, thinking there'd be an opportunity to get him out. We tried it, and François was shot through the foot."

"Damned lucky it wasn't my head," François said, lifting his foot out of the hot water so that Danielle could add more and make it steam again. "I was making a dive for the bushes."

"We finally had to decide it wasn't going to be possible," Antoine went on, leaning back against the warm stone at the side of the chimney with an audible sigh of fatigue. "I swear, Soleil, we'd have tried again if it had seemed feasible, but it was obvious something was up among the English. They had twice as many soldiers as anyone would expect, and they were throwing people into prison on the least provocation."

"They hadn't called a meeting, lured the populace into the church and made them give up their arms?" Soleil asked, torn between joy at knowing her husband was alive and apprehension over his future safety.

"Not by the time we left. After what happened at Pisiquid, and now at Grand-Pré, it seems likely the same was slated to happen in Annapolis Royal. The British are determined to rid Acadia of Acadians once and for all and call it Nova Scotia when they populate it with their own settlers."

"Who was this person who saw Remie?" She had to know more details, was eager for any crumb of information they could provide.

"His name was Daigle, and his brother was incarcerated in the same cell as Remie. He went there to take food to him, anything better than the slops he'd otherwise have had to subsist on. He thought the soldiers would have been satisfied if their prisoners all starved, actually." Then, realizing this could hardly have been reassuring to his sister, he added, "The townspeople keep the prisoners fed, whether relatives or not.

Remie is not happy, but he sent word that he loves you, and to have faith. Sooner or later he'll be out of there.''

Soleil's heart gave a guilty leap, for she had *not* been strong in her faith, for a time denying it entirely. Yet at the moment that was the least of her worries. If God knew all, as 'twas said, He must surely understand.

"But there are ships in the harbor even now," she said, "and we await word that when the others arrive we will be loaded onto them and carried away! No doubt the same holds true at Annapolis Royal! What if we are put on different ships and sent to different places?" Already her relief at hearing that Remie was unharmed was evaporating.

Barbe put out a hand and rested it on Soleil's arm. "Even after this evidence of His goodness, can you not trust in God, Soleil? Surely they will not separate a man from his family! When he tells them, they will allow him to be restored to you. Come," she said, reaching out to Danielle and encompassing them all, "let us pray together now and give our thanks that you two have returned safely. And then we will ask God's blessings upon Remie and Papa and the others."

Obediently Soleil dropped to her knees with the rest, thankful tears wetting her cheeks. But just before she closed her eyes she searched her brothers' weary faces and could not be entirely reassured.

35

"WHAT IF THEY don't put the Lizottes on the same ship as us?" Danielle wanted to know. "And you, Antoine, if they put you on a different ship from Céleste? By families, they said, and since none of us are as yet married . . ."

"They're not putting me on any ship if I can help it," Antoine said. He looked better after a night's sleep and a second hearty meal, but the privations of the weeks he had been gone were startlingly evident in his lean face. He rose from the table and picked up the stockings François had discarded upon his arrival, tossing them into the fire, where they immediately sent out the stench of burned wool.

"What are you doing?" Barbe asked sharply, pausing in the act of pouring water into the kettle.

There was nothing of the boy in Antoine's face, Soleil noticed; he was a man grown, tempered by the recent events to a steely core.

"There was blood on them, and a hole from a musket ball," Antoine said in a flat tone. "It won't do to have them found."

There was a moment of silence before Danielle, eyes wide, asked, "But...aren't you going to turn yourself in? They said...if not everyone in the family reported, the rest of the family would be punished...."

Antoine went very still. "If everyone had stood together, they could have resisted the British. We outnumber them by the thousands, but we've pretended everything was going to be better, that their word could be trusted, and most have handed over their weapons! Well, I won't hand over mine, nor will François! They'll have to come and get us, and we won't be sitting here waiting to be manacled and humiliated. Louis chose to go elsewhere, to a place where the British may leave him alone. François and I and the few others who aren't already sitting in that prison they've made of our holy church can't take the country back from the bastards now, though I'll always believe we could have held it against them in the first place if we'd stood together. But we won't be loaded on their ships and carried off to be slaves somewhere else in their bloody colonies!"

"Slaves?" Danielle moistened her lips, glancing from Soleil to her mother. "What makes you say...slaves?"

Antoine's words were savage in his frustration. "What else do you think will happen? Acadians will be dumped ashore in a place where they have no land, no money, no one to speak for them or defend them. They will do what they have to in order to survive, and that will mean working for a roof over their heads and a bowl a day of that swill the English call food. What else would you call it but slavery? I'd rather be dead, and—" he reached for his musket "—that's what I may well be. But I won't be a pathetic excuse for a man, on my knees groveling before the British."

François, though he said nothing, also rose from the bench and picked up his weapon.

In the awful silence, Barbe's voice trembled. "What are you going to do?"

"Reconnoiter. See how secure that church is."

"There's a stockade around it, and more soldiers than you've ever seen in one place," Soleil said, but her heart was beginning to pound—whether in hope or fear, she could not have said.

"What could the two of you do against an army?" Barbe asked, and there was only fear in her face.

"We won't know until we see the place. Surely there are a few inside who would help now, even if they have to do it with their bare hands, if we can find a way. Tell no one we were here, or they may extract a price from you. Remove every trace of our return. No extra dishes—" he waved a hand at the uncleared breakfast table "—no unexplained garments, no unmade bed. As far as you know we are still in Annapolis Royal, trying to find our brother-in-law."

The women were in a renewed state of shock when the twins had gone. And, as it developed shortly, they had left only in the nick of time.

Half an hour after their departure, a dozen soldiers marched into the clearing, and two of them strode into the house without knocking.

Their faces were arrogant, their attitudes suspicious. "Where are the others?" the leader demanded.

Momentarily struck dumb, none of the women replied.

"The men who did not appear as ordered," the man elaborated in his mutilated French, consulting a paper he carried. "François and Antoine Cyr."

Soleil saw indecision play across her mother's countenance. A bold-faced lie to the authorities was to Barbe a sin, and quite possibly she could not manage it. Soleil stepped into the breach before Barbe could summon enough wit to reply.

"My brothers went weeks ago to Annapolis Royal to look for my husband, who had gone there to visit a dying priest who was an old friend. Do you have any word of that place? Has the populace there, too, been put under arrest?"

She realized immediately that her rapid French had been largely unintelligible to him, and she repeated her words more slowly, adding, "Can you tell us anything of what happens there?"

He ignored her concerns. "Your brothers have surely returned by this time."

"No," Soleil said at once, lying brazenly as she looked the man directly in the eye, "they have not. We are much concerned for them, and fear they may have been imprisoned in Annapolis Royal."

"We will search this house," the soldier said, and a moment later the redcoats were swarming over the place, looking in the curtained bed cubicles, under the beds, inside the chest where Barbe kept her linens. Thank God, Soleil thought, they had followed Antoine's orders and removed all trace of the twins' presence.

"What is that smell?" the leader asked at last, gesturing to the fire. "What have you burned?"

Again it was Soleil whose wits were quick enough to come up with an answer. "I dropped a ball of yarn by accident onto the hearth, and it rolled into the coals. It was only a small ball of wool."

She knew he didn't believe her. He wanted an excuse to take out his anger on her for having been ordered to march all this way to search for fugitives. Yet there was no tangible evidence of wrongdoing on her part.

Obviously furious at finding nothing to justify an arrest, the soldiers left the house. Through a window the women watched as they searched the barn and the chicken house, even jamming their bayonets deep into the loose hay that was piled beside the barn door. Soleil closed her eyes, grateful that the twins had not had to take a hasty refuge there.

No one relaxed even when the soldiers had gone. They might yet find the twins in the woods, though the English were by no means the woodsmen the Acadians were. They tended to walk in groups rather than singly, crashing their way through the underbrush, noisily crushing twigs beneath their boots; a single Acadian on snowshoes could outmaneuver a regiment of British soldiers, Antoine had once observed in a lighthearted jest that now seemed from another time.

And even if the soldiers did not find the twins, what would the outcome be? If the twins avoided deportation with the rest of the family, it would mean permanent separation.

"How can God allow this to happen to us?" Soleil demanded passionately. "If He really cares for us, as we've always been taught, why doesn't He strike the British dead?"

Barbe had no reply to this, only a gentle, sad look that made Soleil immediately contrite enough to hug her mother wordlessly. But the bitter rebellion still simmered in her heart and her mind.

The day was a long one, and there was little to do once the dishes were put away. The cows had been milked and turned out to pasture; a dozen cabbages had been delivered to the pigs; the bread was rising. There was no point in chopping more firewood or carrying it into the shelter of the entrance passageway. Barbe sat mending garments that they would probably not be able to take with them. Danielle walked aimlessly through the house, worrying about her Basile, of whom she had had no word since his imprisonment, speculating endlessly on their fate until Soleil snapped at her to stop.

"If you must pace, go out for a walk!"

Danielle burst into tears. "Not everyone can be calm in the face of catastrophe," she wailed. "I can't help it if I'm upset!"

Soleil was immediately conciliatory. "I'm sorry, but I'm upset too! Everybody is, Danny. Come on, let's both go for a walk. Mama, do you want to come?"

"No. It's time Vincent went down for his nap." A tear trickled down Barbe's cheek, one of the few she had allowed, and Soleil knelt beside her, stroking her hand, wishing she could think of something comforting to say.

Barbe groped for a handkerchief and blew her nose with an apologetic grimace. "Isn't it odd? I'm used to working hard, but now that I've nothing much to do, I'm more tired than I've ever been in my life."

"And I," Soleil agreed. "I could go to bed and stay there forever."

Barbe managed a wan smile. "I always felt that way when I was carrying a baby. As if I could sleep and sleep. Oh, what is to become of your little one? What is to become of us all?"

To their dismay, Barbe began to cry in earnest, the anxiety and grief catching up to her at last. For a little while as they endeavored to calm her, Soleil and Danielle put aside their own concerns.

Later on, walking alone along the dyke after Barbe had fallen asleep with the little boy, Soleil lifted her face to the open sky.

Was God up there? Was He watching over Remie, as she was again praying that He would do? Or was religion all some monstrous joke the priests had been perpetuating over the years, designed to keep the people docile and content?

Her own tears flowed then, unchecked.

Dear God, would she ever see Remie again?

BARBE WAS HER OLD self-contained self when they were seated for their evening meal. No mention was made of her break-down, though the girls watched her covertly for any further sign that she had reached the limit of her endurance. They had taken an extra-large amount of food to the church the previous day, so the walk to town had not been necessary today; they had given up going every morning in the hope that they would be allowed to see Papa and the others. The English allowed them nothing.

Soleil's restlessness finally made her reach for a shawl as twilight fell. She knew that if she didn't escape the oppressive atmosphere in the house she would be pacing in the same way her sister had done. "I'm going to walk toward town. Maybe I'll meet the twins on the way home."

"They won't be on the path," Barbe said. "There may even be soldiers watching for them. Be careful."

"I will," Soleil said, and slipped outside.

She, too, was able to move silently after all that practice with Remie. It hurt to think of him, yet it was impossible not to think of him; either way, she thought, she could not hold back the tears.

At one point, in the shadows cast by a row of fir trees, she paused, uncertain for a moment what had disturbed her.

Tobacco. Someone not far away was smoking a pipe.

Panic washed over her, then an unnatural calm. Not the twins. They would not be smoking in the woods, not now. Who, then?

She stood very still, listening, hoping that she herself was hidden. And after what seemed a very long time, she heard an incautious movement, a rustling of leaves underfoot, perhaps.

The minutes stretched out, and still she did not move, trying to control her breathing, feeling as if whoever it was could hear the racing of the pulse that pounded so loudly in her ears.

The voices, when they came, were low but carried clearly to her. The words were in the hated English of which she understood nothing except her own last name and the name of the community to the south.

"This is a waste of time. No doubt the missing Cyrs were caught up in the net at Annapolis Royal. With any luck, someone shot them."

"Aye," came the response, close enough to her to make Soleil jump. "What's a Frenchie or two, anyway? A pair of them can't make any difference in the long run. What're they going to do, tackle the entire British Army?"

There was low laughter, then silence.

Heart thudding, Soleil began to move again. Cautiously, silently, she made her way along the familiar path so as not to let them know she was there. There were soldiers, at least two of them, waiting to ambush the twins if they showed up.

How could she intercept her brothers to warn them? They might not be wary this far from town, thinking they had eluded their would-be captors. It would be just like them to be singing or joking as they walked into the midst of a volley of musket balls.

No, Soleil amended as reason reasserted itself. The twins were foolish youths no longer. They would be expecting guards to be set around the house. The question was, were there others? More than the two she had heard?

She had walked at least a quarter of a mile, aware of the growing darkness but reluctant to return yet in case she might still encounter her brothers, when she walked into an ambush herself.

She followed a bend in the path, around a huge oak that was turning color, its yellow leaves a faint light halo above her, when she was suddenly seized from behind. A hard, callused hand clamped over her mouth, another went around her waist, and she was jerked back into the deeper shadows.

Instinct made her fight after the first paralyzing seconds, and she kicked backward, trying to break free of the powerful embrace.

A moment later a voice hissed in her ear, "Shut up, you idiot! They'll hear you!"

She sagged in relief, and Antoine removed his hand from her mouth, though he continued to hold her upright against him. She could feel his heart, hammering like her own, against her back. He reached for her white apron, whipped it off and stuffed it between their bodies; realizing why he had done it, she grabbed her cap as well and crumpled it in her hand.

Soleil suspended her breathing, and then she heard the soldiers coming. Not from behind her, but ahead.

This pair, too, were incautious, believing themselves on a fool's errand when they might better have spent the evening drinking with their mates.

They approached, no doubt thinking themselves quiet. They did not talk and passed within a few yards of the pair watching from the depths of the shadow—or, rather, the trio, for Soleil now felt the presence of the second twin behind them and slightly to their left.

The soldiers noticed nothing. They went on by, and after a time Antoine's arm eased his pressure on her ribs.

"They're gone. Changing watch with another pair, no doubt. We'll wait until the second pair has gone off duty."

"They're perhaps ten minutes away—where the spongy damp place is in the path," Soleil whispered.

"Ah, you saw them then, and they didn't see you." There was almost the old amusement in Antoine's voice. "That's our girl! Come on, while they're out of hearing we'll get farther off the path. Get rid of all this white, they might spot it."

"Did you see Papa or Pierre?" It was a vain hope, but she had to ask.

"No. There's no way of getting through to the church. You'd think the entire British Army was camped around it. We'll have to think of something else."

"What?" she breathed, but there was no reply.

The soldiers who were going off duty could be heard speaking in low voices as they came through the deepening darkness.

Soleil was afraid, but not as frightened as she'd been earlier. With one twin at each shoulder, and Antoine's arm around her waist, she felt a surge of what she knew to be irrational hope.

Maybe, after all, the twins would be able to think of something.

36

IT WAS FULLY DARK by the time they reached home, having made a circuitous route around the soldiers positioned to intercept the twins. Although this new pair of soldiers no longer talked between themselves, they seemed to have trouble staying in one spot, so that it wasn't difficult to tell where they were. "As noisy as the swine they are," François proclaimed, though without satisfaction.

Soleil approached the house from the direction of the water, as if she'd been out walking there. The twins remained at the edge of the woods behind the log structure long enough to be sure that the soldiers stayed where they were. Then they snaked over the ground on their bellies, a wide distance apart, and eased silently through the outer doorway, waiting until Soleil had put out the candles inside before entering the kitchen.

There was still enough light from the hearth to make them all nervous, and they dared not cover the windows for fear of attracting immediate attention. The twins settled wearily into a corner between the fireplace and a solid wall, where no one could possibly see them without coming right to the nearest window and being visible themselves. Danielle kept an eye on that window for anything resembling a pale English face, while Soleil and Barbe quickly brought the men food, which they gulped hungrily.

"We'll sleep in the barn," Antoine said through a mouthful of bread and cold beef. "It'll be safer there, less dangerous to you in here. They won't be able to approach without our hearing them. I've never heard such clumsiness. This pair must be straight off the boat from England, used only to London streets, by the sound of them. All the better for us, anyway."

Barbe's eyes were bright in the dim light. "Did you see Papa? Or the others?"

Antoine leaned back against the warm stone with a sigh. "No. They do let the prisoners into that damned stockade for a few minutes at a time, a dozen or so at once, but you can't recognize any of them. And you can't get close to them."

Barbe's mouth drooped in disappointment. "Then there is nothing to be done."

"I didn't say that." Antoine reached for another chunk of bread and chewed for a moment. "We can't get into the church to them, so we'll have to wait until they're brought out...when Winslow gives the order to load their damned ships."

Soleil could tell by her mother's face that Barbe immediately pictured, as she did, the beach of Grand-Pré—broad red sands stretching for an impossible expanse of open area toward the water with nothing to provide cover of any sort.

"Not the beach," Antoine said, following their thoughts. He wiped the crumbs from his hands on his thighs. "It will have to be before they get that far...where there are still trees, or at least houses. You'll all have to be prepared to run—and to leave everything you're carrying. Take as much as you can, make it look as if you've filled a cart with everything you own, then abandon it the moment you get our signal."

"But—" Barbe went no further, her jaw slack as she contemplated what her son was proposing.

"We'll hide out food and a few blankets far enough from here to be safe, but even if we can't make it there to pick up our supplies, we'll live off the land. The important thing will be to travel as fast as we can."

Danielle was thinking about leaving Basile and the rest of the Lizottes behind, and Antoine knew that, too. "We can't figure on getting anyone free but ourselves. We may not even get all of our own family away."

There was a deadly silence. Soleil's breath was caught painfully in her chest.

Barbe made a small choking sound. "Where can we possibly go that they won't find us?"

"They don't have enough soldiers to load the ships *and* patrol the woods, too, not all at the same time. We'll head north, and when we've crossed the Minas Basin we'll figure out where to go. Maybe to Île St. Jean if there are any canoes readily available to cross the strait. The Indians may already have gone on into Canada. If not, they'll help us.''

''No,'' Soleil said slowly. ''Not Île St. Jean.''

''Where, then?'' François asked.

''Across the Petitcodiac. No, wait,'' she said, holding up a hand against the argument she saw forming on her brothers' faces. ''I know the British are all over up there, too, but the woods are thick, and as you say, they're not woodsmen. They attack settlements on well-traveled paths or on the coast. We can take to the woods—I know the way Remie took us—and beyond the isthmus there's a whole continent of forest! We can go the way I went with Remie—up the St. John to the Madawaska Valley.''

And, she added silently, if Remie ever escapes from them, he will go there, too.

The twins considered. ''It sounds reasonable,'' François said at last. ''As good as anything. At least it's heading away from the enemy into Indian territory, where we'll find friends.''

Antoine yawned. ''We'll talk more about it tomorrow. They're watching the house around the clock, so we'll have to be careful. We'll work out the best plan we can. Now let's get some sleep.''

A moment later they were gone, slinking through the night. For a full five minutes the women waited, praying they would not hear English voices shouting or the sound of musket fire. There was nothing, and finally Barbe rose from the stool where she had been sitting.

''They must have reached the barn by this time. Come, let us have prayers before we retire.''

Soleil knelt with the others, but her thoughts were so chaotic that she heard little of what Barbe said. It seemed to her unlikely that any rescue of her father and brothers and little Henri could be carried out, and that if such an attempt was made it was likely that someone would be killed. It was even possible that no one of the Cyrs would survive.

But if they did, and if Remie, too, were able to flee, was it not at least remotely possible that they might eventually be reunited in that place Remie had chosen to live one day?

THE CAPTIVES in the church had little to do except think and talk. In the days after they were locked up, they requested pen and paper, and those who could write put down the thoughts of the others, to be delivered to Colonel Winslow.

"At the sight of the evils that seem to threaten us on every side, we are obliged to implore your protection and to beg of you to intercede with His Majesty that he may have a care for those amongst us who have inviolably kept the fidelity and the submission promised to His Majesty," the document read.

"As you have given us to understand that the king has ordered us to be transported out of this province, we beg of you that, if we must forsake our lands, we may at least be allowed to go to places where we shall find fellow countrymen, all expenses being defrayed by ourselves, and that we may be granted a suitable length of time therefore, and all the more because by this means we shall be able to preserve our religion, which we have deeply at heart, and for which we are content to sacrifice our property."

Pierre gave his approval, like the others, but unlike Émile, who held genuine hope that the British commander would consider their petition and pass it on to those higher up, he expected nothing.

"They won't let us go, Papa," he said in a tortured way, his eyes dark with compassion for his father. "To do so would mean not only continuing to practice our religion, which the English regard as papist heresy. It would mean allowing us to join their enemies in Canada—the French, the Indians—and thus make them stronger. The British have always feared to fight against the lot of us who were on these shores ahead of them, and if we join together we will outnumber them by a tremendous margin. It doesn't matter that the Acadians have been a peaceful people for over a hundred years. If we join the French, who are not passive, and the Indians, who can be fiercely aggressive and every bit as ruthless as the British themselves, their position in the New World seems threatened. They will scatter us to the winds, hoping that not enough of us will ever come together again to constitute any sort of threat to anyone."

Émile's face had grown deeply lined in the short time he had been incarcerated. "I hope you are wrong, my son. It is reasonable, what we ask. We must pray that God in His wisdom will open their hearts to hear us."

Pierre shook his head. "Who is to decide? The king of France cares nothing for us, and we came from his own people. Why should the king of England give a damn for us, one way or the other? He wants only the riches of the New World, our fish and our furs, and a place to send out his own settlers. No, Papa, don't break your heart praying for something that will not come to pass."

Yet he knew that Émile did pray, and did hope, and Pierre wished that hope were possible in his own breast, for it was not. He hugged his younger son close to his side and thought of the younger one at home as he stared at nothing through a blur of tears.

THE ORDER came from Winslow that the first of the Acadians were to be loaded onto the ships anchored at the mouth of the Gaspareaux River.

For the first time since they had been locked up, every man and boy went outside at the same time, blinking in the autumn sun, bewildered and apprehensive.

"Perhaps," Émile suggested eagerly, "they have read our petition and decided to allow us to return home, to prepare ourselves for departure to destinations of our own choosing."

Pierre said nothing. His guts were in a knot, and he hoped he would not disgrace them all by throwing up; he kept a tight grasp of Henri's small hand and shuffled along as they were directed through the stockade into the open, where it appeared that every British soldier assigned to Grand-Pré had assembled before them.

No, he thought, raking his gaze over the cold English faces, noting their muskets held at the ready, they had not been called forth to be given their freedom. He had believed his stomach already as tense as it could be, but as he looked beyond the soldiers to the ships waiting offshore, he felt as if an iron band had been tightened within him, barely permitting him to breathe.

Not even Émile could retain his optimism in the face of what took place next. A young lieutenant and perhaps eighty officers stepped forward, indicating those in the straggling line of prisoners who were to step to one side. Bertin was one of them, and he cast a frightened look at his father as he obeyed.

"What is happening, Papa?" Henri whispered, but Pierre could not answer. There went Basile Lizotte, too, and one of the Dubay brothers. One, Pierre thought numbly, only one. They promised that we would be deported by family, yet they chose only one from each of those families.

He glanced at Émile and saw that his father had not yet grasped the enormity of what was happening. It would be kinder of God to strike him dead than to allow him to witness what appeared about to take place.

Colonel Winslow was there in his scarlet coat and his white wig, and when one hundred and forty or fifty of the young men had been set apart, he gave the order. Not even those who knew not a word of English misunderstood it.

"March, to the ships."

Consternation swept through both the young men and their elders who remained in the original group.

"Not without our fathers!" someone shouted in protest. "We were told that we would remain with our families!"

A ripple, then a roar of agreement ran through the ranks of the captives, but another order was given. "Fix bayonets! Advance on the prisoners!"

A sickening sensation such as he had never known swept through Pierre. Bertin gave him a last wild, pleading glance before he was prodded by one of the bayonets and forced to step out with the others. Georges Picot, who was only fifteen, began to weep, refusing to move, until Colonel Winslow himself put a hand on his shoulder and shoved him forward. Hesitatingly, unwillingly, the young Acadians were forced forward toward the waiting ships.

The women of the village had begun to gather, and as they, too, comprehended what was happening, their voices rose in lamentation, at first in disbelief, then in anguish. The British remained unmoved by any of this, keeping their bayonets at the ready, prodding any in the line of young men who lagged.

It was a mile and a half to the ships. The agony went on and on, step by step, and there was not a dry eye in the entire assemblage of Acadians. Émile comprehended at last, and Pierre put an arm around his shoulders, fearing that his father would collapse, for he had gone very pale.

Grand-père, too, was shaking, and Jacques pressed close against him, as much to receive comfort as to give it.

Pierre tried to keep Bertin in sight as long as he could, until finally the marchers were too distant to be distinguished one from the other; until he had to blink away the moisture in his eyes, knowing in his heart that he would never see that brother again.

Émile had realized the same thing. He slid abruptly to his knees, leaning forward with a choking plea for the mercy of the Almighty. But there was no roll of thunder, no crash of lighting, no divine intervention.

And in the distance the young men were loaded into small boats and sent off to the ships.

37

"THERE ARE NO SOLDIERS watching the house any longer," François reported the following morning, but he did not sound pleased about it. "They must have called them all in. One of you had better go into the village and see what they're up to."

"I will," Soleil offered at once, for she felt she would go mad if she sat any longer listening to the twins' plans; they sounded more like dreams than anything with a chance of success. "I'll take something to Papa and the others to eat, and some tobacco."

"I'll go with you," Danielle added quickly, and they set off at once, each with a basket on her arm for the captives.

They had not reached the village, however, when they met Céleste Dubay, weeping and stumbling blindly. The other girl fell into Soleil's arms with a renewed outburst of sobs.

It was several minutes before Céleste could control her despair enough to tell them what had happened.

"Two hundred and thirty have been loaded onto the ships," she said finally, mopping swollen, reddened eyes on a corner of her apron. "Not Papa. I saw him when they were herded back into the stockade. But all my brothers have gone, and not even onto the same ship! It was as if the British intentionally separated members of the same family! Mme Dubois asked if she and the younger children would be allowed to join the older ones, and the soldiers would only shrug and say that it's in God's hands! How dare they blaspheme in that manner?''

Soleil's legs were threatening to give way, so that she put out a hand to a tree trunk to steady herself. "And our Papa? Did you see him?''

"Yes. He and Pierre were still together, and little Henri. Only Bertin of yours was embarked, I think.''

"Bertin?'' Soleil whispered her brother's name. "All by himself?''

"Yes.'' Céleste's gaze flickered unhappily toward Danielle. "And the Lizotte brothers, all but the little one. I doubt they went onto the same ship with one another, either, though I couldn't be certain.''

Danielle clutched at her bosom as if she had been stabbed. "Not Basile! Oh, please, God, not Basile!''

Soleil felt dizzy with horror, her fingernails digging into the bark of the beech tree. The sun was warm, and somewhere in the distance she heard the familiar cries of the gulls, but she was cold and set apart from everything she had ever known.

"It's true, then. They really are going to send us away to some other place, and they are not even going to allow us to stay together with those we love.''

Céleste looked at her piteously. "How am I going to break the news to Mama? What can I say?''

Danielle had given in to weeping, her face buried in her hands. Soleil tried to draw herself together, to reason, to speak. There must be something to say, but she could think of nothing.

"If only Antoine were here,'' Céleste managed, "but then I suppose he would be locked up with the others, and when there are so many ships it's unlikely we'd be together—''

"The twins are at home,'' Soleil said in a low tone, in case anyone lurking in the woods might overhear. "But not a word of it, understand? No one must know! The soldiers have been guarding the house until this morning, watching for them in their loutish way, but they must have returned to Grand-Pré to help in the embarkation. They are trying to plan something, but oh—'' she reached again for her friend, seeing the hope leap in

Céleste's face "—I do not see how they can succeed, not against all those armed soldiers!"

"But they might," Céleste countered, clutching Soleil's hands. "God willing."

Soleil's own face was bleak. "God willing," she echoed, but heard no faith in her words or her voice.

THEY EXPECTED THAT at any moment the order would come, summoning them to the beach. They had loaded a cart with bedding and clothes and kitchenware, and plenty of food. It was ready to go when the word came.

Then they waited. And waited. And waited, until the slightest sound was enough to send them to the verge of hysteria. And still the order did not come. Every other day the girls walked to the village with supplies, and less and less did they trust that the food actually reached those for whom it was intended. There had been no more ships, and since the British depended upon their cargoes for supplies, they had to fall back upon the populace to feed them.

Colonel Winslow was reportedly in a foul humor, and not only about the lack of fresh supplies. How was he to transport more than two thousand citizens on eight small ships, when even the eleven vessels he had been promised would have been barely adequate?

Besides that, the discontent among his prisoners had taken on a nasty edge; in spite of the fact that they were unarmed and had been fairly docile up to the time he began to separate them from their sons, he now judged it wise to watch them carefully, and he doubled the guards.

Denied the church in which to worship and petition their God, the women of the village knelt openly in the square or in the yards before their houses. They prayed tearfully and earnestly... and aloud. Throughout the days and sometimes into the nights, their lamentations could be heard throughout the village.

Every day a group of women gathered on the beach within sight of the ships that held their sons and knelt in the wet red sand, pleading with God to save them. But the days slid into October, and there was no miracle.

François and Antoine spent most of their days in the woods, setting up caches of supplies in various locations, going over and over their plans to attempt to rescue whichever family members they could reach.

"And Céleste," Antoine said. "If possible, we must rescue Céleste."

François went very still. "Will she leave her family? We cannot take them all, even if we could get them away."

"No. Only Céleste. And she'll come with us," Antoine said with conviction.

Not only did the additional ships fail to arrive, three of those standing in the harbor were ordered to Pisiquid, much to Winslow's rage. Finally, on the 8th of October, the British commander gave up waiting for more ships or supplies. He gave the order: the rest of the citizens would be loaded onto the ships, as many as could be crowded into the holds.

Soleil thought her chest would burst with the tension. Along with Barbe and Danielle, she kissed the twins and they all wished each other luck, then the women and Vincent headed for town, their cart loaded with belongings. Antoine had urged them all to eat, for God knew when food would again be available, but only small Vincent could swallow anything. They made their way along the path with leaden feet, unable to talk, and for the moment beyond tears.

Soleil couldn't have said if her faith in God had truly revived upon hearing that Remie was still alive. But the habit of a lifetime was strong. The litany ran through her mind as she plodded beside the cart. *Please, God. Protect us. Help the twins to save us.*

A cold wind swept in off the water as they left the woods. They had been joined by the Dubays and several other families, exchanging subdued greetings or none at all. No one gave any sign of having slept for days.

So much depended upon events completely beyond their control, Soleil thought. If only the men—Papa and Grand-père and her brothers—came out of the stockade at the right time! Already the women of her own family were leaving the shelter of the forest, and if Antoine and François took any action it would have to be in plain sight of the soldiers who were even now opening the gates of the enclosure around the church.

Danielle murmured something, but Soleil's blood was pounding so loudly in her ears that she was unaware. Lips parted, she waited for the prisoners to emerge, praying that her father and the others would be among them. If not, she must find a reason to slow their own pace.

The village streets were full of people, and there were more gathered on the beach beyond. Everyone they met was weeping or had been weeping. The children were frightened, silent. A dog howled, sending a spasm of distress through Soleil. The dogs and cats, like the cattle, sheep and pigs, must be left behind to fend for themselves.

And everywhere were the redcoats with their muskets and bayonets. Hundreds of them. How could their plan possibly succeed in the face of all those armed soldiers?

The Acadians moved slowly, some of them glancing back at their beloved woods and fields, the only homes most of them had ever known. But a larger number simply plodded toward the ships at the mouth of the river, unable to see through their tears.

One shrill voice carried to the Cyrs as they approached the stockade: Mme Thibault, demanding almost hysterically, "Will I be on the same ship with my husband? Have you kept a record of which ship he is on?"

The nearest soldier made no reply, only prodding her on with the straggling line of women.

Dear God, Soleil thought, hell can be no worse than this, even if it's filled with flames. Nothing could be more searing to these souls than the grief and anguish they were undergoing right now.

There was Papa.

He had just emerged from the stockade. He hesitated, blinking as if grown unaccustomed to the light of day. Then he saw them.

Barbe made a gasping sound and began to run toward him, only to be stopped when one of the soldiers held up his musket as a barrier between them.

Where was Pierre? Grand-père and the younger boys? Soleil could not find them in the mass of humanity that spilled out of the church and through the gates of the stockade. Dear God, they had counted on the family being together, but she saw now that the soldiers were not allowing that as they directed the men and little boys into one line or another.

She glanced wildly around, trying to spot either of the twins, but she didn't know exactly where they would be. They had wanted confusion, and there was certainly that, but the captives were so scattered that Soleil could see no way the family could be pulled together, could be rescued as a unit, even if rescue were possible.

She saw Céleste Dubay and her mother, clinging together—saying goodbye, Soleil thought—and she caught her friend's eye. Tears flowing, Céleste turned from her family and came toward the Cyrs. For a moment it seemed that the soldiers would stop her, but their attention was drawn to an old man who stumbled and fell, and Céleste came on.

Now was the time for the twins to act, if they were going to.

None of them saw the arrow. Antoine had decided that musket fire would be counterproductive, drawing the attention of every British soldier on the scene. Instead, he'd said, he would create a diversion among the soldiery closest to Émile and the others—only the others had not yet come through the gate.

Glass exploded in the windows of the house across from the church where Colonel Winslow was quartered. Even though the women had been waiting for this signal, valuable seconds were lost before they could get themselves into motion. Soleil, as ordered, turned and raced for the woods. She heard Céleste, her breath coming in choked sobs, right behind her.

In the split seconds before she turned her back on them, Soleil had seen her parents fall into each other's arms; she wanted to wait for them, but Antoine had been insistent that she leave with him, and against her own instincts she obeyed. She had a fleeting moment of wondering if this pell-mell dash endangered her baby, but the woods seemed so far away, and there was no time to worry about that now. There would be no saving the baby if she died herself of a British musket ball in the back.

She reached the fringe of trees beside the main path; when she staggered to a halt to catch her breath, Céleste stumbled into her and they clung together, looking back.

François's arrow had found its mark, and it had indeed created a diversion, throwing the soldiers into momentary confusion. With the second one, he had warned them during their final planning session, the distraction time would probably be even less, and the soldiers would be able to get a fix on his own whereabouts.

He was proved correct. A shot sang past Soleil's head and she jerked, then was moving again without need of her brother's shouted admonition: "Run!"

There was no time to see what was happening behind them. Soleil and Céleste ran for their lives.

DANIELLE had spotted Grand-père only seconds before the first sounds of breaking glass. Had she remembered exactly what her brothers had ordered her to do, she would have run for the woods with the other girls, dragging the terrified Vincent with her. Instead, she reacted instinctively by racing forward a few yards to grab the old man by the arm. Grand-père was not a young man, but surely he would try to escape with the others, doing his utmost to keep up.

She hadn't counted on what a nearly five-week incarceration had done to the old man. Inactivity had allowed his joints to stiffen; a limited diet and despair had done the rest.

Grand-père could not run. He was dazed, uncomprehending, and he faltered, then went down.

It was enough. A pair of soldiers, their attention already turning back to their prisoners from the broken windows and the ire their commanding officer would have over the shards of glass scattered across his desk, brought the little group to a halt.

They were angry at this attempt to escape. One of them brought the stock of his musket in a vicious swing against the side of Grand-père's head, sending him sprawling. The other caught Danielle's shoulder.

She cried out in pain, involuntarily releasing her tight grip on Vincent's small hand as she was knocked down across the old man. The soldier stood over her with a furious scowl.

"Try anything like that again and you're dead," he said, kicking at Grand-père's exposed face.

The only word she understood was "dead," but it was more than enough. By the time she got to her feet, weeping with utter hopelessness, Danielle knew it was too late. Confused, despairing, she looked for Vincent, but she had lost him in the tumult around her. She could only pray that he had managed to run free to join the others; perhaps the soldiers would not bother with so small a boy.

A glance told her that Soleil and Céleste had made it to the trees, and that Antoine was hurrying their parents in a slightly different direction. She heard the blast, saw her father stagger and go to his knees, recognized the blossom of red on Émile's shoulder as blood, then was jerked around and thrown forward into the line of stunned women and children.

In spite of this, she turned again. Antoine had dragged Émile to his feet, and with Barbe on her husband's other side, all three were moving again.

The soldier who had fired ran toward them, then suddenly keeled over and lay still, tripping a fellow officer who fell, as well. Danielle saw the arrow protruding through the first man's back, then was thrust ahead with the others.

"My grandfather," she protested, for the old man was still sprawled on the ground. One of the British gestured angrily, and two others came forward to haul Grand-père to his feet; one of them disgustedly continued to hold him upright, steering him along on the walk to the ships.

Blood streamed from the old man's head, but he walked willingly enough. In truth, he did not even know where he was, or why he walked, nor did he feel the wound inflicted by the stock of the musket. Grand-père had long since given his soul over to God. His lips moved almost soundlessly in the old familiar prayers, comforting him.

There was nothing to comfort Danielle. She stared ahead at the masts of the ships as they drew closer and hoped that the shots she heard did not mean the rest of her family were already dead.

She did not turn again to see.

38

GRADUALLY the musket fire and the shouting died away behind them, and François allowed the girls to slow to a rapid walk. Soleil had a stitch in her side that had become excruciating, and she was gasping for breath.

François, unwinded, paused to look back, but there was no sign of either a British pursuit or the rest of the family.

"I'm going back," he decided, "to see if I can help Antoine."

It was too late for that, Soleil thought, despairing. Even if the shots they'd heard hadn't killed the others, they had probably been taken prisoner. Yet she had neither the breath nor the heart to argue.

"Keep going," François told them. "You remember where I told you we left the caches of supplies?"

Soleil nodded, unable to speak.

"Head for the nearest one, near the bee tree, Soleil. Hide there and wait."

Céleste, her cap lost and her hair plastered with sweat to her forehead, managed enough wind to speak. "What if you don't come back?"

François gave her a long, measured look. "Then you go on without me."

Céleste swallowed. "Where do we go?"

"Soleil knows where. Across the Chignecto into Canada. There will be others. They'll help you. If we survive, if any escape from their damnable ships, we'll head up the St. John to the country Remie talked about. Oh, and get rid of those aprons, and your cap, Soleil. Don't throw them away—we may need the material for bandages—but get them out of sight."

He spun around then and was gone.

Silently the girls obeyed, folding their aprons and tucking them into their bodices before they went on.

The boys had ranged these woods since they were no older than Henri and Vincent. They knew every inch of them for miles around. The girls had played in them less recently, but they, too, were familiar with the general area. They had rested briefly and now set a good pace.

Dear God, dear God, Soleil thought, and could not form the other words of her petition. She did not think that God was listening to Acadians on this black day, yet she could not erase a lifetime habit of calling upon the Almighty in time of trouble.

FRANÇOIS FOUND his father in the depths of a thicket by a small stream. Barbe knelt beside him, trying to bathe his face and his wound with a bloodied scrap of apron.

Émile opened his eyes and blinked. "François. Soleil, did she get away? And Danielle and the others?"

"Soleil is all right, and Céleste. I don't know what happened to anyone else. How bad is it?" Barbe made way for him as he knelt to examine his father's injury. "You're lucky, Papa. The ball went clean through your shoulder, and the bleeding could be worse." He reached for the wadded apron and tore several strips from the bottom of it. "Here, Mama, make two pads of this part, one for the front and one for the back, and we'll try to fasten them on. The sooner we get moving the better."

Barbe was very pale but calm. She affixed the pads, secured them with the strips and looked questioningly but with trust at her son.

"All right. The two of you go on. Papa, do you know where you are? Can you find your way to the bee tree, near where we always pick the blueberries?"

Émile sat up, wincing, and spoke with indignation. "I was hunting these woods from the time I was weaned. What are you going to do?"

"Find out what happened to Antoine." François spoke quietly but with determination. "Was he shot?"

"I don't know. He headed us into the woods, then turned back for the others," Barbe told him. "We did as he said and did not wait to see."

François nodded and stood up. "All right. I'll meet you and the girls at the bee tree as soon as I can. If I don't show up within an hour or two, go on to the next cache we left. Soleil will know where it is."

With the lithe agility and the silent grace of an Indian, he left them without looking back.

So much had happened, yet not much time had passed. The sun was as yet only midway up in the eastern sky. François wished he knew whether the soldiers would follow them. He guessed they would leave the stragglers, the few escapees, until after they had loaded the ships. Then, no doubt, they would scour the woods, running them down as if they were no more than wild animals to be destroyed.

François moved rapidly, used to traveling considerable distances in a hurry, slowing only when the trees began to thin out. Impossibly the exodus from the church and the stockade continued, and the ragged line of weeping, praying women still stretched across the sand toward the ships.

There were no bodies on the ground between his observation place and the village proper. It gave him hope that Antoine had escaped, too, even if he had been shot. François did not think the soldiers would have moved a murdered or injured man; he was more valuable as an object lesson if he lay in plain sight discouraging others who might be considering a similar attempt at escape.

And then François's heart lurched. For there was his twin, coming out of the house into which he had shot the arrows, under an armed guard of four soldiers. For a matter of seconds Antoine paused, looking directly at where François stood, though he could not possibly have seen him hidden there in the shadows of the trees.

Two of his captors prodded Antoine simultaneously with the muzzles of their muskets, and with some force, for he nearly fell.

A murderous, impotent rage filled François until he trembled with the force of it. Would that he could kill every one of them!

When Antoine had regained his footing, he stepped out ahead of the guard, but not before he looked again directly at François for the last time and shook his head. *No.*

François knew what Antoine would say, had they been close enough together so that he could hear.

"Do not further endanger yourself on my behalf. See to the others."

Another jab sent Antoine nearly to his knees. Then he faced the tall-masted ships and marched as commanded.

All his life François had followed his twin's lead. He had been born only minutes after Antoine, and they looked so much alike that few outside the immediate family could distinguish one from the other. Both were quick and bright, but François had always known it was Antoine who was the quickest and the brightest. When they disagreed on a course of action, it was, for the most part, Antoine who won out.

The impulse to join his brother, even into captivity and deportation, was strong for those few moments, almost as compelling as his desire to fire the musket blindly into the hated redcoats, reloading and killing as many of them as he could before they cut him down.

But Antoine's shake of the head had been definite, and François knew what it meant. Finally, as he always had, François followed his brother's lead.

From now on, he thought, there would be only his own lead. Papa was injured, and he'd grown more than a few weeks older during the time he'd been locked in the church. The leadership would have to be his own if he were to get his parents and his sister to a safe place.

He withdrew cautiously from the edge of the woods, then began to move faster to overtake the others, his thoughts so wild he wondered how long his head could contain them without tearing itself apart.

For in addition to losing his twin and the rest of his family being loaded on the ships, there was the matter of Céleste.

For a long time, ever since they were all very young, there had been a teasing friendship between the three of them. François couldn't have said when it began to go beyond that for him; when he began to know that he loved this pretty girl with the soft brown hair and the hazel eyes fringed in thick dark lashes.

They had had so much fun, the three of them, and he'd taken as much delight as Antoine in tormenting the girl with tricks made possible because she hadn't been able to tell them apart. But as time passed, some of the hoaxes no longer seemed funny, and Céleste didn't laugh at them anymore. She had grown up enough to want a husband, not mere friends. The one she had chosen had been Antoine, so François had stepped aside, as he always had when Antoine bested him at something—with good grace, with a humorous quip, with an ache in his heart that he tried to pretend was not there. No one, not even Antoine, had suspected.

He swallowed frequently, trotting through the woods, pausing occasionally to listen for any sign that he was being pursued, striving for the control that was so difficult to achieve. For Antoine was gone into the hold of one of the hell ships, to be taken God knew where. And he, François, was the only one left to see that Céleste was safe.

He had regained his wind, and he fell into as fast a run as the woods would allow. For a time, at least, he could not afford to think about Antoine, nor could he dwell upon Céleste as a girl that he loved. He had to get those he had stolen away from their enemies to a place of safety, and he had to do it all by himself.

SOLEIL AND CÉLESTE crouched low to the ground, well off the trodden path, totally silent once their chests had stopped heaving and their gasping breaths had subsided. They did not talk. They did not even look at each other, for that made the terrible thing they had just witnessed more real.

Soleil rested while she could, knowing that she might have to walk until she collapsed once they started again. Only, please God, she pleaded silently, let it not be just the two of them, herself and Céleste.

She put her hands on her stomach, which was still flat, showing no sign of the child that grew within her. She'd heard of miscarriages caused by far less than what she had endured these past few weeks, and she prayed that it would not happen to her. Not to Remie's child.

A small sound made her open her eyes and discover a rabbit looking at her. When Céleste stirred slightly, the creature leaped for cover. Poor thing. It, too, faced an uncertain future in a world where it was a food source for so many other creatures in the wild.

And then the sound was not small enough to be a rabbit. Soleil froze, putting out a warning hand to touch Céleste, who didn't need it. She, too, crouched lower, her eyes wide, her lips parted in the attempt to breathe inaudibly.

François joining them at last? Or . . . a patrol sent out from the village?

Something heavy fell, followed by a smothered oath in a voice Soleil recognized with nearly hysterical delight.

"Papa? Oh, is that you?" She scrambled from hands and knees to her feet, rushing forward to see her mother trying to help Émile up.

He looked terrible, with a great bloody hole in his shirt and a gory bandage protruding through it, but he was alive, and he was free. As was Barbe, who appeared uninjured.

Émile had tripped over a trailing root, but upon seeing the girls he decided not to get up and leaned instead against a tree trunk, panting. "We can rest here for a time, can we not? Is there any water, child? We've been on short rations ever since they locked us up, and now this running..."

"It's the blood he's lost," Barbe surmised worriedly, checking his bandages. "And all that while without exercise."

"I'll see if I can find something to carry water from the creek," Soleil offered. "I think we packed a gourd with the bread and meat—yes, here it is." She pulled it out of the pack François had hidden at the base of the bee tree and ran to fetch a drink for her father from the tiny stream a dozen yards away.

He drank thirstily, then closed his eyes. "Thank you, girl. Now I need to rest until it's time to go on."

Soleil looked at her mother. "François and Antoine?" she asked quietly, and knew that Céleste waited as tensely as she for the reply.

"We don't know. François sent us here. He went to see if he could help Antoine, but..."

Barbe didn't finish the sentence, and no one asked any more questions. They slumped on the ground, together yet each in a private purgatory for which there was no relief.

Remie, Soleil thought longingly. Where was he? Would they ever see each other again?

For the moment she had not even the strength to cry. She sat waiting for whatever was to happen next, and prayed for the will to endure it.

THEY KNEW AT ONCE from his face that he had not succeeded in rescuing Antoine or any of the others.

Gone, all gone, Soleil thought dully. *We'll never see any of them again.*

Later, she knew, the pain of it would be overwhelming. But at the moment she had thought about it as much as she could bear, and she willed her mind to go blank, to shut it out. Because if she could not do that, she feared she would go mad.

No one asked François any questions. He inspected the amount of blood that had soaked through Émile's dressings, then stood up and reached for the bundle of food at the foot of the tree.

"Can you walk, Papa? The farther away from here we can get before dark, the better off we'll be. As soon as the ships depart, they'll have patrols in the woods."

Émile's face was a distressing color, a grayish tinge underlying his natural tan, but he grunted assent. "Let's go," he said, and they were off, single file, with François leading and Soleil bringing up the rear.

Twice they stopped to rest, and not only on Émile's account.

They spoke not at all. And always, in every mind, was the thought of the soldiers who for some reason hated them enough not only to deport them from their land but to separate families, wives from husbands, children from parents.

Soleil did not look behind her to see if the soldiers were coming. At the moment she scarcely cared. She continued to walk through the woods, and after a time her mind seemed almost to float free, allowing the peace and quiet to soothe her.

When François finally let them stop for the night, she dropped to the ground and fell instantly asleep, and she did not dream.

39

THERE WAS NOT enough room on the ships for all of the citizens. Those who had been loaded were packed in like herring in the barrels destined for France, in the days when they had been allowed to trade with France.

Somehow Danielle managed to keep hold of Grand-père, though it was clear that he did not know who guided him or where he was being taken. They were left to carve out their own space in the hold of the ship, a dark place smelling almost at once of human perspiration and excrement as well as bilge water.

Danielle, too, was in shock, yet her concern for her grandfather kept her functioning on at least an elementary level. They found a place in the densely packed compartment, and somehow she managed to shut out the whimpering, the crying, the helpless rage of those around her. She drew Grand-père into her arms and held him, for it was all she could do.

One the morning of the third day—she *thought* it was the third day, though the darkness had wiped away her sense of time—the hatch overhead was opened to allow in some light, and she looked down into Grand-père's unseeing dark eyes. Dried blood caked his face, but it was at peace.

A familiar voice spoke to her out of the surrounding dimness, though her mind was too dazed to identify it. "He's dead, child," the woman said softly.

Danielle continued to cradle the old man, speaking softly to him. Finally someone came and took him away; she did not turn her head to watch him being carried up the ladder, out of sight.

Another day and night passed, and the ship continued to rock gently at anchor. At intervals water and unpalatable food were brought; Danielle never remembered whether or not she ate and drank.

When the order came to take her turn on deck for a bit of fresh air, she would not have bothered to go if someone had not prodded her sharply and insisted. Danielle stumbled as she came into the open air, which was sharp and cold; the light hurt her eyes, and she had to close them and get used to it gradually.

Then she saw the little boy huddled on deck, his cheeks streaked from days of crying, his mouth slack except for an occasional quivering of his lips.

Danielle staggered, then caught herself against the rail. "Vincent?" she said in a whisper. And then she repeated his name louder, so that the boy turned his face in her direction. "Vincent, is it you?"

They flew into each other's arms, and she nearly crushed him in her embrace as they clung together, both sobbing and laughing in their relief.

Grand-père was gone, but she had Vincent, Pierre's little boy. She was not totally deprived of her family.

From that moment on, Danielle began to think again, to plan. To hope.

Two ships away in the vessels anchored just offshore, Pierre listened to the plotting of the small group of young men.

"Are you in, Pierre?" one of them had asked after outlining his idea for escape.

Pierre's arm tightened around his young son. There was no way he could take part in such an attempt, no way he could leave Henri here alone.

"No," he said after a moment's wistful contemplation. "I can't go with you. But if there's anything I can do to help you from here, you've only to name it."

Henri had lifted his face to look up at his father, though it was too dark for them to see each other. "Papa, where are we going?"

"I don't know, son," Pierre told him with great tenderness. "But wherever it is, we'll go together."

The child's voice was small, so small. "Will we ever see Grand-maman again?"

Pierre's hand rested on the soft hair, stroking it. "I don't think so, Henri."

"Or Vincent? Or Grand-papa?"

Pierre's throat closed; he could not speak. He pressed his son's face into his chest, holding him close as he fought to control his own emotions.

Henri did not ask again.

The weather turned bad, as it had a way of doing in October. The wind blew, cold and wet; the ships tugged against their restraints, and those in the holds added nausea to their miseries. There was not room even to lie down, yet there was little complaint from one captive against another. They simply endured.

That night while the British were either engaged in securing their vessels or taking refuge at some village fireside—since so many of the houses had now been abandoned, there was no need to suffer the storm in their tents—twenty-four young men managed to escape from one of the ships. Jacques had heard their plans, and he longed to go with them, for he still hoped that some of his family might be contacted. But when he asked, rather timidly, if he might be allowed to go, they silenced him.

"It would only needlessly endanger you," one of them said. "You are too young."

Jacques listened but said no more as the men made their way up the ladder, and he was glad for them when he heard no shouted cry of alarm from the watch. He wondered how far the ship would take him, and if there would be food and warmth when he got there. Then he closed his eyes and leaned against Guillaume Trudelle, who put an arm around him until he fell asleep.

COLONEL WINSLOW was very angry about the escape. He ordered out soldiers to search for the deserters, as he termed them, and when the young Acadians were discovered, there was a brief skirmish. Two Acadians were killed; the others escaped again, and Winslow's fury mounted against them and his own inept soldiers.

The word went out: if the men did not voluntarily return, there would be reprisals against their families, who were held responsible. When the first execution was threatened, the young men began to trickle back, and this time they were manacled before being thrown once more into the hold of the ship.

The others all heard and were afraid to try again. What good was freedom if it cost the rest of your family their lives?

On October 11, word swept through the captives in low voices. Seven more ships had arrived from Annapolis Royal. Three of these were sent to Pisiquid to be loaded with those citizens; the others were now available to carry the remaining inhabitants of Grand-Pré, and Winslow wasted no time in seeing that as many as possible were put aboard. He still did not have quite enough room for them all, but the order was given: the ships raised their sails, and the interminable wait was over. They were under way, exiled to God knew where: five thousand Acadians, most of them forcibly separated from their family members.

THEY WOULD HAVE MANAGED fairly well, Soleil thought bitterly, if it had not seen fit to storm. Even Émile was able to keep up a reasonable pace, though his color was bad and he was in obvious pain.

But there was no shelter except for boughs of fir, and no furs or skins to warm them. Soaked to the skin, chilled by the cold wind, they might all have taken ill instead of only Émile.

It was hard to judge how far they had walked. The food the twins had hidden was eaten only too quickly, and François did not dare fire the musket for game, fearing it would bring the British down upon them like a swarm of hornets. He had two arrows left, however, which enabled him to bring down a few rabbits, and the streams provided a few fish, which they ate nearly raw.

They halted for the night in the place she and Remie had camped early last spring, on the red bluff overlooking the Minas Basin. Soleil's eyes stung, remembering how happy they had been.

Though the canoe was still there, it wasn't adequate for five. "We'll have to make two trips," François said. "I'll take Mama and Papa over first, then return for you two." He carefully averted his gaze from Céleste, unable to bear the sight of her grief for her family and Antoine.

But in the morning Émile refused to rise.

"Go on, my son. Take your mother and your sister and Céleste to a safer place." He coughed, and the spasms left him notably weaker. "I cannot walk any longer. My shoulder burns as if it had a hot poker through it, and it's hard to breathe. Go, leave me, and do not waste time discussing the matter. I have made up my mind. I'll not endanger the rest of you by keeping you here, and I cannot go on."

Barbe's face was white and already thinner. "I'll stay here with you, Father," she said, almost matter-of-fact.

"You'll not," Émile countered. "You will go with the others. I would have you safe."

"You don't know me very well," Barbe told him, "if you think I would leave you here to die alone."

He contemplated her stubborn mouth, then sighed. "Very well then. I'll agree not to die, if you'll go with the others."

"I don't trust you not to die," Barbe said steadily, "so I will stay."

"Enough of this talk of dying," François said abruptly. "I agree, however, that Papa cannot go on. So I will take Soleil and Céleste across the channel, and we'll decide when I return what's best to do. If only there were some sort of shelter where you could be dry until you feel better... We can leave you the remainder of our provisions. It should be safe to shoot something once we've crossed the basin, so the rest of us will be all right."

"In a few days," Émile said, "we will follow you."

"Yes, of course. Though I'll be back tomorrow to see how things stand. I'll bring you some more fish if I can," François added.

But when he returned for them the following day, there were only the small remains of a fire and some fish bones.

Émile and Barbe were gone.

François spent only a brief time looking for them. He respected his father's wishes and understood them. Yet it was with a heavy heart that he descended the red cliffs and crossed the Minas Basin.

FROM A SAFE DISTANCE Émile and Barbe watched their son for as long as they could see him.

"God grant them a safe journey," Barbe murmured, and Émile made the sign of the cross, adding "Amen."

Then he turned, pausing to look to the south. The lines that cut so cruelly into his face deepened, and Barbe swung around to follow his gaze.

On the horizon hung a dark haze.

Émile stared at it, heartbreak in his brown eyes. "I never thought God would allow it to happen," he said. "They are burning Grand-Pré."

40

SOLEIL AND CÉLESTE stood on the north bluff, watching the approach of François's canoe. They too saw the smoke and correctly interpreted it.

"They've put the torch to the village," Céleste said. In only a few days she had aged years; there were bluish smudges under her hazel eyes, and her hair was tangled and wild.

Soleil supposed she looked no better. She didn't want to watch the smoke, didn't want to remember what it had been like skirting Beaubassin when that settlement, too, had been burning from the British torches. But she did remember: the acrid smell, the smoldering remains of what had been some family's home, the broken doll, the dead dog. She shivered, and didn't know if it was because of the memories or the chill of the wind that cut into her flesh beneath the black shawl she clutched at her throat.

She couldn't smell *this* smoke. It was much too far away for that, and the wind was from the wrong direction, but she felt as if she could. Today it was the village of Grand-Pré; tomorrow, or the next day, would the soldiers reach the Cyr farm with their torches? The barn would go first, easily fueled by the hay already inside, and then the house...the beautiful house in which she had been born, in which she had been so happy...the one where she and Remie had spent their wedding night....

Céleste, who like Soleil had remained silently trapped in her own mournful thoughts, spoke suddenly, drawing Soleil out of her reverie.

"He's alone."

"What?" Soleil shifted her gaze from the billowing dark smoke in the distant sky to the speck on the water below them, which had grown larger while she was absorbed elsewhere. Céleste was right. There was only one figure in the canoe.

She had thought she had become inured to pain, to grief, to loss. Yet it swept through her anew; the figure blurred, and she blinked. How many tears could one set of eyes produce? Was there never to be any end to them?

Céleste was biting her lip. "What's going to happen to us? Might we as well have stayed with the others, gone on the British ships? Could it have been any worse than this? Worse than being out here with no supplies, no clothes, and winter coming on?" She too drew her shawl more tightly around her, but it was not enough to provide warmth even now; what would it be like when the frost came, and then the snows?

With an effort Soleil pulled herself together. "There's an Indian village a day's walk from here. They'll help us," she said, and hoped to God she was right.

They waited until François was nearly below them, then scrambled down the path to meet him.

He hauled the canoe up above the high waterline and came toward them with a grave face. "I couldn't find them. They'd gone."

"They couldn't have gone far," Soleil bleated. "Not with Papa as weak as he was."

"Perhaps not," François agreed. "But he didn't want to be found. He didn't want to slow us down, to be the cause of our being caught." He glanced back at the smoke, which was undiminished. "They may not be content with simply deporting anyone they catch. British punishments tend to be harsh."

Céleste was shaking, and François adjusted the pack on his back and stepped forward. "Come on. The faster we walk, the sooner we'll be warm."

But warmth was hard to come by, for their clothes were slow to dry when a rain squall passed over them, and the wind never ceased to blow, and the opportunities for a fire were few.

Soleil had told them about the Indian village, and they quickened their steps the last mile or two, only to find the clearing deserted when they reached it.

Disappointment struck like a blow.

"They've moved on, and not long ago," François observed, testing the remains of a cooking fire with his hand. "Probably when they saw the smoke. Look around. They may have left something we can use."

The Micmacs, however, had discarded almost nothing of value. François found a moth-eaten deerskin robe, which was better than what they had; he rolled it tightly and Céleste carried it on her back. Soleil found a string of the Indian sausages—made of fat, berries and moosemeat stuffed into a casing of intestine—which had recently been hung in a tree after smoking; it made her mouth water, but she refrained from cutting into it yet. It would keep well, and they'd best save it for the time when eating off the land became difficult.

That was all there was, and they went on.

If there were other refugees, they did not meet them. Days became one long blur; it seemed to Soleil that all she could do was put one foot before the other, and that she fell asleep before she had time to lie down beneath the deerskin robe. In some distant corner of her mind she found time to be thankful for François's ability to bring down small game and his ability to kindle a fire to cook it, for that would have been beyond her.

After the third time she told them of some cabin where they might find help, only to arrive and find nothing left of any value, she stopped remembering aloud what lay ahead of them.

Once, in a small cabin that was undamaged though as bare as the others, Céleste had looked around with longing. "We could stay here for the winter," she said. "It has a good fireplace."

François shook his head. "It's too close to the British. They'll be combing the woods by this time, looking for us, for others like us. If they saw smoke rising from the chimney they'd be on us like scavengers over a wounded animal."

That's what they were, Soleil thought. Wounded animals, with no place to rest or hide.

"I wonder if it's worth it," she said aloud as they prepared to spend the night in the little cabin. "Living, I mean. Going on living . . . running, hiding . . . when everyone else is gone."

François gave her a level look as he spread out the deerskin on the board floor. "They would want you to go on living," he said. "As you would want for them, if it had been us who were carried away in the ships."

"Besides," Céleste added softly, "you're carrying Remie's baby. You have to live for him. And maybe Remie is safe, maybe he escaped the deportation. He might be waiting in the Madawaska Valley when we get there."

"If we get there, you mean," Soleil said in a dismal way, but the thought of Remie did restore a little of her courage. And of course there was the baby. The baby who was all she had left of Remie, unless some miracle brought him to the Madawaska.

THE CELL into which they had thrown Remie held perhaps a dozen men. It was filthy with vermin and human waste; he became more or less accustomed to the smell after a while, but it continued to disconcert him when a rat ran across his feet. He would awaken at night to hear one gnawing nearby, and wait tensely to feel it on his own person. And all the while he lay there he was cursing the British.

And cursing himself.

Father de Laval had died within hours of being brought here, and Remie's protests on his behalf had been valueless. Challenging the authorities had gained him nothing but a bare board bench on which to sleep in this stinking place.

He thought of Soleil constantly, dreamed of her at night. She was the only thing that kept him sane, he sometimes believed. For her sake, and the sake of the child, he had to stay alive. Had to get out of here.

For so small an offense as protesting the removal of an old priest from his deathbed, they surely could not lock him away forever. Yet the guards were indifferent, saying they did not know when he would be released, and his requests to see someone higher in authority went unanswered.

Requests, not demands. There had been no violence in either his manner or his words. He did not want to risk delaying his freedom by showing how he felt about them.

God in heaven, what would Soleil be thinking had happened to him? Remie, who seldom had prayed for himself, knelt every day to ask for protection of his wife and unborn son.

There was no indication that God listened, to Remie or to any of the others imprisoned with him. They were all, with the exception of one sullen Abenaki Indian, devout Acadian Catholics. No one who had been locked up when he arrived had been released, and several more had been added, so that there was scarcely room for them to stretch out to sleep at the same time.

The first day Remie was locked in the cell he had sat apathetically in a corner cursing his own stupidity. By the second day, however, he was too restless for apathy. He got off the bench that was making his behind ache and began to exercise as best he could in the confined space.

"What are you doing?" asked one of the prisoners, a man named Daigle.

"I am keeping fit," Remie said, "so that when one of these bastards gives me the opportunity, I will be able to break his neck and escape."

There was a murmur of approval. Daigle stood up. "I believe I will join you, Monsieur . . . ?"

"Michaud," Remie said without stopping his energetic gyrations, "Remie Michaud."

Within a minute he knew every name except the Indian's, and four others joined the exercise.

By the third day, all the Acadians were exercising. On the fourth day, when Remie started his routine as soon as he'd gagged down the abominable English food, the Abenaki also stood up. They had assumed that he did not speak French, because he had said nothing to anyone.

But this day he addressed Remie. "Kill redcoats?" he asked, and made a twisting motion with his big hands as if wringing the neck of a goose.

"Kill redcoats," Remie agreed, and the Abenaki grunted. When the exercising continued, the Abenaki joined in with the others.

The guard outside scowled at them, these jumping, swaying, panting prisoners. "What's going on?"

Without pausing, Remie replied in exaggeratedly bad English. "Sorry, I speak only French."

The guard cursed and spat and walked away, no doubt convinced that all Acadians were feebleminded.

From that time on, at least several hours a day were spent stretching, lifting and running as best they could in the confined space. Occasionally the Abenaki would make the twisting motion with his hands, and a slow smile would appear on his ordinarily stolid face.

Most of the other Acadians were local men and were allowed visits from their families. It was a good thing, because the women brought food that was far more palatable than anything the British cook produced, and after that first few days, most of them shared with Remie and even the Abenaki.

Remie tried to keep track of how much time had elapsed by making marks on the wall. Soleil must be frantic by this time, probably imagining him dead, and he prayed that it would not cause harm to either her or the baby. He tried to get one of the visitors to carry a message to her, promising that Émile would pay the messenger, but the man shook his head.

"I'm sorry, *monsieur*, but it is too far, and traveling is too dangerous. Something is brewing among the English, and this is not a good time to leave my family unprotected."

Remie's mind fastened on that phrase. "What's brewing? What's happening?"

The man shrugged. "Who knows, *monsieur*? With the English, anything is possible. Yet something is up. There are more ships than usual in the harbor, and there is an air about them that I distrust. As if they know something we don't know, and you can be sure it's to their benefit, not ours. No, *monsieur*, though I sympathize with you, I cannot run your errand."

"Do you know anyone who might?"

He shrugged again. "I will ask, but I am not hopeful. This is the harvest season, every hand is needed in the fields. There is wood to be cut for winter. And there are the British, who are not to be trusted with our women and children." He spat onto the wall.

So there had been no message to Soleil, no way to ease her mind. Remie exercised harder. When the opportunity came, he would be ready, he told himself. He was quite prepared to kill a soldier or two in order to escape, if it came to that, and since they had confiscated both his musket and his knife, it would have to be with his bare hands.

When he thought that, he looked across the cell at the Abenaki and made the twisting motion, and the Indian grinned and nodded.

For the first two weeks Remie was there, he was visited by the chubby priest, Father Dubois, who brought him meat pies warm from the oven.

Remie thanked him profusely.

"You're welcome, I'm sure. You did your best for Father de Laval, and I know he thought of you as a son. I will try to come again day after tomorrow, God willing."

And then, abruptly, the visits ended.

"Has something happened to Father Dubois?" Remie asked Mme Daigle after a week had gone by with no sign of the priest.

The woman glanced furtively over her shoulder to make sure there was no guard within hearing distance. "He's been arrested. He's under house arrest at the church, with the others."

"Arrested? What for?" Remie gripped the bars and wished they were the neck of the Major John Handfield, the local commander of the British soldiers. "What others?"

The woman's voice dropped to a whisper. "Every priest in the entire area. No one says why. We only know they are no longer permitted to conduct mass."

It was a disturbing turn of events. It looked more and more, to Remie, as if he were unlikely ever to be set free from this place. He would have to break out, only there had not yet in three weeks been any opportunity to do so, since they were not allowed out of the cell even for a few minutes of fresh air and exercise in the yard.

And then that same afternoon Daigle's brother came, having smuggled in—after bribing a guard—a bottle of French brandy. It was a close fit between the bars, and Daigle handled the liquor as if it were a lover.

"Ah! You are a brother in spirit as well as in blood," he breathed, stroking the bottle with reverence.

His brother leaned his face close to the bars that kept them apart. "I have a message for the one called Michaud."

Remie reached him in two long strides. "Yes, *monsieur*? A message for me?"

"From two who look as alike as two bones in a fish. They say they are related to you."

Revitalizing hope surged through him. "Antoine and François! You talked to them?"

"They approached me as I came today to visit. They asked if I knew of you, and I confirmed that you were a prisoner, like my brother, *monsieur*. They asked about getting you out. I had to tell them I knew of no way to do that. The British are vigilant, and while they will accept a coin or a bottle of French brandy as a bribe, I do not think they can be bribed to let a man escape—not even with a shipload of French brandy, for such treachery could lead to a firing squad. I could only tell them you were well."

Remie exhaled a long breath. "Well, they can deliver that message to my wife, at least. And they're inventive young devils. Maybe they'll think of some way to get me out."

Daigle had uncorked his bottle and was smiling at the aroma that arose over the stench around them. "God grant they do, M. Michaud. We will all be happy to join you if they manage to overpower the guards."

For several days Remie remained in a state of constant tension, constant alertness, waiting for whatever the twins would do.

And then, on the dark night when the shooting took place, he knew that François and Antoine had failed. Not that the guards told them anything. Obviously they had no suspicion that Remie was the target of the rescue attempt, though he was sure of it. The guards returned the musket fire, there was a yelp of pain, then silence.

The prisoners tried to see out of the single high window in their cell, but there was no light. No further sounds.

Had the twins been injured? Killed? Or did they survive to return to Grand-Pré with at least the reassurance that Remie was still alive?

There was no way of knowing, but Remie's determination increased. One way or another, he would make his escape and find his way back to Soleil.

41

THERE WAS TROUBLE AFOOT. Remie could feel it in his bones. Their guards were even more tight-lipped than usual, but an indefinable excitement surrounded them, and there was tension in the very air.

Remie went through his paces without conscious thought, his mind racing. Something was going to happen, and soon, and when it did, he had to be ready for it.

The other prisoners sensed the changed atmosphere, too.

"Whatever it is," M. Daigle said restlessly, "it's only good for the English. And what's good for the British is bad for Acadians. When my wife comes, she may be able to tell us something."

But Mme Daigle did not come. There were no visitors that day. The uneasiness within the prison did not abate but grew stronger. Illusive yet almost tangible, the tension increased.

The Abenaki seemed to feel it more strongly than the others. His dark face wore a perpetual scowl and he muttered to himself, "It is not good."

Remie had to agree. If only he had a knife, anything that could be used as a weapon! The conviction grew that something of great significance was going to occur soon, and common sense told him that if he missed a step he might never have another chance to escape. And he might never see Soleil again.

The very idea was a pain that slashed through his heart and made his bones ache.

M. Pitre had spent a month so far in their miserable cell for "failure to show respect for a British officer"—"I spat on him," Pitre had explained with a mild show of satisfaction. Now he stretched himself to peer out their sole window, grunting when he saw nothing of interest beyond the bars. "But it's there," he said, "whether we can see it or not. I myself am going to ask the Blessed Virgin to protect us from whatever it is the British would do to our people."

He knelt beside one of the bench-beds, and within seconds everyone else in the cell had joined him, including the Abenaki, who also called upon his own ancient gods of the earth and the sea and the air, for they too were powerful.

Remie had never prayed more earnestly in his life. He prayed for his own escape, for Soleil and the baby she carried, for the twins, whom he feared had been wounded or killed in a well-meaning attempt to free him from this place.

They had seen nothing of their guards since morning, and now it was evening. There had been no midday meal, and so far no supper. When the guard finally came, his voice startled them, interrupting their prayers with his harsh, badly accented French.

"Hey, you! The Indian, Micmac, you are free to go!"

For a moment no one moved. Then the prisoners rose slowly to their feet, turning toward the bars as the guard jingled his keys, opening the door. Remie's heartbeat quickened, but other guards, fully armed, stood beyond the first. They appeared alert for trouble, yet it seemed unlikely that any would originate behind these bars. So where did they expect the trouble to come from, then? Remie tensed, ready to strike quickly if the opportunity presented itself.

The Indian moved slowly, speaking in his own language, which Remie, at least, understood. "The British fool cannot tell

Micmac from Abenaki. The redcoats are an ignorant, ill-mannered lot.''

"Amen to that," Remie murmured as the Abenaki passed him. "Good luck, my friend."

"God bless you," the Abenaki returned, for he knew that was the most respectful goodbye an Acadian could bestow on another.

"Come on, come on, move," the guard said, shoving the Indian as he passed through the opening. But the other guards were there, muskets ready, and no one else dared attempt to pass through the doorway with him. A moment later the prisoners were once more securely locked in.

"Hey," someone yelled after the guard, "when do we get something to eat?"

The redcoat paused long enough to grin over his shoulder. He spoke in his own language, but most of the Acadians, in spite of their contempt for the British, had picked up enough English to understand him. "Eating will be the least of your worries, you troublesome bastards, before the morrow is out."

Tomorrow. Whatever was happening would be concluded tomorrow. Remie inhaled deeply, exhaled slowly, his fists unconsciously clenching and unclenching, as if around British necks.

Tomorrow, quite probably, he would either manage to make good his escape . . . or die in the attempt. For Soleil's sake, he prayed it would not be the latter.

An hour or so after the Indian was set free, there were scattered shots, a short silence, then another volley of musket fire. In the distance men shouted, a single additional shot was heard, and then only silence.

The imprisoned men waited, but after a time, when nothing else happened, they slumped down again in disappointment and frustration. "Some poor devil ate the British musket balls," M. Daigle said with dissatisfaction. "I tell you, if they ever turn me loose from this place, I've had enough of the damned redcoats. I'm going to take my wife and my children and my boat and head straight west and go up the St. John. I've heard there is plenty of land over there, the other side of Fundy, and the very hell of a lot fewer Englishmen."

There was a murmur of agreement. Someone's empty stomach rumbled noisily, but no one commented. Their bellies were empty, too, and it was hard to be amused about musket fire.

"No midday meal, and no supper, and no visitors to supplement the excellent English food we should have been given," M. Daigle said wryly after a time. "Well, I suppose we'll not know what they have in store for us until they march us to the gallows for our monstrous offenses. I, for one, intend to have a good night's sleep so that I may look my best when I face my Maker."

"With any luck," said M. Pitre, "we will take some of the redcoats with us on that occasion."

There was more of the jail humor before they settled down for the night. Remie, for once, did not join in. Every nerve, every muscle, was attuned for the opportunity when it came, the chance to break free and return to his wife.

He had long ago attained the ability to fall asleep at once, whenever a moment was to be had, and he managed it now, only to be awakened a short time later by a scratching sound over his head.

Remie was instantly alert, rising to his knees on the bench. "Is someone there?" he asked softly, facing the window, through which a cold wind blew between the iron bars. "Antoine? François?"

"I've come back to give you news, my friend."

The voice was that of the Abenaki, not, as Remie had hoped, one of the twins. "What is it? What's going on?"

"Then English ordered all white men to the church for a meeting," the Abenaki said softly, his face touching the bars. "They were suspicious, however, and many of them instead sensibly took to the woods. There were shots fired, and I saw two dead redcoats in the street. I don't know if any Acadians were killed, but there is much resistance to what Major Handfield wants. And there is one other thing."

Remie waited, aware that the men who shared the cell were awake and listening as well. It seemed to him that his blood was boiling through his veins, and his inability to act was driving him wild.

"There are ships in the harbor. Many more ships than usual. And some people have been driven aboard, forcibly, by bayonet. I don't know what it means, my friend, but I thought you would want to know."

Remie was breathing heavily, for he could make a good guess. "I thank you, friend, for risking your neck to return and tell me. God bless you."

"God bless you," the Abenaki said in return, and then he was gone.

"Ships, and our people forced on board," said one of the men in the surrounding blackness. "What do the devils do now?"

"What they've been planning for months, no doubt," Remie said bitterly, turning away from the window and its cold wind. What must this place be like in winter, when the snow sifted in between the bars? "They want Acadian land and cattle, and it seems they'll ship us elsewhere to get them."

There was an undercurrent of protest, of anger and help-lessness. These men had families outside, families who needed their support and protection, as Soleil, for all that she had a father and brothers, needed him.

"By the good Christ, they'll never put me on a British ship!"

Remie didn't know who spoke. He was scarcely aware of the words, immersed instead in his own dark thoughts. There must be a way out, a way to outwit the soldiers.

But how to do it?

MORNING BROUGHT an icy wind and scorched porridge; shiv-ering, the men ate while angrily protesting that they fed their pigs better than this.

Remie had finally set his bowl aside in disgust, fearing the slop would not stay in his stomach, when the musket fire be-gan again.

Sporadic, yet unsettling. What in hell was taking place?

Half an hour later, six guards appeared. Their faces were grim, suggesting that some of their own might be among the possible casualties of the recent hostilities.

"Take no chances with them. Shoot to kill if any try to es-cape," the young lieutenant ordered. "There aren't enough ships to hold them all, anyway."

"Where are you taking us?" Remie demanded as the key was turned in the lock.

"You'll find out soon enough," he was told. "March!"

They were farmers and fishermen, not soldiers. They shambled out of the frigid prison in a ragged line, joining others outside who had not been imprisoned. The cold wind ruffled Remie's hair and beard, but he was unaware of it.

There were women and children among those being herded like cattle toward the waterfront, and most of them were weeping.

"Where are you taking us?" he demanded again, and this time the young lieutenant replied with unmistakable satisfaction.

"You are being loaded onto the ships, to be sent where you can cause no more difficulties for the crown," he said. "Your lands and your belongings have been confiscated for the use of His Majesty's loyal subjects. You will finally learn that you cannot defy the king of England!"

Consternation swept through the newly released prisoners. "My wife! My children!" M. Daigle cried out in dismay.

"Your family will also be loaded on a ship," the lieutenant informed him.

M. Daigle cast a wild glance at the masts clustered in the harbor. "But will it be the same ship as mine? Good God, man, not even an Englishman would be so cruel as to separate a man from his wife and young children!"

The soldier shrugged. He did not care one way or the other if the man was reunited with his family. M. Daigle sought out acquaintances in the group of people around him as they headed toward the sea. "My family! My wife, does anyone know about my wife?"

Though there was sorrow and distress on every countenance, there was also compassion. A murmur of dissent ran through those nearest him. No one had seen Mme Daigle.

Remie suppressed the urge to leap on the British officer and strangle him, for he knew he'd never accomplish the feat before he was run through by one or more of those bayonets.

"I'm not from Annapolis Royal. I've left my wife at Grand-Pré. Is this happening there, too?"

Again there was a display of sardonic satisfaction. "It is happening everywhere throughout Nova Scotia, *monsieur*," the officer said, with a mocking emphasis on the French form of address. "In Beaubassin, in Pisiquid, everywhere. All Acadians will be deported by orders of the king. They have refused to submit to the proper authority, and their insubordination will be tolerated no longer. His Majesty's patience is finally at an end, and high time, too, if you ask me."

Remie moistened his lips. "Where are we being sent?"

"Who knows? To the British colonies, according to rumor, to be dispersed among enough loyal British subjects to dilute your papist fervor, your impossible language, your rebellion, *monsieur*."

Another soldier stared Remie in the eye, feeling safe enough behind his fixed bayonet. "You may be lucky enough to be sent to a better climate than this godforsaken one, to Virginia, perhaps, or North Carolina. Or maybe to Boston or New York."

The enormity of the situation made it hard for Remie to breathe. "My wife is with child, for God's sake! If the ships go to all those places, how will we ever find our own families again? What will become of the women and children who have no husbands and fathers to care for them?"

This time there was no answer. The faces of the soldiers around them expressed their feelings: the Acadians deserved what they were getting, and the soldiers did not care if wife never again saw husband, if father never knew whether his children lived or died.

The lieutenant must have seen in Remie's face what he was feeling, however. He raised his own musket so that the fixed bayonet touched the front of Remie's shirt, the same one he'd been wearing for weeks.

"Try it, *monsieur*," he taunted softly. "Try to escape, if you dare! You Acadians are a lily-livered bunch at best. We have sheep at home in England who have more courage than you Frenchies! But if you think you can win out over muskets and *this*, it will give me pleasure to educate you, and you may set an example to bring the others into line!"

Remie had to blink in order to see the other man through the reddish haze of rage and impotence that had formed before his eyes. He might well have taken up the challenge, had not the lieutenant added one final gibe. "Your wife will never know that you have been left with the rest of the carrion for the wolves to pick your bones, and she'll spend the rest of her days waiting for you to find her in some distant spot! Is that what you want, *monsieur*?''

The haze began to recede. The mention of his wife sobered him; Remie had more at stake than killing this man would accomplish, even if it were possible.

He turned away from the scorn in the lieutenant's face and swallowed his wrath, though it nearly choked him.

Someone shoved him from behind. Remie stumbled, righted himself and then, his head lifted high, he allowed himself to be propelled toward the waiting ships.

Somehow, he vowed, with God's help or without it, he would find a way to return to Soleil.

As fate, or perhaps God, willed it, the ship on which he was dispatched was the *Pembroke*, though he could not know at the time that it made any difference.

42

OF THE MORE THAN three thousand inhabitants in the vicinity of Annapolis Royal, at least half escaped the British net, fleeing to the woods. A lesser number managed to elude capture and deportation in other areas.

Winter was coming on, and those who had left would find it difficult to sustain themselves without their normal sources of food. The order went out to the military commanders in the field from Colonel Lawrence: "You must proceed by the most rigorous measures possible, not only in compelling them to embark but in depriving those who shall escape of all means of shelter or support by burning their houses and destroying everything that may afford them the means of subsistence in the country.

"If these people behave amiss, they should be punished at your discretion, and if any attempt is made to molest the troops, you should take an eye for an eye, a tooth for a tooth and, in short, a life for a life, from the nearest neighbor where the mischief should be performed."

Acadia was to exist no more; henceforth, it would be called only Nova Scotia and legally inhabited solely by citizens loyal to His Majesty George II, king of England.

FOR DAYS THE TRIO WALKED, talking little, doing what was necessary to keep themselves fed and sheltered, when possible, for the night.

Only the thought of Remie's child kept Soleil going. If by some miracle Remie lived, she could not allow him ever to be greeted with the news that she'd given up, that their son had died with her here in this once-beloved homeland.

François was plagued with uncertainties about his own ability to carry through what he had begun. A venture that had seemed perfectly feasible in the planning stage now overwhelmed him without Antoine. He voiced none of his fears, however. And he managed to keep the three of them fed, though their diet became so restricted that he decided it was necessary to brew the tea of fir bark and needles that the Micmacs used to prevent scurvy.

Céleste looked almost as worn and exhausted as Soleil, who was pregnant. François rested his gaze upon the girl whenever he did not think she was aware of him, watching her beauty dim with the hardships she endured daily, but never entirely flicker out.

Sometimes he caught her watching *him*, and always he quickly averted his eyes. He knew what she must be thinking: it was Antoine she loved, Antoine who should have been here with her instead of Antoine's twin. He wondered if she would ever forgive him for being the one who was not deported, the one who was now responsible for her.

The horror of finding—even in remote areas—the burned-out cabins, the torched fields, the ruined weirs that had been destroyed to prevent any renegade Acadians from having an easier time of procuring food, gradually faded to a dull acceptance. They could not afford to be apathetic about approaching each new turn in the path, however. The very fact that homes had been burned to the ground so far from the major outposts indicated quite clearly that the British were devoting their time to making sure that all Acadians who remained behind would starve or, in a short time, freeze to death.

The travelers' clothes were in shreds, and without new ones, without warm robes and moccasins to replace those on their feet, they could hardly survive much longer, François thought in desperation. He could bring down a deer whenever they needed the meat, but how could they stay in one place long enough to dress the hide, to fashion garments and footwear? Yet the frost came at night, and the moth-eaten deer hide was not enough to keep them comfortable, no matter how closely they curled together, always in the same position: François and Céleste on the outside, Soleil in the middle.

"God will surely provide," Céleste said bravely one morning when François voiced his concerns. "He helped us get away from the British, didn't He? He won't fail us now, you'll see."

Soleil said nothing. God had already failed them time and time again, she thought. Everyone she had ever loved, except for this one brother and her friend Céleste, had been left behind. For all she knew, by this time her father had died of his wounds and the cold; what would have become of her mother if that happened? And what of the others, scattered throughout the fleet of ships, heading for distant places where there would only be more Englishmen, and no one to care what befell them, whether they lived or died.

Yet *she* still lived, and whether she still trusted in God or not, she was determined to go on living the best she could, for the sake of Remie's child.

At midmorning, under a sullen sky that threatened snow, Soleil suddenly stopped. They had finally left the funeral pyre of Grand-Pré behind, and Beaubassin had burned months ago, but once more she detected smoke.

"I think it's time we left the trail," she told François. "There must be soldiers nearby."

François nodded. "I've been smelling the smoke for half an hour now. Do you know which way to go?"

"Remie swung out to the north. We weren't on a real trail, but we shouldn't get lost, either. The deer have made paths of a sort. This road will stay to our left, and if we stray too far we'll end up on Northumberland Strait, though that's not likely. I'm not sure I can remember enough to take the exact path we took before, but I'll go ahead and try."

François nodded. "Whatever's burning is off that way, to the south, so swinging north makes sense."

Céleste hesitated. "I wonder if they're still there—the British, I mean. Once they've put their torches to a house, would they stay to watch it completely destroyed, or go on to the next clearing? It would be so nice to get warm again, even if it means holding out our hands to someone else's burning house.''

Neither Soleil or François made any reply. After a moment Soleil led the way, and with a sigh Céleste fell into step behind her.

Twenty minutes later Soleil came to an abrupt halt, turning with a finger on her lips to warn the others.

"British," François mouthed, and gestured toward a dense thicket ahead.

They moved quickly, pushing through low overhanging branches into the very heart of the stand of cedars, crouching together, hearts pounding, as the voices came nearer.

There were half a dozen soldiers slashing about with bayonets in the underbrush, clearly not worried about being ambushed by the enemy. Had they not, after all, disarmed and starved the Acadians into either flight or submission?

The men came within a dozen yards of where the trio struggled to control their breathing and their pounding hearts. Not until a good five minutes after they had passed did Soleil dare to move, and then it was only to relieve a cramp in one leg.

When she moved, her foot encountered something soft and yielding, so soft that for a grisly moment she feared she'd touched a human body.

She eased around to see what it was and strangled on a soft cry. "Someone's left a bundle here, see, a blanket? Maybe several blankets!"

"Whoever it was is probably long gone," François speculated, crawling over to help her investigate. "Regardless, we're going to help ourselves to it, unless the owner shows up in the next few minutes."

"Blankets!" Céleste breathed. "Oh, praise God! Didn't I tell you He would provide? And if it hadn't been for those dreadful soldiers, we'd never have found them! Is there anything else?"

There was. Besides four blankets, there were two loaves of bread, no more than two or three days old, a chunk of cheese and a head of cabbage.

François tore apart one loaf and divided the cheese; they ate greedily, licking their fingers for the faintest of remains. Then, not hearing any further sounds of the soldiers, François transferred the remaining food to Céleste's pack and handed each of the girls a blanket.

"Put them around you like capes," he said, rolling the spare one for his own pack, "and I'll do the same." He flashed Céleste his first smile since they'd left Grand-Pré. "Keep praying, girl. This time, try for moccasins that don't have holes in the bottoms of them."

They went on their way again, stomachs eased, and the blankets shutting out much of the cold. They moved with caution yet as rapidly as they could, for there was still a long way to go before they could consider themselves to be safe.

They slept more comfortably that night with the extra blankets and bellies full of the fish François had speared with an arrow in one of the streams they crossed. And the following day they found the moccasins.

The scene hardly seemed an answer to a prayer. Soleil, still in the lead, had slowed her steps because she got a whiff of charred wood. Not a blazing fire, but the remains of one that had been here recently.

Ever so carefully she eased forward after holding up a warning hand. She caught a glimpse, over her shoulder, of François bringing up the musket, ready to fire if need be. His ammunition was limited, and shooting might well bring down the British on them, but if necessary he would pull the trigger.

What had burned was not even a house, only an improvised shelter. The four victims had been surprised around a camp fire, feasting on the rabbits they had roasted on sticks; their murderers had left them as they lay. One, scarcely older than Jacques, had fallen into the fire, but he had been dead before he pitched into the flames.

Soleil swallowed the nausea that rose in her throat. With each new scene of atrocity she had feared finding bodies. She swung away from the awful sight, closing her eyes as François let the musket drop and caught her against his shoulder.

"The beasts," Soleil choked, and heard Céleste gagging beside her.

François released his sister almost at once. His voice sounded strained, but he was under control. "Happened this morning, I'd guess. The predators haven't found them yet, so it can't have taken place too long ago. Probably the soldiers saw the smoke from their fire. I'm surprised they left the meat on the skewers. There must be enough there to keep us from going to bed hungry, and we can save the last loaf of bread for tomorrow.''

Soleil swayed, then pulled herself together. ''There's blood over here. Maybe one of the soldiers was injured and they had to attend to him, so they didn't bother with the meat. I suppose you're right. We can't be . . . too sensitive to eat if there's food, can we?''

''And they're all wearing better moccasins than ours,'' François said with a grim satisfaction.

Céleste made a small protesting sound, and the look he gave her was quelling.

''It's going to snow before morning. You want to go on barefoot? Sit down there, and I'll see which ones will fit you best.''

The boy's footwear was taken from his stiff feet and laced onto Céleste's. The men's moccasins were large, but François quickly improvised thongs to secure them for both his sister and himself. The spare pair went into one of the packs they carried on their backs.

Then he handed over the sticks with the meat on them. Céleste again made a small sound, but she took hers and after a moment bit into the rabbit.

After they had set off again, it occurred to Soleil that the grisly scene they had encountered might be considered the answer to Céleste's prayer for shoes and food. She wasn't sure she wanted any more prayers answered, if it had to be this way.

Yet the blanket was warm around her, the moccasins felt wonderful on her cold, sore feet, and the meat rested comfortably in her stomach.

And at that very moment the child within her kicked.

For a few seconds she didn't understand what had happened. She came to a halt, hand pressed to her belly, and after a moment François whispered behind her, ''What is it?''

The kick came again, or perhaps the babe rolled over. A look of sheer delight spread over Soleil's face as she turned toward her companions.

''The baby,'' she said. ''He's moving! He's all right!''

The horrors of the past weeks melted away, at least temporarily, and Soleil's dark eyes were luminous with happy tears.

43

THE ACADIANS who had taken to the woods and attempted to provide for themselves fared no better than those on the British ships. October and November were the wrong time of year to live off the land. There were some who in despair gave themselves up to the enemy and were imprisoned, only to learn that conditions were little better than what they had encountered in the forests; although they had the shelter of a British compound over their heads, they remained cold and hungry.

Ever since their occupation of this land, the British had been fed primarily by the Acadians, who had been keeping themselves in considerable comfort and produced enough extra to supply the British as well. What could not at once be converted to British use after the deportation was destroyed to prevent its falling back into Acadian hands, including the fodder that would have kept cattle alive through the winter.

There was beef, pork and mutton for those remaining on the shores now indisputably called Nova Scotia. Little of it accompanied the exiles, however.

A pound of flour, half a pound of bread per day and a pound of beef per week to each captive were deemed sufficient to sustain their lives. Yet more captives were loaded onto each ship than had been intended, and not even those meager rations were actually available to the involuntary passengers.

In addition, there was such a delay before the ships ever set sail that many of the supplies were much depleted before the captives left the harbors. And at that time of year, storms delayed arrivals at their varied destinations.

In the interim, the old and sick and the very young frequently died. The stronger ones survived, to be delivered in foreign harbors to societies that had not been warned of their arrival and were ill prepared to cope with these people. The citizens of Boston and New York and other cities to the south looked upon anyone of French descent with the same horror they would have felt had a load of red-skinned Indians been deposited on their doorsteps. Not only did the newcomers speak an unintelligible language, they were known to be Catholics. They were not welcome among the Puritans and Protestants who were having a difficult enough time providing for themselves. The English colonists had no desire to share with presumed enemies.

The Acadian nightmare had only begun. For many, it would never end.

TWICE MORE THE TRIO HID from soldiers before they traveled around what had been the settlement of Beaubassin. They became more or less inured to the charred remains of what had once been homes and barns, to blackened fields, to dead animals.

"Why do they hate us so much?" Soleil mused once, standing on the edge of a dozen acres of scorched hay that had been deliberately destroyed.

"Because they want our land," François said at once. "And now they have it. We should have fought for it, treaty or no treaty. What do kings have to do with land that has belonged to us for centuries?"

For the first time Soleil confronted her brother directly on the matter. "You *did* fight for it, didn't you?"

Startled, François hesitated, then nodded. "Yes. Antoine—" he had to swallow, because his throat had suddenly and painfully closed "—Antoine thought we should, because we didn't have Papa's faith that the British would eventually leave us alone, let us live in peace. But what good did it do us? We should *all* have fought them, and then we'd have had a chance of winning."

Céleste held the blanket-cloak tightly around her to keep out the wind. "Perhaps if everyone had signed the oath, they might have left us alone."

Again François's gaze was rapier sharp. "At the very last, many did agree to sign it, in spite of not being allowed to qualify their fidelity to the British Crown by an agreement that they wouldn't have to fight fellow Acadians or friendly Indians. Colonel Lawrence said it was too late, and he gave the order to deport our entire population."

Soleil sounded almost dreamy, detached. "It's as if he didn't really *want* us to take the oath. As if he wanted to destroy our villages and our fields."

"He wanted our land," François said, and turning his back on the blackened hay field, he went on.

They were not making as good time as she had with Remie, Soleil realized. Being pregnant, she seemed to tire more easily, and though she walked many miles each day, it was with considerably more effort than before. In spite of the blankets and the moccasins they had acquired, they were not dressed warmly enough, and food was an increasing problem. On her trip with Remie there had been plenty of fish in the weirs, and except in the area close to the British outpost they had dared to shoot game. Now the weirs were gone, and even when François brought down an animal with the bow, they dared not build a fire to cook it except under cover of darkness, and even then they knew the smoke could carry to British noses.

Twice they searched for and found root cellars at burned-out houses; they ate of the cabbages, carrots and turnips stored there and carried with them what they could, hoping something else would turn up by the time those were gone.

Of the scattered cabins along the Petitcodiac, nothing remained but ashes and charred timbers. On the previous trip there had been canoes waiting; now there was nothing.

When Soleil stolidly turned to follow the bank of the river, François glanced up at a watery sun. "The river goes more north than west. Isn't it possible to cut across, take a more direct route?" So far they had felt only a light flurry of snow a few times, but he feared a full-fledged winter storm when they were without shelter.

"I only know this way," Soleil told him, sagging in weariness. "If there were a passable trail directly west I think Remie would have gone a shorter way."

François hesitated, then nodded. "All right. I suppose it's the sensible thing, to stay with the river."

That night it snowed in earnest. They woke at dawn, shivering and damp in spite of the blankets and the deer hide, and François knew they had to have shelter and some decent food. It nearly broke his heart to look at Céleste's pinched face, her lips blue with cold, her fingers stiff as she tried to hold the blanket around her, resolutely putting one moccasined foot ahead of the other along the bank of the river they had as yet no way to cross.

"We'll walk until noon," he announced. "I want to get a little farther away from the British than this. Then we'll stop and build a shelter of whatever we can find, get warm, and I'll bring down a deer and butcher it. If they don't find us, we'll stay long enough to cook up a real meal or two."

The look of unspoken gratitude in both girls' faces made it worth trying, he thought, and prayed to the good God that the British would hole up during the cold weather, too, and not find them.

They came upon their shelter shortly after François's noon deadline, though since the sky was gray and there were a few hard, dry flakes of snow, it wasn't possible to see the sun to gauge the time with any degree of accuracy. They had found another root cellar, dug into the side of a low hill a slight distance from a stone chimney that marked the recent site of a settler's cabin.

No doubt in summer the opening to the cellar had been nearly covered in vines and brush, but with the leaves gone and a light coating of snow over everything else, the door of rough boards caught François's eye when they came within a few yards of it.

He jerked open the slanting slab door and peered inside. It was icy cold, worse than outside, but he turned toward the girls with an exclamation of satisfaction.

"Here's our new home for a few days! Someone else has been here before us, and they've had a fire and even left a little wood that the English didn't find! I'll try to get a fire started, if the wood isn't too damp—look around and see if there's anything else useful."

Not much had been left behind by the previous visitors—or perhaps the family that had been burned out—but there was a bag of dried peas that had fallen near the door, and a small pot that would do for cooking if a fire could be kindled.

The wood was indeed damp, but François was an expert on kindling fires under adverse conditions. Within an hour the cellar was warming to a temperature that allowed them to set aside the blankets; and the peas, although a long way from being soft, were lukewarm, promising soup eventually. As soon as the fire was burning satisfactorily, François left them there to enjoy it while, bow in hand, he headed for the woods that stretched away from the river.

It was several more hours before he returned, but he was grinning broadly, looking almost like the old François. "Here! Let's cut off a chunk of this to go into the soup!" he cried, lowering a generous chunk of venison to the floor of the root cellar.

Soon the aroma of cooking food made their mouths water. Even before the soup was actually done they took turns drinking the broth from their only utensil, a gourd they had carried with them from home.

By evening they had *real* soup, and they slept that night in comfort, taking turns rousing to fuel the fire and to stir the kettle propped over it on stones brought from the river.

Soleil dreamed that night of Remie.

He was caught in some dark, dank place, but he was smiling. "Don't worry, love," he told her. "I'm coming."

She woke smiling, and again she felt the baby move. For the first time in weeks she began to feel that life might be worth living.

DANIELLE AND VINCENT held tightly to each other's hands as they descended the gangplank to the wharf in Boston Harbor. They were wan and little more than skin and bones, and as apprehensive as the others before and behind them.

What was to happen to them now?

At first there was only confusion, and the voices that shouted at them, directing them this way or that, were English voices. English words. Words that meant nothing to most of the refugees.

Then a man who spoke passable French shouted out at them. "Listen! Pay attention! You will form a line, so, here! And your prospective masters will pass before you to select which servants they will take into their homes! Because you chose to bury your riches rather than bring them with you, you now arrive penniless, so you must work for your keep. And understand this! Once you are bound by contract to your English masters, you may not leave your assigned territory without a special pass. You are to be clean, industrious and obedient! You are instructed to learn the English language as quickly as possible. The practice of the Catholic religion is forbidden in the colony of Massachusetts. Should one of your priests, having escaped the proper authorities, enter into this colony, he will be subject to be put to death. Should any of you give aid to such a priest, you will also be subject to severe punishment.''

Vincent leaned against her, his small fingers digging into Danielle's. His eyes were wide and round, staring about at the ships in the harbor and all the people and the town beyond, which was very busy in spite of the cold.

They shan't take him from me, Danielle thought, yet her heart was pounding with apprehension. What could she do about it if they did? And once Vincent was separated from her, how would she ever find him again? What chance would there be that she could ever take him home?

"You," said a crisp English voice, "what is your name?"

Uncomprehending, fearful, Danielle stared at the woman.

"What are you called?" The woman, who was in her mid-thirties and prosperous looking, spoke more loudly, as if that might overcome the language barrier.

"She is asking your name." The speaker, a man she did not know, was behind her; he must have come off one of the other ships, for he was clearly an Acadian, speaking her own tongue. Danielle looked around at him and saw a youth of perhaps twenty, a man who had undoubtedly been muscular and good-looking before he'd spent weeks on short rations in the dark hold of a ship.

He smiled faintly, encouraging her, and Danielle moistened her lips. "Danielle Cyr, *madame.*"

The Englishwoman's mouth tightened in disapproval. "We do not use that form of address. You will call me Mistress Monroe."

Again the young man had to translate.

"Mistress Monroe," Danielle repeated, the name awkward on her tongue.

"Danielle?" the woman asked of the translator. "What sort of name is that? I'll call you Martha. I need a girl to help in my house. You will have a place to sleep and be fed. Come along."

When that, too, was repeated in her own language, Danielle's jaw sagged in consternation. "I can't leave my nephew. He is only three, and someone must look after him."

Vincent peaked out from behind her skirts, and something shifted in Mistress Monroe's face. "Three, you say? Does he also speak your abominable French?"

Her interpreter's dark eyes flashed something that only Danielle saw, which was probably just as well. Without waiting for Danielle to respond, he said with at least superficial respect, "He speaks French, mistress."

"What is his name?"

"Vincent, mistress."

Somehow, through the fear that enveloped her, Danielle understood what information was being conveyed. She did not remember having seen the young man before, but if he knew Vincent's name, and that he was able to talk, perhaps he had been on her own ship, after all. Perhaps he had watched them during the brief periods when they had been allowed on deck for exercise, when apathy had kept her from noting anything around her.

"Tell him to say something," Mistress Monroe instructed.

The interpreter squatted beside the boy. "Can you say 'hello' to Mistress Monroe? Like this, in English?"

"'Allo, Mistress Monroe," Vincent echoed.

The woman broke into a smile. "And he's three, you say?" She turned to speak over her shoulder to a companion Danielle had not previously noticed. "He's a charming little fellow, isn't he, Charles? And at that age, he surely can't have been totally seduced by their papist religion, would you think? Perhaps . . . ?"

She let the sentence trail off, waiting. The man was a few years older than she was, and extremely well fed; his jowls reminded Danielle of a pig fattened for slaughter.

"Perhaps. Take him home, if you like," the man said indifferently. "If he doesn't work out, we can always get rid of him." He turned away to speak to someone else in the crowd that lined the wharf, inspecting the Acadians as if they were cattle.

"Very well. Come along, both of you." Mistress Monroe started to move, then paused to address the young man who had served as interpreter. "Where did you learn to speak English, young man?"

"From the soldiers, when I was in prison, mistress. I had nothing else to do."

Her sharp features tightened. "Why were you in prison?"

"Because I am Acadian, mistress."

She considered his reply. "Do you by any chance read and write?"

"Only a few words in French, mistress."

"If you can read and write in French, you can learn to read and write in English," the woman proclaimed. "Charles, this young man knows how to write a little. He might be of some benefit to you, if he's willing to be taught."

Danielle, catching at least the import of what was being said, stifled the resentment that rose through her fear. This woman and the other Bostonians around them spoke as if the Acadians were not human beings at all, but chattel to be bought and sold. As they now were, she supposed, with a surge of hatred.

"Is that right?" Charles Monroe returned his attention to them, viewing the tall young man through a quizzing glass. "What is your name?"

"André Lejeune, *mon*—Master Monroe."

André was considerably taller, and the Englishman had to tilt his head to look at him more closely. "Are you willing to be taught to read and write English, if you're capable of it?"

André Lejeune suppressed the desire to spit in the man's upturned face. "Yes, sir."

"Good. Good. Come along, then. We'll see to the contract papers," he said, and led the way.

Danielle followed, almost dragging Vincent in an effort to keep up. A moment later André Lejeune swept the boy up in his arms, making it infinitely easier, and Danielle gave him a grateful look.

What she saw made her glance linger. He had sounded passive, almost docile, when speaking to the Monroes, but there was nothing passive in the strong lines of his face. Nor in his eyes.

For just a moment a slight conspiratorial smile touched the corners of his wide mouth, making her catch her breath, and then it was gone.

But she had seen a flicker in those dark eyes that sent a wave of something—a renewed interest in living?—through her. As they paused long enough to give their names to the fellow who was drawing up the papers that virtually made slaves of the Acadians, Danielle decided she was glad that André Lejeune had offered to translate for her.

Basile was gone from her forever, but she would not be locked alone, except for Vincent, in a world in which she could not communicate, a world where she was an outcast and an alien on an unfriendly shore. A little of her fear abated—but only a little.

44

THE PEMBROKE HAD REACHED Annapolis Royal later than the other vessels, disabled after losing her main mast in a storm. Whatever the English thought of the Acadians in other ways, they were admittedly good workers. They had kept the British garrisons supplied with food for years, even sending substantial quantities of valuable goods back to England, as well. So it came as no surprise when the English called upon an Acadian to replace the ship's mast.

Charles Belliveau was chosen for the task, which he did most competently. However, when no payment was then tendered, he demanded to be compensated for his work.

No doubt the officials on the ship saw little reason to hand over good money to the man, knowing as they did that all Acadians who could be rounded up would shortly be dispersed to the colonies, where they would be in no position to demand anything. And so they refused M. Belliveau's request.

At that, Belliveau took up his ax with a brawny arm and threatened to cut down the new mast if he were not paid at once. The ship's captain capitulated, but he had his revenge: Charles Belliveau was imprisoned in the hold with two hundred and thirty-one other Acadians when the *Pembroke* belatedly set sail on the eighth of December. It was an action that Captain Fontaine would live to regret.

Remie Michaud had already spent a week in the stinking hold while the mast was replaced. He had thought prison miserable beyond description; the *Pembroke* was far worse.

In the prison he had been cold: here he was chilled to the bone twenty-four hours a day, for the passengers were packed so closely together there was no possibility of exercising to keep warm. He had eaten slops in prison; aboard ship he was lucky to eat at all. He had longed to be free of the stench of unwashed bodies and human waste; now he felt suffocated not only by the smells but by the very lack of breath, for when the hatches were closed upon the *Pembroke*'s unfortunate prisoners, the fetid air was not sufficient to sustain them all, and they feared they would expire.

A few of them did die before the ship ever left port.

Charles Belliveau was an angry man when he was pitched down the ladder to join the others. He fell heavily against Remie with a muffled oath, then muttered an apology as he tried to find room to plant his feet.

Remie drew up his legs to make a space. "Sit, friend. At least you brought a whiff of fresh air with you. We thank you for that."

"By the good Christ, you've need of it!" Belliveau sank down beside Remie with another oath. "They say they've orders to take us to North Carolina? How far away is that?"

There was a silence, for no one knew, then Remie said through gritted teeth, "It's too damned far for these conditions."

"You're right there, mate," someone muttered in the darkness.

A child whimpered and was soothed; someone went into a coughing spell so severe that Remie unconsciously held his breath, expecting the victim to choke to death.

"Is this place full of rats?" Belliveau asked gruffly after the coughing had finally ceased. "I've an aversion to rats."

"No self-respecting rat would stay in this hold," Remie assured him grimly. "There's scarce enough air for the fleas, let alone anything larger."

A baby began to wail and could not be comforted. There were more children aboard than adults, some of them without parents or grandparents to see to them. How many would die, Remie thought, before this voyage ended?

And then, as he always did, he thought of Soleil. Was she, too, trapped in some rotting hulk, the baby already dying within her because there was insufficient food and not enough air? The cold alone could cause an end to life, and there was no heat except what their own bodies could provide.

The prisoners lapsed into silence. They had already said what there was to be said.

Remie dozed, then woke because of stiffness in his limbs and the compelling need to stretch out his legs. He drifted off again, and the next time he woke he knew at once there was a difference in their condition.

The ship was under way.

As the wind filled the sails far above them, its force was transmitted to the hull so that it creaked and groaned like a thing alive. Remie groaned, too, without realizing it. Where was Soleil? How would he ever see her again? How would he survive, or want to, if he did not?

Beside him someone—Belliveau—cursed, then fell against him as the vessel careened to one side. "If they capsize this tub it'll put an end to our misery, at least."

A woman's voice came out of the pitch blackness around them—fearful, pathetic. "Do you think it's likely? Can't any of us swim, I don't think."

Belliveau was immediately reassuring. "Not unless they snap the main mast, and since I made it myself, it's not likely. No, they'll probably get us to this North Carolina, wherever it is. It sounds cold, but it has to be south of here, so mayhap it'll be warmer than we are now."

There was a sudden cry and a woman began to sob loudly. "He's dead! My son is dead!"

For a few minutes they listened to the pitiful creature, and finally the women surrounding her tried to calm her down, but for the rest of the night Remie heard her anguish echoing in his ears.

What was happening to Soleil? God grant she was not in straits like these, he thought, and knew that his prayer was unlikely to be answered.

BY MORNING those who were seasick added vomit to the pervading miasma of illness and despair. The air was so thick it seemed to invade the throat and the nostrils in a smothering wave.

Remie recognized M. Daigle's voice as his fellow prisoner suddenly hammered with his fists on the inside of the hatch cover and shouted, "Hey! You English bastards, there are people dying in here, and we've got to have some air! Open up!"

For a time there was no indication that the crew paid any attention. Daigle continued to pound and shout, however, and when his fists grew sore someone else took his place, until finally a crack of daylight appeared overheard.

As luck would have it, Charles Belliveau was the one leaning against the ladder, nursing his bruised knuckles, when a sailor's face appeared in the opening.

Belliveau sought to keep his voice level, though he was seen to be trembling with rage. "Is it your intention, then, to cause the lot of us to die for lack of breath? Will there not be questions if you arrive at your destination with a hold full of dead and dying, all but about thirty of them women and children? Surely even the English will find such treatment to be inhumane!"

"I got orders to keep you all belowdecks," the sailor said, flinching from the odor that assailed his nostrils.

"Well, see your captain, then, and tell him that if we aren't allowed some air, and soon, it will no longer matter. We will all have suffocated. No doubt *he* will be held personally responsible for more than two hundred needless deaths."

The sailor stared into the dark hole, then withdrew, allowing the hatch cover to thump back into place.

Belliveau verbally consigned the sailor to the devil and slumped back to the deck of the hold. "If there is any divine justice, Captain Fontaine will burn eternally in the afterlife."

Remie rose to take his place, hammering and shouting beneath the hatch. He had begun to feel panic himself, for two more infants had died in the past hour. How long would it be before the entire complement of prisoners had expired?

A few minutes later he heard feet above him, and again the crack of daylight appeared. Though it was only a slice of sullen gray sky, the air was fresh, and Remie inhaled greedily; it made him slightly dizzy, and then his head rapidly cleared as the cover was thrown aside and Captain Fontaine stared down at him.

Immediately Belliveau was beside him. "We are dying, Captain. There is truly no breathing in this place." He watched as the man reached for a handkerchief to hold over his nose. "Let us out on deck long enough to air out the hold. Whoever gives your orders must expect that you will deliver at least some of your prisoners alive, and they're dying down here like flies. Children and a couple of old people, so far, but the rest of us won't be long in succumbing, as well."

The captain stepped backward so that less of the smell could reach him. "Very well. You may come up, half a dozen of you at a time. Walk twice around the deck, and then go back down so that the next six may take your place. And if you try anything, you'll be cut down like the savages you are."

"Good," Belliveau said, turning toward his fellow captives. "Who will be first? Six of you?"

It took a long time to get through them all, and some were too weak to manage the walk even with help. Remie took with him a small girl with curly hair, now matted with filth; she squinted against even the limited gray light as he carried her around the deck. "Where is your *mama*? Your *papa*?" he asked, but she only stared at him. She either did not understand, or did not know.

Remie's rage at those responsible for their plight left him shaking when he reluctantly descended once more into the hold.

M. Belliveau returned a few minutes later. "Did you notice, Michaud, that we sail with a reduced crew?" he asked softly, close to Remie's ear.

"I did," Remie confirmed. "I saw only eight or nine men."

"Correct. I counted eight. And they're Englishmen."

His tone was heavy with meaning. Remie stiffened.

"If they let us on deck six at a time—"

"And we go six *men* at once," Belliveau said. "We are certainly *better* men, are we not?"

"A damned sight better," rumbled a deep voice from the darkness before them. "I want to be one of the six."

There was a current of sudden tension throughout those nearest the hatch ladder. A spark of hope that was fanned by "And I," "And I," grew rapidly to a conflagration of determination.

Their opportunity came almost before there was time to thoroughly plan their course of action. If the sailor who released the captives took exception to six men emerging at once, rather than a mixture of women and children, it would make their chances of success less favorable. But Remie knew in his gut that they would go through with their attempt one way or the other. Better to die trying than not to try, he thought.

Always floating in his mind was the image of his wife, smiling at him as she had smiled the night their child was conceived. Beautiful, beloved Soleil.

Remie was the fourth one up the ladder the next time the cover was removed. He would have given his very soul for a weapon of any sort, but there was, of course, nothing. Nothing beyond bare hands, doubled into fists.

The sailors of the *Pembroke* were too complacent for their own good.

M. Belliveau swung at the nearest one, with Remie a close second to act, and behind them the sailor tending the hatch was knocked off his feet so that the other men in the hold swarmed up the ladder and into the fray.

Captain Fontaine gave a roar of fury, but it was too late. His own men were quickly overpowered; the rebels were already trussing them like fowl for the market, and he himself was thrust aside from the wheel and tied up, as well.

"Where to?" demanded M. Daigle, who had seized the helm.

Belliveau and Remie spoke in unison, without hesitation. "West," they said.

"This is mutiny!" screamed Fontaine, and Remie grinned down at him.

"Quite correct, Captain," he said with the most satisfaction he had felt about anything in months. "Consider yourself lucky that we have not elected to throw you overboard—so far—and enjoy the rest of the voyage!"

The wind was very strong and the sails billowed, the ropes strained, and the deck creaked beneath them as the *Pembroke* was turned around. Belliveau, an experienced mariner, gauged the weather as he took over from Daigle and shouted above the wind, "Do any of you know how to handle the rigging? We need full sail!"

Several men sprang to obey, and the tremor of the vessel rose up through their feet so that Captain Fontaine screamed a warning.

"Stop! You're going to break my main mast!"

M. Belliveau did not hesitate. "You are mistaken, sir! I made this mast, and it will not break!"

"As no more will Acadian spirit!" Remie added.

Already the fresh air, cutting though it was, had infused them with optimism. Their minds were clearer, their muscles tingling from the burst of violent exercise, and they were headed away from the British forces.

Now all that remained, Remie thought, was to find Soleil. From what he had heard, he feared that she and her family had been put aboard another such ship and transported to the British colonies to the south.

But if Antoine and François were still alive, and he knew enough of them to believe it was possible, they might well have managed to rescue some of the Cyrs, including Soleil.

If she were not a captive, if she were free to move about, Remie thought he knew where she would go.

There was no point in returning to Grand-Pré. By this time it was no more than a ruin.

If she could, Soleil would go to Madawaska. And that was where he would go, too.

As he lifted his face to the full force of the wind, Remie no longer noticed the cold. All he felt was freedom.

45

TWO DAYS' JOURNEY up the Petitcodiac River the tattered trio came upon barking dogs, two boys of perhaps twelve or thirteen, armed with muskets, and a small community of undamaged houses.

Soleil moved eagerly behind her brother to meet the citizens who came out of the houses: three men and two women with babes in their arms and a cluster of younger children tugging at their skirts.

The boys had already lowered their muskets, for clearly those three, half frozen and limping, were not a threat.

"Hello!" François called out before the two groups met in the middle of the snowy clearing. "Is it possible the redcoats have not reached this far?"

The patriarch of the group came to a halt a few yards away. "Oh, they've come this far. Three of them are buried over there." He gestured with a callused thumb. "That's where we'll put the rest of them when they turn up, too." His discerning scrutiny assessed them. "Where have you come from?"

"Grand-Pré."

The man nodded grimly. "Thought so. Everybody who got away from Beaubassin left weeks ago. Not that many did, I reckon, since last spring. Loaded everybody on a ship and took them away."

"That's what happened at Grand-Pré, too, and at Pisiquid, from what we heard."

Soleil could hardly contain herself at this evidence that someone, somewhere, continued to live a more or less normal life. "Are we truly beyond the reach of the British, then, *monsieur*?"

His breath was a white vapor on the still air. "Well, that would be an exaggeration. As I said, we buried a few of them. Lost a few of our own, though, doing it. We hope we've held them off until spring, anyway. Got a woman due to give birth any minute. My son didn't want to take the chance of walking his wife off to the wilderness now. If we can stay free of the soldiers, we'll be moving on when the weather turns better, after the babe comes and the children can walk without snow up to their necks. We got four too young for snowshoes."

One of the women moved forward, smiling shyly. "Papa, they're cold, and I shouldn't wonder if they're hungry, too, by the look of them. Invite them in."

A few minutes later they were ushered into the largest of the cabins, installed near the hearth where they could soak up the most warmth they'd had in weeks, and served a savory stew and real bread with butter.

Nothing had ever tasted so good. The men exchanged news and predictions, but Soleil and Céleste were content to sit close to the fire and eat, relaxing and, for the time, forgetting to be afraid.

The Robichauds were generous hosts and urged them to stay. "Your clothes are worn out," they were told, "and you need new footwear as well, and a bit of fattening up."

"Besides that," the old man added, "there's a weather front moving in. You won't get far in a blizzard. Best to sit it out here."

He was right about the weather. It came in a blinding curtain of snow that fell all day and all night and all of the next day, blowing into three-foot drifts around the houses and the barn.

Soleil thanked God for it. She was warm, she was fed, and the baby moved frequently now. The young woman who was due any moment studied her, then smiled. "You, too?" she asked.

"Yes. Not until April, though."

"Ah! By then you will be where you are going. It is somewhat frightening to think of giving birth in the woods, in the winter."

"Very frightening," Soleil agreed with feeling. "Please, tell me what I can do to be of help."

There were plenty of women to keep the house, she was told. But if she and Céleste wanted to repair their garments there were needle and thread available. They even brought out dresses of their own to give them. "We will not be able to take them with us when we leave in the spring anyway. We did have cloth to make new garments, but there have been a number of travelers who needed them worse than we did. These are all we have left."

The clothes that remained were in far better shape than what Soleil and Céleste wore. They accepted them gratefully and were even more delighted with the moccasins that were stitched together for them before their visit ended. They were not decorated, like the beautiful ones Running Fawn had embroidered for her, but Soleil expressed her most sincere thanks. They were sturdy and would last for many miles.

The Robichauds gave them gifts of food for their packs and presented them with additional items, as well: snowshoes for the three of them.

They left the tiny settlement on the fourth day, feeling invigorated and heartened. At least among Acadians there was still generosity and compassion.

By the end of a week most of their elation had dissipated, though they chanced on several vacated cabins where it was possible to spend a warm, dry night and to cook provisions to carry with them. Still, the distances were great; it took far longer to reach the little chapel at the bend of the river than it had taken Soleil and Remie.

Things looked different in the winter, too. It was hard to judge where they were. Had it not been for the river, Soleil would have been hopelessly confused.

They lost all sense of time. They had long since given up worrying about feast days and fast days. "We have enough involuntary fasting to worry about the proper days," Céleste remarked with a touch of vinegar in her voice. Yet, while they had the chance, they had knelt in the little church to ask God's help and protection.

Soleil prayed guiltily. Whether she believed anymore or not, there was always the chance that if God were there, if He had not totally abandoned the Acadians, He would bless her child. And Remie, wherever he was. She prayed for Remie, too, and the others. But she could not pray for herself—not after what He had allowed to happen to her family.

WITHOUT THE SNOWSHOES, Soleil thought, they would have died there in the wilderness.

Even with them, it was hard going. Game was scarce, the smaller streams were frozen over so they could catch no fish without first chopping a hole in the ice, and they carried no tools except for François's knife.

Occasionally they encountered other fugitives like themselves, from Beaubassin, Pisiquid, even two heavily bearded brothers from Annapolis Royal. Soleil eagerly asked about Remie, but they shook their heads. They knew nothing of him, though they recognized the name of the old priest, Father de Laval.

"He was thrown in prison, where he died," they told her. A pain ran through her, along with repudiation of that fate for Remie. He had not been old and sick; there was no reason to think he had also perished in that British jail. Somewhere, Remie yet lived. Her need for him was a physical ache that sometimes diminished but was never wholly assuaged.

The English ships had taken away many people, the brothers told her. The rest, they assumed, were starving or freezing in the woods. One of the men had lost a wife and two children in the deportation, the other a young woman to whom he was betrothed.

Like all the other refugees, they were ragged, thin and exhausted. Yet the light of hope still burned in most of them.

"We go to Québec City," they said. "We have heard that there is food there, and that a man can make a living building boats for other men to fish."

Soleil's hope had flared and died. "Yes, that's true," she told them. "There are boats being built along the shore, at any rate."

"You've been there, *Madame*?"

"Yes. Last summer." It seemed years ago, eons. She had been so happy, except for worrying about becoming pregnant, and then *that* had happened, too. She felt the sting of tears. "With my husband."

They asked questions about the city, and she answered them as best she could before the men went on after gravely thanking her.

So grim, everything was. The news, the hunger and weariness, the grief in nearly every face—so grim.

How they had laughed, she and Remie, throughout last spring and summer and into the fall, until he had gone away to visit the dying priest.

She wondered if she would ever laugh again.

MOST OF THE TIME they walked steadily, stopping only to sleep or to eat, when there was anything available to eat. The cold was a constant misery. They had not washed in weeks. Their blanket-coats were thin, and there was no way to replace them. Still they kept going.

From time to time they came across graves, marked with stones or wooden crosses, unblessed by any priest. The priests had all been thrown into jail and no doubt deported by this time, unless they had escaped to Québec City. Céleste yearned for a priest to hear her confession, to bless her, but Soleil did not think a priest could warm the stone she carried where her heart ought to have been.

Only the vigorous kicking of the babe kept her going, kept her caring whether or not she lived or died.

Miraculously they reached the St. John, all three of them still alive, though little more than walking skeletons. Now there were scattered cabins, but while these people took them in for a night spent snugly under a roof—being near a fire was enough to make both Soleil and Céleste weep with gratitude—they had few provisions to share.

"There's no trade anymore," the settlers reported. "The English destroyed so many crops and most of the boats. Nothing comes to us from across the water, and they have pursued those fleeing the deportation across the Bay of Fundy as if they were so many vermin to be exterminated."

Still, most of them shared what little they had. The simplest of hot meals was more than the travelers were used to. Twice more they sat out blizzards in some isolated cabin while meat roasted on the hearth, and Céleste would murmur, "Thank God we're not out in that."

Soleil remained silent. She stared through the window at the falling snow and thought that if they were out in it they would probably fall in exhaustion, be buried and die, and it no longer seemed such a terrible thing to happen.

And then the baby kicked again, and she knew that she had to stay alive for the child.

They came upon bloody footprints in the snow as they trudged up the St. John, then a cairn of stones to mark another grave; the ground was frozen too hard to allow for digging one. Céleste knelt to say a prayer beside the marker, and François stood watching her. His love and concern were clearly written on his face for his sister to see, and her heart wrenched within her.

Céleste seldom mentioned Antoine anymore. When she did, François's pain was as great as her own. Perhaps more so, Soleil decided, for he both grieved for his brother and longed for this girl who had been his twin's intended bride.

Antoine was gone, Soleil thought in a mingled rush of love and sorrow. But Céleste and François were still here, and the girl had had difficulty in choosing between them in the first place. Perhaps, when this ordeal was over, if they survived, Céleste and François would yet find some measure of happiness. Yet the girl showed no awareness of François as a man, treating him no differently than she would have treated one of her brothers.

In fact, Céleste was quite aware of François. During the first few days, when they had fled the nightmare of the beach at Grand-Pré, she had suffered agony over Antoine's capture. And then, in the following weeks, she had seen Antoine in François at every turn. Even in the final carefree days she had known, she had been fooled by their trickery, unable to tell the two apart. Yet she had at last been sure it was Antoine she wanted, and they had talked of marriage.

Why, then, did she now watch François as he coaxed life into their infrequent small and reluctant fires, or when he skillfully butchered the game he was able to bring down with an arrow, and feel the same sort of longing to be touched? Why, when her gaze fastened unwillingly on his mouth—no longer laughing, but sober—did she wonder what it would be like to be kissed by *this* brother?

François *looked* like his brother, but each twin was a separate person, a man in his own right. How could she have these feelings, these emotions? Guilt sent her often to her knees, praying for forgiveness, for guidance. Praying for deliverance from this terrible journey, from these crushing circumstances.

"What will we do when we get there? When we reach this Madawaska Valley?" she asked. "It will still be winter, and there is no one there, is there? No house, no supplies. How will we survive until spring, when the rivers run again full of fish, and where will we get seed for a garden?"

"We'll build a cabin," François said.

"With what? You have only a knife, not even an ax."

"Soleil says there are Indians in the vicinity, friends of Remie's. Failing their help, I'll make do with the knife. Or failing *that*, with my teeth." There was a disturbing intensity in his expression. "I'll see that you have a place to live, I promise. And since we'll be out of earshot of the British there, I'll bring down game with the musket."

He had scarcely any ammunition for the musket. They knew that. Yet his voice carried conviction. François would manage, somehow.

However, they didn't get as far as the Madawaska Valley that winter, for Céleste fell ill. It began with a cough, then pain in her chest, then progressed to fever.

Soleil discovered the fever in the morning when they had all three been kept awake by the coughing. They had nothing to give her for it. It had snowed lightly, covering their deerskin robe with a dusting of white, and Céleste's hair also had a frosted appearance where she had not burrowed beneath the covering.

Soleil had sat up, shivering, loath to arise yet knowing that she must, for her brother was already up, and they must be on the trail soon or they would lose valuable hours of daylight. The only way to avoid freezing was to keep moving.

The woods were very still around them. Steamy vapor issued from their mouths, but the snow had stopped, and it looked as if the sun might emerge from its cloud cover.

Soleil slid out of the improvised bed, wrapped her blanket around her, and fled to the woods to relieve herself. When she returned, Céleste still lay sleeping.

"Come on, get up. The sun is rising, and François has laid out the last of the fish he caught through the ice—"

Céleste didn't move, and Soleil bent to shake her shoulder. In so doing, her cheek brushed against her friend's cheek and felt seared by the heat of it.

Soleil spun in alarm toward her brother. "François! Come quickly, Céleste is burning up with fever!"

He came at once, frowning with concern as he knelt beside her. At his touch Céleste opened her eyes, but they were glazed and vague.

"Antoine?" she murmured, sending a spasm of pain through both her companions.

"No, it's François," he said softly. "Can you get up?"

"Yes, of course," she replied in a drowsy way, but she didn't stir. "Are we there yet? At the Madawaska?"

François's eyes met Soleil's across the girl's form, communicating his own alarm.

"No. We have to move on. Do you think you can walk?"

"Of course," Céleste said again, but when they tried to help her sit up she was limp and weak.

Soleil swallowed and spoke in a low voice. "What are we going to do? Clearly she can't travel, and another night here in the open like this . . ." She sounded as if she were about to cry.

"No. She can't stay here. Where are we? Do you have any idea how far it is to the next settlement? The next cabin?"

Soleil glanced around at the trees and the rim of ice along the river. "I don't know. There's nothing for a landmark, and everything looks alike—" She felt so helpless!

François hesitated for only a moment. "We'll have to carry her."

Soleil was appalled. "We can't! I can't lift her, and you—" She couldn't tell him how pathetic he looked, gaunt and debilitated from lack of adequate food.

"Not on our backs. I'll have to fashion a travois, like the Indians use. Crawl in beside her, keep each other warm while I look for the poles."

"But she's already scorching hot," Soleil said, even as she crawled back under the robe.

"Keep her that way, and she'll warm you, as well. I'll be back as soon as I can."

Soleil wrapped her arms around the other girl, and soon the warmth began to seep through their combined clothes. Céleste seemed to have fallen back into a stuporous sleep and did not rouse at the embrace, although once in a while she coughed, a deep, racking, harsh sound on the quiet air.

Soleil, not in the least sleepy, stared upward at the winter sky and spoke as if she could see God's face above her.

"If You hear me," she whispered, "help us to save her. Don't let her die out here after what we've been through. Don't let any of us die."

Almost as if in response, the baby in her belly kicked.

Soleil bit down hard on her lower lip and tasted blood. She waited for François to return.

46

IN EARLY DECEMBER, off the southwest coast of England, the *Violet*, carrying nearly four hundred deported Acadians, began to take on water.

Its passengers were almost all debilitated by deprivation and cold. The elderly and many of the very young had already died, and for the most part those who remained had little spirit for the future that lay ahead of them: exile and probably imprisonment in a land where they could expect no welcome.

Still, when it became obvious that their unseaworthy ship was listing to one side, many of those who had given up now found a new desire to live.

Bertin Cyr was one of those. He despised himself for his cowardice, for the fact that he had begged and pleaded with both his captors and his God for mercy. One had shown as much compassion as the other, as far as he could tell. He hated the weakness that had made him cry far into the night so many times, when there were those around him who did not cry. Papa would be so ashamed of him, Bertin was convinced.

He didn't know how far off the coast they were, though they had been sailing for weeks and surely must be nearing the end of their voyage. However, he could not swim, and even had it been otherwise, there was no way out of the hold in which he had been locked with the others so long ago.

Shouts and running feet on the deck above his head told him that his terror was justified. The *Violet* was definitely sinking.

Others were jolted awake around him when the vessel shifted sharply, throwing them into a heap against one of the bulkheads. Women cried out, children began to weep, and Bertin felt paralyzed with the certainty of impending death.

"What is it? What's happening?" Joseph Trudelle, his friend since childhood and just as bereft of family as Bertin, roused from sleep and clutched at his arm. "Dear God, we're going down!"

A voice rose over the wailing and the clamor, loud enough so that some fell silent to listen. "Almighty God, we commend our souls into Thy hands! Give us courage, Oh Lord, to die like the men we would be, rather than the wretched captives we are!"

Bertin found Joseph's hand and squeezed it tightly. Yes, he thought. He had been a coward, and now was his last chance to redeem himself. Papa would never know, at least not on this earth, but if Papa felt any particle of pride in him, Bertin would now make it an honest pride.

He sank to his knees, drawing Joseph with him, feeling the icy waters of the North Atlantic sloshing around him, but no longer aware of the chill.

He was still praying when the water had reached his chest, when the *Violet* suddenly rolled onto her side and sank completely beneath the waves.

He never knew that his brother Pierre was only yards away on a sister ship, and he never heard the blast when that ship exploded, sending debris over a wide area.

He was, at the last, no longer afraid, for he had finally remembered what he'd been taught from the time he was able to stand alone: to have faith in God, even to the end.

PIERRE HAD TAKEN Henri on deck only moments before the captain of the *Duke William* became aware that a sister ship, the *Violet*, was settling into the sea.

Henri was shivering violently, and though it was no warmer belowdecks, it was at least out of the wind down there. Pierre held the boy in his arms, wrapping his own coat about him as best he could.

"In a moment, son, we'll go back down, but let's have a few more fresh breaths before then," he said, and cradled the child's head against his own neck. He was glad that Aurore had died years before, that she had not been among those subjected to this degradation and torment, for she surely would have suffered more in life at being torn from her children than she had suffered in dying.

He didn't know what had become of Cécile Meignaux, the pretty, shy young girl he would have taken for a bride. He didn't know about anyone in the immediate family but Henri. He was in the midst of neighbors he had known all his life, and they helped one another as best they could, but the misery was so overwhelming that most were lost in it, unable even to help themselves in any meaningful way.

Pierre turned to walk along the deck, the raw wind at his back to shield the boy, when he heard the shout from the rigging. He looked up into the gray sky, not understanding the words but quickly gathering the implications as the sailor scrambled down from the crow's nest.

The youngest of the Dubay brothers, deprived of his wife and infant daughter, knowing not whether they lived or were dead, was walking the deck, as well, and paused near Pierre.

"Trouble of some kind, or has he spied land? Are we about to get off this stinking tub?"

"Trouble, I think," Pierre said as the sailor hit the deck and was off on a run for the helm where the captain stood. "He wouldn't act that way if it were the land we are headed for."

"Another ship," Étienne Dubay guessed, and they stood together watching as the captain shouted orders and wrenched the wheel.

They were changing course. The wind came at them now with renewed violence, making Henri wince and bury his head in his father's beard. Pierre was unaware, though he continued to hold the child tightly. "There! On the horizon, see? Another ship!"

A few minutes later it was clearly visible, listing badly.

"It's one of ours," Étienne muttered. "Has our people aboard. Damnation! There's no sign of land, and they won't have boats to save more than the crew!"

Pierre's teeth were bared to the wind. "And all those poor devils locked in the hold, no doubt, the same as they keep us most of the time! Jesus, God and Mary, have mercy on them!"

Ordinarily the prisoners would have been quickly returned to their crowded quarters within ten minutes or so, but at the moment they were forgotten. Sailors jumped to attention and laid on more canvas, and the *Duke William* shuddered under their feet.

The men looked at each other in rising alarm. At first Pierre thought that the tremors were caused by the ship turning so abruptly, and that in his haste to reach the sinking vessel the captain of the *Duke William* had called for too much canvas. Beside him, Étienne exhaled a ragged breath.

"Surely we're canting too much to starboard! God bless us, is *this* tub in trouble, too? It wasn't enough that the English

committed this monstrous crime of separating families and
tearing us from our homeland, they sent us rotten ships to cross
an ocean?''

A moment later and there was no doubt about it. The captain, distracted from the plight of the *Violet* by a report from
his own men, gave the order to lower the longboat.

Sailors swarmed into the smaller craft, and the trio of prisoners exercising on the deck moved with them, almost too
stunned to react, had not they been jostled by a crew too
frightened to take note of the men they swept along with them.

Pierre heaved Henri into the longboat and fell in after him,
propelled by the men behind him. The sailors, following orders, released the ropes. In their panic, they let down the bow
too quickly and nearly spilled out the passengers before the
stern rope dropped, too. Pierre, hugging his son, caught a diz-
zying glimpse of pewter-colored water rising and falling below
them, and closed his eyes.

But they were not destined to die immediately, after all. The
longboat dropped and was caught by the waves. Those who
manned the oars threw their backs into it, and they began to
pull away from the doomed *Duke William*.

Pierre turned to look back. They were so low in the water
now that the other ship was barely visible above the heaving
waves. It was going down, he thought in despair, perhaps even
his own family and friends among the hundreds of people
trapped belowdecks, and there was nothing to be done for them
except pray that their end came quickly.

The explosion was totally unexpected, and debris rained
down on their heads so that they all ducked and cowered. A
flaming bit of wood landed in Henri's hair, and Pierre knocked
it into the water, unaware of the burn it left on his hand.

And then the ships were both gone, sunk beneath the waves,
and it was quiet except for the gasping effort of the rowers.

Étienne Dubay wept openly. "Dear God! Seven hundred
people, it must be, and gone in an instant! Every one of them!"

Pierre was shaking. He crushed his son against him, thanking God that Henri was saved. But, of course, he was *not* saved,
only from the watery grave of those others.

There was still England, if they could reach it without the
longboat swamping with them first, and he had no reason to

believe the English in England would have any more compassion for an Acadian than those who had loaded them on the ships.

Pierre leaned forward so that his face was very close to Étienne's. "When we reach land—*if* we reach land—I'll not be taken captive again, my friend. They'll either kill me, or I'll run free."

Étienne wiped his ragged sleeve across his face. "And I," he agreed. "There are ships going both ways across the sea," he said. "And if I cannot gain passage on one going west again, then may I join those other souls in heaven."

Wordless, then, they clasped hands and sat that way, waiting either to sink or to reach land.

47

THEY DRAGGED THE TRAVOIS carrying Céleste, bundled in the blankets and the deer hide, upriver. The St. John itself would have made an easier road, but though there was ice along its banks it had not frozen over, and there were no canoes available. Once they thought they had come across one, but when Soleil ran to it, she saw that it was damaged, with a hole punched into its side.

Around noon on a bleak day that was reflected in their spirits, they were hailed from the trail ahead. Two men as ragged as themselves had brought down a deer. Soleil's mouth began to water at the sight of it, but there was a more important consideration.

"Hello! Is there any shelter nearby?" François called. "We have a young woman who is very ill. We need to get her warm as soon as possible."

"There's a cabin a half mile upstream," one of the bearded men said, rising to his feet from where he had been gutting the animal. Tendrils of steam rose from the creature and wreathed their faces. "You're only about a mile from St. Anne."

"St. Anne? A town?" François felt as if a great weight had been lifted from his shoulders, though there was still the matter of nursing Céleste through what appeared to be a serious illness. He felt responsible for the fact that she'd been inade-

quately fed and warmed; somehow he was certain that if Antoine had been in charge, he would have managed those things
even under these adverse conditions.

"Yes, *monsieur*, a town, such as it is." The fellow strode over
to them, still carrying his bloody knife, staring down at Céleste on the travois. "Do you need some help, perhaps?"

Soleil, whose fingers and toes ached with the cold, watched
François hopefully, and he nodded.

"We are very tired and hungry. And our friend runs a high
fever."

The stranger put out a hand to touch the girl's face. "You are
right. Hey, Jacques! You finish with the deer and get it home.
I'll help these folks!"

The other man nodded and went on with the task of caring
for the meat, while their rescuer took over Soleil's position on
the travois. She felt positively limp with relief.

Jacques, the younger man was called. She thought about her
own brother Jacques, who was less than twelve years old and
who had, as far as she knew, been separated from every member of his family. Where was he now? Did anyone care for him?

Remie had been on his own since he was little more than
Jacques's age, except for the couple of years he'd spent with
Father de Laval. She hoped to God there was some such kindly
person in her brother's life, and despaired of ever seeing the boy
again. Damn the British! she thought in a burst of hatred that
almost had the heat to warm her a bit as she trudged after the
men.

A short time later they angled away from the river on a nearly
indiscernible path, and ten minutes beyond that, arrived in a
clearing where a cabin of square-cut logs sent up a ribbon of
smoke.

There were women in the cabin, an older one and a younger
one, and four small children. Soleil managed a smile of gratitude when they were ushered into the house, when other hands
took over the tasks of unwrapping Céleste, making her a pallet
before the fire and spooning soup into her.

Soleil was given a bowl of her own and left to eat it while the
women chafed circulation back into Céleste's limbs. "She is
very ill," the older woman said with concern.

Soleil was too tired to reply, too tired even to lift the spoon at first. Gradually, however, the warmth of the bowl brought her fingers back to life, first with stinging pain, then with stiff movement, and she ate.

"I am Mme Gaudet, and this is my daughter-in-law, Geneviève. Where do you come from, *madame*?"

"From Grand-Pré," Soleil murmured. She looked around the room at the coziness of handmade quilts and candles, at the shelf of plates and mugs, at the rugs upon the floors to keep the drafts from coming through the cracks, and her eyes filled with tears. For the first sixteen years of her life she had taken such things for granted, the comforts of a home of her own. Would she ever know such luxury again? Or was she destined to go on walking, freezing, starving, until she died in some remote place, alone? Without ever knowing what had happened to Remie and everyone else she loved except François and Céleste?

Céleste muttered something, and Geneviève bent over her with the spoon. "*Mademoiselle*, try to take some of this. It will warm you from the inside," she urged.

Mme Gaudet saw the tears in Soleil's eyes. "It is a long way from Grand-Pré," she said kindly. "But you are luckier than some, *madame*. So many have died, and continue to die."

"I don't feel lucky," Soleil said, and the tears brimmed over, running unchecked down her cheeks.

Mme Gaudet clucked understandingly. "Ah, you'll salt your soup too much, young *madame*, if you cry into it! Perhaps you need to rest and grow thoroughly warm before you eat, eh? At least the British didn't take your scalps. You have that to thank the good God for, do you not?"

"Scalps?" Soleil lifted her wet face and saw the woman bite her lip.

"You have not heard?"

"No."

"The British pursue those who escaped the great deportation. They are said to be killing those they find and scalping them. And they call us and our Indian friends barbaric! Ah, well, no doubt the good Lord will deal with them in His own good time!" She turned to her daughter-in-law. "Geneviève, don't feed it to her so quickly, girl, she'll choke! Let me do it!"

Scalping Acadians, whose only crime was to try to escape the cruelty of the British deportation.

Soleil put aside the bowl of soup, feeling sick to her very soul. Would they do that to Mama and Papa if they caught up with them? Or had Papa died long since of the fever? And in that case, what had become of Mama?

They should never have left them there beyond the Minas Basin, she thought. François ought to have looked for them—they could not have gone far from where they had all camped the night before—and insisted that they come along.

She doubled over her knees, seated on the low stool, and could no longer hold back the sobs that racked her frame. She felt a friendly hand on her shoulder but did not look up.

There was no God, she thought angrily. There could be no God such as she had believed in all those years, or He would have struck the British soldiers dead when they committed their terrible deeds. Scalping innocent farmers and fishermen was more savage than the animals in the forest, who killed only in order to eat.

Later, when the Gaudet family knelt in evening prayers, Soleil listened dully. She was exhausted in mind and body. Even the fact that Céleste had taken the broth and was now sleeping peacefully did not make her feel any better.

Her gaze settled on her brother's face, and she read nothing there, either, except the same exhaustion. His eyes were glazed, as if they looked far from this place, saw things beyond this warm, cheerful room.

François felt her eyes upon him and shifted his own. For long seconds they stared at each other, each reading the other's grief and sense of abandonment, each unable to offer anything in the way of solace to the other.

Then it seemed that François went away, though he did not move. He is with Antoine, Soleil thought. Antoine was so much a part of him, and now he has lost him. Without Antoine, he has nothing.

Except, perhaps Céleste. Soleil turned her head a bit to look at the girl on the pallet. She was still too pink, and she occasionally coughed so that Geneviève would rise to give her some sort of tonic Mme Gaudet had brewed up. But she did seem better.

If Céleste lived, perhaps there was hope for her and François, even if there was none for herself.

And with that thought, Soleil unknowingly had taken the first step back to caring what became of the three of them.

THEY SPENT A WEEK with the Gaudets, for Céleste was simply too ill to be moved.

The first night, when she was in and out of delirium, Soleil dozed off and on beside her, soothing her with the mixture Mme Gaudet had offered when she coughed, spooning broth into her from time to time.

Since the cabin was small and already filled with people, there was no sleeping space for the newcomers except rolled in their own blankets on the floor of the main room, which they shared with two young boys.

Considering the temperature outside, they were thankful to be under a roof, but Soleil was almost too weary to take note of the blessing.

Once during that first night, when Céleste's coughing had roused her, Soleil saw that François, too, had been awakened. The firelight cast a reddish glow over the room and she saw that his eyes were open.

"How is she?" he whispered, after his sister had laid a hand on Céleste's forehead.

"Very hot," Soleil murmured. She wondered how long a person could sustain a fever like this without dying of it, or, like old M. Forêt at home, being sent into imbecility, which had lasted the rest of his life.

Céleste moved restlessly, muttering, and only two words came out clearly. "No, Antoine!"

Soleil brushed back the damp hair from the other girl's forehead, hoping her brother had not heard that weak cry, fearing that he must have. She was so tired, Soleil thought, near tears of sheer fatigue. If only Céleste would rest, so that she could, too!

When Céleste finally subsided, sinking once more into uneasy sleep, Soleil curled up in her own blanket and prayed—out of long habit and not from any conviction that the prayer would be answered—that she would able to sleep until dawn, which was not far away.

Some time later she woke, disoriented and with her heart pounding, for there was a bulky presence between herself and the fire. After a moment she realized it was François, kneeling to bathe Céleste's face with a cloth Mme Gaudet had given them.

As Soleil raised up on one elbow, she saw that Céleste's eyes were open, staring up at François.

"It's all right," François whispered, unaware of Soleil beside him. "You're safe, and you're going to get well. Go to sleep now. I'll take care of you."

For a few seconds longer Céleste stared upward, then, obediently, she closed her eyes.

Soleil eased back into her sleeping position, watching François in profile, silhouetted against the fire. The sadness and concern on his face made the tears come again, and she thought of Remie. Dear, precious Remie, whom she had thought to have beside her for the rest of her life! Was he, too, in some cold and distant place, unable to sleep, thinking of her?

She pretended to be unaware of François when he finally moved across the room and crawled once more into his blankets. And this time, answer to a prayer or not, she *did* sleep until dawn.

BY THE FOLLOWING MORNING Céleste's fever had broken. She lay limp, unable to lift her head to sip at the broth, but she did look better.

"Definitely better," Mme Gaudet said, pleased. "She is young and strong. She will recover, I think."

Recovery, however, was not rapid. And as Céleste rested and took nourishment, Soleil and François became more aware of their surroundings and the kindness of their benefactors.

They had both put themselves to work carrying in firewood, and they paused in the bright morning sunlight for a moment of private conversation.

"We must move on as soon as we can," François said, adding another length of wood to the stack already balanced on his arm. "We impose here, I'm afraid."

Soleil nodded. "I know. There is plenty of wood—thank God for that—but food supplies are low. I saw into the bin when Mme Gaudet last opened it for peas for the soup. And she's worried about wheat for bread. There is little of that, too. Yet I fear to move Céleste too soon. She seems quite fragile still.''

François was sober. ''Too fragile to set off through the woods again in this kind of cold,'' he agreed.

That afternoon François disappeared for several hours, returning at dusk. He stood before the welcome heat from the fireplace, rubbing circulation back into his hands. Soleil saw that the snow from his feet did not immediately melt on the pine board floor, and she pulled the shawl more closely around her.

''*Monsieur, madame*,'' François said, addressing their hosts, ''you have been most generous and hospitable. We thank you sincerely, and we realize that our being here has reduced your own supplies. The only way I can repay you is with meat, and I'll do that before we move too far. I saw a moose this morning, right on the river. But I've been in St. Anne today and have found a small house where we can go until our friend has fully recovered. We won't impose on you further.''

The Gaudets were undoubtedly relieved to have the visit at an end, Soleil thought. It was humiliating to be at the mercy of strangers, especially when they had so little to share, yet the Gaudets had done it ungrudgingly.

''A house?'' M. Gaudet asked. ''There are so many refugees coming through, and I'm aware of no empty house.''

''It's not empty. It belongs to the Widow Cormier,'' François said. ''She is alone and suffers from lack of a husband to cut her firewood and bring in meat for the pot. I've agreed to perform those services in exchange for a place to stay until Céleste is strong again.''

Soleil immediately sensed something in the atmosphere. Did *madame* and *monsieur* exchange a guarded glance? Or had she imagined it?

''The Widow Cormier,'' M. Gaudet repeated, sounding oddly wooden. He cleared his throat loudly.

Madame was definitely biting her lip, though after a moment she managed a smile and broke the small silence by saying, ''Well, a moose would be a welcome addition to the larder, M. Cyr.''

François seemed oblivious of any hesitation on the part of the Gaudets, though Soleil was certain she detected an undercurrent of disapproval in their voices.

When the opportunity arose, she asked Geneviève in private, "Is there something...peculiar about the Widow Cormier? Is there any reason why we should not move into her house for a few weeks?"

Geneviève turned bright pink. "Why, no, Mme Michaud," she denied at once with too much vehemence. "I'm sure the move will be a sensible one. Excuse me, Mama has asked me to skin those rabbits at once."

Soleil stared after her, bemused, then shrugged. What did it matter if Mme Cormier was an eccentric old lady? It would not be for long, anyway, and a roof over their heads was better than sleeping in the woods with the snow dusting them every night.

She did ask François, however, on another of their excursions to the woodpile, if there was something odd about the widow.

François shot her a sideways glance. "Odd? Why do you ask that? No, she's an ordinary woman who has lost her husband and has no children to help her. Here, can you carry this one more?"

It wasn't until they had bid the Gaudets goodbye, with profuse thanks, and arrived in St. Anne that Soleil finally made sense of the reactions of their hosts.

They had bundled Céleste up and pulled her on the travois again, for she was too weak even to walk across the kitchen by herself. Once or twice Soleil dropped back to make sure her friend was all right.

"Where is it we're going?" Céleste asked. "To St. Anne? That has a nice sound to it, doesn't it?"

"Yes," Soleil agreed without thinking about it. "We're to stay with a kind old lady who can use some help. Then, when you're strong enough and the weather eases a bit, we'll go on toward the Madawaska Valley." She hesitated before adding wistfully, "If Remie was able to escape, too, it may be that he'll go there."

"I hope so." Céleste managed a wan smile. "We're very lucky, aren't we, that François found a kind old lady!"

St. Anne was a small village, much smaller than Grand-Pré. Still, it seemed good to be in a town again, a place with a church—though no priest—and dozens of people going about ordinary tasks. It was almost possible to forget the atrocities of the British soldiers, at least for a time.

The house that was their destination was on the far edge of the village, set apart from its neighbors, and as François had said, it was very small. Once again they would be sleeping rolled in their own blankets on the floor, but that idea didn't bother any of them in the slightest. Compared to the frozen ground, it would be heavenly.

And then François knocked. The Widow Cormier opened the door, and Soleil stood stunned while François untied their patient from the travois and carried her across the threshold.

Mme Cormier was no more than twenty years old, and though she was dressed in black, there all resemblance to the widow of Soleil's imagination ended. She had a full bosom that strained against the black wool, a tiny waist and only a wisp of a cap on a wealth of rich chestnut hair that fell in curls over her shoulders. Mme Cormier's lips were a glossy pink, her eyes a sparkling blue, and her complexion of a perfection seldom found in anyone other than a healthy infant.

Soleil stumbled on the sill, but no one noticed. The others were busy installing Céleste in a chair before the fire, which crackled cheerfully. The aroma of roasting meat wafted across the room to her—either François had already fulfilled his part of the bargain by bringing in the venison that sizzled on the spit, or the widow had another benefactor—and although it was not yet dark, a candle had been lighted to welcome them.

"Come in, make yourselves comfortable," Mme Cormier said in a sultry, seductive voice such as Soleil had never before heard.

And then she observed the smile that the young widow turned on François, heard the sugary voice. "Don't worry, *monsieur*, we will take good care of your sister's friend. We will nurse her back to health, no matter how long it takes."

Now Soleil understood the meaningful looks exchanged between the Gaudets. At least she thought she did.

48

THE *PEMBROKE*, its captain and crew in chains, arrived in St. John Harbour a few days before Christmas.

During the crossing, which had been stormy and rough, Remie had had plenty of time to think. He had remembered the difficulties Soleil had had on their trek to Québec City and knew that without him, in the winter, another such journey could be suicidal.

Of course, if by some miracle she had escaped the deportation, she could have company, the twins, perhaps. They were quite capable of getting around in the wilderness even in the dead of winter—if, that was, they hadn't been shot attempting to free him from the prison in Annapolis Royal.

He didn't think they had been. The guards would have boasted of it if they'd killed any of the rebellious Acadians.

Instead of setting out on such a trip ill prepared and without adequate supplies, the twins might have chosen to hole up until spring. Any of the Micmacs encamped deep in the forest would have befriended them if they'd been able to get that far.

What if he went up the St. John River, Remie thought, only to learn later that his wife had never made it that far, had perhaps never even started?

By the time the *Pembroke* had reached port, he had changed his mind about his course of action.

He would return to Grand-pré first, in case Soleil was still in that vicinity.

The first fisherman he approached looked at him as if he were mad.

"Grand-Pré, *monsieur*? But there is nothing left of it! They say the fires burned for six days in the village alone! And after that the soldiers scoured the countryside, destroying everything in their path. There are only the English there now, and they have orders to kill any Acadian they find—a duty they find only too easy to carry out. No, no, *monsieur*, I understand your grief at the loss of your family, but I would as soon shoot you here and now as take you to Grand-Pré."

Every man he spoke to around the harbor told him more or less the same thing. "The English are taking scalps," one dour fisherman informed him, making Remie's own scalp tighten.

"In retaliation, no doubt, for the raids the Abbé Le Loutre and his Indians made on the British settlers. I've no wish to risk my own scalp, *monsieur*, not with a wife and twelve children dependent upon me."

Remie was becoming desperate.

"I have no hard coin on my person, but my wife had some," he stated, unable to give up. "If her family escaped, they may have taken it with them. If they didn't, they may well have hidden it in fear the British would confiscate it if they carried it aboard the ships. At any rate, when I take the next load of furs to Québec, there will be coin to pay for them. I'll pay you whatever you ask, *monsieur*, up to the whole of my earnings for an entire year!"

The man puffed on his pipe, shaking his head. "I'm sorry, my friend. You would find nothing, and we would be extremely lucky not to lose our hair and our lives. If the British didn't kill me—" and he showed a quirk of the mouth that he made a macabre joke "—my wife would, for trying it."

"Your boat, then," Remie countered. "Let me take your boat."

"Ah, you are an experienced sailor? Oh, I know, you are one of those from the British ship, but that is a far cry from a boat such as mine, and this is no time of year to take a small craft out onto Fundy. No, no, you'd never make it across, let alone return, and without my boat, how do I make my living for all those mouths? I grieve for you, *monsieur*, as I grieve for all who have lost everything, but I cannot help you."

The more resistance he met, however, the more determined Remie became. Somehow he would reach Grand-Pré.

And then he encountered a young man just setting out in a small boat for the Petitcodiac, a youth who reminded him of the Cyr twins. Simon de Vitre was seventeen, with a shock of thick black hair and eyes that challenged the newcomer with amused tolerance.

"To Grand-Pré, *monsieur*? You are either very brave or very foolish." He spat over the side of the boat into the bay.

"Perhaps a little of each," Remie conceded. "But mostly I am concerned for my wife. If it is possible on this earth to find her, I'll do so, one way or the other. Where are you heading for after the mouth of the Petitcodiac?"

De Vitre shrugged. "Wherever fate takes me. And we make a major assumption, *monsieur*—that the British will not intercept my boat before I reach the Petitcodiac. They burned out Chipoudy, and even if I go past there at night there is always the chance that they will catch me. On the other hand—" his grin showed a crooked tooth "—they're stupid bastards, and they don't like to come out in the cold. But I don't know about taking you to Grand-Pré. It is a big risk. Bigger than I'm used to."

"Then take me as far as you're willing to go," Remie said. "I'll get the rest of the way on foot, if I have to."

De Vitre regarded him with interest. "This wife of yours, she is very special, eh?"

"Very special," Remie agreed, and to his dismay felt his throat close and moisture sting his eyes.

The youth's hesitation lasted only a moment, then he waved a hand. "Oh, what the hell! Come aboard, *monsieur*, tell me your name and about this special wife, and we will see what happens when we have gone as far north as we can go. If I'm in the mood, we may then try east and south, who knows? Perhaps the good Lord will give us a sign, eh, that I am to help you on this errand. And if not, well, you'll be no farther away from your destination then than you are now."

Remie scrambled into the boat, which was small and old but appeared seaworthy. "God bless you," he said, trying not to sound as choked with emotion as he felt, and Simon de Vitre grinned again as he cast off the rope and faced the mouth of the harbor, sailing toward the Bay of Fundy.

IT TOOK THEM TWO WEEKS to reach the place where the Minas Channel emptied into Fundy. Several times they had slipped silently past British patrols during the night, and once when they were pursued by the enemy they ran far up a small stream and lay hidden in the reeds throughout a stormy afternoon.

"A close call, eh?" Simon asked cheerfully when they were once more on their way north, and Remie had to grin back because the youth's spirits managed to raise his own. Yet the apprehension he felt never entirely left him.

"I thought the prison at Annapolis Royal was cold," he told the boy as the freshening wind tore at his hair, "and it's a wonder we didn't all have frostbite in the hold of that stinking ship. But I've never experienced cold like this!''

"It's cold on the water," Simon admitted. "There's always a wind, and it's sharp. You can't keep moving, the way you do in the woods, to keep warm. But I was born on a boat, and it's all I know. Keep an eye out now, mate, for they'll be patrolling the mouth of the Petitcodiac for certain. They want to keep the settlers upriver from any illegal trading, starve them out, you know.''

Remie's eyes ached from searching both shoreline and the surface of the water. "You mean there are settlers left they haven't burned out yet?''

"Oh, they've tried! But that batch up there—'' Simon paused to pull his knitted cap farther down over his ears "—are a feisty lot. Well armed and plenty of ammunition, and they're good shots. They've buried full half of the soldiers sent up there to torch their houses and their barns, and this time of year I almost feel sorry for the soldiers, eh? They can't walk on snowshoes, they're not used to this kind of cold, and by the time they get up there, their hands are too frozen to fire their muskets. Besides—'' and he laughed again, looking to assess his sails "—in those red coats, they make mighty fine targets against the snow and the firs, eh?''

"And you're to do a little illegal trading, is that it?'' Remie didn't care one way or the other, as long as the youth took him closer to where he wanted to go.

"Everything's illegal these days. I've got relatives up the Petitcodiac, all Papa's brothers. Fourteen of them. Dead shots, every one of them. They'll send what food they can spare back with me. Plenty of people going hungry in Saint John this winter, I'll tell you, *monsieur*. The place is full of people who ran ahead of the English, and there's no food coming in the way there used to be. Cape Breton still belongs to the French, but they say the English don't let any French ships through these days, nor any of ours, either, and those in Louisbourg are starving, too. What the British couldn't use immediately they destroyed, and Papa says they've overdone it, they'll be hungry themselves before they get their own settlers in and working the land. England doesn't want to send food to the New

World, they want the New World to send wealth of some sort to *them* and there's naught to feed us all, eh?''

"If everyone moves west, there will be," Remie murmured. "If they can get through the winter. Come spring, they'll be all right."

"If the British don't come after them. They're like a nest of hornets stirred up with a stick, angry over the ones who escaped their treacherous deportation plot. Papa says—" Simon scratched through the beard he was trying to grow with only limited success "—they look on Acadians like rodents. Leave any of us and we'll breed fast, so they'll be dealing with us again. They want to exterminate us, every one."

Remie turned so that the worst of the wind was at his back. "Does your papa think any of the exiles will be back to reclaim their lands, their houses, their boats?"

"No. Even if they come back—and split up the way they are, how are they even going to find their children, their wives?—the land won't be waiting for them. The enemy settlers will come in, build new houses, take over the fields. They say those around Grand-Pré had dyked thousands of acres, reclaimed them from the sea, and that it's valuable property now. You've seen it, I take it, Monsieur Michaud?"

"It's impressive," Remie said. "They ought to have fought for it, treaty or no treaty." He thought of Émile. "They didn't really believe it would ever come to this. They thought they would go on as they had for years, squabbling, maybe, but not to an end like this. It might have been kinder if the British had stood them up in rows and shot them than to have separated their families, torn babies out of their mothers' arms, made orphans and widows of thousands."

Simon seemed not to have heard. He was squinting off into the distance. "Is that a sail over there? Or only a bit of low-lying cloud?"

They went on, moment by moment expecting to be discovered. A part of Remie would have welcomed a confrontation. He'd acquired a new knife—nowhere near the quality of the one Émile had given him for a wedding present, but better than no knife at all—and he'd have liked nothing better than dispatching a few redcoats. Common sense overruled that primitive urge, however, and he kept a sharp watch along the shore for any sign of the enemy. He would be of no use to Soleil if he took an English musket ball between the eyes.

Once they'd entered the wide mouth of the river, they proceeded only under cover of darkness until they had safely passed the stretch where Simon said the patrol boats would be. After that they made a straight run, reaching the de Vitre settlement upstream without incident.

While Remie helped load the small boat with bags of grain and dried peas and even a quantity of precious maple sugar, he thought about Soleil and the rest of the Cyrs. Were they hungry? Were they without shelter? And would Simon take him any closer to Grand-Pré so that he could try to find out?

He didn't ask until they once more reached the mouth of the river. If they were spotted by the patrols, they could either head along the western shore for Saint John or take the more dangerous route down Chignecto Bay, increasing the risk of being intercepted.

Remie was not aware that furrows had been deepening in his brow as they approached the moment of decision. He turned when Simon laid a hand on his arm.

"Now we know what I am made of, eh? I run safely home with the supplies my uncles have provided, or we tweak the nose of the English murderers."

Remie had already made up his mind not to beg. The food they carried would save lives in Saint John before spring, and he'd come to like and respect the younger man. "If you want to put me ashore here, I know my way. And I'll thank you for the favor."

"It would be easier for you to go to land east of the fort they now call Cumberland, eh?" Simon hunched his shoulders within his coat, the only sign that the cold was bothering him, too.

"It would be safer," Remie conceded, beginning to hope.

"My papa will undoubtedly have me drawn and quartered if I don't deliver the supplies safely. But what is another day or two, eh? I'll tell you what, my friend. I will carry you to the mouth of the Minas Channel. We will wait for the tide to be right so that we are not caught in the infamous bore, and I'll put ashore on the far side. After that, the best I can do is ask the good God to keep you safe, and help you find your wife."

Remie gripped Simon's hand. "No friend could ask for more."

"Good." Simon grinned, showing the crooked tooth. "Then it is done, eh?"

THE PATHS WERE FAMILIAR, and there were memories at every turn. But there were changes, too.

No welcoming smoke rose from scattered chimneys, though it was clear that for a time there must have been plenty of smoke. Only the chimneys themselves remained, and the charred timbers around them were covered with snow.

Remie saw no footprints but his own. He hoped that meant the British had given up regular patrols in this part of the country; he was ill equipped to take on half a dozen redcoats at once.

He felt more confident of his ability to look out for himself than when he had left Saint John, however. Simon's relatives had been generous to his friend. They had provided Remie with snowshoes, food and, most reassuring of all, a musket and a supply of shot. When he got the chance to acquire a bow and arrows, he would consider himself a complete man again.

He came upon Grand-Pré at dusk. The wind howled through the trees, and a few dry snowflakes had begun to fall. Excellent, he thought. The British, who loved their drinks with the warmth of a hearth, would mostly be inside.

In spite of what he'd heard, Remie was unprepared for Grand-Pré.

Under a leaden sky the slate-colored water washed the shore beyond the skeletal remnants of blackened stone and charred timbers; only a few denuded willows, whipped by the fury of the rising wind, moved in what had once been a lovely village where hundreds of people had lived out their contented lives.

The devastation was complete. Not even the skim of snow that had fallen earlier could mask the ugliness, the destruction.

Breathing was physically painful. Remie's hope began to drain away.

How could anyone have survived this? How likely was it that the soldiers who had touched the torches to these homes would have left alive any who managed to slip through their net? They would have combed the woods, seeking out the fugitives. He had a sudden sickening image of Soleil, her beautiful dark hair streaming around her terrified face, as the soldiers took her scalp in the same way as the savages they purported to despise. . . .

He shook his head, clearing it, and began to withdraw into the nearer trees. There was still a chance, however slim, and he would search for her. Whatever had happened to his wife, he had to know, or he would never rest.

IRONICALLY THE MORNING dawned bright and sunny. The forest was beautiful under its new frosting of white; when he inadvertently brushed against a heavily laden bough it would spring upward, scattering its burden in a miniature storm.

It was the kind of day Remie had always reveled in, crisp and cold and promising adventure.

Today there was no joy in it. And during the following days, when he sought out survivors in the woods—and there were survivors, though from the look of them their suffering surpassed belief—nothing happened to give him hope. No one knew of the fate of the Cyr family, though a few had seen a member or two being driven toward the ships.

"Maybe they were taken in by the Indians," Remie mused, but the heads had shaken negatively, the thin, pinched faces leaching away from him even the faintest of possibilities that he would find any of the Cyrs here.

"The Indians have long gone. Moved out, every last one of them," he was told.

And so at last Remie was forced to give up. If Soleil lived, she was not here amid these wretched, starving people. Only the fact that no one knew of her death kept alive the tiny trickle of hope that had almost expired in his heart.

There was still the chance, faint though he must admit it to be, that Soleil had gone on to the Madawaska Valley. And that was where he must go, too.

49

WITHIN HOURS OF ENTERING Mme Cormier's house, Soleil despised the young woman. Yet she was as much fascinated as repelled. She had never known anyone who looked or behaved the way Odette Cormier did.

While promiscuity was not unknown among the Acadians, it was extremely rare. There had been whispers about one woman, considerably older than this one, in Grand-Pré, but no open talk that Soleil had ever heard. A childless widow after some twelve years of marriage, the woman from her village had seemed very much like any other woman: quietly friendly yet reserved, never pushing into any conversation unless she was invited, keeping to herself and her small house, which, like Odette Cormier's, was somewhat isolated. There had been curiosity about her among the young people, but not revulsion.

Their hostess had begged them prettily to call her "Odette," and there was nothing reserved about her. At least, Soleil amended after they'd been there for a day, not as far as François was concerned.

She fluttered her eyelashes at him, her eyes sparkled and her smile was animated whenever he looked in her direction; her pouting mouth smiled at him to such an extent that it made Soleil's hackles rise. And the woman's sugary voice was enough to set her teeth on edge, as well.

Odette hadn't completely ignored Soleil. The smile for *her* had been what Soleil thought of as surface warm and skin-deep. After their hostess explained that she'd made ready a pallet before the fire for the invalid—and invited Soleil to do the same for herself when she liked—her attention was fixed on François.

She was like a great fat spider waiting to eat her mate—after they had mated, Soleil decided. The idea was enough to shake her to the core.

Odette Cormier was a stunningly beautiful young woman. And François, Soleil decided with considerable annoyance, was a gullible—no, *stupid*—young boy who took her glowing smile and honeyed words at face value.

He didn't seem to mind that the woman trailed her fingertips across his hand on the slightest pretense, or that she found it necessary to lean close to him to whisper in her throaty manner the most innocuous of comments. And when he was seated at the table and she was serving a surprisingly ample supper for one who had claimed to be in need of a man to bring in the meat for her, Odette managed to press her bosom against his shoulder as if by accident, though it stayed there long enough to convince Soleil the action was quite deliberate. François *did* notice *that*, for a touch of pink suffused his face, visible even in the firelight.

What a brazen display of immodesty, of impropriety! What had begun as suspicion hardened into certainty as Soleil noted signs in the small house of recent male occupancy: a hat that had fallen behind a bench, a pipe that smelled as if it had been lighted within hours before their arrival, an ax beside the door, and the stack of firewood that had been piled beside it for convenience.

Odette Cormier had never wielded that ax, Soleil decided, nor had she carried in the firewood, which still dripped with melting snow and had dropped bits of bark and debris on the floor. The widow was dressed as if for church, and no moisture nor clinging sliver of bark marred that enviable expanse of bosom.

When she asked how long M. Cormier had been dead, Odette turned to her with a swirl of the rich chestnut curls about her shoulders and said sweetly, "Oh, it's past a year now, poor dear."

In a year both the pipe and the cap would have been discovered and put away, Soleil thought wryly. And the snow would have melted and dried if it had been even as long ago as yesterday since *that* had been carried in.

There was nothing to complain of in Odette's hospitality. She set a good table, though admittedly it was more meat and turnips than anything else. "Supplies have been cut off from everywhere beyond our own region," she apologized. "So I've brewed up a lot of fir tea to make up for the lack of other things. And of course since my husband died I've neither furs to trade nor cash money to buy anything."

François was staring at her with sympathy and admiration, and Soleil wanted to kick him under the table, but she couldn't quite reach him. She rose from her end of the bench, saying,

"The venison is quite delicious. I think I'll see if I can coax Céleste to eat some of it."

"I'm sure it's been very difficult for you," François said, and Odette shrugged—she did that prettily, too—and admitted that it had, but she did the best she could. Her smile was enough to melt the icicles on the eaves outside the window, and François was acting as if he'd never seen a woman smile before.

Céleste had awakened and managed to sit up long enough to feed herself, though the effort tired her. Her hazel eyes, dark in the firelight, shifted toward Odette. "She's very beautiful, isn't she?"

"Very," Soleil said through her teeth, and wondered how Céleste, as well as François, could be so obtuse.

That night as they lay rolled in their blankets on a floor that remained chill in spite of the fire, Soleil was the only one who heard the tap on the door.

Though she was instantly alert, she stayed where she was. A moment later the young widow tiptoed out of her bedroom on bare feet and silently eased open the door. Heedless of her undressed state, Odette put her face into the opening and hissed, "Not tonight, you idiot! I told you!"

There was a mumbled masculine response—perhaps slurred by too much wine?—and Odette closed the door. Through slitted lids Soleil watched her sharply scrutinize the three figures on the floor, then she pattered back to her bed.

Soleil heard François give a small snore, and she curled her hands into fists in frustration. This proved it beyond all question: the widow was not the respectable female she had led François to believe, and it was no wonder the Gaudets had been startled by his announcement that Odette Cormier would take them in. How could he be so blind to what the young woman really was?

Céleste's obtuseness did not last for long, however. By the third day there she was feeling much better, well enough to sit on a stool close to the fire and mend various garments that were threatening to disintegrate. Once, while Odette was busy in the lean-to bedroom, having asked François to secure a shelf there that threatened to fall, Céleste had given Soleil a perceptive glance.

"I think we've not known a woman like Mme Cormier before."

"Get well fast," Soleil suggested, "before the lovely spider has drawn François into her web once and for all."

Startled, Céleste cast a glance toward the doorway, where mingled male and female laughter suggested that François's task was not too onerous. Her brow furrowed. "Do you think that's what she's after? François? He said...she needed someone to provide meat and do chores...."

"Who do you think did them before François came here? There was meat aplenty when we arrived, and he didn't provide that. And look at her hands! She doesn't work with them, not outside the house, yet she's enough firewood stacked to see her through until spring. Besides," Soleil said, and lowered her voice to relate the rest of what she had observed.

Céleste's face revealed her shock. "Do you think she really...does it with...?" She couldn't quite put it into words.

"Don't you? What other explanation is there, especially for the man who came to the door late at night? Obviously he expected to be let in!"

Céleste moistened her lips. "But she wouldn't...with François?"

"He's a man, isn't he?"

Céleste clutched her worn shawl at her throat. "But François wouldn't...would he?"

"How do I know? He was raised in a God-fearing way, but men have—" she tried to think of a delicate way to put it to an unmarried girl "—men have strong impulses, Céleste. And not always perfectly good sense where women are concerned. Besides, I'm not sure that all she wants is to...seduce him."

Céleste blinked. "What, then?"

"Well, if she has a...certain reputation here in St. Anne, then the local citizens aren't too likely to respect her, I'd think. A man looking for a wife, for instance, wouldn't consider a...a loose woman."

Comprehension seeped into Céleste's face. "You mean you think she wants to *marry* François?"

Another burst of hilarity in the adjoining room made Soleil glance uneasily in that direction. "I'm only guessing, but the way she's acting *could* indicate that. After all, François would be a good catch, wouldn't he? He's young, good-looking, strong. He'd be a good provider. No doubt that's what she wants. Someone to see to her needs. A husband would be more reliable that way than a series of... visitors.''

Céleste's mouth sagged. "I don't believe it. You've always had so much imagination, Soleil—"

She was interrupted by a small crash and more laughter.

"Now we'll have to start all over again, *monsieur*," Odette said gaily, and Céleste shut her mouth with an audible click of her teeth.

"What are you going to do about it?"

"I? I'm only his sister. What can I do?"

"He's so... innocent," Céleste said, sounding wistful. "He doesn't know what she is."

"Would he believe us if we told him?" Soleil's tone was dry.

Céleste's throat worked. "If only Antoine were here! He always listened to Antoine...."

"Antoine isn't here. He's managed without Antoine for months," Soleil pointed out, trying to ignore the ache in her throat that mention of any of her missing family always evoked. "He'll probably never have Antoine to be the leader again. But you're right, he is innocent. And I think it quite likely that he needs a woman in his life, a woman of his own." The ache deepened as she remembered the times with Remie, alone together in the dark, laughing and loving.

Céleste's hazel eyes had darkened. "I know. Everyone needs someone." She swallowed, glancing toward the doorway. Replacing a simple shelf seemed to have become an incredibly amusing task. "I'll never have Antoine, now. And I feel so strange... about François."

"How do you feel about him?" Soleil asked softly.

"I don't know... or, rather, I do, sort of. You remember what it was like. I had so much fun with both of them, and I was half in love with each of them, and then..."

"Then you chose Antoine."

"Yes." Céleste was troubled. "Or maybe it was as much that *he* chose *me*. François never said anything, except to make jokes, and he didn't keep trying to kiss me, the way Antoine did." Her voice softened. "François has been very good to me since we left Grand-Pré. Very sweet."

"He's in love with you," Soleil told her bluntly.

"Oh, no! It's only that he's trying to take on Antoine's responsibility... and he'd have rescued *anyone* under those circumstances...."

"Yes, of course he would, but what does that have to do with the fact that he's in love with you? I think he's always been in love with you, but he wouldn't say so when he thought you wanted Antoine, and Antoine wanted you."

Céleste's voice was so faint it was barely audible. "You must be mistaken, Soleil. He's never said the slightest thing to make me think he cared for me, and he's never touched me except when he had to carry me somewhere, or when he helped take care of me when I was so sick. I assure you, he's never made the slightest advance toward me!"

"Because he thinks you're still grieving over Antoine—that it's Antoine you're in love with. Are you?"

Color rose up Céleste's neck and flooded her face. "I'm grieving over Antoine, yes. Over everyone, Mama and Papa and—" She choked, then regained control. "I'll grieve forever. But now I wonder if I even knew what love *was*, the kind of love between a man and a woman. I thought I loved Antoine because he made me laugh and he was such fun. But now I see that he was a boy, and I was only a silly girl. François has become a man these past few months. And what I feel for him is... different than what I felt for Antoine."

"If you want him," Soleil said with all the wisdom of an old married woman, "you'd better do something about it."

Céleste was helpless. "What can I do?"

"Tell him."

"Tell him! That I love him? Soleil, I can't do that! Not when he's given me not the slightest reason to think he cares for me that way! What if you're wrong? What if he thinks of me only as a—a sister—or a friend?"

"He loves you!" Soleil insisted. "Do you think I don't recognize the way a man looks at a woman he truly cares for? I had..." Her voice broke suddenly, and she covered her face for a moment, then wiped at her eyes with the heels of her hands. "Listen to them in there! That silly giggling! If you don't want François to end up marrying her, or at least going to bed with her, you'd better say something to draw his attention back to you before it's too late!''

"But if he really cared about me, he wouldn't marry her, or—or want to go to bed with her!" Céleste objected.

"Men sometimes want to go to bed with women they don't intend to marry," Soleil told her. "And they sometimes wind up marrying them, too! Céleste, for the love of heaven—"

There was no time to finish the thought. Mme Cormier and François were finally emerging from the other room, talking as if they were old friends as she profusely thanked him for his help.

Soleil watched her friend watching *them*. She saw the distress in Céleste's face, saw her gaze fasten almost hungrily on François.

Soon, Céleste, soon, Soleil urged silently, and hoped it would be soon enough.

50

ONCE AWARE of the true nature of Odette Cormier's hospitality, Soleil found it humiliating to be staying under her roof. The weather was both a curse and a blessing. When she ventured out, she invariably encountered other residents of St. Anne, whose looks and attitudes reflected their knowledge of the young widow's activities.

The women's stances ranged from cautiously neutral courtesy to uncertain suspicion to outright aversion and hostility. The very idea that these women might consider Soleil and Céleste in the same light as a woman who sold sexual favors—or traded them—made Soleil's skin crawl.

What was even worse, in a way, were the glances of a few of the men she passed on the path—speculating, lewd glances. Did they think that *she*, too, was available for a price?

Soleil would hurry past them, completing her errand, interrupting her already brief period of exercise to avoid those probing eyes, the suggestive smiles.

The only thing she knew to do was to hold her head high and ignore them—or, when the occasional woman actually spoke to her, to pretend innocence of the situation.

It wasn't easy to express gratitude for Mme Cormier's kindness in taking them in until Céleste regained her strength, not when she was inwardly seething against the woman herself. There had been a steady stream of refugees traveling upriver to Québec City or to anywhere they might be safe from the British. Many villagers had taken some of them in for a few days or a few weeks when they might otherwise have died. Why did *they* have to have landed in *this* household?

When the storms raged through the depths of winter, when she was kept inside by the fire, Soleil at least was spared the embarrassment of meeting people who were wondering about her own virtue.

At times she felt an overwhelming resentment against her brother for having put them in this impossible position. How could he not see what Odette was?

Yet she knew he did not. To François, Mme Cormier was only a pretty woman, widowed at an early age, managing as best she could. His chivalry toward her was the result of his upbringing; respect for females and a protective attitude toward them had been ingrained since he was weaned.

"But he's so stupid sometimes!" Soleil once raged, when he had gone outside to rescue Mme Cormier as she carried home a bag of dried peas she had obtained in exchange for some of François's fresh meat. "She's so transparent, a child could see through her, and there he is, making a fool of himself over her!"

Céleste, having tired of sitting up during the morning, reclined once more on her pallet. "He isn't making a fool of himself, Soleil. He thinks she's just what she says she is, and he's a kind, sweet man."

Soleil gave her a smoldering glance. "Kind and sweet don't rule out stupid," she said, but she knew Céleste was right. "We ought to tell him."

Céleste's smile was rueful. "I'm not sure he'd believe us. And besides, what would that accomplish? We'd be back out in the snow."

That was where her impulse to expose Odette Cormier evaporated. Because if they told François, or if there was any sort of confrontation between the women, they would have to leave her home. And being on their own in the open in this weather, with Céleste still not over her cough and so weak that walking around the little house left her alarmingly exhausted, could prove fatal.

Soleil held her tongue, though with difficulty. Surviving came first, ahead of everything else.

They were eating regularly and fairly well, and they'd begun to regain some of the weight they'd lost since their departure from home. The clothes that had hung on Soleil as if on a stick had grown tight, especially around the waist. It was now obvious to everyone that she was with child, and when the village men watched her with lascivious eyes she wondered if they thought she was a loose woman, like Odette Cormier, who only professed to have had a husband. It made her cheeks burn to think about it.

Barbe had always said she'd never felt better than when she was pregnant, and her deliveries had always been much easier than those of many women. "Except for Louis, who was the first, it was never more than three or four hours from the first twinge until they were suckling," Barbe had laughingly told Soleil when she had returned from Québec with her own news that she would have a babe in the spring.

To judge by the way the wind blew and the sullen sky continued to produce dry, hard flakes of snow, spring was still a long way off. Yet they were into the New Year, 1756, and April was drawing closer with each passing day.

Soleil's conviction grew that when the time came to give birth, she must have reached the Madawaska Valley. Perhaps, she thought with longing, Remie would find her there.

She found herself praying again. *Please, God, let it be as easy for me as it was for Mama. And don't let me be alone when it happens. Let Remie be there.* She didn't know if she trusted that God heard, or that He cared, but she *wanted* to trust, as she had in the past, before God had allowed the English to destroy her people.

Céleste, too, was struggling internally. She *was* getting better; most days it seemed that she felt stronger. She was able to sit for longer periods between naps, able to be on her feet a little more. But the improvement was relative. She knew she might easily have died with the fever, and that she would still be at risk if she left the security of this house she'd come to hate.

She watched François and Odette, the woman brazenly flirting, enticing, and François falling over his own feet in his gratitude, trying to prove that they were worthy of having been taken in.

Well, to be fair, what man was likely to resist the flattery, the admiration, the warm smiles? François had had his share of interest from the village girls at Grand-Pré, but no one had ever before devoured him with her eyes or found so many ways to make supposedly accidental physical contact with him. Certainly, Céleste admitted sadly, *she'd* never done so. They had been like children, playing together, dancing together, teasing and making jokes and playing pranks. The three of them. She and François and Antoine.

Soleil had insisted that her brother was in love with her friend, but Céleste saw no indication of any such thing. He had been kind to her, as he would have been kind to anyone in distressing circumstances, but it was Odette Cormier who sparked his romantic interests.

Céleste watched with rising jealousy as Odette playfully tickled François under the chin with a feather and he held her wrist to make her stop, both of them laughing as if no one else were around. He had once done that sort of thing with *her*, though there had been only innocence between them then. Céleste was still innocent in the sense that she had no experience of anything more than playful kisses, and those had been few in number—stolen by Antoine, for the most part. Perhaps François was still very naive, but as for Odette, every wriggle, every smile, was calculated to inflame masculine interest.

Céleste slid her gaze away from the pair, wishing she could crack their heads together and bring François to his senses. She saw that Soleil had been watching them, too, and the message, though unspoken, was clear on her friend's face.

If you want him, do something about it.

Céleste suddenly knew that she *did* want François. She wasn't sure that she loved him—she had *thought* she loved Antoine, and now she was confused—but she was quite certain that she did not want Odette to claim François. Not even for a furtive half hour in the lean-to bedchamber.

She didn't know what to do about it, though. She had never learned those coquettish tricks that seemed to come so easily to Odette.

She said as much, later, to Soleil.

Soleil thought of herself and Remie, of how easy it had been between them, right from the first. "I don't think you have to be like her to make him notice you. Honesty and decency—and virtue—are values a man wants in a wife."

"But he doesn't know she isn't virtuous. And she is beautiful," Céleste pointed out wistfully.

"So are you. And he cares about you, Céleste. I know he does."

"I'm a pale, skinny hag," Céleste said, making a face.

Soleil shook her head in disgust but said nothing else, and Céleste knew she was back where she had started.

If she wished to save François from an undeserved fate as a second husband to a woman for whom the villagers felt nothing but contempt, it was up to her, Céleste, to do something about it.

That night she prayed for guidance, and in the morning she had an idea.

Odette, of course, had an idea first. Immediately after the morning meal she suggested to François that, since the snow had stopped, they might walk to the miller's with the last haunch of venison and see if it could be traded for some flour, if he had any left.

François accepted immediately. And then Céleste, her mouth dry, pasted a stiff smile on her lips and made her own bid for attention.

"Will you be long, François? I'd thought, perhaps, if you weren't busy—" She hesitated, but he was waiting for her to finish with no sign of impatience. "I'm feeling ever so much better, and I thought I might begin to get back my strength by walking a little. Every day, you know. If," she added in a rush, before her courage deserted her, "you had time to go with me, to make sure I didn't overdo and become too tired to get back."

Odette's good humor had vanished with Céleste's first words, but François was smiling encouragingly. Céleste thought he looked more like an older brother than a prospective suitor, though, and felt discouraged.

Yet he said, "Of course. In fact, why don't you come with us to the mill? It's probably not too far, and we're in no special hurry, are we *madame*? We could walk slowly and rest if you need to."

Thunderclouds were gathering in Odette's lovely face. "You are still very weak, *mademoiselle*. You would not want to risk a setback by going out too soon."

At that point Soleil came to her friend's rescue. "I think some exercise outdoors is an excellent idea. The more you sit around the house, the longer it will take for you to be well again. By all means, go with them, Céleste. I'll see to the fire and tend the spit." She pulled the shawl from around her shoulders. "I'll loan you this to make sure you're warm enough."

"Yes. It wouldn't do to take a chill," Odette said, sounding flat.

In that obtuse manner men often display in such situations, François nodded. "Bundle up warmly, then, and we'll go. You, too, Soleil. The exercise will do you good. I think it's even a little warmer today. There are icicles forming on the eaves, did you notice? It must have thawed a bit."

The excursion was not a total success, for Odette managed to dominate the conversation and direct their steps. But one of her attempts to monopolize François backfired.

"You are rather pale, Mlle Céleste," she said. "Perhaps this is too much for you. There is a stump here. It might be wise for you to rest until we come back this way."

Céleste was feeling rather pale, for she had not walked this far in weeks, but once more Soleil intervened.

"I've a better idea. François can take her arm and make it easier for her. I'll carry the venison."

François shifted the haunch uncertainly on his shoulder. "I don't know, Soleil. It's heavy."

"Not as heavy as Céleste, in spite of the fact that she's skin and bones. Here, let me try it."

The meat *was* heavy, but it gave Soleil great satisfaction just to see Odette's face as she was forced either to lead the way or fall behind the group, for there was no room for three abreast on the path. Céleste clung to François's arm and even, in a bold move empowered by exhilaration, pretended to slip several times on the softening snow. From then on he put his arm around her for support, and by the time they'd returned home she didn't have to pretend to need it.

"I told you you would overdo," Odette said brusquely as they stamped the snow off their feet before entering the house. "You must take it much more easily, Mlle Céleste. Tomorrow you may have to forgo a walk in favor of more rest, for you are quite out of breath."

On the following day, however, Céleste was determined to walk again. True, she had been very tired. But she need not walk quite as far as before, and once she'd had time to recuperate she truly felt stronger for having made the effort.

Besides that, the surge of pleasure brought on by the nearness of François, by his touch, and especially by the realization that *he* was feeling something, too, made it worthwhile and more.

Odette was left behind on the second day and on the third, as well. Soleil hummed as she went about the kitchen while their hostess fumed impatiently.

It was going well, Soleil thought. François was looking at Céleste again the way he had before she fell ill, as if she were someone special.

And then something happened to convince Céleste that she must take an even bolder step.

She woke late at night, knowing the temperature must have dropped again, for she was cold. Even before she stirred, she realized that François was up, putting more wood on the fire, quietly so as not to disturb anyone.

Céleste opened her lips to whisper her thanks when she heard the creak of a floorboard and shifted her gaze toward the bedroom doorway.

Odette stood there in a flowing nightgown, her chestnut hair catching the light from the fireplace, her bosom prominently displayed when she held an arm close against her body so that the fabric was drawn taut.

"Monsieur François," Odette breathed, and beckoned him closer with a crooked finger.

Like a sheep, Céleste later told Soleil, François stepped toward her. He was fully clothed, but did not hesitate because *she* was not fully dressed.

"Oh, you have already put wood upon the fire! Thank you, *monsieur*. It is very cold tonight, isn't it? On a night such as this, a woman misses a husband, eh? She longs to have a man's warm arms around her—"

The next thing Céleste knew, the audacious widow had slid her arms around François, who allowed himself to be drawn close without resisting, and then she put up her hands to pull his face down to hers and kissed him fully on the mouth.

He didn't resist that, either.

Céleste knew in a blazing moment of clarity that if she didn't do something, and at once, the hussy would have him in her bed, mesmerized by her beauty, her tantalizing figure and her seductive kisses.

Whatever she did would have to be extremely effective.

Céleste suddenly rolled, crying out as if in a nightmare, and flipped the corner of her blanket onto the hearth. A moment later she was on her knees, where it was possible to assure that the blanket caught fire in the embers nearest her.

"Oh! Oh, help, François, Soleil! My blanket is burning!"

She let her voice rise in quite a satisfactory shriek.

Pandemonium lasted only a moment or two, for François quickly stamped out the fire. The smell of burning wool filled the room as he knelt beside her.

"Are you all right? Did you get burned?"

"Only a spark, right here." She extended her hand with a pinkened spot where she had quickly bitten it; in the dim light, it would pass for a burn. "Perhaps if I had a bit of snow to put on it—"

He moved at once and brought back a compacted icy ball, then held her hand while he applied it. "There. Does that feel better?"

"Yes. Thank you, François." She decided, as she gave the widow an apologetic smile, that she was becoming quite an actress. "I'm so sorry, *madame*, for waking you. And you, Soleil. I was having a bad dream, and when I moved I was too close to the hearth . . . I might have burned up in my sleep!"

"But you didn't. You think you can go back to sleep now?" François asked. "Shall I bring in more snow?"

"No, no," Céleste said, sounding as brave as she could. "It's only a little burn, after all. Go back to bed, everyone. I'll try not to disturb you again."

It was too dim for her to see Odette's eyes clearly, but Céleste knew that they would reflect fury and frustration. "Good night," Odette snapped, and disappeared, while François crawled onto his own pallet, farthest from the fire.

Smiling a little, Céleste rewrapped herself in the scorched blanket, not minding the pungent smell. From that time on, whenever she noticed where the corner had burned off, she would feel again the amused satisfaction of that moment.

And she knew that starting first thing in the morning she would seriously plan her own campaign to prevent François's being caught in the widow's web.

Soleil knew it, too. She was close enough to have seen Céleste shoving the corner of the blanket into the fire, and while she didn't yet know why her friend had done so, she, too, was amused.

The baby kicked, and she curled up in a fetal position of her own, content for the moment to feel the child and to relax into a warm sleep.

51

BAD NEWS TRAVELED FASTER than good. Everybody knew that. Yet it was many weeks after the deportation of the Acadians from Nova Scotia, as their land was now called, before news of it reached Île St. Jean.

Charles Trudelle, brother of Guillaume of Grand-Pré, told the Cyrs. He came to the tiny one-room cabin Louis had built in a sheltered cove, and Madeleine knew at once that something dreadful had happened, for Charles had been weeping unashamedly.

She feared at first that it was his wife Marie, who had recently been brought to bed with her third child, or perhaps the babe had died, though she had seemed healthy enough when Madeleine had visited a few days earlier.

Louis had opened the door to his knock, and the man had stood there, just inside, twisting his cap in his big hands, tears glistening on his cheeks as they slid down to disappear into his dark beard.

"For the love of God, man, what is it?" Louis had to touch his arm to draw him close to the fire.

Madeleine's two sons were like baby birds with mouths open, waiting to be fed, but she held the spoon poised in midair, the children forgotten. "Marie?" she whispered.

Charles shook his head and accepted the cup of fir tea Louis had quickly poured. Brandy would have been more to the point, from the look of their friend, but there was none. Indeed, there was nothing in the house that they hadn't made themselves, and little enough of that.

"Everyone in Grand-Pré," he told them after his throat had worked painfully for a few moments, "has been loaded onto British ships and taken away. And everyone in Beaubassin, and Pisiquid, and Annapolis Royal, everywhere there was a settlement. They have been deported, every one."

They stared at him in shock. "Deported?" Louis echoed. "To where?"

"No one seems to know exactly. To the English colonies, a few even to England, 'tis thought. But they've gone, every Acadian, and the villages have been burned, with only the chimneys and the wells still standing. And not only that, they were not even allowed to go as families; they were separated and put into different ships. We will never see any of them again on this earth."

Louis and Madeleine moved closer together, shoulders touching. "Everyone?" Madeleine repeated, almost inaudible. "My parents? My brothers? Mama and Papa Cyr?"

Louis moistened his lips. "Surely some escaped. They couldn't all have been rounded up like sheep—"

Charles related what he knew, unmindful of their horror through his own grief and dismay. "Some, no doubt, got away into the woods. But how long could they live through the winter with no shelter, no supplies? If Guillaume had been among them, he would surely have come here—" His voice failed.

The baby cried, and Madeleine picked him up without conscious thought, jiggling him to calm him down. "We should never have gone away and left them," she said faintly. "We should have been there to help them—there might have been something we could have done—''

Louis shook his head. "No. Staying would have done no good for them or for us. What I should have done . . . was to persuade Papa and the others to come with us. Except . . . this was not necessarily a good place to come. I never dreamed food would be in such short supply, and even the firewood is not as plentiful as we were used to.''

Nothing, Madeleine thought bitterly, was plentiful, as it had always been at home.

Charles blew his nose. "It would be, had not so many people fled here to get away from the English. Even the Micmacs, 'tis said, are leaving in droves, heading west.''

Louis inhaled deeply. "That's what we should have done, I suppose. Gone west. Remie talked of that place, up the St. John River, toward Québec. It might have been better.''

His wife looked at him in alarm. She was much thinner than she had been when they left home over a year earlier, and deprivation had taken its toll on her prettiness. She had been lonely here, for their closest neighbors, Charles and Marie, were too distant for frequent visiting. Even this tiny cabin, coupled with the care of two babies, was too much for her to manage without falling into bed each night in an exhaustion so great that it was nearer to illness than fatigue. She missed both her own family and the Cyrs with an intensity born of desperation, and she feared falling truly ill when there was no one to help. Even her prayers were most often said when she was on the move, cooking or changing the baby, or after she'd gone to bed at night, and then she often fell asleep before the devotions were completed, adding to her sense of inadequacy.

Yet fear of the unknown was greater than her apprehensions about this place.

"We won't leave here, will we?" she asked, and Louis put an arm around her in a comforting hug, though his mind was on those English ships and their human cargo. "No, no. We came here, and here we'll stay. Charles, your news is staggering. I can hardly believe it. God knows, we've had reason to hate the English for years, but this surpasses the imagination for pure evil! You're sure it's true?"

Charles's gaze held raw agony. "As sure as I can be. 'Twas related in considerable detail by one who saw Grand-Pré after it had been razed. He lost his entire family. We had no reason to doubt his sincerity or his accuracy."

"But he escaped," Madeleine pointed out, clinging to Louis with her free hand while balancing the baby on her other hip. "So there must have been others! Louis, maybe some of ours—"

Louis himself held no hope, but he could not bear to crush the tiny spark in his wife's eyes. "Perhaps. Well, they know where we are, and if any survived, they know where to find us. They'll come here."

After Charles had gone they held each other and wept for their losses, for everyone's losses. For a time Madeleine comforted herself with the memory of Louis's words: "If any survived, they know where to find us. They'll come here."

But day by day that optimism dwindled, for no one came, and the news they heard only confirmed what Charles had said, as winter eased on toward the longed-for spring.

DANIELLE STRAIGHTENED from her scrubbing, pausing long enough to massage her aching back before she went to the door with the bucket of dirty water. To think that she had once regarded her mother as a hard taskmaster! she reflected. Compared to Mistress Monroe, Barbe Cyr would qualify as a kindly saint.

The only good thing about this place was the food; Master Monroe was well-to-do, and his larder was plentifully supplied. The comparative luxury of the Boston home did not impress her; her own log home had been cozier. She missed Grand-Pré with a deep, longing ache, and with an endless yearning remembered the firs, spruces and maples surrounding the house there. The city streets here, which might have intrigued her had the people who walked them spoken—or even tolerated—her own language, were alien, unfriendly, without beauty.

Though the citizens of the Massachusetts Bay Colony had not wanted the Acadian exiles, they were willing to exploit them. Acadians made good servants. And, Danielle thought, mouth tightening as she heard the front door open and close and the sound of happy childish laughter, they even made welcome adoptive children for childless couples when they were young enough to have the French blood in them suppressed and were converted to proper little Englishmen.

Vincent was too young to understand any of it. He couldn't be blamed for the fact that the Monroes doted on him, treated him as the son they had never had. Already he'd stopped asking about Papa and Henri and Grand-maman and Grand-papa. He had picked up the new language so quickly, though it was so difficult for her. She often asked him to translate, when André wasn't around.

The thought of André sent a flood of warmth through her as she hurried to relieve the mistress of her winter cloak and the bundles she would be carrying. Without André Lejeune, life in this house would be intolerable. She thought she was falling in love with André, though the realization was not one of unalloyed joy. She doubted that she would ever be allowed to marry André, even if he wanted her.

That, of course, remained a big question. André was very handsome. Even the simpering English girls rolled their eyes at him. He was unvaryingly polite to them, though behind their backs he made faces so that Danielle had to smother her giggles in her apron. And of course he was older than she—twenty-one to her fourteen. Still, she knew he *liked* her.

He liked Vincent, too. He was good for her nephew, better for him than Charles Monroe, who spoiled him rotten and discouraged him from speaking French or even remembering anything of his own background, his own family or homeland.

Sure enough, Mistress Monroe was loaded down with packages. "Oh, Martha, there you are! Takes these, please! And take Master Vincent, too, and wash his hands. They're sticky from the sweets."

Danielle wanted to point out that the sweets would have spoiled Vincent's appetite for the dinner that was even now simmering in the kettle, but she knew better. The mistress did not take kindly to observations from the servants.

"Oh, and, Martha, he'll need a clean shirt before supper. The Ridgeways are coming. Be sure there's plenty of claret out, as well as the brandy."

French brandy, and smuggled at that, was good enough for them, Danielle thought, easing the bundles onto the table beside the door, though everything else that smacked of Frenchness was treated with contempt. Including people of French ancestry.

Except for Vincent. Even his name had been accepted, though they pronounced it differently. Mistress Monroe had tentatively considered calling him Peter, but Vincent had thrown a royal fit, and she had backed off. Danielle had marveled at the way he'd done it, knowing if he'd tried anything like that at home Barbe would have taken a switch to him and given him a bit of her tongue, as well.

Oh, yes, Vincent would do all right in this society as the adopted son of a prominent couple.

"Oh, and, Martha," Mistress Monroe called after her as she led the little boy toward the kitchen, "don't forget to see there's plenty of wood for the parlor fire. We'll be sitting up later than usual this evening with our guests."

Their guests be damned, and the Monroes too, Danielle thought, yet she knew she would do as she was told. The mistress was a formidable adversary and a strict disciplinarian.

Vincent pulled away when she attempted to wash his face, but she persisted. "There. Now you can be seen by the company," she told him finally.

"I had sweets twice today," Vincent informed her. "And Mama bought me a new pair of shoes. See? Real shoes!"

"She's not your mama," Danielle reminded him, troubled by his easy acceptance of this new role as a favored child. The Monroes were, after all, part of the hated race that had destroyed their own people. "Your mama is dead. And your papa and brother were sent off on a ship somewhere. Don't you remember your papa? And Henri?"

"Yes," Vincent said vaguely. "But now I am to call *them* Mama and Papa. I want an apple."

"It's almost suppertime," Danielle said, hearing her mother in her own voice.

"Oh, let him have what he wants," Mistress Monroe said from the doorway. "I'll wear my blue gown tonight, and it's rather crumpled. Have it ironed for me to put on after I've rested for a bit. And Vincent, lamb, do play quietly for a time so that Mama can take a nap, will you, like a good boy?''

"Yes, Mama," Vincent said obediently, and trotted off with her. Danielle stared after them for a moment, resenting the orders, which were always issued without a "please" and accepted without a "thank you." Vincent knew from which direction the wind blew.

Behind her the door into the backyard opened, and André stuck his dark head around the edge of it. "Ah, there you are. Is the mistress home?"

Danielle's heart bounded. It wasn't often that André was allowed to come home so early, for he was kept busy at the accounting offices of Master Monroe.

"She's gone to take a nap. There will be guests for supper. With no more notice than five minutes ago," Danielle observed. "I'm to prepare for two more."

André came in and closed the door. "An easy matter for one of your talents and abilities. Put more turnips in the soup."

In spite of herself, Danielle giggled. "We aren't having soup."

André shrugged. "Cut the bread into thicker slices. Listen, my beautiful fellow slave—" for a moment she almost lost the sense of his words, for he'd never suggested before that she was beautiful "—I have important news."

"Oh? What?"

He came closer and lowered his voice, losing his jocular air. "I overheard Master Charles discussing me today. He has all sorts of plans for me."

"Really? What?"

"More responsibilities at his place of business, for one. And he seemed quite receptive when Master Leighton broached a serious subject—that of my being allowed to marry his daughter, Priscilla."

Danielle's heart plummeted. Her mouth went dry. "I thought you didn't care for Priscilla."

"I don't. I can't bear simpering females, and that lapdog of hers is enough to make me want to throttle the pair of them."

The knot in Danielle's stomach eased, though it didn't go away. "So are you going to marry her anyway?"

André helped himself to an apple from the bowl on the table and bit into it. When he spoke he sounded like one of her brothers. "Of course not. I'd be just another lapdog, and can you imagine having her mama for a mother-in-law?" He aped the way that Mistress Leighton surveyed the world through her quizzing glass, and Danielle felt a bubble of mirth form in her throat. It was too soon to relax, however.

"So how are you going to get out of it?" she asked cautiously.

"They spoke in terms of a summer wedding."

She waited, and when he only took another crunchy bite of the apple Danielle became impatient. "Well? There must be more than that!"

André looked her directly in the face. "I don't intend to be here in the summer."

A trickle of something, half excitement, half apprehension, tickled her veins. "Where are you going to be?"

André was serious again, looking past her to make sure there was no listener at the door, then drawing to the very far side of the kitchen, again pitching his voice low. "In the spring I am going to leave Boston. Without, of course, asking permission."

Danielle pressed a hand to her suddenly racing heart. Punishment for running away was severe. The Acadians who had been brought here were not better off, had no more control of their own destinies, than the black slaves on the plantations in the Carolinas.

She waited for the rest of what he had to say, hearing the blood in her own ears.

"I am going to head north and walk until I reach a place where someone says to me, 'Good day, *monsieur*,' and I will know I have walked far enough."

Her eyes stung. "They burned our villages. We smelled the smoke for days before we sailed."

"They didn't burn all of Canada. There are still Acadians in Québec, on the Gaspé, in the woods behind Saint John. I'm leaving when it turns warm enough so I've a chance of getting there without dying of cold and hunger." He stopped, and now there was none of his customary teasing humor in either his face or his voice. "Will you go with me, Danielle?"

For a moment she listened to the meat on the spit, the cat mewing to come in, her own rapid breathing.

He was waiting, and she had to find her own voice. "Yes," she said, sounding strangled. "I'll go with you."

"They'll whip us, or worse, if we're caught."

"I'll go with you," she repeated, and suddenly her spirit was singing, her heart soaring. "I'll go, André, I'll go!"

"You'll have to continue to appear to be your usual sullen, sulky self," he warned, the smile coming back into his dark eyes. "Otherwise the mistress will suspect that something is up."

"I'll snarl at her every day," Danielle promised tremulously, "even if she beats me for it."

"Good. And now I have one final surprise for you." He produced a scrap of paper, which she recognized as having been torn from a newspaper, though she couldn't read it when he thrust it in front of her.

"What is it?" The printing meant nothing to her.

"It is an advertisement that was published only today. Shall I tell you what it says?" He read it aloud with profound satisfaction. " 'Wanted: Information about any of the Cyr or Trudelle families of Grand-Pré. Contact Guillaume Trudelle or Jacques Cyr.' And they are here, or close to here. In Cambridge, which is only a few miles away."

"Jacques!" In her astonishment and joy she had yelped the name aloud, and André clapped a warning hand over her mouth.

"Shh! You must learn to be more careful! Think before you speak, or you'll give us both away!"

His face was very close to hers, so that she could have counted the hairs in his eyebrows. Danielle went very still and after a moment André removed his hand from her mouth, where it had made her lips tingle.

And then, very slowly, he bent his head and kissed her.

Danielle's bones seemed to melt within her like candles left standing on the mantel when the fire has been built too hot. The only thing holding her together, she thought vacuously, were the hot threads that seemed to extend throughout her body, into her limbs, everywhere.

Footsteps sounded in the adjoining room, and André whirled and was gone, closing the door behind him without a sound.

"Mama says I may have some cider," Vincent piped.

Danielle turned, barely capable of comprehending, of acting. Bemused, numbed, she sought to pull herself together to dip the cider from the barrel.

Only a few months ago she had felt so alone, so abandoned, so terrified by these English who insisted she be someone, something, she was not. Even the memory of Basile had dimmed, for she knew she would never see him again. And now she felt warm all over; her heart continued to race, though it was not frightening this time, and she wanted to shout and sing.

For now there was André.

52

FRANÇOIS WAS NOT QUITE as naive as Soleil and Céleste imagined him to be.

He, too, had been aware of the reaction from the Gaudets when he mentioned Mme Cormier, and he had guessed the reason for it more quickly than Soleil. What, however, could he do about it if the woman had an unfortunate reputation? He knew that Céleste must be kept warm and dry and well fed if she were to survive the winter; he also had been keenly aware that the three of them were making deep inroads into the Gaudets' food supplies, using up staples that probably could not be replaced as long as the British continued their blockade.

He had met Odette Cormier quite by accident when he went into St. Anne to scout out alternatives to their imposing any longer on the Gaudet family. He had been deeply concerned for both their benefactors and his own two charges, for whom he felt totally responsible, and he'd been thinking about Antoine, who'd have shared that burden if they'd both escaped the deportation.

God in Heaven, how he missed Antoine! The entire time they had been growing up it was almost as if the two of them had continued to be joined as closely out of the womb as they had been in it. They had slept together, played together—even, he thought with bitter amusement, fallen in love with the same girl together; it was probably the one thing about him that Antoine had not known—and he'd have given up his right arm, or one of his eyes, rather than his twin.

How many hundreds of times over the past months had he wanted to say something to Antoine? Knowing that Antoine would be thinking the same thing, and that they'd laugh over it, or grapple simultaneously with whatever problem there was to be dealt with.

Losing Antoine made him feel as if the heart had been torn from his breast and the bleeding continued. And the irony of being the one who had rescued Céleste, rather than Antoine, whom she loved, was a constant pressure within him.

He saw the girl ahead of him on the path, moving briskly, carrying a basket. He was only a few yards behind her when she slipped on an icy spot and went down; the basket flew into the snow beside the path, its contents scattering...a turnip this way, an onion that way.

François heard a decidedly unladylike expletive as she sprawled before him on the ground, and he dashed forward to help her.

"Are you hurt, *mademoiselle*?"

She sat up, rubbing the back of her head, her eyes squeezed shut in a grimace of pain. "I think I've split my head! And it's *madame*, not *mademo*—"

She opened her eyes at that point and stared into his face. Her own altered perceptibly as she took in his dark curls and the brown eyes, now showing concern on her behalf.

"Ah, *monsieur*, you find me in a very unattractive position! Kindly assist me to my feet and help me just a bit farther to my house, so that I don't fall again!"

François complied with alacrity. He pulled her up, then refilled her basket with the items that had sunk into the snow. By this time he'd had several good looks at the young woman, and he saw that she was stunningly pretty.

Although he had committed his love to Céleste long since, even knowing she preferred his brother, he was not totally immune to other feminine beauty. "Where do you live, *madame*?"

"Over there. In the tiny little house." She had a melodic voice and a rippling laugh. "It's big enough for one, though."

Her gaze met his from beneath thick dark lashes. "My husband left me that much when he died, thank God, or what would have become of me? As it is, living is difficult for a widow, particularly in these times." Confidently she tucked her mittened hand in the crook of his elbow and allowed him to carry the basket.

"You are widowed, then."

"More than a year ago," she confessed, leaving François to wonder why no one had yet made her a wife again. She was young and healthy and quite the most beautiful woman he'd ever met.

"Ah, here we are! Thank you, *monsieur*, for your kindness. It is cold, isn't it? Would you care to step inside for a cup of tea? I have only fir tea, I'm afraid, but it *is* hot."

That was how it had begun. Innocently, at least on *his* part. When they had talked for a few minutes over the tea and learned a little about each other, it didn't seem suspect that Mme Cormier might make an offer to help solve his problems. Everywhere they had been there had been kind and caring people, sharing what they had with the refugees.

However, it hadn't taken long after they'd actually moved in for François to realize that he'd made a tactical error in describing Céleste as his sister's friend, though he didn't see how else he could have designated her. My brother's betrothed, when his brother had vanished, God knew where, and would probably never be seen again?

He was not quite as shocked as Soleil upon comprehending that the Widow Cormier supplemented her meager resources by entertaining various gentlemen. Back home, in the carefree days before the black ones that followed, the twins and other young men in the village had joked and speculated about visiting such a woman. None of them had been brave enough to do it—indeed, they hadn't much to offer, as they thought, to the only such female they knew of, a woman twice their age and having none of the looks of this one.

Still, at first he hadn't thought it mattered. *He* had no intention of taking advantage of Mme Cormier's generosity, only of keeping his charges safe until Céleste was well enough to travel again, and he would earn their keep by filling the cooking pot.

He hadn't quite counted on how Odette would make him feel, though. Not like an inexperienced boy at all, but like a man. He'd felt some of the same longings and urges before, but never with the knowledge that if he cared to indulge them, the lady would be more than willing to oblige.

He wasn't quite naive enough to think that what he got would be for free, either. He, too, had caught the signs about her house of previous male visitors, and far more recently than a year ago when M. Cormier had died. She wasn't angling for a romp in exchange for a buck for her spit; she wanted another husband.

François wondered if she would be satisfied with one man if she remarried, or if she'd been faithful to M. Cormier when he was alive. There was no need, in Acadian society, for a woman to sell herself to survive. The entire community would band together to see that a lone female, or one with children, was fed and her roof mended when necessary. So why did Odette Cormier do it?

Admittedly, the idea of taking her to bed was exciting. And while he didn't initiate the episodes like the feather tickling and the touching that sent jolts of tremendous sensation through him, François didn't pretend not to enjoy them. If it hadn't been for his sister's presence, and Céleste's, he might easily have succumbed to Odette's overtures.

In fact, he damned near had, that night when he'd got up to rebuild the fire and she'd come walking out in that nightgown that revealed virtually everything about her lush, round figure.

If Céleste hadn't had a nightmare and thrashed around so that her blanket started to smolder . . . François grinned every time he thought about it, but there was a tinge of regret mixed with the relief.

Sooner or later, if they stayed here long enough, Odette was going to get him into a situation from which he wouldn't be rescued—willingly or unwillingly—and in the daylight, when that delicious breast wasn't pressed into his shoulder or his arm as she bent near him in some seemingly innocent act, he knew he'd be better off staying away from her.

In the long run, he'd be better off making love to Céleste, except that it would seem like adultery with his brother's wife, he thought wistfully.

But the winter was a long way from being over, and he didn't see how they could leave yet. François called upon the Blessed Mother for the power to resist temptation, yet couldn't help wondering if She were up to the task.

SOLEIL WAS INCREASINGLY restless. Céleste no longer required actual nursing, and that left her with little to do to occupy her time. Had there been materials available, she might have made new garments for the three of them, for they were in rags.

There was no cloth—Mme Odette did not even own a spinning wheel and there was no indication that she was a seamstress—and no money to buy any.

Soleil might have made friends in the village during the weeks they were in St. Anne, but she was convinced the other women looked at her askance because she was staying in the house of a harlot. She averted her gaze when they stared at her with curiosity, and she despised Odette for being what she was.

And there was no mistaking just what that was. Twice more since that first time, men came to the door late at night. On both occasions, like the first, they had been drinking, and Odette sent them away with bland explanations to the girls, who kept their faces carefully neutral.

Soleil continued to walk; she was determined that they would go on as soon as possible. She wanted to stay in good condition, and she wanted her baby to be born where it had been conceived, miles upriver from here. April seemed far away, and the village remained locked in an icy winter, but her burgeoning belly was a constant reminder that her time was approaching.

She made it a point not to walk with François and Céleste on what had become their twice-daily excursions. Céleste was regaining her color, and there was a sparkle in her hazel eyes that made Soleil both glad and wistful. She, too, had no doubt looked that way when she and Remie were courting.

Céleste had made up her mind that she *did* want François, and while they walked they talked. Deliberately, in spite of the anguish it caused, she led the conversation to those they had lost, including Antoine.

"You miss him terribly, don't you?" she murmured, putting a hand over François's in the boldest gesture she had made so far.

"Like half my soul," François said unhesitatingly.

"I miss him, too." Céleste hesitated. Then, taking a page from Odette's book, she leaned closer to him so that their shoulders were touching, though they wore too many clothes for the warmth to come through them. "Only it's strange, François. I loved him, but it seems like a dream, not something real. We were children, playing at loving. And now..."

"Now?" François prompted, pausing to stare down at her with an inscrutable face.

"Now we're grown up," Céleste said softly. "How could we not grow up, after all that's happened? I don't feel like a little girl any longer, I feel like a woman. And you proved you were a man when you got us out of there, off the beach at Grand-Pré. Actually, I suppose you proved it before that, when you were fighting the British, only none of us knew about it."

"Except Antoine." The sunlight glinted off the snow so that François shifted position to rest his eyes from the glare. "That's what I can't get used to. Antoine always knew everything I did. Everything I thought. Now it's as if... half my brain is gone, as well as half my heart."

Céleste gave a sad, twisted little smile, but her own heart was beginning to thump rather loudly, for the way he was looking down on her sent a prickle up her spine. As if perhaps he *did* find her more than passingly attractive.

"I remember that Mama and Papa used to be almost able to read one another's minds. One of them would start to speak, and the other would finish the sentence. Or sometimes they would speak together, and then laugh, because they didn't need to finish. They *knew* what the other was going to say. Sometimes it's like that with... with married people. Almost the way it was with you and Antoine."

François hadn't thought of it that way. "I guess my mother and father did that, too, sometimes. I never paid much attention. I miss that the most about Antoine, I guess—that closeness."

Her pulse racing, her mouth dry, Céleste lifted her face to study his. "A man and wife can be very close," she said.

She was not to know how François would have responded to that. For coming through the woods along the trail they had left in the snow was Odette. She called out cheerfully, interrupting the moment. *"Monsieur! Monsieur François!"*

Whatever expression had been forming on his face was erased as he turned to greet Odette. "Yes, *madame*?"

She was like a butterfly, light, airy, fragile. Céleste stifled her annoyance. Curse the woman's timing, anyway!

Odette had a way of honing in on any male in the group, cutting out the females with a meaningless smile before she dismissed them. Until now Céleste had not fully appreciated what a detestable manner it was. "I hope I do not interrupt anything," Odette said, and did not wait for a reply. "I have need of your services, and quickly! A bird or some other creature has apparently gotten into the chimney, and the house is filling with smoke! I am at my wit's end to know what to do before we are all driven out into the cold!"

François hurried back to the house with her; Céleste followed more slowly, meeting Soleil, her face smudged with soot, outside.

"There really is an emergency, then," Céleste greeted her.

"Oh, yes, though I've been wondering if the woman climbed to the roof and threw a poor bird or even a rabbit down the chimney. Honestly, Céleste, though I suppose I should be grateful that we aren't sleeping on the ground, I don't think I can take much more of living with Madame Cormier! I dislike her more with each passing hour."

"Yet François remains at her beck and call," Céleste observed with an unhappy smile. "I thought, for a moment, that I might be getting somewhere with him, and then *she* came running after him. It's impossible to have a private conversation with him for more than a minute or two, and then *madame* appears, and I no longer have his ear. How can I compete with a woman like her?"

Soleil did not know what she was going to say until she had said it. "There's only one way that I can think of. I don't think she's actually managed to lure him into her bed yet."

For a moment she was stunned, then Céleste moistened her lips. Soleil watched as the idea filtered through her friend's head, but instead of denying that such a thing was possible, as Soleil had half expected, Céleste spoke uncertainly.

"How would I go about doing that? I don't know about such things!"

Soleil's lips quivered in mischievous delight. "I didn't know, either, until Remie taught me. But he taught me well—oh, no, I won't cry, I promise I won't—and I'll tell you how to go about it."

There was a shout from the house, and Odette came to the doorway, flapping her apron to fan the smoke outside. The girls were scarcely aware of her.

Céleste's face was red, but she was fascinated as well as appalled.

"What would I have to do?"

"He hasn't kissed you yet, has he? I thought not. Even a simple, chaste kiss can lead to... much more. François is an honorable man. If he believes he has seduced you, he'll feel bound to do the right thing by you."

"But I can't..."

"Don't you want to kiss him?"

"Yes, of course I do, but—" Céleste was torn between longing and the embarrassing fear that if François *wanted* to kiss her he would already have done so.

"He still thinks of you as Antoine's bride-to-be," Soleil told her, as if reading her mind. "You have only to convince him that you don't feel that way anymore. Get close to him, reach up to him and touch him, brush your lips across his—" She gave a choked little laugh. "I can't tell you how many times, without meaning to do any more than that, a gesture of affection or even teasing led us to—" Her breath caught on a gasp. "No, I won't talk about Remie and me, but it's true, Céleste. You don't have to be so terribly forward, just give him a chance to kiss you, that's all it will take."

"Do you think it would work?"

"If not, then he's not worth wasting your time on," Soleil pronounced. "There's no time to delay. She's closing in for the kill, I'm sure of it. Tonight, Céleste. Tonight I will sleep very soundly, and you must pretend you are alone with François, and show him you are as much a woman as Madame Odette.''

Still flushed, Céleste said, ''I'm not sure I am.''

''Oh, don't be silly! You have everything she has—''

''But she knows how to use it!''

''And François probably doesn't know all that much, either—not from personal experience! Just give him the opportunity, and I'll wager he'll take over from there.''

''If I do what you suggest, then he will think that *I* have no more virtue than she has!''

''No, he won't. A man wants a woman he loves to need him, too, and once in a while, at least, he likes her to show that she wants *him*. Let him think that he was the one who lost control of his passions and swept you off your feet. I doubt he'll know the difference, and the end result will be the same. In these times there's not even a priest to cry the banns, nor to marry, yet people aren't waiting to fall in love and be together until priests are available again. We may go the rest of our lives without seeing another priest, if the English have their way. Tonight, Céleste!''

''You can come inside now,'' François called over Odette's shoulder. ''We got it out, it was only a small bird.''

''Tonight?'' Soleil pressed quietly.

Céleste didn't reply. She felt frightened and excited and as if she might be sick.

But she hadn't said no.

53

REMIE MOVED OVERLAND, northward, edging to the west, staying alert for British forces but otherwise trying not to think of anything. Yet the memory of the charred remains of Grand-Pré weighed heavily upon him.

He had left a considerable amount of money with Soleil, the proceeds from last year's trapping. Had she carried it away with her, wherever she had been taken or escaped to? Or had she, like so many of the others he'd heard about, buried it to prevent it falling into British hands, with the idea that one day they would come back for it? And even if she had it, or any part of it, would she be able to buy what she needed to subsist?

If he allowed himself to dwell on such thoughts, worrying about where she was and how she was, Remie feared he would go mad. A part of him knew he should accept the fact that he was most unlikely ever to see her again in this life, but a smaller yet vital part could not quite give up the hope that a miracle might take place. Father de Laval had once told him that *he* believed in Holy Miracles. They happened every day, every time the sun rose, every time a baby was born.

Father de Laval had died in prison, alone, forsaken by God as by man.

The thought was a mental blow as he tramped through the Nova Scotia wilderness. He had lived in this country all his life. He loved it. It would, he told himself, eventually work its healing magic upon him. He'd survived what should have been a fatal attack by a bear, hadn't he? He'd survived a British prison and escaped from a British ship. Miracles, every one, the good Father would probably say.

Yet the priest's last words to Remie had been, "Do not concern yourself for me, my son. I am in my Father's hands."

How did a man come to faith like that? Even Christ had cried from the cross where he was dying, "My God, my God, why hast Thou forsaken me?" Even His faith had wavered, at least momentarily.

"I will have faith," Remie said through set teeth, plodding on through another sullen day that promised more snow. "I will believe I'll find Soleil, and I'll keep looking until the day I die."

Without her his soul would shrivel within him, and that would be worse than dying from a bayonet or with a bear's hot breath in his face.

The scars were there in his flesh, proof that one miracle had occurred. There would be others. He would make his own miracle if need be.

By himself, in familiar territory, he moved swiftly. The weather, no matter how bad it was, did not bother him unduly.

The soldiers were another matter. They were a constant threat as he worked his way around their new Fort Cumberland, at what had been Beauséjour, outwaiting them, outwitting them, but finally he made it safely across the isthmus of Chignecto.

The question then was what to do next.

The closest route to the mouth of the St. John was by boat, but he had no boat. He met straggling bands of refugees, tired, cold and hungry; none of them had boats. If there were many of them fleeing through the forest, along the rivers, they would be desperate for food; no doubt the game had been decimated by these starving people, though probably most of them were less adept than he was at bringing it down. If there had been signs of Indians he would have sought them out, obtained a canoe, but the Indians, too, had gone to safer places.

The western coast of the Bay of Fundy consisted of high cliffs and unexplored wilderness. There were no trails, and it was impossible to move along the shore because of killer tides that rose up those sheer rock walls with unrelenting regularity, leaving a traveler no way to elude them. Much as Remie wanted to go that way—the shortest, quickest route—it was clearly impossible.

He turned yet farther to the north, when every fiber of him protested the delay. But he had no choice.

He passed through a clearing where smoking remains indicated that the British had managed to penetrate just a bit farther upriver. Damn them to hell, anyway. He prayed that the raiding had not extended as far as the de Vitre holdings, and knew with a twinge of guilt that if they offered him something to eat besides meat, he'd accept it. If, indeed, they were still there.

They came out to meet him, welcoming yet with unsettling news.

"Simon was captured after he left you at the mouth of the Minas," one of the youth's uncles informed him, ushering him inside. "Here, no doubt you can use a warming drink." He produced a bottle of brandy and a cup. "We heard about it from a man who escaped them at the same time. They confiscated Simon's boat—my brother's boat, actually—and there it sits. For the British to use to patrol the waterways, if they've any who know enough to use it. Fundy can prove treacherous to those who don't know it well."

Remie was, indeed, hospitably treated by the de Vitres. The anticipated twinge of guilt became a torrent. Simon would never have fallen into British hands if he hadn't taken Remie almost to Grand-Pré.

He looked around at the family group, whittling clogs or wooden plates, mending snowshoes or harnesses, and settled on one youth whose name he remembered as Joseph.

"Do you know the layout there at the fort? How difficult is it to get to the prison? Could a couple of good men get into it and get Simon out?"

Seeing that Remie had singled him out, Joseph began to grin. "Yes, *monsieur*, I know the layout, at least from the outside. If you would have me as companion, I would go with you. I am not afraid of the English!"

"The more fool you!" one of the women said bitterly, but no one paid any attention to her.

As quickly as that, it was decided. Remie regretted the delay, for if Soleil and any of the others had managed to sneak past the British patrols, she could be far into the western interior by this time. But he couldn't abandon Simon. Not after the risks he'd taken on Remie's behalf.

At evening prayer, blessings were asked for on the rescue expedition, and there was a chorus of fervent amens.

The following morning he and Joseph were headed back down the river into the territory of their enemies, and for a time Remie scarcely thought of Soleil at all.

THE BRITISH WERE OBVIOUSLY not expecting anyone to break into their stockade. It was a bitterly cold night, unfortunately moonlit, but there were occasional clouds that gave the rescuers moments to move swiftly across the open area surrounding the fortifications.

Remie had made a good choice in Joseph. He was young enough to move quickly, an expert in the woods from stalking game, and he had a determination equal to Remie's own. He was also willing to let Remie do the planning and give the orders, though not without initiative of his own when it was called for.

Darkness fell early in Nova Scotia in midwinter. The frigid temperature held most of the redcoats inside by the fires; the sentries were unenthusiastic about their jobs—indeed, about being in this godforsaken place to begin with—and not as alert as common sense might have dictated.

"You take that one," Remie whispered from their vantage point only yards away from the building where Joseph had indicated the prisoners were kept, "and I'll take this one."

Joseph's teeth flashed briefly in the moonlight. He nodded and looked up at the sky. "As soon as that cloud touches the edge of the moon."

Remie concentrated on his own man. He had never killed a human being before, and he had feared that he might, at the last minute, suffer pangs of conscience that would stay his hand for critical seconds. When the time came, however, he thought of his months rotting in Annapolis Royal with the hated redcoat guards, of the unnecessary cruelty of Father de Laval's death, of the fact that these soldiers or others like them had separated him from his wife and child, perhaps forever. There might not be a declared war between the Acadians and the British soldiers, and the Acadians wore no uniform, but it was war, nevertheless.

His knife blade, which he had spent last evening honing to a razor edge, slid between the man's ribs as easily as it would have gutted a deer. The soldier made a gasping sound and slid onto the snow, and Remie did not linger to see the dark blood pool around the body.

Only then did he turn to see how Joseph was doing with the second sentry. The moon had already emerged from behind the protective cloud; Joseph was wiping his own blade off on his trousers and ducked closer to the building. "Will we have to kill the other pair, too?"

How much time had passed? Would the other sentries round the corner at any moment, or could they cross that remaining open space in time?

"Go," Remie decided, and they ran.

They stood against the rough log wall long enough for their breathing to slow somewhat, praying the dead sentries would not be discovered too quickly and an alarm given. When, after a minute or so, there was no sign of additional soldiers, they moved again, the two of them working together to raise the heavy bar on the gate to the prison itself.

The stink of the prison brought back bitter memories and firmed Remie's resolve. It was cold, so damned cold, Remie thought, his own fury warming him, when there was plenty of firewood to be had with little effort. The English wanted their prisoners to die, no doubt, so they wouldn't have to be fed.

Over the muted sounds of slow breathing and a snore or two, Remie said, "Simon de Vitre, are you in here?"

Immediately there was total silence. No one could sleep deeply in such a place, at such a temperature.

The voice that replied was familiar, cautious and incredulous, yet hopeful. "I am de Vitre. Who asks?"

"Remie Michaud. There's no time to waste. Two of the sentries are dead, but the others will give the alarm any minute," Remie said tersely. "The gate is open. There's at least a chance the lot of you can reach the woods before they can load their muskets, if you run for it."

The scrabbling sounds that ensued were a reminder of the rats he had heard in that other prison, but Remie didn't dwell on it. When Simon's hand encountered his in the blackness, he grasped it and tugged. "Come on! Let's get the hell out of here!"

The moon was out again, and this time there was no convenient cloud moving in the right direction, at least not one close enough that they dared wait for it.

Men poured through the gate behind them, scattering in every direction, silhouetted against the snow. Remie ran, concentrating on reaching the edge of the woods, and heard a shout go up in English, then another and another.

Somewhere off to his left he heard gasping breaths, and to his right Joseph swore blasphemously. They reached the trees and the dark shadows closed around them, and Remie cried, "We've done it!"

Seconds later, the musket ball took him full in the back.

He was conscious of no pain, only the blow that sent him pitching forward between the unseen trees. He heard someone yell in pain, and more gunfire. Then there was nothing.

54

DUSK SETTLED OVER the village of St. Anne and the glow of candlelight flickered behind frosted windowpanes. François and Céleste walked slowly homeward in what he thought of as a contented silence, and what *she* knew was a creeping terror of the proposal Soleil had made earlier.

She would never be able to carry it through. She had been a fool to consider it, even for a moment. She was not a seductress, she was a simple country girl. It was not that she was ignorant of the ways between men and women. She had seen animals mate in the farmyard and been aware of stifled giggles and deeper persuasive voices late at night within the curtained cubicles that provided the only privacy to be had in a large household. Three of her brothers had spent their wedding nights in such beds only yards from her own.

No, she wasn't afraid of lovemaking, either. Her own body gave off signals more exciting than fear-provoking. The problem was, François had given no indication that he thought of her except as a friend, and Soleil could be wrong about him. What if his controlled attitude had nothing to do with her betrothal to Antoine? What if he simply didn't find her attractive in that way?

She couldn't imagine a more unbearable humiliation than offering herself to François and being rejected.

If only there was a way to test Soleil's theory somewhere other than in Mme Odette's house!

Ice snapped under her feet as it broke, and François put out an arm to encircle her waist, though she had been in no danger of falling. Céleste wanted to lean into the strength of him but could not bring herself to do it, and a moment later he withdrew his arm. Tears of frustration stung her eyes and she blinked them away before they could freeze on her lashes.

They had been late in going for their walk because there had been a mess to clean up, soot settling on every surface after they'd gotten rid of the bird in the chimney. It was late enough so that no one else was out and about, and she might have contrived a way to get François's arms around her, to have kissed him, without an audience. Yet she hadn't been able to do it, and now they were nearly home. It was too late.

Of course they wouldn't have been able to do anything but kiss, anyway. And Soleil's idea was that, to be really successful, the kiss must lead to lovemaking.

François spoke softly in the evening stillness. "I always liked coming home at night in the winter and seeing the candles through the window. Smelling supper cooking."

"Only it's not our home," Céleste reminded him, and was chagrined to hear the tears in her voice. "I do miss everyone so!"

Good God, that wasn't what she ought to have said! He would think she meant Antoine, so she added quickly, "Mama and Papa, and the boys, and my sisters-in-law, and the little ones—"

François heard the emotion in her voice and attributed it to fatigue. "I shouldn't have asked you to walk so late in the day. Now you're overtired, and you still aren't well."

"I *am* well," she contradicted at once. "In fact, I think I'm well enough to go on, François! We only intended to stay with Mme Cormier until I recovered from the fever, and these walks have helped me to get my strength back ever so well. I know Soleil is anxious to leave, too—"

François came to a stop, staring at the house just ahead of them. "I understand why she wants to get to the Madawaska Valley she and Remie talked about, but it's still winter, and there's no shelter there except what we can build. What if Remie isn't there, if he doesn't come? That's far more likely than that he got away from the British and traveled so far as this."

The diluted candlelight from the window touched his strong face, highlighting the crisp black curls, the straight nose, the wide Cyr mouth that made her melt just to look at it. Céleste was nearly overcome with a rush of love for him, and it had nothing to do with the fact that he was Antoine's brother; it was because he was François.

A flood of memories swept through her: François fishing her out of the water when she'd slid down the wrong side of the dyke when she was ten; François using his knife point to get the splinters out of her hands so she wouldn't have to admit to her mother that she'd been out in the forbidden boat, which had overturned and left her clinging to its rough sides; François trailing a slimy eel across the back of her neck so she'd shrieked and flailed out at him with the hand that happened to be holding a rather larger stick. That had left him with a great purple welt, and he'd never told anyone how he got it.

"Soleil has to hope," she said with a great tenderness that would have astonished him if he'd known it was directed at him rather than at his sister. "It's all she has left, François."

He was uncharacteristically moody. "She's going to have a baby. I'm not prepared to deliver it miles from civilization, maybe without even a roof over our heads. Are you? At least here in St. Anne there are other women around, women who know about such things."

Céleste's stomach lurched, but her reply was reasonably confident. "Most babies come of their own accord when they're ready, whether there is anyone around to see to the matter or not."

"Then why did Mama leave her own home so many times to attend someone in childbirth? And I remember when Jacques was born, there were three women in attendance, and they made a great to-do about sending us outside for the day."

Céleste smiled a little. "That was only to get you out from underfoot. Your mama always had her babies easily. I've heard her tell my mama so half a dozen times. It will be the same with Soleil." She hoped she was correct about that, for she, too, had grown uneasy as she saw her friend's belly expanding. "I know she wants to be gone and is only waiting for me. Well, I'm ready. I would be delighted if we left tomorrow."

If she got François out of this house, he would forget about Odette Cormier, and she wouldn't have to take any drastic sort of action on his behalf. She could then afford to let matters take their own course, which held far more appeal than what Soleil had proposed.

François drew her forward so that the light fell upon her face, too. "Are you sure? You really want to go on? You think you're strong enough?"

She was acutely conscious of his hand holding hers, and though both wore mittens she imagined she felt a tingling sensation that was not the cold but François's warmth. "Yes. The sooner the better."

For a few seconds they stood there looking into each other's faces in the muted light. Céleste was sure of the tingling now, for it raced through her entire system, and she swayed toward him as if the movement were beyond her control.

François bent his head slightly—to kiss her?—and then they jerked apart as the door was thrown open a yard or two away.

"François? Céleste, is that you? I thought you were never going to get here."

François dropped her hand and swung toward the lighted rectangle, the steam from his breath hanging on the frigid air. "Is something wrong?"

Soleil didn't sound particularly alarmed. "Well, Mme Odette has taken to her bed. She's not feeling well, though I doubt it's anything serious. She didn't want to eat, but I'm starved, and the food's ready to dish up." She stepped backward, allowing them to enter, and gave Céleste a rather wicked smile that her friend didn't immediately interpret.

"I shouldn't wonder," Soleil offered as they divested themselves of their outer wraps, "if I might not sit up with her tonight, just to be sure she's all right."

François gave her a brotherly, distrustful look. "I thought you just said she didn't have anything seriously wrong with her."

"Probably not." Soleil was already dishing up from the pot over the fire. "But I wouldn't want to take the chance that she has the same thing Céleste had. If she goes into a fever, I'd want to get some tea into her and bathe her forehead."

François lifted one leg over the bench at the table, then stood straddling it for a moment before sitting down. "Odd," he said in a voice too low to carry to the bedroom, "I've had the idea you didn't care much for Odette."

"I don't," Soleil said. "But she has been kind enough to take us in while we had to nurse Céleste through a serious illness. It would prey on my conscience not to care for *her*, if she needs it."

Again, as François maneuvered into his place at the table, Soleil sent Céleste one of those sly smiles, and this time her meaning was clear.

Mme Odette was sick in bed, and Soleil would move into the bedchamber with her on the pretext of caring for her; Céleste and François would have the main room to themselves this evening.

Céleste's face was flooded with heat as she took her own place, her appetite vanishing. She couldn't say anything until later, however, when François went out to bring in a supply of firewood.

Then she leaned across the table and practically hissed: "I can't do it! I'm not that kind of person!"

"What kind of person?" Soleil countered, quite calm but firm. "Every woman is the kind of person who can make a man want her, if she tries hard enough. Even the ugliest one can find acceptance in the dark, and you're far from that. There'll never be a better chance than tonight, Céleste."

Suspicion made Céleste bite her lower lip. "Did you do something to her to make her ill?"

Soleil laughed. "No, but I might have, if I'd thought of it. I'll stay in the bedroom with her for at least an hour. That should give you plenty of time."

"I can't! I've thought about it all day, and I simply can't! I can't do those things that *she* does, not when I detest her so!"

They were unable to speak further, for François had returned with an armload of wood, which he dumped unceremoniously in the box beside the fireplace. Immediately Odette called from the adjoining room.

"Monsieur François? Would you attend me, please?"

François stepped obediently to the doorway, holding aside the curtain that covered it. "Yes, *madame*?"

"It is so very cold in here. If you wouldn't mind drawing the curtain aside so that some of the heat may enter?"

"Yes, of course." François complied.

"It is getting colder, is it not?"

"I think so, yes, *madame*."

Céleste could imagine her smiling at him in that odious way she had. Her voice certainly didn't sound as if there were much wrong with her.

"If you'd be so kind as to keep the fire up tonight. The water in my pitcher was frozen last night, right here beside my bed. My throat seems to feel better if I can sip once in a while."

"I'll keep the fire going," François promised, "even if it means getting up several times. I'm going to bring in one more armload of wood before we retire."

"Oh, I do thank you. I'll feel much better, knowing you won't let the heat die down. Oh, and Monsieur François, if you *do* get up to feed the fire, perhaps you'd check? Just step in here—it won't disturb me, I promise—and see that my water hasn't frozen?"

This time François hesitated, then finally said, "Whatever you like, *madame*."

The two girls, still seated opposite each other on the benches at the table, waited in a frozen silence until the door had closed behind François. Then they spoke in soft but explosive voices.

"Oh, that woman is impossible, I *hate* her!" Céleste exclaimed.

"You see? Even when she says she is ill she still tries to entice him into her bed! For the love of heaven, Céleste, if you care anything about François, save him from *that*! Do you want to be responsible—and have the rest of your life to think about it—for him being trapped into marrying her? I wouldn't put it past her to tell him she is with child, if she once can lure him into sleeping with her, to hook him like some poor stupid fish! He'd marry her in a minute if she told him that, and what kind of life would he lead then? At her beck and call, and looked upon with contempt by the decent people in St. Anne. And think of his humiliation when he learns what sort of woman she really is!"

"Is there something wrong?" Odette called from the bedroom.

In the silence, during which they heard the wind rising around the eaves and the crackle of the fire, Céleste sat dumb, for she had not considered the matter in exactly that light before.

"No, *madame*," Soleil called after a moment. "All is well."

"Oh. I thought I heard someone talking, but I couldn't make out the words."

Soleil gave Céleste a sardonic smile and rose from the bench. "We were only discussing the weather, *madame*. The water is boiling. Would you like a cup of tea, perhaps?"

"Oh, yes, thank you," Odette agreed.

Soleil moved to dip hot water into the teapot. As she got down cups for the four of them, François entered the house and she mouthed at her friend, "Tonight. Before it's too late!"

Céleste's heart was hammering, and not even the usually soothing tea could calm her. She could not look at Soleil, who was giving her those challenging glances, nor at François, who caught her gaze and asked, puzzled, "Is something wrong?"

"No, no, nothing," she denied, willing her hand not to tremble on the cup. When the tea had been drunk, and they were arranging their pallets for the night, Soleil made her announcement, very casually.

"I believe that I will wrap up in my blanket and sit with Madame Odette for a time, just to be certain that her fever does not rise as it often does at night when one is ill."

"That's not at all necessary, *mademoiselle*," Odette said at once. "I assure you, I am not seriously indisposed."

"I don't think so, either," Soleil addressed her from the doorway to the inner room. "But I wouldn't want to take a chance on it. I will sit there in the corner, just for an hour or so, and then if you are sleeping and not showing signs of fever I'll take to my own bed. But of course if you waken and need anything, be sure to call me. Perhaps, since you've been lying there for several hours already, your back is tired? Mama used to say that I gave very good back rubs."

"A back rub? Well, that does sound appealing. Very well, Mlle Soleil, but I wouldn't want you to lose your own sleep because of me."

That time François intercepted the speaking glance his sister sent to Céleste. "What's going on?" he demanded as Soleil lowered the curtain back into place in order to perform the back rub in private.

"What?" Céleste turned to him, hoping she looked more innocent than she thought she did. "I have no idea what you mean."

François's extended scrutiny went on for long seconds, so long that she rose and dipped some of the hot water into a basin, then cooled it, and set it on the table. "I'd like to bathe, if you please. Kindly avert your eyes, if you don't mind." She bent her head to blow out the candle, but the fire still gave plenty of light for the new logs were blazing.

Finally François shrugged. "All right. Have your private jokes. See if I care."

He turned away and a moment later said, "I've gone to sleep. Bathe all you like."

Her heart was thudding as if she'd run a mile along a dyke. After she had washed herself—checking periodically to make sure François still had his back turned—she stood uncertainly. She wanted to go to bed and go to sleep—and she wanted to go to François. And she didn't want Soleil to castigate her in the morning for her timidity and lack of concern in the matter of saving François from Madame Odette.

"Céleste, will you take this, please?"

She swung around to accept the teacup Soleil had brought to give her. "Do it!" Soleil urged in a whisper.

"I don't know what to do!" Céleste sounded to her own ears as if she were whimpering.

"Get close to him, and *he'll* do it!" She glanced over Céleste's shoulder at her brother's back as he lay on the pallet.

Céleste looked that way, too, then quickly aside, knowing he could not possibly have fallen asleep this quickly. Her face was piteous; anyone with less determination than Soleil would have given up on her by this time. "But what if he doesn't know what to do, either?"

"He will!" Soleil said in an almost nasty voice, and went back into the bedchamber.

Céleste was shaking, verging on anger. She recalled how Soleil had always made her do things she hadn't wanted to do: climb a tall tree, balance on a log from which she had fallen into the creek, eat forbidden green apples until they'd both been sick. Why hadn't she ever thought of it before, how bossy Soleil had been? Just as Antoine had always been to François, taunting him, daring him, until he won out over François's better judgment.

Yet she did want to go to François. Her whole body felt on fire with the wanting. Why was she such a coward? And it was for his sake as well as her own, before he went into Madame Odette's room to see if her water was frozen, and *madame* reached out—

Her imagination refused to go any further. She had had these stirrings before, but never with such intensity. Her nipples tingled, and in the secret part of her body was a fire as hot as the one that made shadows dance throughout the room.

A spark flew out and landed within an inch of her pallet. She gave a smothered cry and jerked the blanket away from it, and as she did, she heard François roll over toward her. "What's wrong?" he asked.

And then the idea came to her, as if from the Blessed Mother herself. Surely it was an omen that this was right, that this was the way it should be?

"Oh, I flipped my blanket away from the hearth and something . . . something went into my eye!" She covered her eyelid and pressed against it, almost convincing herself that it was so. "Oh, François, it hurts!"

He reached her in seconds, drawing her hand away from her face. "It wasn't hot, was it? Not from the fire?"

His touch was searing. She had trouble finding her voice, thinking of words; her voice trembled. "No, only from the blanket. A bit of bark, perhaps."

"Come here, sit down closer to the hearth and let me look."

Since her legs didn't want to hold her up anyway, it was easy to allow herself to be maneuvered into a kneeling position on the pallet, with François before her. "Now, tip your head this way and let me see."

One hand held her chin; the other lifted her eyelid, and he brought his face very close to hers, so that she seemed to view him through clear water that magnified every detail.

His fingers were large but very gentle. It hurt her chest to breathe. "Roll your eye up. Now to the left. I can't see anything, but this damned light isn't very good—maybe I should light the candles again, and perhaps—"

"No," Céleste said quickly. "No. It feels better, truly it does. It must have been very small, and it's been dislodged when I moved my eye—"

He still held her chin, and he was still very close. She stared into his eyes and saw something change in them, and she did not have to pretend to be giddy as she swayed toward him ever so slightly.

He seemed to be swaying forward, too, and her eyes closed of their own accord, seconds before his mouth touched hers.

The kiss was light, no more than a feather brushing her lips, and then his arms came around her, and she was drawn into an embrace that was almost painful, yet from which she sought no escape.

She heard him groan deep in his throat and for a moment feared she had done something wrong, then, as his mouth became more insistent, her lips parted of their own volition to allow him what he wanted. She was dizzy, heat and sensation suffused her entire body, and somehow she was no longer kneeling but lying back on the pallet, with François mysteriously hovering over her without crushing her.

He groaned again, and her hands fluttered to his arms, where she felt the muscles bunch and strain, and then he *was* crushing her, though she made no protest.

Soleil had been right. Her own body told her what to do, to lift her face and slide her arms around him, inside his shirt. When his hands fumbled with her fastenings, she barely had the wit to help him, for she was sinking into what was both lethargy and excitement, combined in a way she would not have thought possible.

By the time their hindering garments had been disposed of, Céleste had stopped worrying about whether or not François would know what to do.

Every touch of his hand and mouth and body seemed exactly right.

THE SOUNDS WERE SMALL, furtive, barely heard over the crackle of the newly fed fire. If she hadn't—against her conscious will—been listening for them, Soleil would never have heard them.

Did Madame Odette hear them, too? Hunched in her blanket, Soleil tried to see the woman on the bed, but it was too dark in the room to make out whether her eyes were open or not. At least she didn't move.

She was glad Céleste and François were together, Soleil thought, shivering. She wondered how long she would have to wait before she could go out to her own bed in the warmer room. She knew the firelight would be playing over their naked bodies, they would be locked in an ardent embrace, and they would be sealed together forever. Madame Odette, in spite of her wiles, would not be the ruination of François now.

She heard a moan of pleasure—Céleste's, or her brother's?— and suddenly felt rent by an anguish such as she had thought finally behind her. Soleil doubled over, awkwardly muffling sobs in her blanket-wrapped knees because of her protruding belly.

They had been so happy, she and Remie! They had loved each other so much! Surely, if he lived, he must be feeling this same grief, this same need, and God only knew if it would ever be eased. She wanted him so badly, to touch him, to make love to him, to see his smile again!

She lifted her wet face as if she might penetrate the darkness and see God up there above her, a God who could give Remie back.

"Please, God! Please," she begged in a whisper, then wept again—helplessly, hopelessly. And this time not even the vigorous kicking of the babe made her feel any better.

55

IN THE AFTERMATH of passion Céleste lay contently spent, smiling at the man who leaned on an elbow beside her, studying her face in the firelight.

Mother of God, but he was handsome! And never had she felt such tenderness, such fulfillment. She stretched out a hand and ran a finger from his ear, across his cheek, to the sober mouth, and held it there.

François kissed her fingertip, then put her hand aside to speak in a low tone. "Are you sorry?"

"Sorry? No, I'm glad!"

There was no answering smile, only a faint tremor in his voice. "I don't think I could bear it if you were sorry. If I had to feel guilty about . . . taking you."

Perhaps someday she would tell him how she had deliberately brought him into her bed, but she sensed that now was not the time. She traced his face again, loving the feel of him. "You only took what I wanted to give. I love you, François."

She had never said that to anyone before, and she knew, so close to him this way, aware of every breath, every muscle, every change in his dark eyes, that no one else had ever said it to him, either. She wanted, quite desperately, to hear him say the words to *her*.

"I've wanted you for years," François said. "Since we were children, when I was only beginning to understand what can be between a man and a woman, long before I was a man."

The intensity of his words caused her to wonder; when she was so relaxed, so happy, why was he so serious? He sounded almost frightened of what was taking place between them, which was puzzling, because it didn't frighten her in the slightest.

"You never said anything to me," Céleste pointed out. "You put bugs down the front of my bodice, and that eel on the back of my neck."

He still didn't smile, nor react to her hand as it moved down over his chest, teasing the darkly curling hair. "For a while I kept hoping that you would choose me, though I knew there wasn't much chance of that. Antoine was ..."

"Why did you never speak to me? You acted like one of my brothers. I thought you teased me because I was your sister's best friend, and you treated me the way you treated Soleil."

"If I'd said anything, and you rejected me, you'd have taken away my hope. And I couldn't think of that, couldn't see how I'd live with it—"

She was astonished and dismayed to see genuine pain in his eyes, even as they lay here together after the most intimate moments it was possible to have with another person. The depth of his emotion stirred in her something very different from the passion of a few minutes ago, something just as strong but protective now, fiercely protective.

Céleste lifted her arms to encircle his neck and drew him down to her so that their lips were nearly touching. "I love you, François. I shall always love you!"

His eyes were black, unreadable, looking into hers, and then he kissed her.

She had thought their lovemaking to be the ultimate in rapture, but there was a sweetness in this kiss, a fervor, that transcended what had come before.

She closed her eyes and let it sweep her away, and she did not think of Antoine at all, but François did.

SOLEIL'S EYELIDS FELT swollen and puffy in the morning, and she thought someone would ask about that, or at the very least send her a speculative glance. Of course, in these days when so many had lost so much, no doubt there were plenty of tears that weren't discussed or particularly noticed.

Soleil saw as soon as she rose that Céleste and François noted no one but each other. She was glad for them, but it hadn't occurred to her before she'd urged her friend to take the steps her brother hadn't made that it would hurt so much to watch them.

Not that they did anything untoward, she had to admit. There was no touching, not so much as a tender word, yet what had taken place between them last night shone in their faces for any but the blind to see.

Belatedly Soleil realized that Odette was certain to be aware of it at once, perhaps with unfortunate consequences.

Mme Cormier rose late, taking advantage of her mild indisposition to wait until the others had taken care of the usual morning chores, then requesting a cup of tea to begin her day.

She had not bothered to dress—or more likely had consciously chosen the dressing gown she wore to the table for François's benefit. Where had she gotten such a garment? Soleil wondered in envy. It had to have come from France, a creation in scarlet silk that set off Odette's dark beauty to perfection and emphasized her physical attributes as her widow's weeds did not. Some other man in her life had bought it for her, and it was her ultimate weapon to use on François—aside from her own body, of course.

The trouble was, François scarcely noticed either his hostess or her stunning dressing gown. He saw only Céleste, and though he was not especially obtrusive about it, Odette was astute enough to recognize the situation immediately.

Her perceptive dark eyes flashed from one of her guests to another, not bothering to assess Soleil's appearance in any depth—after all, she was breeding—but fastening her attention with rapacious ferocity on the other two.

Anger boiled within her. His *sister's* friend, she had been told when François had mentioned the need for a place to stay. His sister's *sick* friend.

Well, obviously the sick friend was feeling better and had now become *his* friend, his *intimate* friend. The extent of the intimacy was unmistakable; it virtually oozed from them both.

She had felt so sure of François, so confident that she could bring him to heel. She didn't dislike the life she had led since her husband's death. In fact, she had begun it earlier than that, though discreetly, of course. But there were advantages in having a man of one's own. And this François had the youth and the looks and the virility that M. Cormier had lacked, so that perhaps for a time she would not have felt the need of additional male companionship.

Righteous indignation swelled in her bosom. How could she not have seen it, that the little slut was after him? And from the look of the pair of them, he'd taken her to bed last night, right here in her own house, the ungrateful wretch!

She was so upset she could not drink the tea, and no one noticed, which made her angrier than ever.

Soleil, watching Odette, saw that their days in this household were at an end. Whether they went on upriver or not, they had to be out of this place, and quickly.

She followed her brother outside when he went to chop wood. He hefted the ax, testing the blade and deciding it did not yet need sharpening. He finally noticed her eyes. "Is something wrong?" he asked.

"We have to move on, François. Mme Cormier has grown tired of having guests, if you aren't going to succumb to her charms."

He was so startled at that idea that she couldn't doubt his surprise was genuine. "Me? Succumb to... You must be joking."

"Why do you think she invited us to move into her house? She would have liked to become Madame Cyr, and now that—" She stopped short of mentioning that she knew what had happened last night. "Well, she isn't winning you over, and she knows it, so—" She shrugged expressively.

"Has she asked us to leave?"

"No. But I suspect she will, if we don't announce plans to do so very shortly. Today, in fact. Céleste is well, and I...well, I'm better able to travel now than I'll be in a few months' time."

François was unconvinced. "Céleste is better, but she's still somewhat fragile to be out day and night in this kind of weather. And you need clothes. You can scarcely squeeze into those anymore." He flushed, a little embarrassed to be speaking to his sister of such matters.

Soleil rested her spread hands on her rounding stomach. "I know. But what's to be done? We've no money to buy anything even if there were garments or dress goods for sale. I'll make out for a bit longer, François. Please, let's tell *madame* we are making plans to leave."

"No doubt you're right." He gave in more easily than she'd anticipated. "Let me do it, though, eh? I guess it's time I talked to someone else in St. Anne besides Mme Odette. We might find an alternative to moving on quite yet."

"As long as we get out of her house," Soleil agreed. "Getting through one more day here may prove impossible."

François stared after her as she returned to the house. What was the big hurry? Why *today*, when they'd been here for weeks with no trouble?

He raised the ax and brought it down with a satisfying *thunk*. There was no understanding the way women's minds worked. But maybe, he thought, a smile curling the corners of his wide mouth, he'd come a little closer last night to understanding at least one of them.

He chopped the wood in record time, simply because he felt so good, then headed into the center of the village.

THE DAY WAS AN uncomfortable one, because Mme Odette made no secret of her sudden displeasure, though she didn't spell out for them why they had lost favor.

"Do you think she *knows* about François and me?" Céleste asked, her cheeks pink, as soon as Odette had withdrawn into the bedchamber.

Soleil's smile was rueful. "I'm afraid anyone who sees either of you will guess at once," she confirmed. "You look so happy. There aren't that many genuinely happy people about these days. It sort of... shines out of both your faces."

"I believed she was…after him, but I didn't think how she'd react if it became obvious that he wasn't interested in her."

"Nor did I." Soleil's mouth twisted wryly. "I'll be amazed if she doesn't toss us out, bodily, now that it's clear she isn't going to get what she wanted. I've put on the meat for the soup, and I've no wish to sit here under her baleful looks the rest of the day. Do you feel up to a walk—a good, long walk?"

"Of course! It's a beautiful day, and I feel so full of energy—what are you laughing at?"

"Have you peeked out the window at the 'beautiful day,' my friend? It's gray as pewter and starting to snow again!"

Céleste had to laugh, too, but she stuck by her statement. It was a wonderful day, and she prayed with all her heart that in spite of what had happened in the past there could be some joy ahead. It was only when she looked at her friend that sorrow touched her again.

If only God would bless her, too. If only Remie would eventually find them in the Madawaska Valley.

THEY SPENT THE ENTIRE morning out-of-doors, unmindful of the scattered dry snowflakes that landed on caps and eyelashes, simply walking together and talking. When at last they headed for home, driven by hunger and the cold that had insidiously crept inside their wraps, they met François on the path.

His smile was broad. "We move this afternoon," he greeted them.

"Upriver?" Soleil asked quickly.

"No. The weather is still against us. I don't want to be caught out in another storm without shelter, and there are no real settlements above St. Anne. But I've found another house where the owner would welcome guests on the same terms as Mme Odette—that I keep the place supplied with meat and firewood."

Their dismay must have been evident in their faces. François laughed aloud.

"Not another widow this time! And not young, either. M. Ayotte is seventy-four, a widower whose sons have gone off to a life of fishing on the Gaspé, and he's been having a difficult time this winter because he's taken to his bed twice because of congestion in his chest. No, no, he's not an invalid, he doesn't require nursing care, but the cold sets badly in his lungs, and outdoor chores are something he'd gladly relinquish in exchange for a part of his house.'' François was looking so pleased with himself that both girls hoped there was not a catch to this. ''And the best part is—''

''Well, what?'' Céleste demanded when he paused.

''It is a larger house, with a bedchamber that has not been used since his wife died and he moved into a bed in the main room. And there is a lean-to that can easily be converted into a sleeping room, as well, and which backs onto the fireplace, so the water doesn't freeze there at night! How's that for palatial quarters?''

Soleil was more cautious in her acceptance this time, after the experience with Mme Odette. ''And what is his temperament, this M. Ayotte?''

''He reminds me of Grand-père,'' François said, in such a gentle, affectionate tone that tears stung Soleil's eyes. ''A nice old man who will be glad of the help and the company. He is very lonely.''

And so it proved. Moving out of Mme Odette's house was an easy matter; they simply wore all the clothes they owned and rolled up the extra blankets. They did not take any of the venison that François had brought in a few days earlier, because he intended to go hunting at once for more.

Without regret on either side, Mme Odette ungraciously bid them farewell and they walked through the now steadily falling snow to the house of M. Ayotte.

He was, indeed, a nice old man. He made no demands on them, seemed grateful there were females to cook and sweep his floors, which he could no longer see well enough to do, he confessed to them in apology. He was also, rather conveniently, almost deaf. Private conversations could easily be held in his presence; if his attention was desired, one only raised one's voice and looked directly at him.

While Soleil made a visit to the outhouse—it seemed to her that she was doing that very frequently these days, because of the pressure of the growing child within her—François took advantage of a private moment with Céleste.

He was carrying the extra blankets but did not immediately put them down. "I asked about a priest in the village, and of course there isn't one. It has become the custom, during weekly public gatherings at the church, for a couple to announce their intentions to live together as man and wife. The union will eventually be blessed, if a priest ever comes, or not, if there is no priest."

Céleste swallowed, looking up at him. "I would be your wife, François, if I could. If not within the church, then outside it."

The smile began in his eyes and spread to his mouth. "Good. Tomorrow is the Sabbath, and we will make our own announcement. I have already told M. Ayotte that you are my wife."

So it was that when Soleil reentered the house, she found them cheerfully making up the curtained bed in the privacy of a real bedroom and was left to prepare her own in the lean-to that took heat from the back of the fireplace.

It was, in fact, a rather nice snug space, or would be nice when she'd had time to clean it out a bit. She would have thought it marvelous if Remie had been there to share it with.

A few hot tears fell onto her hands as she spread her blanket right up to the stones that would warm the room. Would she ever get over this feeling of loss, of longing, of unendurable pain?

She heard laughter in the adjoining room, and old M. Ayotte's reply to something they had said. She was determined not to spoil their newfound happiness. It wasn't their fault she had lost Remie; they had suffered losses, too, and she must somehow put on a brave face.

She had finished with the improvised bed and looked around the tiny room, ducking her head below the slanting roof. Within her the infant kicked, which it had seemed to do almost constantly for the past week or so. Her time was drawing closer, and she knew that Remie would expect her to love and care for the child, to provide for it the affection he'd been denied for much of his life.

"He shan't have a mother who is all tears and dripping nose," she swore to herself. "I must learn to laugh and sing again."

It was beyond her at the moment, though. Hearing François and Céleste only intensified her own sense of desolation. Once, she remembered wistfully, she had found comfort in prayer. Was it possible that she might somehow find that inner peace again?

On impulse she dropped to her knees on the thin pallet and bowed her head. Her prayer was brief and fervent: for her baby, for a way to return to good spirits and to find joy in something, and lastly, a plea that she might yet be reunited with Remie.

She did not feel the relief of relinquishing her burdens to a Higher Power, nor any subsequent lightening of mood. But she was able to emerge into the main room of M. Ayotte's pleasant house and join the others without dampening *their* happiness.

Maybe, in time, the answers would come.

56

REMIE GRADUALLY BECAME aware of a searing pain that seemed to encompass most of his body. It came in jolting stabs, and after a time he figured out that he was being carried, and that the worst of it occurred simultaneously with the sounds of feet hitting the earth.

He faded in and out of consciousness, but the pain never quite went away. Afterward he would remember only bits and pieces of conversation— "Your M. Remie is a heavy bastard," and, "Watch your footing now, it's slippery as hell." Once they fell with him, sliding down an embankment, and he was plunged into water so cold he thought he had surely reached the nether world and everyone had been mistaken about the temperatures there.

There was much muttered cursing at that point. A strange voice said, "That ought to have done him in for sure. Look, he isn't going to survive anyway, with the hole he's got in him, and now dunking him in ice water, that didn't do a thing for his chances. Dragging him along is slowing us down something fierce—"

There was the sound of a blow, and low, angry voices. One of them, familiar though he couldn't quite place it, said, "Damn your soul, he got you out of that prison and you're still alive and on your way home! Help us get him as far as the boat, and then you can look after your own worthless hide, but I swear to God I'll cut your throat if you abandon him before that!"

They went on through the blackness. It didn't seem to matter whether his eyes were open or shut; Remie saw nothing. The pain was unremitting, and in some remote corner of his mind he thought he must be dying. It didn't seem to matter very much. Except for Soleil; he had hoped to see her once more, to be assured that she was safe and well. But then, he would see her eventually in Heaven, he supposed. That idea was more easily accepted than he would have thought.

He prayed that the agony would end soon. He prayed for his own soul, too, but there was no true concern about that. He remembered telling Soleil that he had no need of speaking to God in a church, for he was secure in his own relationship to the Almighty. Father de Laval had given him that.

Father de Laval was dead. He had died in prison. Remie wondered if the priest had felt this cold while he was dying. His fingers brushed against his garments and he felt the wet wool freezing into rigid contours against his thigh.

Soleil was so warm and soft. He drifted, remembering how they had curled together under their protective robe, and how her hair had glistened with frost early in the morning. How beautiful she was! How much he loved her!

He resented the grunting, heaving effort when he was lifted, maneuvered and finally dropped onto what must be the deck of a boat. Why did he hurt so badly? He couldn't figure it out at first, then finally it came to him.

He'd been shot. The British soldiers had been firing at him and the others as they fled toward the woods.

"Is there anything to put over him? He's going to freeze to death before we get out of here," someone said. Joseph, it was Joseph speaking. A good man, Joseph.

Something rough and heavy was laid over him, yet he felt no warmer. He wondered how long it would take to die, and hoped it would be soon.

There was motion beneath him now, he was on a boat, and it was moving.

"Has he got a chance, do you think? The poor bastard, it's a good thing he's unconscious."

Not unconscious, Remie wanted to say, but no words came out.

"I don't know." That was someone he knew, too. Simon. Simon de Vitre. "But we're going to do everything we can to try to keep him alive. Give me a hand here, will you, before the soldiers realize we've taken the boat and come after us?"

"They won't come this far, not on the river at night. They're not boatmen, and it's blacker than the depths of Hades. We're away, Simon, thanks to your friend Remie."

They didn't talk much after that, and Remie slid in and out of awareness, but always there was the pain and the cold, and always the wish that he would die and get it over with.

HE DIDN'T DIE. They got him home, to where Joseph lived with the rest of Simon's uncles and aunts and cousins, and they peeled the frozen clothes off him and put him into a bed. A real bed, with pillows and blankets, and hot bricks wrapped so they would not burn him were placed against him.

The women were dubious, soft voiced, concerned. "It is very bad," they said, not knowing he could hear them. "It is a miracle he's lived this long."

"I think he stopped bleeding because the blood froze when it hit the air. He's going to live," Simon insisted, "because he's got a beautiful wife he has to find. I need another boatload of supplies to carry home—the English benefited from the last load—but I'll be back for M. Remie in a month or two, and you'd better have him on his feet by then."

There was a pressure of a hand on his shoulder and Remie felt Simon's breath on his cheek as the youth bent close to him. "Remember your lovely wife, *monsieur*, and for her sake get well. I will be back for you."

IT WAS FORBIDDEN that Acadians assigned to the Boston area cross the boundary into even so near a community as Cambridge. Danielle had been in a state of excitement that was difficult to conceal ever since André had shown her the advertisement in the newspaper from Jacques, and she could hardly wait to go and find him.

"You can't do it," André said when she finally found a private moment to broach the subject. "It's too dangerous. The night watch is alert for anyone abroad after curfew, and the punishments are severe. We can't risk it."

She stared at him in dismay. "But I must see him! He's with Guillaume, obviously, but he must be as desperate to find some of the rest of the family as I am! I *must* go!"

They were in the kitchen, after the family had gone to sleep, finishing up the daily chores.

"No," André said calmly, "you must not. I'll go. Luckily, Master Charles thinks nothing of sending me on errands at late hours and I have a pass that will probably get me through Cambridge as well as Boston. I'll find your brother and tell him of our plans to leave at the earliest opportunity. Be careful, child. Don't give us away by looking the way you are looking now. Mistress Monroe would not consider you her biddable Martha if she saw you at this moment."

Indignation made her draw in a sharp breath that caused her bosom to rise proudly, which did not pass unnoticed by her companion. He was grinning even before she said, "I'm not a child! Don't treat me as one, André!"

"You are a child, a beautiful little girl. When you grow up I am going to marry you, I think. If we can find a priest ever again, that is."

His assertion took the wind out of her sails regarding her age. "André, please—"

He laid a finger across her lips. "No. You speak no English, or at least not enough, and you don't know your way around. If I get into a tight corner I don't want to have to worry about getting you out of it as well as myself. I'll find your brother and report back to you, and when we're ready to leave, you'll be together. In the meantime, there is something you can be doing. You must begin to store a quantity of food to take with us, food that will not easily spoil. You'll have to keep changing it, no doubt, because it may be many weeks before the time is right, but it must be ready on a moment's notice. Point out to Mistress Monroe that your shoes are in need of replacing, so that you'll be ready to walk. And have a warm cloak ready at hand." His smile flashed, having its usual effect upon her. "One of Mistress Monroe's should do nicely, perhaps the green one lined in beaver."

The idea of stealing that exquisite cloak kept her reasonably content while she remained at home in Boston the night André went to Cambridge.

She knew at once, seeing him the following morning, that he had found Jacques. She could tell by the air of suppressed excitement as he met her gaze across the kitchen.

"Martha, Master Charles and Master Vincent are waiting for their breakfast! Why are you dawdling? I never saw such a bird-witted girl!"

"I'm taking it in now, ma'am," Danielle said in her accented English, lifting the tray she had prepared and heading for the dining room. Her accompanying prayer was answered when Mistress Monroe joined her husband and adoptive son at table, for that meant Danielle was free—though precariously so—to speak to André as he ate his own meal in the kitchen.

"Tell me!" she demanded at once upon returning there.

Tantalizingly, André buttered a thick crust and took a bite, which he chewed before replying. "Your Jacques is fine, though very thin. I think he's not being fed as well as the rich Cambridge lawyer for whom he polishes boots and andirons. I spoke to your friend Guillaume, too. It's lucky the boy was under his protection, such as he could offer, or his ordeal might have been worse. Pour me a bit more of that tea, will you? It's vile-tasting stuff, the English drink, but at least it's hot."

"Can they get away to join us when we leave?"

"M. Trudelle does not intend to leave. He and his wife have three of their children with them, all too young to travel so far. They are hopeful of locating other members of their family through notices in the newspaper, though Guillaume admitted to me as I was leaving that the hope is small. Still, they have no one left in Acadia, and nothing to return to. Jacques is another matter. He will be ready when we send word."

Danielle bit her lip, staring down at him as he continued to eat. "Guillaume's children are no younger than Vincent," she said in a hollow voice.

André stopped chewing.

Danielle sank onto the bench opposite him. "André," she said in a whisper, "I can't leave Vincent behind. If I ever find Pierre again, or Mama, how could I tell them I'd left Vincent here with the enemy?"

André spoke deliberately. "Vincent is treated as a favored son. I shouldn't wonder if they legally adopted the boy in time. If you leave him in Boston he'll live his life out in luxury and plenty." After a moment of silence he added, "It will be a very long journey back to Acadia."

Danielle was stricken. "But how could I face Pierre and Mama?"

"He is also a very spoiled brat," André pointed out bluntly. "Already he does not mind what you say, and he's forgetting his French."

Her eyes blurred. "But he's Pierre's son. He is by birth Acadian!"

For a moment she waited, fearing that André would refuse altogether, fearing that if Vincent must stay behind, she also would feel compelled to stay.

Perhaps he read this in her eyes. After a long time André sighed. "You can't mention it to him ahead of time. He would never be able to keep his mouth shut."

The tears of relief spilled over and she wiped at them with the corner of her apron, too choked with emotion to express her gratitude.

"Martha, what on earth are you thinking of? It's time to clear the table, and here you sit as if you were mistress of the house!" Mistress Monroe stood angrily in the doorway.

Danielle leaped to her feet. "I'm sorry, ma'am," she said, and scurried past the woman to take up her duties. She pressed her lips firmly shut to hold back the retort that she wanted so badly to make, that she was not *Martha* and never would be, and that before long she would not be a servant, either.

Vincent, wiping at his chin with a white linen napkin, was just getting down from the table. Master Charles was already pulling on his coat to leave for his place of business and did no more than nod absently in her direction.

Vincent was a handsome child. He looked just the way Pierre had looked at that age, Mama said. Because Aurore had died when he was an infant, Mama had been more mother than grandmother to Vincent.

If she ever found Mama again, or her brother Pierre, she must have Vincent with her. Her heart swelled with love for the little boy, even though he was rapidly growing away from her in this new family.

That feeling of tender affection lasted until the night that she woke in darkness to feel a hand over her mouth and heard a whisper in the voice she had come to love. "Shh! Don't make any noise! We are leaving tonight."

"Tonight? Already?" She was incredulous. "But you said *spring*, when we wouldn't freeze, walking so far—"

"We won't be walking, or at least we won't start out that way." He was so close she could feel his breath on her cheek, yet she could barely make out his words. "I've helped myself to a tidy sum from Master Charles's cash box and bribed a sailor to smuggle us onto an English supply ship heading north at the turn of the tide."

Horror rose in her throat in a scalding wave, but again his hand covered her mouth, stifling the sounds she made.

"We'll travel faster that way, by far, and with less effort. Come on, hurry! Jacques will be there ahead of us if he gets past the watch with no trouble, and we don't want to leave him waiting and worrying about us."

The thought of her youngest brother was an additional spur. She dressed by touch in the warmest gown she owned—it was a sturdy woolen one that had once belonged to Mistress Monroe—and with a candle lighted from the fireplace headed for the room where Vincent slept.

The boy looked like an angel, the dark curls falling over his forehead, a thumb trailing from his small mouth. Danielle's heart caught in her throat. If they were caught, would Vincent, too, be punished?

But no, of course not. Who would hold a child, barely four years old, responsible for running away? It was only she and André and Jacques who would be flogged, or perhaps hanged, for all she knew, and even that threat did not stop her. The prospect of freedom was worth the risk.

André loomed behind her, reaching for the candle. "Get him dressed. If he doesn't waken fully until we're out of the house, so much the better. Just keep him quiet!"

Vincent was limp as she struggled to pull on his small trousers and poke his arms into his sleeves; momentarily she despaired of ever accomplishing it without his conscious cooperation. And then André was handing her the warm coat and the knitted cap that would cover his ears, and the mittens knitted by Mistress Monroe herself, and still Vincent slept.

"I'll carry him," André said brusquely, returning the candle. "You get a wrap and the food you have hidden, and we'll be on our way."

Even under such terrifying circumstances, Danielle felt a surge of satisfaction in taking the cloak down off the hook near the door and securing it around her; its rich beaver lining would be warmer than anything she'd ever owned. The bundle of food came next, and then she slid aside the bar and they stepped out into the winter night.

It did not feel as cold as she'd expected, though perhaps that was due to the dark green cloak. Mist drifted around them in faint wisps as they moved quickly along the silent street toward the docks.

Vincent did not awaken until they heard their own footsteps on the wooden wharf. He stirred, twisted, and cried out in alarm.

"Shh!" Danielle cautioned him, putting her face close to his where it rested on André's shoulder. "It's all right! We are going home, Vincent, to find your papa and Henri and Grandmaman! We are going on a ship, where we must hide for a time, and you must be very quiet!"

She was appalled when he let out a shriek of rage. "I don't want to go away from Mama! I don't want to go on a ship! I *hate* ships!"

It was not as late as she had thought, for there were still lights on in the public houses along the way, and a few men moving about on the wharf itself. The seamen were drinking up their wages, no doubt, against the dawn when they would sail beyond the reach of anything but their shipboard grog, considerably watered down. She prayed they were too drunk to notice a couple with a young child out at this time of night.

"Stop it," André ordered, giving the boy a shake. "You'll have the watch on us! Hush, I said!" He shifted his grip on the child and clamped a firm hand over the small mouth when Vincent would have cried out again. Danielle had never imagined André could sound so menacing. "I mean it, lad. If I have to throttle you to keep you quiet, I'll do it! Our lives depend on getting on that boat without being caught, do you understand? *Our lives!* It's a good thing he spoke in English," he said over his shoulder to Danielle, "or he'd have given us away for sure! It's only a little farther, see, where the tallest mast is, there? I'm going to keep my hand over your mouth, Vincent, because you must not talk, but once we're aboard then you may whisper. Let's get on with it!"

Danielle fought the compulsion to run, though she was almost as afraid of getting on the ship as of not reaching it. The memory of weeks on a crowded vessel, of the cold and the lack of food and sanitary arrangements, of the polluted water that had made everybody sick, was vivid in her mind. There was no sign of Jacques, and her anxiety began to mount.

"About time, mate," said the man who stood in the shadows at the foot of the gangplank. "The lad's been here for an hour gone. Ye got the rest o' me money?"

"I'll give it to you when we're settled in, and you promised us decent quarters, remember? None of that stinking hold business."

"Don't stink no worse'n the rest o' this tub," the man said cheerfully. "Follow me, and watch yer step. Won't do to disturb the captain, though he's drunk enough to make it unlikely he'll stir for less'n a cannon. This way."

Danielle, her heart pounding, was aware of nothing but maintaining contact with André by hanging onto the tail of his coat, and the fact that Vincent was struggling until his captor gave him a solid smack on the behind.

"Ye didn't tell me was going to be no little kid along," the first mate said, disgruntled. "I got to charge you extra for another kid."

"You'll get your money. He's not going to take up much extra space."

"But he's going to increase the risk, man. He makes a noise and ye gets caught, ye sneaked on board by yourselves. Ye don't implicate me, that was the agreement."

"It's still the agreement," André assured him. "And the child won't give us away." There was such an ominous note in his voice that Vincent went quiet.

Several times Danielle stumbled, and then the mate picked up a lantern, which made it easier, and they went down a ladder; rough hands guided her, and at last they had to lift their feet to clear some unseen obstruction at the same time as they ducked for an overhead beam. "Here ye are, and if ye stay quiet ye ought to be safe," the mate told them. "I'll see't yer fed and there's a slop bucket wedged into the corner, like. I moved out most o' the cargo that was stored here and made up a sort o' nest at the back. Now, I'll have the rest o' me money, if ye don't mind."

André counted out the coins, and Danielle watched the avaricious smile of the mate and hoped he would turn out to be more honest than he looked at that moment.

"There. You'll have the same amount again when we're safely landed ashore." André put the pouch into his pocket, and in the dim, flickering light he, too, had an almost evil grin. "Just remember that if you betray us in any way, the money is the first thing that will go over the side. You won't get it off my body, dead or alive, whichever it may be."

"Hey! I wouldn't do nothing so foolish as that!" the man protested, and then he was gone, leaving them in darkness. A drowsy voice issued from a few yards away.

"That you, Danielle?"

"Jacques? Are you all right?" She groped her way toward him, leaving André to follow with Vincent.

"I fell asleep," Jacques said. When she hugged him she felt his bones through the garments that were not nearly as heavy as her own. "It's not half bad in here, a lot better than the ship I came to Boston on. That you, Vincent? You'd best not snivel that way, in case anybody comes to this part of the hold."

Danielle lowered herself onto the improvised bed and drew Vincent with her. "Come close, we'll keep each other warm," she told him gently, feeling the tremor in his small body.

"Is . . . is André going to throw me overboard if I don't be quiet?" he asked, sounding very frightened.

"No, of course not," Danielle reassured him. "He's trying to save our lives, and we must do exactly what he says."

"I don't want to be on a ship." She could tell he was crying. "I want to go home, to Mama."

She hadn't bargained for his attitude, though she told herself that she ought to have guessed he wouldn't want to leave the luxury and indulgence he'd become accustomed to in Boston.

"We're going to our real home, Vincent. To Grand-maman and Papa, if we can find them again."

She hugged him against her, wrapping the cloak around him. "Your uncle Jacques is here, too. Remember Jacques?"

The child pushed against her petulantly. "I don't like you. You took me away from Mama."

"Come over here," Jacques invited. "I've fixed a place where we can stretch out together and keep each other warm."

"André struck me," Vincent said. "Papa Charles never strikes me."

André's voice came out of the adjoining darkness as he settled against Danielle on the other side. "I am not as nice a person as Papa Charles," he stated with an implied threat, and slid an arm around Danielle. "Go to sleep, Vincent."

After a short time she guessed that both the boys had indeed dozed off again. André's muscular body was a welcome warmth against her, and their quarters were not as objectionable as she'd feared.

Besides that, they were safe for the moment. André's arm was around her, and she could hear his measured breathing.

It was silent in the hold except for the distant scurry of an unseen rodent. They were apparently well away from the sleeping quarters of the crew, and the ship rose and fell ever so gently on the rising tide.

Though Danielle was tired, she had never felt more wide-awake. After a short time André's arm tightened around her shoulders, drawing her toward him. He reached up with the other hand to tilt her face, then he kissed her, ever so softly.

"I, André, take thee, Danielle, to be my lawful wedded wife," he whispered, and let his lips brush her temple.

Danielle's throat tightened with emotion and it was a few seconds before she could reply. "And I, Danielle, take thee, André, to be my lawful wedded husband."

André had a delicious low chuckle. "There's room to stretch out ourselves. It wouldn't have surprised me if the mate had stacked us up like a cord of wood. We might as well be as comfortable as possible."

Danielle yielded to his unspoken guidance, then, welcoming his embrace as he drew her down beside him, pillowed her head on his arm.

"Will we really get away, André? Will we really find my family, and yours?"

"Mine are all dead," André told her with a sigh. "But I think we may find some of yours. And we'll have each other, little Martha," he added teasingly.

Danielle made an exclamation of disgust. "I don't ever want to hear that hateful name again!"

He laughed.

"And so you shall not. From now on you will be Madame André Lejeune, and we will speak only French, eh?"

"Only French," Danielle agreed, and then, as his arms came strongly around her beneath the spread-out warmth of the beaver-lined cloak, she said, "I love you, André."

He made no reply in words, but his response was eloquent nevertheless; for a while she forgot where they were, and the dangers they faced, and even the difficult quest that lay ahead of them.

She was content in André's arms.

57

FAMILIES, REMNANTS OF families and individuals fleeing the British continued to trickle up the St. John, even through the worst of the winter. Some of them were heading for the distant walled city of Québec in the hope that they would find safety there. Many decided to sit out the coldest weather in St. Anne, even though food was in short supply and housing was limited, as well. There was some comfort to be had simply in the proximity of other people.

Old M. Ayotte was not the only one who took in refugees. In fact, François reported with a cheerfulness that reassured Céleste considerably in regard to Mme Odette, their former benefactor already had six people staying with her.

"Six!" Soleil echoed, picturing them sleeping wall to wall on the main room floor. "A family?"

"All men—single men—I heard," François said. Behind his back the two girls exchanged glances. "Well, at least we're out of there. M. Ayotte is a more satisfactory host."

He was, indeed. They liked him, and though he didn't have much, he shared what he did have. Which included something as valuable as it was unexpected.

The old man had taken chill and requested of Soleil that she bring him another quilt. "Should be one in that chest there in the corner," he said.

Willingly she went to the chest, which was also used for seating, and found the quilt. She had started to lower the lid on the chest when she realized what she was looking at. Thoughtfully she carried the quilt to the curtained bed and spread it over him.

"*Monsieur*, the rest of the chest is full of clothes," she observed.

"Oh, yes. They belonged to my wife, God rest her soul."

"Have you no use for them? I mean, I hesitate to ask more of you when you have been so generous with us, but we have not had new garments in so long, and ours are so worn—"

M. Ayotte's eyesight was no better than his hearing. He peered more closely at her. "You're in need of clothes? By all means, Mme Michaud! Take whatever you like! What is an old man to do with a woman's garments! Help yourselves!"

That afternoon, while *monsieur* took his nap, Soleil and Céleste examined the contents of the chest, their excitement rising with every layer removed. Mme Ayotte had been shorter than they, and a bit stouter, but the garments were in excellent condition. The chest was made of cedar that had kept out the moths, so the warm woolens were ready to be worn again.

"I do believe," Soleil said, "that this will go around me without pulling up in the front, and though it's not quite as long as I'd like, it will cover more than the rag I'm wearing."

Céleste had a sparkle these days like the gemstones Soleil had once seen in the callused palm of the traveler who had told her one was the eye of the Micmac god, Glooscap. "This one is of the same material, see? We can take the bottom from it and stitch it onto the hem of that one and make a very acceptable gown, don't you think?"

They emptied the chest, spreading out the cedar-scented garments around them, planning, trying them on, then cutting into the ones they could best modify for themselves. François came home to find that dinner had been forgotten in the excitement of creating new clothes, but he was good-natured about eating bread and cold meat for supper. It was worth it to see Céleste so happy and even his sister looking less strained and sad.

For days thereafter they cut and stitched, creating new wardrobes for both of them and fashioning attire for François, as well. It not only kept them busy, but raised their spirits enough to brighten his.

There was laughter in the house over simple things. Soleil watched Céleste and François, wishing them well, trying not to envy their happiness together. Yet there were times when she had to retire to the lean-to room to relieve the exquisite torture of being reminded of her own joy in being Remie's wife. And at night, lying in her lonely bed, she longed for his arms about her, his lean, hard body pressed against hers, perhaps laughing with him over the way they no longer fitted together so well because of the size of her belly. At night she could not stop the tears and was grateful that in the mornings no one commented on the evidence of them, though it must have been plain to see.

One morning Soleil woke very early and was strangely alert. For a moment she thought she'd overslept, that someone else stirred in the next room.

But there were no footsteps, no creaking of floorboards, no sounds of a log being dropped onto the fire. There was only a dripping sound.

She sat straight up in bed, then threw off the covers and ran into the main room. M. Ayotte still slept behind his drawn bedcurtains, and from the other direction François muttered in his sleep.

Soleil crossed to the door and threw it open, and now the sound was louder. Water dripping. The snow was melting from the eaves.

Exhilaration swept through her, though the wind that blew in chilled her.

Spring was coming! The snow was melting!

By the time the sun was fully up it sparkled on dozens of icicles decorating the edge of the roof, and the dripping became a veritable chorus, a music sweet to her ears. Soleil laughed up into her brother's face.

"Now we can go on to the Madawaska," she said.

FRANÇOIS REFUSED TO BE moved quite so rapidly as she'd had in mind, for as he pointed out, the icicles refroze every night. Nonetheless he conceded that the time grew close, for at least single men were going on past St. Anne and none of them were coming back. They were either getting through to Québec or stopping off somewhere up there in the wilderness. Or dying there, François thought with a momentary stab of doubt, but he didn't mention that.

Indeed his spirits lifted, too, for the winds grew warmer. The snow shrank in upon itself, becoming wet instead of crisp. Overnight the melted snow created hazardous icy patches on the paths, which did not always soften before the day was out, so it was safer to walk around those spots, thus creating new ones. Yet every day the signs of spring grew stronger.

If only Antoine were here, François thought wistfully. The two of them together had seldom had doubts of any kind, about anything. Yet there was no Antoine, and though the girls' lives as well as his own might well depend on what he decided, he would have to act on his own.

He made up his mind abruptly one night at the supper table when he was acutely aware of his full belly and of what a transient condition that might be. He looked across the table at his wife and his sister. "We'll go day after tomorrow," he said. "Tomorrow we'll gather together what supplies we can manage, and be ready."

He read the mingled emotions in Soleil's face, the anxiety beneath the eagerness to be off. The Madawaska Valley was a magical place to her; he could tell even without knowing all the reasons why, though he could guess at some of them. Strongest, of course, was the hope that Remie would somehow find her there.

He wished the child were not so near to being born. It made him extremely uneasy to think of it entering the world far from any town, from any female except Céleste, who knew no more about the business of birthing than he did. She'd had no personal experience, for all her brothers were older than she was; she had never been present when her own mother gave birth.

He supposed one could only trust in the Good God to see them through whatever lay ahead. It troubled him that Soleil's faith had been so severely shaken. Though she didn't talk about it much, he knew it was true. And because he'd struggled with his own dark doubts since that terrible final day at Grand-Pré, he couldn't help her much. He had no more answers as to why the Almighty had allowed such a catastrophe to destroy the Acadian people than she had.

But there was an air of optimism as they set out again at last, a sort of electricity in the air between the three of them such as that he'd sometimes felt before a storm that brought thunder and lightning to the skies. François made a point of pausing on the riverbank before launching the canoe he'd managed to acquire to kneel and ask God's blessing on their journey.

He couldn't tell how his sister felt about that, but she knelt, too. He hoped that her faith was returning, not only because he feared for her eternal soul but because to be without faith could be a terrible thing.

François and Soleil paddled, and they moved up the river far more easily and swiftly than when they had walked. The sun that first day was warm on their backs and later in their faces, and though they didn't talk much, there was a contentment among the three of them that had not existed for a long time.

THE GOOD WEATHER HELD. It was cold at night, but in warm clothes and with ample blankets and robes, they slept comfortably enough in the shelters François devised from the sweet-smelling boughs. They had cooking pots now, supplied by M. Ayotte, which made it possible to have hot meals at least part of the time. The first few nights their arms ached from the unaccustomed exercise with the paddles, but very soon they became conditioned to it and Céleste tried her hand, too, so they could spell each other.

The St. John swung in a mighty curve from its westerly direction and headed north. They overtook no one, and no one overtook them; they traveled through the silent land as if in a dream, and as long as they were on the river there was no need for the dream to end.

Soleil lost count of the days. She didn't have to think about paddling; it came back to her quickly and naturally. When one midafternoon she began to feel twinges in her back, she attributed the discomfort to having overdone the day before.

The twinges came and went. By evening she was tired but otherwise felt fine; the best she'd felt in days, actually. They camped beside the river and ate their fill of fresh rabbit, and because the sky was clear, they didn't bother with a shelter but slept in the open.

The following day Soleil woke with a backache. What a nuisance, she thought as she rolled up the bedding and loaded it into the canoe. She was ravenous when Céleste called her to breakfast and wondered wistfully how long it would take to raise the seeds M. Ayotte had given them so that they could have bread and wheat and peas again.

By midmorning the backache had diminished and she was back to feeling twinges again. But when they stopped an hour or so later for a hasty meal, Soleil was decidedly uncomfortable.

Céleste caught a glimpse of her face as they pulled the canoe out of the water. "What's wrong? Aren't you feeling well?"

"Oh, I'm a little tired, I guess." She rested a hand on her protruding middle. "This one gave me no rest last night, kicking the way he does, though he seems to have stopped now."

Céleste smiled. "That means he's strong and healthy, doesn't it?"

"I hope so. Come on, let's eat, so we can get going again."

She knew the other two sometimes regarded her with pity for wanting to press on so steadily. They knew she was hoping that Remie would find her there where the Madawaska and the St. John came together, that maybe he would even be there ahead of her.

She knew as well that they had less hope of that than she did. Well, she *had* to hope, and without even realizing it she had begun to pray for it again. Sometimes the prayers had no words, no formed thoughts, only the plea, *Please, please, please*.

Every turn of the river brought memories. For the most part she didn't share them with her traveling companions. There was the bend in the river where they'd seen a moose and a calf. Here they had camped for the night and made love beneath the stars. Around the next bend they had struck a submerged snag and nearly capsized, ending up in a laughing embrace.

Perhaps she was getting stronger, Soleil thought, or adjusting to her losses. She could, at least part of the time, think of Remie without weeping.

Yet the silent litany went on in her mind. *Please, please, please*.

That night it clouded over and even snowed a little. Soleil was unaware of it until morning, protected by the cedar branches François had woven above them. She had slept deeply and well and rose feeling refreshed and ready to travel on.

They were not concerned by the powdering of snow. It melted as soon as the sun was well up, and there was a definite smell of spring in the air.

That day she felt fine. She was energetic, in good spirits, and that night again she slept soundly, dreaming of Remie, waking with a smile that faded only when she realized that it *had* been no more than a dream. Even then she felt sadness rather than the anguish that had so often ravaged her over the past months.

They had been on the river for an hour when Soleil lifted her paddle for another plunge into the clear water and suddenly felt as if a knife had slashed through her belly.

She forgot to paddle, more surprised than alarmed at first, because the pain was gone almost before she realized what it was.

Cautious, she swallowed and waited, but it didn't happen again. Her heart racing, she made herself take up the rhythmic stroking again, waiting for the pain to return.

Unlike the backaches, which had come gradually, this pain had been so sharp and so intense that she finally began to consider what was happening.

She couldn't be going into labor already. The baby wasn't due for more than a month—more like six weeks, if she'd calculated correctly in the first place.

It couldn't be the baby.

She said nothing to the others; she was behind them, and when she had to pause occasionally because of another deep, twisting cramp, they didn't notice.

By the time they stopped for the night several hours had passed without difficulties, and she was breathing more easily again. Of course she wasn't in labor. It was simply that she'd been too inactive during the months they'd spent at St. Anne, and she had to reaccustom herself to this much exertion.

That night she scarcely slept at all, though the baby was quiet. The backache returned so that no position she tried was tolerable for more than a few minutes. She got up to relieve herself so many times that she didn't seem able to get warm between risings. In the predawn she looked down with envy at François and Céleste, sleeping in each other's arms, looking contented in a way that she might never be again.

It seemed only moments after she'd finally fallen into an uneasy doze that François was shaking her shoulder. "Come on, wake up, breakfast is ready, and it's going to snow again, I'm afraid. Let's get on up the river and build another shelter before dark."

She knew without his saying so that he was wondering if they'd left the settlement too soon. Northern springs were notoriously unreliable; a warm and promising day or two could be followed by a late blizzard, and if they'd guessed wrong, the results could be catastrophic.

Especially with the way she'd been feeling.

Soleil was groggy, exhausted. She'd have given much to be able to curl up once more beneath the warm covers and rest. She wasn't sure what was happening and was reluctant to alarm the others unnecessarily, but she was beginning to be extremely uneasy.

She stood for a moment on the riverbank when they were ready to shove off, trying to figure out where they were. She didn't remember exactly how long it had taken her and Remie to reach the Micmac village below the falls, and while there were occasional landmarks, much of the forest along the banks looked the same for miles on end. Even the landmarks seemed different now because of the time of year. How she wished that it were summer, when there would be berries and roots and edible plants as well as more plentiful game!

François noted her concentration. "Something wrong?"

"No," Soleil lied, managing a smile. "I was just trying to figure out where we are from the Indian village. I can't be sure, but we must be getting close. They're friends of Remie's. We'll stop and see if they've heard anything of him."

"Good. They might be willing to trade jerky for fresh meat, so we wouldn't have to stop so often to hunt something. Ready, my love?" he said to Céleste. "Let's go, then."

At noon even the lovers, absorbed as they were in themselves, noticed that Soleil was in distress. She stumbled getting out of the canoe, wetting one foot in the icy water, and François caught her arm before she went to her knees.

"It's so awkward, being off balance this way," she said, trying to smile, but the effort was too much. She had to cling to him for a moment to fight doubling over.

"What's wrong?" François demanded, and Céleste guessed at once.

"The baby? Is it coming?"

Soleil had to wait for one of the spasms to pass before she could speak. She felt cold sweat form on her body and she was very shaky. "I think so."

"How long have you been feeling pain?"

She brushed back the hair from her forehead, and that was damp, too, though the breeze chilled her. "Off and on for several days. I didn't realize at first . . ."

François looked up at the sky, appraised its grayness and compressed his lips. "Do you know how close we are to the Indian encampment?"

"Not for certain. I think I remember that fallen tree, but I can't be sure. If it's the right one, we can't be more than half a day from the village of Angry Waters." She prayed that she was right about that, because if she wasn't, this child was going to be born right out in the open, possibly in the snow, if that sky meant what she thought it did.

"We'd better go on, then," François said. "We'll feel better, being where there are other women."

From then on Céleste paddled, and they had to pause more often to rest, but she didn't complain. Soleil sat in the middle of the canoe, enduring the cramps as they came with increasing severity, breathing deeply and raggedly when each one had passed. Sometimes her knuckles grew white as she grasped the sides of the canoe until a contraction had passed, leaving her limp and bathed in that horrible cold sweat.

It was nearly dusk. The snow had held off so far, but Soleil knew that *she* couldn't last much longer. It was all she could do now to keep from crying out when the waves of pain went through her body. Had it been like this for Mama, all those birthings? How she longed for Barbe, for her touch, for her comforting words! Mama, who knew about babies coming into the world, instead of Céleste, who knew less than Soleil herself.

François's words cut through the miasma of apprehension and discomfort. "That big old cedar's quite a landmark, broken off at the top that way. You don't by any chance recognize it, do you?"

Soleil looked up, blinking to bring her vision into focus. "Yes," she said slowly. "Yes, I do! I'm sure we saw it just before we reached the Micmac village! It can't be more than another mile or so now!"

That gave them heart, and they worked more vigorously, heading upstream. Soleil concentrated simply on getting through each of the contractions and on breathing deeply and praying between them. It was too soon for the baby, she was sure of that, and it was coming anyway, as babies always did. Sometimes when they were born too early, they died.

Her prayers became more desperate, that Remie's baby would live, that she would find the necessary courage.

In one of the lulls between pains—the dull ache no longer counted, for she was scarcely aware of it—she remembered how she had tried to bargain for Remie's safety. When he was returned to her, she had said, she would renew her faith in God.

He had not returned. Her entreaties had not been answered. A vivid recollection came to her suddenly of herself as a very little girl, wailing that God had not answered her prayers, and Barbe's calm, smiling response. "God does not always say yes, you know. That doesn't mean He hasn't answered you. He's

simply given you a different answer from the one you wanted—
no or *wait*.

Soleil no longer felt a resentful compulsion to try to strike a
bargain, to renew her faith only if God complied with her
wishes. The baby was the important thing, and on his behalf
she could ask for life, for safety. She couldn't take the risk of
anger against God, not with so much at stake.

"There's a clearing ahead on the bank," François shouted,
and Soleil lifted her head, suddenly jubilant. The Micmac
women were like women everywhere: they knew about giving
birth, and they would see to her.

A moment later, however, her heart plummeted. As the
canoe nosed into the bank, she heard her brother's stunned
words.

"They've gone. The village is deserted."

58

A FEW WINTRY FLAKES drifted out of the leaden sky as the three
of them stood on the bank, staring at the clearing. Angry Waters and his people had obviously been gone for months.

"Well," François said after a moment, "at least they left one
of their big wigwams. I hope it wasn't because there was illness. We're going to have to use it."

No one said the word *smallpox* but they were thinking it. If
there had been smallpox in the village they might themselves
contract it if they stayed here. It was highly contagious. However, François was right; it was nearly dark, and there was no
doubt that Soleil was in labor. They had to have shelter.

François strode forward to inspect the single wigwam left in
the middle of the clearing where fifty people had lived only last
summer. He returned almost immediately. "I can't see anything to show they didn't just up and move to a better hunting
ground. It wasn't recently, anyway. There are signs that others
have used the lodge since the Indians left, so we'll move in.
Let's get you inside, Soleil, out of the wind, while Céleste un-
loads the rest of the canoe. I'll find some wood and try to get a
fire started. Everything's pretty damp."

Soleil made her way into the big council wigwam, trembling with a combination of apprehension and anticipation. She had waited so long for this moment, and now it was here, whether she was ready for it or not. If only Remie were here, too, she wouldn't be afraid. She consciously stiffened her back, lifting her chin. She *wouldn't* be afraid, and in a matter of hours it would all be over.

"It's going to be all right," Céleste said, dropping a bundle just inside the entrance and kneeling to spread out one of the fur robes they had brought from St. Anne. Her eyes were wide and dark in the dimness and, in spite of her encouraging words, reflected some of Soleil's own concern.

"It's too soon." Soleil's voice was unsteady, and she was again bathed in that cold sweat. "I remember when other babes came too early at home; most of them died."

"But not always. We'll ask the Blessed Mother to look after you and the baby. Here, let's get you warm under the blankets. Is it very close, do you think?"

Soleil's smile wavered a little, but excitement was building within her. "Quite close, I think. I'd give anything to have Mama here."

"I'll do the best I can to take her place," Céleste promised, and her voice was unsteady, too. Oddly enough, knowing that Céleste was nervous seemed to calm Soleil; she hugged her friend spontaneously. "It's going to be a long night, no doubt, but in the morning—"

Another cramp hardened her belly and brought her gasping onto the robes, but she was smiling as soon as it had passed. "The babe has kicked so hard that it must be strong enough to be born." Over the past few days she had somehow come to a renewed faith that she and Remie would one day be reunited, and for his sake she would be strong, too.

When François returned, he reported that it was snowing heavily. "Thanks be to God that the Micmacs left their lodge, even if they didn't stay themselves. Outside of having stayed in St. Anne, this is the best we could have hoped for."

Soleil scarcely noted what he said. Her labor had begun in earnest, and she understood now why it was so named. She gave no thought to anything except the need to expel the child from her body.

And then it was over—so suddenly that Soleil could not believe it. There was a mewling cry, and Céleste was smiling and offering her the squirming infant. "We've nothing to clean her with except a petticoat, but she looks perfect!"

"A girl?" Soleil raised herself on both elbows, then rolled to one side as the infant was delivered to her for closer inspection in the firelight. "She's not too little?"

"She's very small," Céleste conceded, "but she certainly appears to be all right! Oh, Soleil, she's beautiful!"

With an exultation that overcame her fatigue, Soleil peeled back the improvised blanket. Dark hair covered the small head, and incredibly tiny fingers groped and curled when she touched them.

Soleil could never have imagined what this moment would be like, seeing this diminutive daughter she and Remie together had created, a new life just beginning. A wave of tenderness and joy made her eyes fill with tears as she touched the softness of the baby's cheek with a single finger. The child's head turned toward her, mouth seeking, working, and Soleil laughed in delight. "Already she's hungry!"

"That's a good sign. If they're too early, sometimes they won't suck," Céleste said, as if she knew all about babies.

"I'm so tired," Soleil told her wonderingly. "No wonder they call it labor. It's the hardest work I've ever done."

"And now you can rest. For as long as you like."

Soleil held the babe against her and, well content with her night's work, slid into a euphoric sleep before she had finished her prayer of thanksgiving.

DURING THE NIGHT the weather changed. It had been snowing heavily when François went out early in the evening; they heard when it started to rain and were grateful to the Micmacs for leaving the council lodge behind, whatever their reasons for doing so.

In the morning Céleste was the first to look out, and she gave a cry of pleasure. "Oh, look! It's lovely!"

The world around them had turned to crystal. Every tree, every bush, every weed had been transformed to a thing of beauty with its coating of ice.

"A good omen," François said, grinning down at his sister in her bed, the sleeping infant beside her. "You ought to come and look at it, Soleil."

"In a moment," she said, snuggling deeper into the furs. "But I'm glad it's beautiful, like my baby."

"What are you going to call her?" Céleste wanted to know, dropping the flap back into place, shutting out the cold air and the glittering wonderland of ice.

"Micheline." Soleil sounded dreamy. "If it had been a boy, he would of course have been named after Remie. We talked about it once, shortly after I knew I was pregnant. He said he didn't want to name a girl after me, that there would be only one Soleil in his life." Her eyes were moist, but she was smiling. "So she will be Micheline."

"It's a lovely name. I think we will call our daughter Victoire, or after both his grand-papas if it is a boy—Georges Émile."

It took a moment for the import of Céleste's words to seep into Soleil's mind. Then her mouth fell open. "Céleste! Are you—?"

"I think so. I'm almost certain. I told François last night, after Micheline was born."

François was grinning like an idiot. As if it had been all his own doing, Soleil thought happily. Well, maybe he would have gotten around to proposing sooner or later, but she was well content that she and Céleste had conspired to help things along. Men could be dense in some matters.

Not that Remie ever had been. She blinked against the incipient tears and cuddled the baby close to her breast, eliciting a tiny, protesting squawk at the change of position. No, she wouldn't weep for Remie, not today. Today she would take joy in her exquisite, brand-new daughter.

THEY STAYED IN THE MICMAC wigwam for a week. At home her confinement would have been twice that long, at least, but Soleil was insistent that she could be up and about sooner than that.

"The Indian women are back at work within hours, sometimes. Am I any less than a Micmac woman? Besides, I feel wonderful. And the sooner we can travel, the better. It will soon be spring, and there will be much to do once we reach the Madawaska.''

The ice had gone and even the snow had melted away except in the deepest shade when they set out once more. François and Céleste paddled; Soleil cradled the baby, infinitely amused and entertained by the changing expressions on the small face, the waving arms, the eyes that crossed occasionally and failed to focus.

In spite of being born a few weeks ahead of time, Micheline thrived. There had been a few anxious days when there seemed to be no milk for her, and then it had come, and the baby was content to be held and rocked to sleep against her mother's breast. At times it seemed to Soleil that her heart would burst with the love she had for this child.

They heard the falls before they reached them, as Soleil had done before, and she told them the story of the Indian maiden who had taken the enemy Mohawk braves to their deaths.

Céleste shivered, looking up at the tons of thundering water as it roared through the gorge above them. It was easy to believe such a story, for surely no one could live through such a wild plunge.

And then, as they made for land to begin their portage around the Great Falls, the canoe hit a submerged rock. They were unprepared for the jolt; the canoe capsized, sending the three of them, and the baby, into the icy water.

Soleil had instinctively clutched Micheline to her and surfaced, gasping with shock and cold. For a moment sheer terror almost paralyzed her, and then she realized she could touch bottom.

She saw François hauling Céleste toward shore and struggled in that direction herself, aware of the baby's wailing. François turned back to reach out a hand for her, and amazingly he was grinning. "Anyone who can howl that loud can't be hurt too badly," he reassured her.

She stared up at the blood streaming from a cut on his temple. "Mother of God! Is everybody all right?"

Céleste had sunk onto the ground, still choking and spluttering. "The canoe—it's gotten away!"

It had, indeed, rapidly drifted downstream. They stared after it in dismay, and then François let out a howl of his own. "All our supplies went into the river!"

Indeed, several bundles were floating after the canoe, and he went running toward them. The cooking pot had sunk right where they had capsized; they could see it through the churning water, and Céleste steeled herself to go back in after it.

"We're lucky," François reported eventually, when he had returned with the undamaged canoe and two bundles of furs and sodden blankets. "The canoe was trapped in some debris at the next bend where a fallen tree was holding the driftwood, or I'd never have caught up with it. We didn't lose everything."

Soleil's teeth were chattering and she was seriously concerned about the screaming baby. "We need to get warmed up, but how?"

"We'll go back to the Micmac village," François decided, having already considered the matter. "There we can have shelter and a fire to dry out our clothes. Come on, let's go."

It seemed a defeat to have to retreat, but there was no other logical course of action. The air wasn't cold enough to freeze the clothes on their bodies, though it felt like it. Soleil pressed Micheline against her own bosom but despaired of producing enough warmth to help much.

They were stiff with misery when they once more approached the clearing around the council wigwam, and it was François who spotted the other canoe, pulled well up onto the bank.

"Hey! We've company! Someone else has taken over our lodge!"

"I pray they're hospitable," Soleil chattered as their own slender vessel nosed in to shore. "I must get Micheline warm and dry before she takes a fatal chill, if it isn't already too late!"

They pulled the canoe above the reach of the water and headed into the clearing, only to stop in total disbelief seconds later.

Their voices had drawn the new occupants out of the wigwam and they all stared at one another for long seconds before Soleil let out a scream of incredulous delight and dashed headlong into her mother's open arms.

59

ÉMILE HAD AGED MORE than Barbe, though both had gone gray, and their faces were more lined. Like the other refugees, they were lean and ragged, but they appeared in good health.

"They told us in St. Anne that you were no more than a week ahead of us, and we feared we'd never catch up with you," Barbe told them when they had finally settled inside around the fire and wrapped themselves in blankets while their clothes dried. She had immediately taken charge of Micheline and now patted the baby against her shoulder. "It was the hand of God that stayed your progress to wait for us!"

No one disputed that. They had hugged and kissed and cried and laughed, and now, as Soleil told them, "We're ready to hear what's happened to you since we left you on the edge of the Minas Basin."

Their story was simple and moving; it did not take long to tell. Barbe related most of it.

After watching the canoe disappear across the red tides, Émile and Barbe had headed into the woods, hoping to find shelter with other escaped Acadians.

"Or at least a place where I could die in peace," Émile interjected. "Only your mama refused to let me give up."

"I knew if your papa died, I should die also." Barbe jiggled the baby. "And so we kept walking until it was nearly dark. And then we saw the fire."

They had, either by accident or by the blessings of Providence, stumbled into a small Micmac encampment.

The main body of their band had gone, heading north and west, deeper into the heart of Canada, away from the English. Those who remained were too old or too young or too ill to travel quickly. Only a dozen in number, they waited while one of their band, a young brave, recovered from a broken leg. When it was healed enough so that he could walk, they, too, would go.

"They took us in," Barbe related, "and fed us, provided us with a place to sleep. There was no *puoin* with them, but all the Micmacs seem versed in healing. They made hot poultices for Papa's wound and brought him potions of herbs, and by the time the brave with the broken leg had mended, so had Papa.

We came on with them, all the way to Saint John, where they went deeper into the wilderness after the rest of their tribe. Papa and I came up the river, asking everyone we saw about you. Finally, in St. Anne, we were sure we were only days behind you, and that the Good God would enable us to overtake you. As, of course, He did."

They had heard the horror stories about English atrocities against the Acadians. They had also heard of exiles who had made their way to safety beyond the reach of the British, at least so far.

"There are many who believe the soldiers will come up the river in the spring," Émile said heavily. "There is no way to say we will be safe unless we go all the way to Québec City. But we give thanks to God that we are together again. And perhaps He'll bring the others back to us, as well."

They fell silent around the fire, smelling roasting meat and wet wool, and Soleil watched her mother with her first granddaughter, and smiled.

Life had once more become worth living, which was a miracle in itself. Perhaps it would yet happen, the ultimate miracle, that they would eventually be reunited as a family, all of them.

SEVERAL THOUSANDS OF MILES away, across the gray Atlantic, Pierre and Henri, hidden in a hold with a cargo destined for the American colonies, set sail once more. It would take them weeks to reach Halifax, and months beyond that to make their furtive and dangerous way across the peninsula of Nova Scotia, but their goal was fixed firmly in their minds.

If any other Cyrs had escaped and survived, they would find them far up the St. John River in the Madawaska Valley that Remie had talked about. They had only to persevere.

DANIELLE, VINCENT, JACQUES and André were put ashore in mid-March on a lonely stretch of beach on the western Fundy shore. That they were not landed in hostile Annapolis Royal was due to a severe storm that drove the merchant ship off course, damaging a mast; the captain chose to seek shelter in St. John Harbour until the winds blew themselves out and his mast could be replaced.

It was a black night except for the stars, they had no supplies, and it was not yet spring. But there was exultation in their steps as they headed inland. André still had some money left, and he was sure he could find someone who would accept English gold in payment for food, arms and ammunition.

Danielle faced the north and west, scarcely aware of the rawness of the wind or the darkness of the night.

Over there, somewhere, she was convinced she would find other members of her own family. And now there was André, who took care of her as she would take care of him, and her life was full.

She knelt briefly on the damp sand to say a prayer of thanksgiving for their delivery thus far, followed by a plea for a safe trip upriver. And then, confident that the prayers would be answered, she stepped out after her husband with a growing joy in her heart.

In the frigid darkness the baby whimpered.

Madeleine stirred, reluctant to get out of her warm bed, but when the sound was repeated she went to him. His hands and feet were cold, and there were no other covers to put over him. She checked on Marc, then, who seemed to be fine, and picked up the baby. She would have to take him into her own bed to coax the warmth back into him.

He seemed content enough once her body heat was communicated to him. But Madeleine could not go back to sleep. She lay looking up into the night, involuntary tears trickling from the corners of her eyes and running downward into her hair.

It was true that Île St. Jean was a lovely place in summer, with its contrasting red beaches and the extraordinarily vivid greens of grass and beech and maple trees.

But in the winter it was so cold, and so many refugees from English tyranny had fled to the island that there was not enough of anything to go around: not firewood, not food, not even fish from the surrounding sea were plentiful enough to fill their bellies. More than once she had fed the children her own portions, and still they looked at her with sad eyes and Marc would say, "Hungry, Mama."

Louis should never have brought them here, she thought, though there was more sorrow than bitterness in her heart. He had done what he'd thought best, and certainly the news from Grand-Pré and other places bore out his contention that there was no future for any Acadian under British rule.

Yet she could not see that there was any future for them here, either. Even when spring came there would be insufficient food, since the customary supply lines were cut off. Louis would fish, although she knew he found it far less satisfying than farming had been. When he caught more than they could eat themselves there were plenty of others who would welcome his catch, but no one had money to pay or goods to trade, and not even money helped much if there was nothing to buy.

"Madeleine? Are you awake?"

She stirred guiltily, not wanting Louis to know she had been crying, but already he was reaching for her, and his lips brushed against her wet cheek.

He didn't ask what was wrong. He held her tight, and she felt a tension in his body to match her own. After a few moments he kissed her and spoke very softly. "The ice is melting, and the harbor will be open before long. I've talked to Michel Duperre about his boat."

Madeleine stirred uneasily. "We've no money for another boat, surely!"

"Not money," Louis told her. "Passage. Michel is leaving as soon as the weather breaks. We're going with him."

Her heart lurched, whether in fear or anticipation she could not have said. "We're leaving? Where do we go?"

"To the Gaspé, probably. At least that's where Michel wants to go. I thought we'd take advantage of the boat that far, at least. And then perhaps we can continue upriver toward Québec, to Rivière-du-Loup. When we get that far we can better judge if we should head for the Madawaska River."

Madeleine was incredulous with an exploding joy that brought her upright in bed, impervious to the cold. "To the Madawaska? Where the others will have gone if any escaped?"

"Come down," Louis said, drawing her flat again, "before you freeze us both to death before we can go. Some of them surely outwitted the British—can you imagine the twins meekly giving in to them? Yes, with God's mercies there's a good chance we'll find some of them there, in that valley Remie mentioned.''

She was trembling as she allowed herself to be drawn into his embrace once more, but this time it was not with the cold. "When?'' she asked unsteadily. "How long?''

"Two weeks, maybe three. We won't be able to take much. The boat is small, and Michel's family is larger than our own.''

She hugged him in elation. "But we will go! That's what's important, that we will go!'' It was longer still before she finally dozed off again, but it didn't matter. Knowing that they were leaving the island, that there was a possibility of finding other members of the family, gave her hope, and before any of it was accomplished or even actually begun, she gave thanks to God.

THE SMALL PARTY REACHED the Madawaska Valley in early April. Spring came late in the north country, but on the day they landed Soleil felt the weather was an omen, a holy promise of what was to come, for the sun was warm on their faces, the breeze fragrant with the scents of grass and fir and spruce. The river had yielded a bounty of fresh fish; a bull moose inspected them without fear from the edge of the forest.

"There,'' François said, pointing. "That's the place for a house.''

"Yes.'' Soleil was smiling, though the deep ache remained a tender wound within her. This was her place, hers and Remie's, and it would never be completely home until he came.

In the meantime, however, there was Micheline. The baby was thriving in spite of the hardships they had endured; she clearly delighted in the attention from her grandparents and the others. Émile and François set to work at once to cut the logs for the first small house, and the women scoured the countryside for edible roots and plants and planned for the things they would do to make the house a home.

As the weather warmed and it was truly spring, there was an uneven trickle of travelers past their front door. Always they shared whatever was in the pot, which was mostly wild game, for there had been no time as yet to raise vegetables or grains.

One day Soleil and François stood together on the river-bank after having bid the most recent family goodbye with cries on both sides of "God bless you! God bless you!"

When the travelers disappeared out of sight upstream, François sighed. "Well, it's back to work for me. I never appreciated how easy it was to plant and sow the seed and harvest at home until I found out how hard it is to break ground here. But Papa is looking happier every day, don't you think? Now that he has land again. I hope to God he's allowed to stay here, that the British never penetrate this far inland looking for Acadians."

She touched his arm. "I hope so, too. I'd best finish my laundry or it won't dry before dark," she said, but neither of them made a move to go. François was staring downstream, where far in the distance they could see a tiny speck on the water that was surely another canoe approaching.

"I pray that someday it will be Antoine who comes," François said softly. "And all the others, of course, as well. But God in Heaven, how I miss Antoine!"

No reply was expected, and she made none. Her throat had closed convulsively, anyway, so that for a few moments speaking would have been impossible. François saluted her in an affectionate gesture and left her to return to his own tasks; she could welcome the newcomer if he stopped.

She knelt beside the water to scoop up the garments she had been scrubbing there, wondering wistfully how long it would be before they could acquire a big kettle such as they'd always used at home to boil the laundry. Her hands felt raw from immersing them in the water that had probably been part of the ice on Lac Temiscouata only days before. She hoped that François would make good on his promise to shoot a bear soon, so that they would have the grease for their chapped hands.

She twisted a shirt to wring it as dry as possible and dropped it into the basket beside her. It was a good day for drying clothes, she thought with satisfaction. They had so few, they must be dried quickly or in some cases put back on damp.

The canoe was a little closer now. At first she was merely curious; she could tell it was a lone man, nothing more.

And then something quickened within her; her pulse began to beat faster and faster.

He was too far away to see in detail, yet surely there was something familiar about him, something...

Soleil stood paralyzed, almost unable to breathe, and her chest began to ache with the strain of it. Oh, Mother of God! Let it be! Let it be him! The man had a full beard and he was thin, but oh, God, the shoulders were surely the same wide shoulders she remembered, the unruly dark curls the same, too!

She started to move toward him, tentatively at first, then more quickly, finally running.

The canoeist lifted his paddle and held it, drops glistening as they dripped from it, and she screamed his name.

"Remie! Remie!"

The paddle plunged in a powerful stroke that sent the birch-bark shell hurtling toward her against the current that tried to hold it back.

The bronze face was split in a grin that showed even teeth, and before he reached the shore Soleil hurled herself into the water, unaware of the temperature of it, reaching for him. "By the Good Christ, woman, have you no feminine subtlety at all? Chasing after a man that way, nearly swamping my canoe?"

And in the end she *did* swamp it, though it was only in a few feet of water by that time. Remie was pitched, laughing, into the river beside her; he reached back to jerk the canoe up onto the bank, and then she was enfolded in the strong arms she had thought lost to her forever, and his mouth was eager and warm upon her own.

He lifted her in an exuberant swing well off her feet, and then they fell together, laughing—Soleil through tears—in the soft grass.

Her fingers reached up to touch the beard, to brush the wide mouth. "Oh, Remie, I must have died a hundred times inside, fearing you'd never come!"

"And I," he said softly, all laughter gone and only tenderness remaining. "Not knowing if you were on one of those hell ships, bound for God knew where. But I knew that if you were free, you'd come here. Who escaped with you?"

She told him, and his eyes darkened as he thought of all the others.

"And the baby? What of the baby?" He was lying beside her, his hand on her flat stomach in the way that sent shock waves throughout her system. "Do I have a son?"

"You have a beautiful daughter, Micheline."

"A daughter. Me! Imagine that! Well, next we'll have to see about making a son, eh? Every girl needs a few brothers to look after her interests."

She tried to sit up, but he was pinning her down. "Can you see the house? Or François in the field, or Papa?"

Remie swiveled his head. "No."

"Then they can't see us, either," Soleil said.

She watched the grin return to his lips.

"You're even more brazen than I remembered," he said, and lowered his mouth to hers. Soleil felt her heart, her soul, her body explode in an ecstasy of loving this man, and there was no more need for words.

Their kisses said it all.

Author's Note

The Acadians wandered for many years, seeking missing relatives and a new homeland where they would be allowed to live in peace. Some were assimilated into the English-speaking colonies; some, like those eventually transplanted to New Orleans, established a new but related culture. There are still predominantly Cajun communities in Louisiana—*Cajun* is a local modification of the word *Acadian*—and elsewhere.

Some of these people did find the family members from whom they had been separated during the deportation. Others never did.

Historians are generally in agreement that the first permanent settlers in the Madawaska Valley were given permission to take up land there in the spring of 1785, thirty years after they had been dispossessed of their original lands and holdings. However, there is some evidence that there may have been a few people there ahead of them, though they did not stay on that land.

Most historians are also convinced that Acadian family members were deliberately separated with the intention of further hindering them from ever returning to reclaim their lands or banding together to oppose British rule. The personal diaries of Colonel John Winslow, the commander who ordered the loading of Acadian prisoners from Grand-Pré, seem to bear this out, though some writers of a later period insist that the separations were a matter of accident. This writer became convinced that the cruelty of dividing families was, indeed, intentional.

In the instances in which historians are not in agreement, I have chosen the course that best suited my own purpose—that of creating a fictional story based on a series of true events.

Although the surnames of the characters in this book are those of some of the Acadians who lived at Grand-Pré and those who settled along the Madawaska River, these characters are fictitious except for the British commanders at the time of the deportation and the Abbé Jean-Louis Le Loutre, who with his bands of loyal Indian followers led attacks upon the English that undoubtedly inflamed them to perform some of the atrocities that were later inflicted upon the Acadians.

**Cloaked behind a family curse
and Irish legend, a madman stalks
his final victim.**

DAN BARTON

When the body of a woman buried alive is discovered, a doctor begins a desperate manhunt to prevent a psychotic killer, who is terrorizing a small canyon community in California, from reaching his next victim!

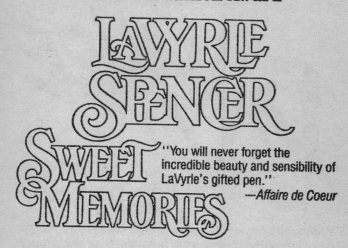